SHIVAREE
THE COMPLETE SERIES

CARA McKENNA

Second Edition

Backwoods and *Shivaree* originally published 2010

Getaway originally published 2011

Edited by Jaynie Ritchie and Kelli Collins

Cover design by Cara McKenna

ISBN 978-0-9977834-7-6

For the fine state of Louisiana, where I enjoyed
the boudin far more than the West Nile virus.

BACKWOODS

CHAPTER ONE

"Evenin', boss."

Shane raised a hand in reply to Jeanne, the afternoon bartender stationed across the way. The door slapped shut behind him and he wandered through the screened-in porch, past empty couches and up a step to the main lounge area. He glanced at the scuffed wood of the dance floor, those same boards he'd played on when this room had been his memaw's front parlor, before his aunt inherited the old plantation-style monstrosity and turned the ground floor into a club.

He headed to the bar, waving at the lone, early drinker camped out by the front windows. Shane tossed a pile of mail on the counter. "You mind sortin' out the junk and tossin' the bills on my desk?"

"You got it, boss." Jeanne started flipping through the envelopes.

He smiled at her. Cute gal. A little heavy, though Shane didn't mind that one bit. Warm smile, shiny brown hair. If he wasn't ten years her senior and signing her paychecks, he'd have asked the girl out by now.

She set a catalogue from Baton Rouge Bar Supply in the junk pile. Shane picked it up, thinking the place could stand some new furniture, some stools that didn't wobble or have stuffing creeping from under the vinyl.

"We got a new musician coming in tonight," Jeanne said.

Shane frowned as the bills stacked up. "What kind of musician?"

It was Lovers' Night, as his Aunt Marie had rechristened Fridays years ago. Shane hated that girlie name but he'd kept it after he took over running the place, just as he'd kept nearly everything his aunt had established. It brought the customers in and he wasn't about to argue with that.

"It's Valentine's week," he added. "I don't want some amateur stinking up my club when folks are looking for foreplay."

"Every night's foreplay around here," Jeanne said.

True. It might be worse for wear, but something about the Shivaree drew amorous folks like a siren song.

"Plus Zach said this guy's good," she said. "Real good. Said he's from New Orleans."

"What's he play?"

"Mandolin, I think."

Shane made a face. "I don't even know what a mandolin looks like."

"It's like…it looks like a ukulele and violin, put together," Jeanne said. "Sort of."

"Don't sound real sexy to me."

"Well, you'll have to just come down later and decide for yourself then." Jeanne disappeared around the corner to the bar's office with the mail. She returned and leaned on the counter, flared her nostrils. "You stink, boss."

Shane put his nose to the shoulder of his work shirt, breathing in motor oil and grease. "You're nuts. I fuckin' love that smell." He pinched the front of his shirt and tugged at the fabric, pretending to waft a cloud of his questionable fragrance in Jeanne's direction.

"You should wring that shirt into a bottle and sell it to Calvin Klein," Jeanne teased. "Eau du Shane Broussard. Eau du Sweaty Auto Mechanique."

"Maybe I should," Shane said, snotty. "Give folks a cologne that actually smells like a man, not all that sporty shit, citrus or sandalwood or whatever."

"You lemme know how that goes, boss. Why don't you go get yourself cleaned up before you scare the customer away?"

Shane knocked twice on the bar and turned, heading back through the porch to the side steps that led to the second-floor balcony. He unlocked the door to his apartment and kicked off his muddy boots, shed his clothes as he made his way through the living room and kitchen to the bathroom, turned the shower on as hot as it went. Forty degrees might not seem bad to folks from places colder than Louisiana, but Shane couldn't stand anything below seventy-five. Heatstroke over frostbite, any day of the week.

He soaped up, washed away the grease and grit, thought about Jeanne's breasts and jerked off, professionalism be damned. Hell, maybe he *should* ask her out. He owned the place. What was he going to do, fire himself?

He stepped out of the tub and toweled off, wiped the steam from the mirror and stared at himself in the yellowy bathroom lights. Not bad. Thirty-five was still young these days. He had another decade or two before his height went from asset to liability and left him with a bad back like his old man and his uncles. He kept himself fit, lifted weights and did sit-ups and chin-ups to stave off the seemingly hereditary paunch overdue to him from the Broussard side.

Dragging an electric razor over his face, Shane considered his hair. It was at the end of this month's cycle, ready for another buzz. He thought about doing it himself but he liked an excuse to go into Baton Rouge and flirt with the girl who ran clippers over his head for half a minute and charged him fifteen bucks for the honor. Another woman he ought to ask out.

He glanced around the counter and scanned the medicine cabinet, found a hair clip and tube of lip gloss, evidence of bygone one-night stands he'd prefer to not advertise to future one-night stands. He buried them in the trash can under a spent toilet paper roll. Best to be safe, in case he got brave enough or drunk enough to make a move on Jeanne or some other willing woman on motherfucking Lovers' Night.

* * *

Shane passed the early evening in the bar's office, paying bills, ordering stock, fumbling through the computer program that balanced the club's books. Eight hours spent crouched under various cars and trying to drill the most basic information into his thick-skulled new apprentice had left him with a sore neck and head. He wished he could just trot upstairs, crack a beer and fall asleep watching the news. But he had a musician to weigh in on and a barmaid to flirt with for as long as it took him to realize he was on the age cusp where that sort of thing went from shameless to plain creepy.

He flipped through catalogues, wondering why the fact that it was the weekend didn't feel like something to be relieved about. Two days spent rattling around this house, keeping himself busy. At night, drinking three beers too many and waking up the next morning with a semi-familiar girl wrapped around him, or maybe just his own right hand. Excuses for why Shane ought to head into the garage tomorrow and get ahead on next week's work flowed easily and loosened the knot in his chest. His seventeen-year-old self would've had a field day with that one—avoiding drunken one-night stands by working overtime.

Seventeen, shit. That was more than half a lifetime ago.

He glanced up at a knock on the door. "C'min."

Jeanne poked her head through, the recorded pop music playing out in the bar leaking in behind her. "The mandolin guy's here. You want to brief him on what sorts of stuff to play?"

"Just tell him to keep it sexy. No lyrics with cussing if he sings. I'll be out in a few."

"You all right?"

"Just a headache. And I gotta work tomorrow," he added.

"Bummer." Jeanne offered a sympathetic frown and closed the door quietly behind her.

Nice girl... Too nice to get hit on by her boss. Plus she'd be moving on sooner or later. She'd get snapped up by some decent young man or realize she was bound for better things, head off to school someplace. Like everybody else around here she'd move on, leave Shane behind to tend to his little territory and await the slow but steady arrival of unremarkable middle-age.

He rubbed his face and temples and when he lowered his hands the clock on the computer told him it was seven fifteen.

Beyond the office, the soft bass thump of the canned music faded away. Shane pushed his chair out and hit the lights, locked the office and walked into the Shivaree's heady, amorous fog.

Even in February it felt like July. Even at suppertime it felt like three a.m. This place made folks sweat, made them itchy to find a warm, willing body to pair off with. His aunt had designed it that way, a place with no pretension, where people could be themselves, dress up or down and drink cheap drinks and listen to free music, get out of their heads for an evening. Old, young, pretty, homely—the differences all faded away under the canopy of colored Christmas lights and crystals strung like vines from the ceiling.

The bar had started filling up in the last couple hours, bustling now with a few dozen patrons. Shane slid behind the counter, filled a handful of drink orders alongside Jeanne before he popped a beer bottle open and took a seat on a stool across from her.

He got his wallet out and laid a twenty on the wood. "Order yourself and Zach some food."

"And you?" Jeanne asked.

"Yeah. Whatever you guys have." Shane glanced to the stage, where the new musician was setting up, his back to the bar.

Zach appeared from the hall, hugging a half dozen liquor bottles to his chest.

"Burgers or pizza?" Jeanne asked him.

He set the bottles along the back bar and nodded a greeting to Shane. "Burgers."

Jeanne called the nearest delivery joint and placed their orders.

Shane took a deep pull off his bottle. "How's school, Zach?"

"Waste of time and money." Zach was twenty-two or -three, baby-faced but handsome, torn alternately between half-assed dreams of rock stardom—talentless—and signing up for the army—no discipline. Big on ambition but lacking on the follow-through. Too damn eager to get himself landed in the middle of some kind of drama, anything with a uniform that girls might shed their panties over.

Shane cast him a little glare. "Well, drop out now and you might find yourself in my shoes in ten years."

"Don't sound too bad."

Shane laughed. "Runnin' your auntie's bar and breathing diesel fumes all day?"

Zach shrugged. "You own one place and you're a partner in another. Gotta be better than studying fucking business management with half the same rednecks I went to high school with. Lucky if I can run a fucking fried chicken franchise when I'm done."

"Watch your fucking mouth in front of Miss Jeanne, son."

Jeanne rolled her eyes at Shane.

Zach jumped on the next drink order, clearly ready to escape the lecture.

The speakers buzzed—the sound of the system switching to the microphone from the stereo. Shane swiveled his stool to watch the stage, held his beer in his mouth for half a minute before he remembered to swallow.

He felt as if he knew the musician.

He didn't. Hadn't ever seen him or anyone like him in his whole life, but something about him rang in Shane's head like recognition, like some instant pang of familiarity despite how relatively exotic the guy was.

The man dressed odd—odd for this region and odd for this century. You could plunk him down in a photo taken in the thirties in some classy European city and he'd blend right in. White dress shirt tucked into dark slacks, shined shoes, one of those old-timey brimmed hats only ancient black jazz musicians and fashionable pop stars wore these days. A watch- or wallet-chain dangled at his hip.

He flicked the mic on and leaned into it. He held his instrument at his chest, a strange little curly guitar, plucked a few quiet notes before he spoke.

"Evenin'."

A couple people clapped politely and the man took a seat on the stage's stool, eased the mic stand down, close to the instrument. He strummed a couple chords and then his fingers began to dance.

The music sounded Spanish, fast and moody and damn sexy in an urgent kind of way. Shane knew jack-squat about mandolins but he suspected this guy was phenomenal. Too good to waste his time playing for seventy-five bucks and free drinks in a backwoods nowhere-club like the Shivaree.

He took another deep gulp of his beer, thinking this would do nicely for Lovers' Night. Goddamn nicely indeed, if everybody was feeling even half as crazy as Shane suddenly was.

It was as if he'd lost control of his own heartbeat, as though it'd been reconfigured to match the rhythm of this stranger's hands. He drained his bottle and slid it across the wood, spoke to Jeanne without turning. "Whiskey."

A glass clacked beside him and he took a sip, let the alcohol burn down his throat as he stared at the musician. Couples formed in his periphery, taking over the dance floor, giving their bodies the physical outlet Shane himself craved as he listened to this song. He wished he could see the guy's face better, get a good look at the man responsible for this eerie atmospheric change in his bar and his head.

The song slowed and faded, came to a close amid enthusiastic clapping and a few whistles. The musician leaned in to the mic and murmured, "Thank you," in a voice that made the hairs on Shane's arms prick up. The man slid the mic higher and started another song, a bit slower and sadder, still sexy enough to fuck with the course of Shane's bloodstream. The guy was placid, as if under his own trance. After a minute of skillful picking, he sang.

A low, awed moan rose in Shane's throat but he sucked it back down, doused it with the last of his shot.

The man's voice was pure audio sex, a raspy baritone singing Spanish lyrics Shane couldn't understand and didn't want to. He felt weird and high, hypnotized and hungry and on edge, all at once. There was a reality somewhere outside of this man's words and the deft movement of his fingers across the strings, but Shane didn't know what it might be. Couldn't give a shit as long as this man was singing. It took a physical intrusion to snap him back into his body and land his butt firmly on the stool, rematerialize the shot glass in his fist. Jeanne had tapped his shoulder again and he turned to her, setting the glass between them.

She pointed to the stage as she poured a customer's beer. "So that's him."

"I gathered."

"He's awful good, huh?"

Shane felt compelled territorially to find fault with the stranger holding court in his little kingdom. "Not the usual sound for Fridays."

"Yeah, but look around, boss. Who cares?"

Shane took stock of the crowd. Friday always attracted its share of horny couples, set a mood conducive to folks retreating into the Shivaree's darker corners to get as close to having sex as they could manage with their clothes still on. On Saturday afternoons Shane often had to send some poor junior staffer out into the backyard with a pair of barbeque tongs and a trash bag to clear the lawn of jettisoned condoms. Lovers' Night meant make-out music, sultry jazz, mostly. One year they'd scored a major coup when a voluptuous black lady from Biloxi came and sang torch songs every week, but this man topped even her.

Shane couldn't be surprised by the friskiness happening out on the wood—the Shivaree did that to folks—but he'd been immune for a long time. Until tonight. Tonight he felt it himself, as though he'd been drugged. Some drug that made his skin warm and antsy with sexual energy.

"Yeah," he muttered, willing his eyes toward Jeanne, away from the stage. "He's good. Long as people keep buying drinks."

Her smile bloomed slow and sly. "He's awful sexy."

Shane cocked an eyebrow at her, protectiveness raising his hackles.

Jeanne laughed. "Is that look telling me I can't fraternize with the hired help?"

"Just don't get yourself mixed up with a musician. They'll break your heart and give you syphilis."

Jeanne made a sputtering noise. "Listen to you, soundin' all jealous. There something you're not telling me?"

Her flirtation was harmless, a ploy to get Shane to admit he might like her himself. He wished that was what his sudden foul mood was all about, but he didn't think it was.

"Just don't want to see you getting mixed up with some stranger on my watch."

"Ha! Wish I could, but that guy's like light-years out of my league."

"Who told you that?" Shane asked, making his voice stern.

"Just a fact, boss. Look at him."

Shane aimed his eyes at the stage again. He was too far away to really see the guy's face in the spangled lights, but he had a good body—tallish, slender, dripping with some kind of grace Shane didn't have a fancy enough word for…all the things women craved once they got bored with a grease-stinking bruiser like Shane Broussard.

He shrugged and Jeanne turned to pour a beer.

The musician finished his song, easing the hot tension in Shane's body by a couple degrees, but not much. He stood from the stool and set his mandolin down, offered the appreciative crowd another thank-you and flicked the mic off. He stepped off the low platform and headed toward the bar. Sauntered—that was the only word for it. He eased himself between the two empty stools to Shane's right and leaned on the wood.

Jeanne turned back from loading dirties in the washer and he smiled at her, the gesture carving deep lines beside his lips and flashing white teeth. He pulled a cigarette case out of his pants pocket, opened it to reveal a small wad of bills and a square paper packet with a picture of a mandolin on it, a smaller plastic square behind that. "I can get a glass of red, please?"

"Course."

Shane swiveled his legs to the side and stood. "Entertainment drinks on the house," he said, to Jeanne more than the musician.

The man straightened up to look at Shane, eyes shaded from the lights by the brim of his old hat.

He was taller than Shane had guessed, over six feet, if barely. Good thing too—Shane hated being level with anybody's eyes, and he had him beat by two or three inches. The guy's build was more substantial than he'd guessed as well, a buck-seventy maybe, none of it fat. He had a dark patch beneath each arm, a gleam to the tan skin of his neck, and tattoos of some kind, snatches of ink peeking from behind his crisp white collar. He was a pretty kind of handsome, but not polished or prissy. Five o'clock shadow, messy black hair curling from beneath the hat. Smelled like cedar and grass and something else—something dark.

"Evenin'," he said in that voice that set pulses humming.

Shane set aside his scrutiny, pulled himself together. "I'm Shane Broussard. I own this bar. See you're our new musician."

"If you want me."

"Heard you grew up in town."

The man nodded again, accepted a glass from Jeanne and took a sip. He tilted his chin up, drawing the shadow off his face to reveal dark eyes, as black as Shane took his coffee.

He set his wine down and offered his hand for a brief, warm shake. "Gabriel," he said. "I like your place." His eyes drifted up, traveling across the sea of colored Christmas lights to the billowy white drapes hung from the tall windows, made from old wedding dresses. "There something about it, here," Gabriel said.

He had a weird-ass accent, as heavy as any Shane had heard in the most backwater corners of the region, but different too. Shane wouldn't ever say it around any of his militantly Cajun friends or family, but Gabriel's accent was so thick he sounded damn near brain-damaged. Looked like every woman's wet dream, though—all the best genes from a big bubbling cauldron of mismatched DNA. High cheekbones and black eyebrows and sideburns, thick lashes, perfect skin. A hundred things Shane wished he weren't noticing. If anybody caught him staring, he hoped it came off as suspicion.

"Gabriel what?" Shane asked.

"Marino-Doucet."

"That's a heck of a name."

"My father's Cuban," Gabriel said with a strange, mischievous smile. "They love their hyphens."

"Right. Well, you keep playing like that and you can have the mic 'til we close up at two. Free drinks, just don't get yourself sloppy while you're on my clock."

Gabriel nodded once, took his glass back to the stage. He clicked the microphone on and leaned in to address the crowd. "Good news. The boss-man say I can stay."

People clapped and someone shouted, "You better, Shane!"

Shane rolled his eyes. "'Nother beer please, Jeanne."

He tossed a five in the tip jar and took his bottle to the other side of the lounge, sinking into a spring-shot couch by the front windows. Gabriel played a sensual, mournful song and a few couples slow-danced, drifting in lazy circles and obscuring Shane's view of the stage. He shifted in his seat, uneasy. He'd put on a sweater after his shower but he felt strangled by it now, too warm and confined. He pulled it over his head and shoved it between his leg and the arm of the couch. The colored lights made the whole damn world look drunk.

Gabriel sang, more Spanish lyrics that left Shane's throat tight, his skin hot. He'd never been affected by music this way before. And it had to be the music, since Shane had never felt the first inkling of attraction to a man in his life, and what he was feeling now…it'd be laughable to pretend it wasn't sexual. Maybe he'd stumbled upon his first real kink at thirty-five, the world's first and only mandolin fetish.

But he stared at those strings and his eyes saw only fingers. He tried to listen to the notes but he only heard that man's voice, memory conjuring his mouth and face and eyes, his smell. Just the thought of those lips and hands drained the blood from Shane's head and sent it rushing south, making his cock heavy and warm.

He tore his eyes off the stage and directed them at the various women dancing and laughing and drinking, but his attention passed over them as if they were furniture, mannequins. His eyes floated back to the stage, to the half-Cuban, half-everything-else spell-caster and damn if it didn't feel good, watching. Fuck if it didn't feel as though a phantom hand were sliding down the front of his jeans to palm his dick.

Jeanne appeared at Shane's side two songs later, leaning her plump hip on the arm of the couch, holding a beer bottle. "You were starin', boss."

"You're too young for me, girl."

She laughed. "Not at me, at him." She nodded to the back of the room. "At Gabriel."

He winced, feeling slapped. "No I wasn't."

"Yeah you were. You looked like…" She turned to the stage.

Shane swallowed, panic rising in his chest. "Like what?"

"Like you caught him with your little sister or something."

He melted into the cushions with relief. "Just wonderin' who I've invited into my bar."

"Well, he's amazing—everybody's saying so when they come up for a refill. Don't go scaring him away." She swapped his empty bottle for the full one.

"Keep 'em comin', Jeanne."

She grabbed a couple dirty glasses off the adjacent tables. "Only if you promise not to get drunk and punch the guy's lights out."

Shane imagined the start of such a confrontation, his hands fisted around Gabriel's open collar. The fantasy didn't end in a punch though, and he felt his face burn, glad it was dim. "Another whiskey'd be appreciated, next time you're in my neighborhood."

"You're the boss."

Yeah. So why'd he feel so goddamn powerless right now?

CHAPTER TWO

"Thank you. Good night."

Shane woke from his trance as Gabriel switched the mic off to furious clapping and set his mandolin in its case, snapped it closed. Shane squinted at the clock behind the bar. One forty-five? When the fuck had that happened?

He stood and felt the clumsiness the last few hours' many drinks had lent him. Customers swarmed the counter, settling tabs and getting final orders in. Shane tucked his sweater under his arm and carried a bunch of empties to the bar, slid in behind Zach and loaded the washer before getting out of the way. He wandered around the porch, tapping the more inebriated-looking folks on the shoulder and doing his nightly designated driver matchmaking shtick. After the crowd thinned he went back to the bar, reached over to pop open the register and counted out five twenties. He glanced around for Gabriel only to find the man standing just to his left. Gabriel took off his hat and fanned his face a few times, sending his smell drifting toward Shane.

Shane held the bills out. "Here you go."

"Ad said seventy-five." Though Gabriel folded the twenties and tucked them inside his cigarette case all the same.

"You're damn good, and the crowd liked what you do. Hoped I might bribe you into coming back, regular as you want."

Gabriel grinned, maybe drunk, maybe supremely relaxed. "Sounds good."

Shane swallowed and did his level-best to keep their eye contact to a minimum. "You live close?"

Gabriel shook his head. "But I'm lookin' for someplace to stay 'round here. Temporary. You know anybody with a couch to let?"

Shane took a deep drink before he replied. "For how long?"

Gabriel raised his shoulders, too graceful to be called a shrug.

"What's that mean? A night? A week? Six months?"

"Maybe a week," Gabriel said.

"I dunno about a week, but I got a couch upstairs. For the night at least."

"You live here?"

Shane nodded. "I'm heading up now. Take it or leave it."

Gabriel left him to go back to the stage, returning with a small, ancient suitcase in one hand, instrument in the other.

Shane shouted over the din to Jeanne and Zach. "You kids good down here?"

"We're fine, boss. See you tomorrow," Jeanne said.

"See you Sunday," Zach added.

Shane glanced at Gabriel and blamed his shiver on the dispersing crowd. He heard and felt the man behind him as he walked through the sunken porch area to the side exit, up the wooden steps to the second floor. He unlocked the door and flipped on the living room lights, actually missing the cold air as they went inside. He'd cranked the heat up and now he regretted it, the apartment feeling oppressive.

"That's the couch," Shane said, pointing. "Bathroom's past the kitchen. Don't steal nothin'."

He turned to find Gabriel smiling, looking around the room. It was Shane's late grandmother's taste, deep yellow walls and old, handsome furniture that was wasted on his bachelor ass. He grabbed the work shirt and grease-smeared jeans he'd left on the floor that afternoon and took them to his room, snatching his shorts off the kitchen linoleum as he went. He poured himself a glass of water and downed it at the sink.

He addressed Gabriel over the counter that separated the kitchen and living room. "What d'you drink? Wine?"

"Sure."

Shane grabbed a bottle from the cabinet above the fridge, one of the three reds the bar carried. He uncorked it and opened the cupboard, eyeballing the wineglasses he'd inherited with the rest of his memaw's classy stuff. The stemware screamed romance to him and he shut the door on it. He strolled to the living room and plunked the open bottle on the side table between the couch and the easy chair and took a seat in the latter. Gabriel took a drink from the bottle and held it out.

Shane only ever drank wine at weddings and family holiday meals and he bet he'd wake up the next day and remember why that was. But it tasted good, tasted like everything about this night. Warm and dark, different than all the things he considered normal.

They passed the bottle back and forth and shot the shit for a while, trading stories about growing up in Louisiana—about Shane's childhood outside Baton Rouge, Gabriel's early life with his crazy, superstitious grandmother in New Orleans, and his late teen years and twenties spent with his father in Havana.

"Explains that fucked-up accent," Shane said, taking the bottle back. "You speak fluent Spanish, then? Or just sing it?"

Gabriel rattled off something Shane didn't understand past "*Sí.*"

"Guess so. Hope it's twice as comprehensible as your English… So that's where you learned mandolin? Is it a Cuban thing?"

"Not really." Gabriel gave the case by his foot a gentle kick. "Found this in my maw-maw's attic when I was tiny. She di'n know where it came from. Let me have it. Taught myself from a book I stole from a music shop."

Shane nodded. "I don't know how to play any instruments."

"I play lots. Saw you got a bluegrass night, and folk and blues. You ever need something down there—fiddle or bass or any kind of guitar—you tell me."

"Sure," Shane said. "Pays even worse than a solo gig though."

"I don' care. I jus' like to play."

Shane took a drink, cleared his throat, feeling shifty inside his clothes. "Fuckin' hot in here." As he shrugged his shirt off he realized what it must look like. He wondered if that wasn't why he'd done it. He had an undershirt on beneath his button-up, but Gabriel didn't. Gabriel slid his dress shirt off his tan shoulders and it was just bare, damp tattooed flesh with no barriers.

"Notes," Shane said dimly, eyes darting across the black and blue ink that etched sheet music all over Gabriel's chest and neck and biceps. "What song is it?"

"All sorts," Gabriel said, predatory eyes narrowing for a fraction of a second. "You have any? Tattoos?"

He shook his head. "Always wanted one, but I don't commit well. Can't ever think of something I guess I'd still want in forty years."

"Mine help me remember," Gabriel said.

"Songs?"

He shook his head. "People."

23

Shane didn't ask him to elaborate. "So…what brings you to Shiloh, anyhow? Why ain't you back in New Orleans, playing there? Cashing in on some of that Carnivale crowd?"

"I don' like going back there anymore."

"So why're you here?" Shane took a drink. "Why not Baton Rouge, at least?"

"I went. A club owner there, he send me here. Said your place is somethin' special."

Shane snorted. "'Special' meaning it's the only place with a liquor license for twenty bog-stinking miles."

"No, it special." Gabriel held his eyes. "You know it, jus' like everybody else down there."

Shane shrugged. "My Aunt Marie opened this place after she inherited the house. She worked for thirty years making weddin' dresses and then her hands started hurting too much to keep going."

He told Gabriel about how she'd intended it to be a fun venue for receptions, over-the-top bridal themed. Turned out it wasn't high-class enough for most brides, but regular old thirsty folks loved it—all the antique framed wedding photos she'd picked up at estate sales, the neon signs from drive-thru chapels, the garters nailed into the window frames to hold the sequin- and pearl-encrusted curtains open. It started out a novelty and evolved into more—into an experience.

"I bartended down there from when it opened 'til I became the owner, two years ago."

"You inherit this place, then?" Gabriel asked.

Shane shook his head. "I bought it from her for a few thousand dollars. She wanted to give it to me outright but I wouldn't let her. Just paid her what I had."

"Why she decide to leave?"

"Got married, actually. Moved to Plano with her new husband."

"Very romantic." Gabriel smiled at that and they passed the bottle between them for a couple minutes.

Shane was finding it harder and harder to remember not to stare at Gabriel. He wanted to blame the wine for what he was feeling, though it'd started when he was totally sober. This man…he was seductive, without making a single flirtatious remark or crossing any physical boundaries. It was in the way he accepted or offered the bottle, how he narrowed his eyes when he smiled, pursed his lips at some comment or other of Shane's. He was more beautiful than any woman Shane had ever been with—hell, than any Shane had ever *seen*—and it made his body ache.

Any minute now, he'd find his sense and turn all this carnal curiosity into male insecurity, quit with the friendliness and get back to good old-fashioned defensive bigotry. Not that he was a bigot. That was the one thing he hadn't inherited from his old man. But he sure as hell wished he could muster a taste of it right now. Might give him the scare he needed to beat it the fuck out of this room and get a purchase on his manhood.

Gabriel set the bottle on the table with a distinctly empty-sounding clank.

"Les watch something," he slurred. He fixed Shane with a long, devious look then crawled to the cabinet beneath the TV, flung the doors open and began rummaging. Shane knew damn well what he was looking for. Only one thing drunk men went looking for with that kind of gusto—unless they were *Star Wars* fans, and he bet Gabriel didn't know an Ewok from his asshole.

"If you're looking for porn you'll have no luck there."

Gabriel turned and cocked an eyebrow at him. "Where, then?"

Shane got to standing, found his wobbly land legs and walked to one of the disused rooms in the back, still piled with his grandfather's things. He heard Gabriel's footsteps behind him. He reached into a paper shopping bag by the overflowing closet and lifted out the stack of ancient fishing magazines that concealed his modest stash.

"Ah," Gabriel said.

"My last girlfriend was kind of a basket case about that stuff." Most of Shane's girlfriends over the years had been...except for a couple who'd been into it, but both of them had turned out to be total psychos in other respects. Always one thing or another with the women Shane seemed to attract.

He grabbed a few DVDs and brought them to Gabriel. "You pick. I need a piss."

He hid in the bathroom for a few minutes, staring blearily at himself in the mirror. Knowing what was going to happen. He tried to picture any one of those psycho girlfriends' faces, but all he could see were black eyes, black hair, tan skin, lips that made his dick stiffen with thoughts he didn't want.

His heart was pounding as he emerged. He opened another bottle and held on to the neck for dear life as he returned to the living room. Gabriel had plugged in the string of Christmas lights that had been hanging around the window since long before Shane moved in. Surely his grandmother had been planning on taking them down after the holidays, but Shane never got around to stuff like that.

He downed three swigs and took a seat on the floor, back against the couch. Gabriel was fucking around hopelessly with the remotes. He didn't even belong in the same century with a DVD player.

"Gimme that." Shane put his hand out. He got the disc playing in seconds flat and Gabriel took the wine from him, settling a couple feet to his left on the carpet, way too close. Way too far away.

They traded the bottle back and forth for ten minutes, Shane barely processing the images flashing by on the TV, none of them having the first thing to do with the ache between his legs. He took a final, deep slug of wine and took them where he damn well knew Gabriel wanted to go.

"I gotta jerk," Shane said.

He didn't wait for permission, just unbuckled his belt and unzipped his fly, shoved his shorts down enough to take his cock out. His periphery told him Gabriel was following suit. He glued his eyes on the screen, as if an arrow might shoot out of a hidden trap in the wall and thwack into his heart if he even thought about glancing to the left.

He watched the movie, an idiotic scene he'd sat through a few times before. He wanted to find the woman attractive, blame her for his arousal, but she registered in his brain as an abstract pile of fake breasts and collagen lips and bleached hair, too-smooth hairless pussy. He was relieved the sight of the male porn star did even less for him. So why were his eyes so fucking hungry, dying to watch the man sitting next to him?

He heard Gabriel moan, a soft, rhythmic sound. He couldn't help himself—he looked. Just a glance, enough to register a nest of curly black hair, those talented, slender fingers wrapped around a long cock. Long, but not huge. Not near as big as Shane. He smiled to himself, smug, then felt immediately drunk and stupid.

You want to fuck the guy. Having a bigger dick's a pretty pathetic attempt at bolstering your manhood, jackass.

And he did want to fuck him. And he knew Gabriel wanted that. To fuck or to get fucked. Better be the latter, since Shane wasn't taking anything up the ass, no matter how shit-faced or horny he let himself get, no matter how hot the guy was.

Spurred by a million hot chemicals racing through his dick, Shane glanced to his left again and didn't look away. Gabriel's eyes slid from the screen to Shane's face, then down to his stroking hand. He licked his lips, the gesture looking more reflexive than seductive. He looked to Shane's face again.

Shane had no clue what to do. He'd gotten into this deeper than his sober self would have ever wanted. Panic made his mouth dry but he let his darting eyes settle on Gabriel's steady black ones, knowing he must look like a pleading man.

Save me, he thought. *Decide for me, so it's not my fault.* He could almost swear the man nodded. Gabriel looked back to the screen and Shane did the same.

The blonde was going down on a cop—actually, a criminal dressed as a cop, if Shane remembered the so-called plot correctly. The blowjob looked painful. Too fast and rough, no subtlety, fake nails glinting like a liability. If a woman ever blew Shane like that he'd say, "Baby, I gotta fuck you right now," just to get away from that scary mouth.

"I suck cock way better than that," Gabriel murmured.

"I'll bet." It took Shane a moment to register Gabriel's words. He snapped his head to the left. "You actually sucked cock before?"

"Yeah."

Shane's hand froze. His brain was unable to coordinate multiple parts of his body at once and it was his mouth's turn now. A dark, defensive part of him wanted to use a slur, but his momma had raised him better than that. Plus it'd take one big fucking hypocritical nerve and he knew it.

"You gay?" he finally asked.

"Not for everybody."

"You bi?" Shane had never really believed people were bi—he'd figured it was just something gay guys said until they got themselves figured out.

Gabriel nodded. Shane had seen Gabriel work his magic on women downstairs and he believed him. Girls had approached him during breaks between songs, and he'd had an easy grace with them, nothing fake about the sexual interest he'd communicated with his body language.

They both turned back to the movie and Shane felt more naked than he had in his entire life. He fisted his cock but didn't stroke. He wanted this man, just as he might want a hot woman. More. And Gabriel's charisma…it had a feminine undertone to it. Shane wasn't attracted to men. He was attracted to *one* man. This one. And this one was beautiful, and Shane wanted to fuck him the way he'd fuck a woman. He repeated the thought a few times, let his fist begin to pump again.

Gabriel cleared his throat, the noise sounding tight. "I suck cock better than that," he repeated, mischief in his voice. "Even big, thick ones like yours."

"That what you like?" Shane asked, eyes aimed straight ahead.

"Yeah."

His grip tightened as his fist sped up. "You askin' me?"

"You invitin' me?"

Fuck you, man, just say yes. "I dunno."

Gabriel moved. Shane turned to watch him get to his knees, letting his underwear ride up to half-hide his cock. He faced Shane, dug one elbow into the couch cushions and propped his jaw on his hand, so casual it was cruel.

"I'd love to suck your cock, Shane."

Shane's heart raced. He shut his eyes, kept jerking until he felt Gabriel's knees nudging his calves open. He groaned as two hands ran up his legs from the ankle to the thigh, squeezing.

"Lemme see," Gabriel whispered.

Shane let him grasp his wrist, pull his hand away and set it to the side. He swallowed deep and almost choked when a warm, unfamiliar fist closed around his base, slender, string-calloused fingers measuring him with slow, appraising strokes.

"Sit on the couch, Shane."

Fuck, that voice. It should dampen the urge, hearing a man speak, feeling a big hand wrapped around him this way, but it only made Shane ache worse.

He opened his eyes, wincing, feeling helpless. He braced his hands on the cushions and pushed himself up onto the sofa. Gabriel shuffled forward on his knees, tugged Shane's jeans a few inches farther down his thighs. Shane watched his face, the filthy concentration in those dark eyes, mouth opening, tongue wetting his lips. Those slow strokes kept Shane burning, kept his entire body hot and hurting. He heard a groan and it took him a moment to realize it was his own.

"Do it," he whispered. He closed his eyes, leaned his head back and fisted the upholstery at his sides. He tried to conjure the woman from the movie, the one still grunting in the background. His eyes opened to stare at the screen but the images felt like an assault and he shut them tighter. Gabriel's hand slowed and his other palm slid up Shane's thigh.

Any second now. He swore he felt hot breath steaming against his dick. Then, wet heat.

He bucked against the cushions, from surprise and pleasure and panic. Lips, firm and tight, slid halfway down his cock then back up, again and again. The hard, slick, expert pressure of the man's tongue pressed the ridge along the underside of his erection. Shane tried again to replace him with a woman. Any woman. Or nothingness, pure sensation. Fat fucking chance.

The heat took him deeper, adding suction—just the right amount. This man knew what a blowjob was about, how to make it equal parts worship and service. Shane realized something in a flash, something so obvious and so frightening it stripped away all his pointless attempts at denial.

He was getting sucked by a man. And who was he trying to kid? He wanted it.

He opened his eyes, pointed them right where they ached to be, on Gabriel's beautiful face. He reached both hands down and pushed the wavy black hair back from his stubbly cheeks, tucked it behind his ears so it wouldn't obscure Shane's view. He kept one palm on the back of Gabriel's head, stroked his own belly with the other.

"That's good. That's so fuckin' good, boy."

He felt Gabriel moan around his dick, a hungry, needy noise.

"Suck me. Suck my cock."

Gabriel's pumping hand sped up, eager. He was getting hot, losing some of his grace, but Shane didn't give a good goddamn. He'd never seen a woman look so hypnotized, doing this to him. Gabriel's skin was flushed, perspiration beading on his forehead. He took more, another inch, another, until he had nearly all of Shane buried in his mouth and throat, until Shane could hear and feel him gagging. It only seemed to excite the man more.

"That's so hot," Shane muttered.

Gabriel paused a moment then pulled back, giving Shane's cock the faintest graze of his teeth as he slid it out. He turned his attention to the head, lapping and sucking, tonguing Shane's slit and stroking the length of his dick with a tight, steady fist.

"Yeah. Don't you dare stop."

Gabriel's brows knitted, a moment of deep, even painful arousal. He freed his mouth, met Shane's eyes and held them. "I'm thirsty, Shane."

The words shot down his spine like electricity, knocked his wind out. That mouth, that voice. Those fucking pitch-black eyes, locked on his.

Gabriel looked away, put his mouth back to work and let Shane catch his breath. Shane tangled his fingers in that messy hair, held Gabriel's head, wanting to possess him and control him, or to cling to such an illusion even as this man had him near to pleading.

"Don't you stop. Keep sucking that cock. Keep sucking me."

Gabriel did as he was told, kept the pleasure coming, kept Shane on the brink longer than anybody'd ever done before. His mouth eased as he took Shane to the edge, holding release just out of his grasp.

"Come on, motherfucker. Make me come." He pulled Gabriel's head close, forced his cock deeper between those sucking lips. The smug, dirty noise Gabriel made threw Shane overboard. The heat and excitement and need pooled and boiled between his legs and he came, pulling his hips back, slipping his head from Gabriel's mouth so he could watch the come shoot between his lips and across his tongue until Shane had nothing left to give.

Sobriety punched him in the head, rearranging reality. He heard himself muttering, "yeah, yeah, yeah," under his breath, felt two mismatched male hands gripping his dick, saw the beautiful, strange musician from the bar kneeling on the rug before him, swallowing Shane's come.

The scrap of rational thought left in his brain told Shane he was supposed to be disgusted and pissed to high heaven, but his instincts had only one agenda.

He shoved a hand under each of Gabriel's armpits and hauled him awkwardly to his feet. "C'mere."

Gabriel got a knee beside either of Shane's thighs, straddling his lap. Shane pulled Gabriel's open pants halfway down his ass, yanked at the waistband of his shorts to expose his cock.

He'd never touched another man before and Gabriel felt foreign and exotic—smooth skin, stiff and pulsing and blazing hot. Shane felt the exact opposite of how he'd guessed with his hand wrapped around this stranger's dick. He felt powerful, big and insanely masculine.

Gabriel moaned at the touch, setting a hand on each of Shane's shoulders and leaning in, making him feel all that weight, smell everything similar and different about their skin and bodies. Shane listened to Gabriel's rasping breaths, wanting more.

"Talk to me, boy." He squeezed his hand tight, drew it up and down Gabriel's cock in long, mean strokes. "Tell me what you're thinkin'."

"Since I first saw you," Gabriel said through his panting, "all I been able to think about is how I can get my mouth 'round your dick."

"Guess you got what you wanted then."

Gabriel moaned his agreement as Shane's pulls sped. He tugged at Shane's undershirt and Shane let him peel it up and off. Warm, damp hands appraised Shane's chest and arms, just as countless women had but so utterly different.

"D'you fuck or get fucked?" Shane held his breath, fearing one answer, fearing the pleasure he knew he'd get from the other.

"With men?" Gabriel asked through a moan. "Get fucked."

Shane's spent cock twitched as he fought to keep from imagining it, to keep from groaning from the dark excitement coursing in his veins.

"Like it rough," Gabriel whispered. "Bet you fuck nice an' rough."

Shane kept silent, bit back every animal promise his body was dying for him to make to this man. He kept pumping Gabriel's cock, squeezing his hard thigh with the other hand. He rubbed his hip and felt the restless tensing of bone and muscle under Gabriel's skin. His palm crept back, back, until his fingers dug into the firm, ripe flesh of his ass. Shane felt the man in his lap burning hotter and felt himself coming apart too, ripping into pieces from the power and helplessness and fear and want. He stared at Gabriel's tattoos and lost himself in those hundreds of black and blue notes, dozens of snatches of music he couldn't translate.

He stroked Gabriel's hard cock, palmed his ass cheek. His fingers slid into his crack, holding steady for a moment as he drank in the guttural moan Gabriel rewarded him with. Behind it was cheesy synthesizer, strangers' grunts and dirty murmurings, the movie's pathetic attempts at eroticism impossibly paled by what was happening in Shane's drunken reality.

Gabriel's hips were eager, thrusting his cock into Shane's fist, clenching the cleft of his ass around Shane's fingertips. Shane didn't think he'd ever seen anybody get so fucking riled up. The man looked crazy, panting and trembling and moaning, and he looked beautiful. Shane wanted to take him to the edge and hold him there, watch him fall, see him wrecked by what Shane could do to him. He wanted to be better than any other guy Gabriel had ever had, wanted him hooked, wanting him fucking *faithful*. Who the fuck's thoughts were these?

Shane edged the tip of his middle finger deep between Gabriel's cheeks. The hands gripping his shoulders squeezed tight, short nails digging, maybe breaking skin—Shane didn't give a shit.

"I know what you want, boy." He took a breath and pressed his fingertip to the puckered skin of Gabriel's asshole.

Gabriel's hips bucked, bringing his body closer to Shane's. One of his hands moved to the back of Shane's head.

"Say my name," Shane said, rubbing the entrance. "Say my name and I'll give you what you want."

"Shane," he gasped. "Shane. Shane."

"Say please."

"Please. Please, Shane."

Dizziness clouded Shane's mind but he had what he needed—the illusion of power. With Gabriel begging, Shane was in control. He drew his hand away and spat across his fingers, brought them back to Gabriel's ass.

"Yeah. Please, Shane. Now."

He rubbed the wetness across the hole, slow and mean.

"Tell me about me fucking you," Shane said.

Gabriel moaned. "On the floor. My hands and knees."

Shane slid his finger in to the first knuckle and Gabriel gasped.

"Keep talking," Shane ordered.

Gabriel's hand went to Shane's dick, half recovered already, half hard. "Your big cock."

"What about it?" Shane forced another finger in, shallow, massaging the tight ring of muscle.

Gabriel's eyes closed, mouth frozen in a silent moan.

Shane squeezed Gabriel's throbbing dick even harder. "Tell me about my big cock."

"You fuck me," Gabriel choked out. "On your floor with your big cock. You're so deep. An' fast, like you want it to hurt."

Shane drove his fingers deeper, not caring if they were slick enough or not. Gabriel cried out in surprise or excitement or pain.

"You come," Gabriel stammered. "You pull out and come on my ass then you lick me clean."

Shane tensed but kept his hands working. "I don't drink come. Not mine or yours or the goddamn pope's."

Gabriel's eyes looked vacant, lost deep in his own pleasure and fantasies. "An' you turn me over and hold me down, and suck me 'til I shoot."

Fear and revulsion churned acid in Shane's gut but he didn't stop. He wasn't about to be the powerless one in this intimate battle. "You keep wishin' that," he said, staring Gabriel down. "'Cause you'll never get it from me."

"I wan' you to own me," Gabriel whispered.

A chill trickled down Shane's body, cooling his fevered skin like ice water. There were things he'd never do for this man, but he *did* want that. He wanted to own him.

He penetrated Gabriel deeper with his fingers, twisted and curled them, coaxing the most beautiful moans he'd ever heard, ten times more mesmerizing than the man's singing. He watched his other hand, the dark skin of Gabriel's swollen head in his fist. He imagined bringing it to his mouth, tasting him. Rubbing the smooth skin over his lips and wetting them with this man's pre-come. He clenched his eyes shut, wanting to drive the thought away. Gabriel's groans were impossible to block out. Shane plunged his fingers deep, aching at the thought of that tight heat wrapped around his cock.

"Shane."

He opened his eyes, gave up and gave in, watched this man coming undone from his touch and wallowed in it.

"Come for me, boy."

Gabriel leaned closer, a sweat-slick hand gripping the back of Shane's neck, the other on his arm. He rested his chin at Shane's cheek, his hot, wine-sweetened breath warming his temple. His body trembled, hips pumping in tight, greedy motions in time with Shane's fist.

"Come on. Come on."

Shane drunkenly imagined someone showing up, some faceless acquaintance coming through his door and finding him with his fingers jammed to the third knuckle up this beautiful man's ass. It should have scared him, but it didn't. The only thing that mattered was making Gabriel moan and buck, making him feel so good he'd never look at another guy, never want anything he couldn't get from Shane. His fist tightened at the idea and he felt Gabriel stiffen against him with a harsh gasp. Hot wetness lashed Shane's stomach and he slowed his hands, still jacking, just as he would if this had been his own cock.

Gabriel's groan tapered off to a low, satisfied chuckle, pure contentedness. He leaned back and Shane took in his flushed face and heaving chest, damp hair plastered to his cheeks, heavy lids hiding those deadly eyes.

Shane took his hands back, wiped them on the undershirt beside him on the couch. He pushed Gabriel's hair from his face and did the only thing his body wanted—he kissed him.

It felt sinful, darker and dirtier than any other act that evening. This strange man's stubble scraped Shane's chin as he deepened the kiss, plunged his tongue into Gabriel's mouth to taste him. He pressed his palms tight over Gabriel's jaw, tilted his head, forced his way farther inside. He wanted to bite him—leave him marked and bleeding, branded. He wanted to hurt him and scare him, make him run away so Shane wouldn't find himself in this position again.

Warm fingers rubbed the come into Shane's skin, an act of possession if he'd ever felt one. He broke his mouth from Gabriel's and yanked his head back. He mopped his stomach with the undershirt, wadded it into a ball. He shifted Gabriel, pushed him onto the next cushion and stood. He tucked his hard cock behind his underwear and zipped up his jeans.

Shane's heart raced as he wandered down the hall to the big parlor he'd made into his bedroom. He shoved the undershirt deep inside his hamper, grabbed a pillow off his bed and a couple blankets from the linen closet, went back to the living room.

Gabriel had tugged his pants back up but he still had that look of lazy seduction plastered all over his gorgeous face.

"Here." Shane tossed him the bedding as gruffly as he could manage, went to the TV and clicked it off. "I have to go in to work at ten tomorrow, so be prepared to leave then."

Gabriel smiled. "Sure. And thank you. For the wine and the couch."

Shane didn't want to think about or acknowledge wine or couches anymore. "It's not a problem. I'll see you tomorrow if you're still around."

That pretty-ass grin again. "Sweet dreams, Shane."

CHAPTER THREE

Shane peeled his eyes open to find his room lit by streaming sunlight. It deepened the ache in his temples and sinuses, exacerbated the drum-pounding force of the blood pulsing in his ears.

"Fuck *me.*"

He squinted at the clock—ten fourteen. So much for getting to the garage early. His mouth tasted like old wine and dried phlegm and he made himself yet another promise to never drink so much again. He looked down at his legs and found he still had his jeans on, belt unbuckled. Then the fear and recollection hit him like a kick in the balls.

He lay still, stared at the ceiling, at the motionless blades of the fan. His heart thumped, sending tremors through his body. He didn't need confirmation that he hadn't dreamt last night. It'd been real.

That man had been real and so had Shane's pleasure, as real as the panic gripping him now. That man was probably on his couch.

Shane entertained a strange, hopeful thought. *Maybe he robbed me blind and disappeared forever.* That'd sure as hell be better than having to face the guy.

He listened to the old house, straining for sounds of a stirring guest. None. He rolled off the bed and his bruised brain flopped to the other side of his skull. He dragged his ass to the bathroom, relieved by the fan's white noise, the murmur of the spray as he turned on the shower. Brushing his teeth while the water heated, Shane felt a little calmer. He swallowed six aspirin and leaned on the sink a long time, counting his breaths.

He felt better after the shower, better once he changed into clean clothes and adjusted to the challenge of walking. He lingered in his room, tidying things or at least moving them around. He got his sac together and ventured into the kitchen, took a deep breath and looked across the counter that separated it from the living room.

Gabriel was stretched on the couch, facing away—black hair against Shane's white pillowcase, bare foot and bare, tattooed arm peeking from under the blanket.

Shane didn't feel as he'd expected. He didn't hate the guy or feel scared. Not even embarrassed. He didn't particularly want him here, but he wasn't all that bothered. He filled the coffeemaker and switched it on, went to the living room. He passed Gabriel and gathered the two empty wine bottles from the floor beside the couch, let them clank together. Gabriel moved, a small, sleepy shifting of his body. Shane opened the screen door, thanked God for the cool winter air for the second time in his life. He filled his lungs with it as he trotted down the steps, tossed the bottles in the huge recycling bin behind the bar's back entrance.

As Shane closed the door behind him, he found Gabriel unmoved. He gave that profile a good long study. Just as handsome as he'd thought last night, not diminished by sobriety or regret. Still, Shane fled back to the kitchen.

He didn't know what he expected to see on that man's face when they inevitably made eye contact. Cockiness, maybe. Triumph, if Gabriel was one of those guys Shane had heard about, the kind who lived to corrupt straight men. Or maybe nothing at all—no sign that anything had gone on between them. And that scared Shane worse than he wanted to admit.

But when Shane rounded the corner from his room to the hallway and came face-to-face with him, Gabriel didn't look like any of those things. His lips curled into a smile, mischievous but not smug. Maybe even a touch shy. He was wearing pants but nothing else and carrying a small leather shaving bag.

"Mornin'," Shane said, determined to act as if he were fine with all this.

"Mornin'. You min' if I shower?"

Shane shook his head. "There's towels in the cupboard by the door."

"Thanks."

Shane poured a cup of coffee and emptied the dishwasher, hands and brain desperate for things to do. He decided to go ahead and make breakfast, just as he would if it were a girl in his bathroom, if only for the activity and the charade of normality.

He was peeling strips of bacon from the package when Gabriel emerged, towel knotted around his waist, pants tucked under his arm. His wet hair was slicked back, all his breathtaking features on full display.

Shane poured him a mug of coffee and slid it across the center island between them with what he hoped was a bored face.

Gabriel's smile conveyed his thanks and he took a sip, setting his pants and bag on the counter. Shane looked to his stomach, tan skin draped over lean muscle, the northernmost point of the soft black hair peeking from behind the low-riding towel…that rose-patterned, ancient bath towel Shane associated with his grandmother sunbathing. He turned his attention back to the bacon, hangover and confusion redoubled.

"Thanks for the couch," Gabriel said. His voice slid down Shane's spine like a warm finger.

"Sure." Shane kept his eyes on the frying pan, laying the strips perfectly parallel, making a distraction of it.

"An' the gig."

Shane nodded.

"I heard tonight is Latin dance night."

Shane looked over his shoulder. "Yeah. Not sure if the band's got any openings though."

"I was more interested in the dancin'."

"Oh. That another thing you picked up in Cuba?"

Gabriel nodded.

Shane went to the fridge to pull out a carton of eggs and a stick of butter. "Well, dance all you want. It's a free country."

"You 'round tonight?"

Unseen to Gabriel, Shane shut his eyes and tried to unravel what that question made him feel…a twisted cocktail of dread and excitement and hope.

"Might be. I usually drop in to check everything's okay with the staff, hang around for a drink." *Or three.*

"Maybe I see you 'round then?"

"Maybe." Shane cleared his throat. "You as hungover as I am?" He looked over his shoulder again.

Gabriel shook his head.

Shane laughed to himself. "Course you ain't." He cracked five eggs into a bowl and scrambled them, turned the bacon over. "I'm not leavin' at ten," he said. "Obviously, since it's pushin' eleven. And I ain't cookin' for one here. Feel free to join me." He kept his tone casual.

"I'd like that. Smells good."

Shane wiped his fingers on a dish towel and turned. Goddamn if the previous night's feelings weren't still there. Just looking at the length of this stranger's raw, lean body, Shane felt his cock rousing.

He'd had this man last night. Had his mouth and hands, had him pleading and desperate, needing what Shane could give him. Heat and tension fisted his heart and he took a few steps, rounded the island to stand in front of Gabriel, remind both of them who was bigger, taller, whose house this was and whose rules it followed. He stared at Gabriel's beautiful face—all that black stubble, those dark irises, molasses brown in the daylight. That mouth and all the pleasure it could give.

"How old are you, anyway?"

"Thirty next month."

Shane nodded.

"I 'preciate everything you done for me," Gabriel said, eyes on Shane's throat. "If there's somethin' I can do to show you how grateful I am, you tell me, Shane."

He reached his hands out, slow, gave Shane plenty of time to knock them away. His fingers traced the slit between the top two snaps of Shane's work shirt. His eyes locked on Shane's and he popped the top snap open then the second, all the way down his belly.

Shane put his hands to Gabriel's face, dug his thumbs into his cheeks and held his jaw. He studied his eyes for a good long moment before he brought his lips down and settled them against Gabriel's. Not a kiss—just two open mouths touching, uneven breath warming the minuscule space between them.

Gabriel's exotic scent was gone, replaced by Shane's too-familiar soap and toothpaste and coffee, the bacon smell permeating the kitchen. Shane missed others scents now, sweat and red wine and sex. He cocked his head a few degrees, drew the tip of his tongue along Gabriel's lower lip. Both their pairs of eyes were half-open and Gabriel's dark irises snapped back and forth between Shane's.

Satisfaction loosened Shane's muscles as he realized this man would never kiss him first. Shane was in charge, calling the shots, the one with the control…or so he decided to believe.

He moved his hand, brushed his thumb over Gabriel's parted lips a few times then pushed it in. That wet, hot mouth closed around his knuckle, sucking gently, tongue teasing. Shane pushed it deeper, made Gabriel suckle for a minute before he took it away and replaced it with his mouth.

Shane kissed him how he'd never kiss a woman—bossy and graceless and filthy, ramming his tongue deep, fucking those hungry lips with it. He reached between them, tugged the towel open and pulled Gabriel hard against him, wanting him to feel Shane's clothes, the bite of his belt buckle against bare skin. He ground his crotch against Gabriel's ready cock, pinned him to the edge of the counter.

Shane let Gabriel unbuckle his belt, open his fly. He let him push his jeans and underwear down and press his body close, their stiff cocks touching and setting Shane on fire. Strong, calloused hands massaged Shane's hips then slid to his ass. He held his breath, let it go, let Gabriel explore his flesh with hungry hands, kneading his muscle.

"So strong," Gabriel murmured.

Shane rubbed his cock against Gabriel's, got a hand between the man's back and the counter and palmed his ass a minute before sliding his fingers into the cleft to tease his asshole. Gabriel made two noises—a soft, awed gasp, then a happy *mmmm* as Shane stroked the spot.

"I loved sucking you last night," Gabriel whispered, mouth at Shane's neck.

"I know you did."

Slow hands continued to knead Shane's ass then one came down with a light smack.

Shane rankled. "Don't forget who's in charge."

He heard a smile in Gabriel's voice as his fingers curled into claws. "Never."

They rubbed their cocks together, touched each other's bodies until the smell of burning meat snapped Shane out of the trance.

"Fuck." He pushed back from the counter and hiked his pants up, jogged to the stove and tossed the smoking pan into the empty sink, twisted off the burner.

He turned to find Gabriel gone. He swore again, flipped the fan on above the stove and prayed the smoke detectors wouldn't go off.

He found Gabriel in his bedroom, running a hand along the back of the couch that helped fill the massive space. Shane watched his naked body in the warm sunlight, forgot the smoke and remembered only the sensation of pressing himself against this man.

"What d'you want?" Shane asked, taking a step closer.

Gabriel met his eyes, held the stare a long moment before speaking. "I wanna watch you."

They studied each other awhile longer, then Shane shrugged his shirt off, let his pants and shorts drop and kicked them aside. He ran his hand down his chest and stomach and gripped his cock, gave it slow strokes and watched Gabriel's reaction. He loved that look—utter worship. If the boy wanted a show then Shane would give him one.

"Lie on the bed," he said.

Gabriel went to stretch across the rumpled covers and Shane followed, feeling domineering and mean and unafraid. He slung a leg over Gabriel's waist and straddled him, took hold of his own dick again, gave it slow pulls designed to torture them both. He stared down at the beautiful man on his bed.

"This what you wanted to see?"

Gabriel's lips parted but he didn't speak. He rubbed his palms over Shane's thighs, in thrall.

Shane reached his free hand out and swept his fingertips across Gabriel's lips before sliding two fingers between them. Gabriel grasped Shane's wrist and sucked hard, that same face as when he'd taken his cock.

"Good... You always take what I give you." He took his hand back, fondling his balls as he masturbated himself, loving the look on Gabriel's face. He let Gabriel touch his thighs again, his stomach and side, his ass.

"You so big," Gabriel murmured. "All of you." He kept squeezing Shane's backside, eyes on his cock. The hungry touch made Shane nervous and he moved, shuffled back and shoved his knees between Gabriel's thighs to spread them wide open.

"Touch yourself," he ordered.

Gabriel fisted his dick, pleasured himself with slow, masterful strokes. "Had to do this 'fore I went to sleep las' night," he mumbled.

"What'd you think about?"

Gabriel moaned. His free hand ran down his belly to between his legs, giving his balls a couple tugs before two fingers rubbed his asshole. "'Bout you, Shane. 'Bout you fucking me." He penetrated himself, fingertips disappearing along with Shane's composure.

Shane imagined his cock in their place, imagined squeezing himself into Gabriel's tight body and riding him right here, on this bed. But not on his back. From behind, so Gabriel wouldn't see how helpless Shane would surely look as he came.

"Fuck yourself," Shane said. "Fuck yourself and watch my cock."

He stroked himself faster and rougher, excited beyond belief by Gabriel's rapt expression. Excited by other things...by the soft-looking dark hair on Gabriel's forearms and the tendons twitching beneath his tan skin. By those fingers, the ones sliding in and out of his asshole and the ones rubbing pre-come over the crown of his cock.

"You're so big," Gabriel said again.

"You think you can handle me?"

"I wanna try. Fuck me now."

"Beg me."

"Fuck me, Shane. Please."

Shane grinned down at him, feeling cruel, high on the power. "Spread those legs wider. Open right up for me."

Gabriel brought his knees closer to his chest.

"Lemme see."

The hand pleasuring Gabriel's ass moved away, giving Shane the filthy, tempting view he wanted. He reached his own hand down and teased the hole, listened to the harsh sound of Gabriel's gasp.

"Reach over your head," Shane said. "In my bedside table drawer—there's lube in there."

Gabriel craned his torso and rummaged, finding the bottle in record time. Shane took it and snapped the cap up. He smeared the cool gel across his palm and smoothed it over his cock, then got more, brought his fingers to Gabriel's ass, easing one in, then two.

"Yeah."

"Get your hand back on your dick," Shane barked. "And keep your eyes on me."

He stroked his slick cock, slow and tight, taunting. He pushed his fingers farther into Gabriel's ass, twisted them, drew them out, forced them deeper.

"More."

Shane added his ring finger and Gabriel's groan made his pulse rocket. "You feel good, boy. Nice and tight. You're makin' me want things I never even thought about before." Things he wouldn't be doing today—maybe not ever—though they still excited him. He slid his fingers out and angled his rock-hard dick, stroked his swollen head over that forbidden place.

"Yeah. Give it to me, Shane."

"You're forgetting who issues the orders around here." He kept his voice cool even as he was fighting his body's every instinct, willing his hips to stay still and not make him do something he'd regret.

"Please. Don' tease me, Shane."

"Me? Tease you?" Shane took his cock away and fucked Gabriel hard with his hand, rough and fast until the man stopped begging and simply moaned. Shane saw lust in every one of his features, in his swollen lips and his glazed eyes and his flushed ears and cheeks. And it was surely just like looking into a mirror.

"Come on," he whispered. "Come. Come all over yourself."

A dozen more strokes and Gabriel obeyed, every muscle tensing, ass clenching around Shane's fingers as his dick erupted, jets of come shooting across his stomach and chest. Shane waited until his body relaxed then eased his fingers out.

"Good boy." He felt powerful and horny beyond belief, staring down at Gabriel's panting, spent form. Then he did something he wouldn't have if he'd bothered thinking about it even for a second. He reached down and touched Gabriel's warm come, gathered it on his palm and smeared it over the length of his own dick, stroked himself until the friction turned sticky.

He sat back and spread his legs. "C'mere."

Gabriel got to his knees, came forward and sank to his elbows between Shane's thighs. His mouth was working before Shane could even give the order, sliding down his shaft to take him deep, greedy hand stroking as he sucked.

"You're so fucking dirty." Shane wiped his hands on the comforter and cupped the back of Gabriel's head, tangling his fingers in that wet hair. "I saw how bad you wanted me to fuck you."

Gabriel moaned around Shane's cock, sucked harder, hungrier.

"God, keep that up. Just like that." Shane closed his eyes and gave in to the sensations, wondered how he'd ever be able to live without this. Then he opened them again, wanting to see that face just as he had last night. "You are fucking beautiful."

Gabriel kept up his motions, catching Shane's eyes with his dark ones from time to time. And Shane didn't care. He wasn't afraid to acknowledge what was happening anymore. All he wanted was this experience, all of this foreign and intimidating pleasure right here in his bed. This man had real and palpable power—in his beauty and his charisma and his talent—and to be able to dictate orders to him, to make him beg, made Shane feel bigger than he had in his entire life.

He kept his palm on the back of Gabriel's head, told him who was in charge. "Good... Now do that thing you did to my head last night."

Gabriel slid Shane's cock nearly all the way from his mouth, locked his lips tight around the crown, sucking, teasing with his tongue. Shane moaned, clamped his hand around his base and stroked. He felt Gabriel's rough fingers close around his fist and something about that intimacy launched him over the edge in an instant.

"Fuck." The orgasm rattled through his body like an earthquake, made his legs twitch as he released for ages into Gabriel's greedy mouth.

He worked hard to find his breath and focus his eyes. "Holy fuck."

Shane made it to kneeling then collapsed, flopping down against the pillows. He looked at Gabriel's face and he wanted him again, only different.

He grabbed his arm and pulled him close, not giving a good goddamn where his mouth had just been. He kissed him, a seduction in reverse—starting out fierce and possessive then fading to a light sweeping of his lips over Gabriel's. He pushed his face against

Gabriel's neck, buried himself in that smell and warmth and circled his arms tight around the man's waist.

"I don't know what you're doing to me," he said, probably just a string of muffled grunts to Gabriel.

A hand stroked his hair and ear and back, something protective in the gesture.

Shane waited for reality to sink in. He had his naked body twined around another man, the smell of their sex heavy in the air, strong as the lingering smoke from the kitchen. He was supposed to feel something different from how he was, but how he felt was perfect. Satisfied and spent and content.

"You late for work yet?" Gabriel asked, a whisper floating past Shane's ear.

He pulled his mouth from Gabriel's damp throat. "No. I don't even have to go in. I just figured I might. Something to fill a few hours."

"What d'you do?"

"I'm a mechanic."

"You take a day off," Gabriel said, stroking Shane's hair again. "You stay in bed with me 'til we too hungry to sleep. Later we go down for a drink and listen to the music."

"No more drinking for me, not for a couple days at least."

Gabriel pulled his face back a few inches and smiled at Shane. "Fine. How 'bout the rest?"

"I dunno. I'm already hungry," Shane lied. He was uncomfortable with how damn comfortable he felt right now.

"You ever been with a man before me?" Gabriel asked.

Shane felt a strong urge to haul back and hit him, revenge for how hard it stung to hear the truth laid out so bare. He swallowed. "No."

Gabriel ran his tongue over his lower lip for the briefest second, smirked, a tiny show of self-satisfaction. "You ever wanted one before?"

"No… I think I better head in to the garage." He shrugged Gabriel's arms off and rolled over, swung his feet to the floor.

Gabriel propped himself up on his hip and elbow, smiling wickedness in Shane's direction.

Shane yanked his shorts and jeans back on, buckled his belt. "What's that shit-eating grin for?"

"Jus' like lookin' at you."

"You love this, don't you? Gettin' the better of straight guys."

"You make it sound like a game, Shane."

"Yeah, well. You make it look like one, sometimes. Like right now. You look real pleased with yourself."

"I'm more interested in pleasin' you," Gabriel said.

Shane narrowed his eyes, found his shirt and tugged it on. "Good. Just you remember that. And don't start forgettin' whose house this is. Who's the guest."

That evil smile again. "'Course not."

"And who's in charge."

"Never."

"Good." Good, since Shane was having a harder and harder time remembering it himself.

"Shane?"

He buttoned his shirt all the way up before he met Gabriel's eyes. "What?"

"I can use your couch again tonight?"

Shane batted a few replies around in his head before settling on cruelty. "We'll see. Now get your ass up. This ain't a halfway house."

Shane made himself busy, pulling on socks at the couch, keeping his eyes off Gabriel's naked body as the man rose and strolled from the room. Shane inhaled, deep, and blew the air out, propped his elbows on his knees and hung his head. It was easier to breathe when that man wasn't close—he was like a fire, sucking all the oxygen out of a room. Shane stood and headed for the kitchen, praying to God he'd get through the day without suffocating.

CHAPTER FOUR

Two weeks passed by in a haze—endless days full of waiting, nights drenched in wine, mornings when Shane woke up with a dry mouth and his arms wrapped around a naked male body.

Somehow it was Saturday again and nearly March. Shane didn't know what he'd accomplished in the past two weeks aside from keeping the barest distance between himself and that one act he wanted and feared so deeply. But every night he managed to resist, managed to corral their encounters into a relatively safe routine—drink like fishes, fool around like teenagers, sleep like a goddamn married couple.

Shane was alone in the garage for the afternoon, free to overthink things to his heart's discontent…which was all he really knew how to do anymore. The emotional pattern had become sickeningly predictable. First, a cold feeling in his gut, shame or fear or a mix of the two. Then something warmer, curiosity and a dark thrill trickling through his veins. Then fear again. Twice in the past two weeks Gabriel hadn't turned up. Shane had busied himself helping out in the bar until last call, stayed up late watching shit TV, left the door unlocked when he eventually gave up and went to bed. Those nights gave him restless sleep, had him waking early, anxiety burning a pit in his stomach.

"Fuck," he muttered, tossed a wrench on the floor and chipped the painted cement, rubbed his temples with greasy fingers. "Shut the fuck up," he ordered his brain, knocking his fist against the side of his head.

He wasn't a man who obsessed. He didn't know how people could live this way, with a constant loop of nonsense running in their skulls like a maddening radio frequency with no tuner or volume control.

He worked harder, poured all his attention into the details. Still, at least twice a minute that face snuck through the mechanical distractions, making his heart and cock throb.

At six he threw in the towel, scribbled some notes in the work log and locked the shop. On the twenty-five-minute drive back to the Shivaree, every bump in the dirt road made Shane's hungover head pulsate with a new vengeance. And still, all he thought about was Gabriel.

Shane had never been in love, but he suspected this wasn't it. This was something worse, hot little flashes of pleasure and excitement amid a cloud of confusion and lust. Obsession. Ugly and uncontrollable. Then the next minute, a spark of joy at the ridiculous thought that maybe it wasn't one-sided. Then—

"Jesus." He angled the rearview and frowned at himself. "Shut the fuck up in there."

He parked his truck on the patchy front lawn close to the house, where it would soon be trapped as the makeshift parking lot filled up with patrons. Nobody lived close to the Shivaree except Shane and the mosquitoes. He still marveled how it attracted the brisk business it did.

"Fucking magic," he murmured and slammed his door.

The screened-in porch was already abuzz with early customers and Shane greeted the ones he knew by name, raised a hand at the ones he didn't. Jeanne was behind the bar reading a fashion magazine between refills.

"That's an interesting look, boss." She gestured at her temples and Shane put his fingers to the grease smeared there. He accepted a bar towel and did a half-assed clean-up job.

He scanned the club, looking for that hat, that face, those hands. Nothing. A few of the band members who played on Latin night were setting up for the seven o'clock kick-off and Shane shivered. He both hated and loved watching that man dance.

"Everything under control here?" he asked Jeanne.

"Yup. Should be a good one."

"Where's the new guy? Brian or Ryan or whoever?"

"Ryan," Jeanne said. "He just took an empty keg out back." She smiled tightly.

Shane raised his eyebrows. "What's that look telling me?"

"I haven't got a look."

"Yeah, you do. You sweet on him?"

She shrugged.

"Don't date a bartender, Miss Jeanne. 'Specially not one I hired."

"You were a bartender, like, forever," she said.

"Yeah, and I wouldn't advise any woman to date me, neither."

"Whatever, Shane." She never called him Shane unless she was on the defensive. "Anyhow, he's cute."

"Thought you said the mandolin player was cute," Shane said.

"No, I said Gabriel's *sexy*. Too sexy. I'm sticking to guys who're less pretty than me, thanks."

"That'd be every guy, Miss Jeanne. And all the girls."

She rolled her eyes at him. Then the man who was more beautiful than any woman Shane had ever seen strolled through the door, making his heart jackhammer.

"Speak of the devil," Jeanne said.

Shane thought it was an appropriate choice of words, considering how blazing hot the room suddenly felt. Gabriel headed for the bar, offering them both a grin and a dip of his brim as he slid onto a stool, provocatively close to Shane.

"Hey, Gabriel," Jeanne said. "You playin' tonight or just dancin'?"

"Dancin'," Gabriel said. "'Less you need me."

"Don't think so. Glass of red for you?"

He nodded. "Please, sha."

"You got it."

Shane aimed a look at Gabriel as Jeanne turned to open a bottle. "You watch yourself, cuttin' in the way you do."

Gabriel offered an amused, too-innocent smile.

"Just watch it," Shane said. "One of these weeks you're gonna step on the wrong man's toes. This place makes people hot-blooded." Even as he said it, Shane felt his own pulse shift, sending warmth southward.

Gabriel smiled again, kept his voice low. "I'm not afraid of hot-blooded men, Shane."

Shane didn't think he'd ever heard a syllable half as explicit as his own name coming out of this man's mouth. And he'd heard it a lot in the last two weeks, mostly when one of them had a fist wrapped around the other's cock on Shane's living room floor.

"I gotta get cleaned up." With that Shane pushed from the bar, defying his body's every instinct and moving away from that man's gravity.

As he headed across the porch and up the side steps, he imagined Gabriel following. He imagined him joining Shane as he shed his clothes, as he stepped into the hot shower. Shane imagined their two tall bodies pressed together, slippery with lather, Gabriel's black hair slicked back to expose every sinful feature on that face. Shane thought about kissing him, rubbing their hard, wet cocks together, turning him around and soaping him up and making the most beautiful mistake of his life. He jacked himself with a tight fist, half disappointed when he came and opened his eyes and didn't find Gabriel there at the edge of the curtain, watching.

He toweled off, shaved, stared at his reflection and half-recognized the man staring back. He dressed in fresh clothes and got downstairs around seven thirty, the energetic music hitting him like a heat wave. Couples were already dancing, a dozen frenetic bodies twirling and dipping and in some cases practically dry humping out on the dance floor.

Shane took a seat at the bar, waved to the new guy. Okay kid, though he had a kind of self-conscious swagger that grated on Shane…acting as if he were tending bar at some fancy Manhattan place, slinging twenty-dollar martinis instead of two-buck longnecks.

"What'll it be, old man?" Ryan or Brian slapped a bar towel over his shoulder as though he'd rehearsed it—probably had—his wide-ass cocky grin rubbing Shane all sorts of wrong ways.

"I'm the most regular regular you got, kid. If you don't know my drink order by now I ain't got high hopes for your future in this business."

Brian-Ryan's face sank and Jeanne muscled by him to plunk a beer and a whiskey down at Shane's elbow. "Don't be a bully."

Shane grinned at her and downed the shot, chased it with a sip of beer. Brian-Ryan made his way to the other end of the bar and Shane bid him a mental good riddance.

As soon as the distraction of the banter faded, Shane's body turned itchy again.

He scanned the colorful shadows for Gabriel.

For half a minute he thought maybe he'd gone, but no, there he was, hiding in plain sight. Shane blinked. Gabriel was leading a young woman on the dance floor in those fast, graceful steps, looking born to it. His white shirtsleeves were rolled up to his biceps, making his tan skin even darker in contrast. He wore a smile Shane knew only too well from their time alone and the sight made all the blood rush up from his cock to flood his neck and cheeks and leave him lightheaded with hot jealousy.

Shane snapped out of his trance as Jeanne spoke.

"What can't that man do?" she asked.

Shane forced his voice into an imitation of casual amusement and drained his beer. "Find a different fucking couch to crash on, for one."

Gabriel's sleeping arrangements were common knowledge among the staff, though Shane was pretty sure they hadn't given anyone cause to guess at what was really going on upstairs. "Anyhow, he told me he lived in Havana for close to ten years. Guess he learned his moves there."

"Explains the funky accent, at any rate," Jeanne said.

Shane nodded and slid his empty bottle across the wood. Jeanne leaned in to get a fresh one out of the bar fridge and Shane stared at her tits, on full display in a low-neck, clingy shirt. He was lost in concentration, trying to muster some glimmer of his withered heterosexuality when she snapped her fingers in front of his eyes.

"Huh?"

"Jeez, Shane."

He shook his head to clear it, knowing he'd look pathetic denying he'd been staring, worse than pathetic if he tried to explain why. "God, sorry."

Jeanne smiled and rolled her eyes, tugged her shirt up an inch. "Well, that's why I bought this top. Guess it's working."

"Yeah." Shane took a drink. "It is."

"Guess I underestimated myself. Now all I need's some dance moves like those and maybe I'd stand a chance with our Casanova." She nodded to the floor and Shane turned.

Gabriel had his talented hips locked with the young woman's, two bodies making art look like sex or maybe the other way around. He led her in flawless movements, thrilling Shane and pissing him off with equal fervor. Every few turns Gabriel's eyes met Shane's over his partner's shoulder, their message intense and pointed but tough to translate.

"He's a dangerous one," Jeanne said through a sigh.

Shane nodded. He thought about the other Gabriel, maybe the *real* Gabriel—the pleading man who begged to be dominated, begged to suck Shane's cock when they were alone. That was the one Shane wanted, not this commanding man in total control of the hypnotized woman he led. Shane needed to see that man on his knees again. He needed and wanted to give Gabriel what he'd asked for that very first morning in Shane's bed, needed to fuck him 'til he pled for mercy and knew with no trace of a doubt that Shane was the only person who could satisfy him.

The song came to an abrupt end and the dancers all turned to clap for the band, then the eventuality Shane had seen coming for two weeks finally arrived.

A tall, beefy regular Shane recognized approached Gabriel and his partner and a tense conversation ensued. It escalated in seconds, seemingly spurred by the boyfriend's drunkenness. A new song started up as things turned tense, the girlfriend clearly telling the boyfriend to calm down just as he did the opposite. He gave Gabriel a sharp shove in the shoulder, knocking him back a pace.

Shane got to his feet.

Gabriel held his ground for a handful of seconds, looking poised to relent. Then he hauled off and punched the boyfriend, caught him with a hook to the jaw that Shane could hear even over the music.

Jeanne gasped.

The song fell to pieces as the band stopped.

Shane crossed the dance floor in a flash, locked his arms around Gabriel's waist as a patron did the same to the boyfriend. Gabriel's body felt spring-loaded, eager to finish this.

"Not in my fucking bar," Shane growled and dragged Gabriel back a few paces, let his middle go and gripped him by the upper arm. He led him gruffly down the little hallway past the office to the restrooms, pushed in the door to the single-person men's room and shoved Gabriel through, slammed it behind them.

The bright light was blinding after the motley shadows of the club and Gabriel seemed taller, starker, a stranger all over again.

"Enjoyin' yourself?" Shane barked. He flipped the door lock then took a step toward Gabriel.

"Very much."

"I told you I seen this comin' for weeks now."

"I know."

"You're here as a guest. You start any more shit in this club and you'll get your ass tossed back out in the swamp, understand?" Shane came close, nearly chest to chest, wanting as always to remind Gabriel who was stronger, who was in charge.

"I upset you, Shane?"

His expression echoed everything Shane knew was true in his own heart—he was ten times more torn up from having to watch Gabriel dance with that woman than he was pissed about the fight.

"No. I just want you to remember whose territory you're in before you go getting yourself in deep with my customers. 'Specially if you want to keep sleepin' where you have been, boy."

He watched Gabriel swallow, black eyes on Shane's mouth. "I sleep wherever you tell me to, Shane."

"Yeah, you do." He brought his face close, their noses touching, breath mingling. Gabriel gasped as Shane grabbed the back of his head, knocked his hat to the ground and rammed his tongue into Gabriel's mouth, cutting off the sound. He kissed him rough for a minute, maybe less, sucked hard on Gabriel's lower lip as he pulled away, releasing it with a faint snap.

"Now," Shane said, voice low and dangerous. He pulled his keys from his pocket and unclipped the one to the apartment, pressed it into Gabriel's palm. "You're done down here for the rest of the night."

Gabriel narrowed his eyes, looking as if he wanted to say something but holding his tongue.

Shane took a deep breath and returned the stare. "Now you go upstairs, and you wait for me. You open up a bottle from over the fridge and you sit in my living room and I'll be up when I goddamn well feel like it."

Gabriel nodded.

"Good." Shane gave his cheek a couple soft slaps and stepped aside as Gabriel unlocked the door and slipped out, letting in a flare of brassy music. Shane flipped the lock again and leaned against the door, feeling as though he'd fall right through the wood, land flat on his back and crack his skull open. Might be a blessing. Instead he steadied himself, took a few deep breaths and went back out into the bar, relieved Gabriel was nowhere to be seen. Shane returned to his abandoned beer and sat back down across from Jeanne. He rubbed the counter's worn varnish with his thumb, losing himself in the motion.

"Everything all right, boss?"

"Yeah. I gave him the boot for the rest of the night."

"Seems harsh. Looked to me like Jesse started it." She turned her eyes to the big boyfriend, deep in an argument with his livid girlfriend by the far wall.

"That man works for me now. I hold the people I hire to a higher standard than the paying drunks." Shane blew out another angsty breath, feeling high, sobriety nowhere in sight.

"You okay yourself? I watch you play bouncer at least three times a week but you never seem shaken up like this."

Shane looked up at Jeanne's round, pretty face and offered his best smile. "Sorry. Haven't been feelin' like myself lately."

"You haven't been lookin' like yourself either. It's not a woman, is it?"

If only. "No, Jeannie. It's not a woman."

"Think maybe you're sick?"

"Somethin' like that."

CHAPTER FIVE

Shane mounted the outside steps nearly an hour after he'd given Gabriel his marching orders. He'd had two whiskeys at the bar and wanted more. Wanted yet another hangover tomorrow, a sour reminder, a punishment for whatever was about to happen. He opened the unlocked door, found Gabriel just as he'd been instructed, lounging on the couch with an open bottle on the side table. As Shane stepped inside Gabriel swung his bare feet to the floor, attentive.

Yeah, you better be.

Shane toed his shoes off and sank into the easy chair. He took a slug of wine, never taking his eyes off Gabriel's. He set the bottle down and wiped his lips.

"I hate watchin' you with those women," he said.

"It jus' dancin', Shane."

He narrowed his eyes. "I don't think anything's *just* anything with you." He'd never have guessed distrust could be such a powerful aphrodisiac, but the more he feared losing this man's attention the hotter his attraction burned.

Gabriel's eyes flicked away and his lips pursed. He met Shane's stare again, shifting in his seat.

"Tell me how I make it up to you, Shane."

He thought about it as he downed another swallow of wine. He stood, stepped close to the couch and nudged Gabriel's knees apart with his own.

"Get me hard."

Gabriel reached for Shane's belt, got it open along with his fly, eased his jeans down. Those fingers, strange and familiar and warm, peeled his shorts down and exposed him, already stiff. His eyes shut for a moment as Gabriel fisted his cock, stroking until it was pounding and thick.

"Yeah." Shane fumbled with his snaps, shed his work shirt and stripped off his tee.

Gabriel's eyes took it all in. He scooted to the edge of the cushions, his free hand surveying Shane's stomach and chest. Warm lips grazed his navel, kissing, tasting. Worshipping.

Shane was close to done already, just from the way Gabriel stared at him. He took a step back, out of reach.

"Stand up."

Gabriel did and Shane yanked his dress shirt out from his pants, took one look and thought, *fuck it,* ripped the shirt clean open in two pulls and scattered half the buttons across the floor. Something flashed across Gabriel's face—Shane had seen it before, all the times they'd fucked around, that mix of excitement and fear that told him this man liked getting roughed up.

Gabriel brought his face close to Shane's, held his eyes. "It gon' be tonight, Shane?"

He didn't answer. He undid Gabriel's belt, wrestled with the clasp on his dress pants, pulled them down his legs.

Shane stepped back to kick his own pants away and grabbed the bottle, sat beside his so-called guest and studied his body. They traded the bottle and rough, mean kisses for a couple minutes. Gabriel took a final, deep swig then nipped at Shane's lips as he set the wine aside. He got himself into Shane's lap, two ready cocks separated by two layers of cotton. Shane tugged him close by the hips, pressed their bodies together until he didn't know whose legs were whose or whose idea this ultimately was. Anger bubbled up to transform the lust—to demand he take it further, tender the punishment Gabriel had coming and make good on the fantasy they both craved.

Shane shoved Gabriel onto the next cushion, yanked his shorts down his legs and pushed him to his hands and knees. He got up and ditched his own underwear, knelt behind Gabriel, ran a hand over his gorgeous bare ass. He took his own hard cock in the other fist, stroked himself as he palmed Gabriel's flesh.

Gabriel turned to watch and Shane met his gaze with a cold glare.

"Eyes forward."

They'd done this the last few times they'd fucked around. Shane gave Gabriel's ass a hard slap, rewarded with a sharp suck of breath. He smacked him again, loving the jolt in the man's body, the reddening flush where his strike landed. He jacked himself with a tight fist and fantasized about taking everything too far, just as he'd been imagining for two weeks. He spanked Gabriel until his gasps became one long, drawn-out moan, then Shane angled his hips, spread Gabriel's cheeks and stroked his slick head over that tempting hole.

"Shane."

"I know what you want." He pressed a bit harder, threatening penetration.

"Do it, Shane. Fuck me."

He teased the puckered skin with slow, mean strokes. "When I'm good and ready."

"Tonight."

"We'll see."

Gabriel groaned, pushed his pleading hips back. "You been keepin' me waitin' for too long, Shane. I won' wait forever."

Fear twitched in Shane's muscles. "Well, fucking look at you, dishin' out ultimatums when here I've been giving you whatever you goddamn want."

"Not everythin'."

Shane pushed hard, felt the very beginnings of that tight heat welcoming his head. Gabriel groaned so deep and animalistic Shane's hair stood up. He backed away.

"Don' tease me, Shane."

"Me, tease?" He tried to keep his voice cool and mean even as his heart pounded so hard he felt faint. "Oh that's fuckin' hilarious, boy."

He grabbed Gabriel's hip, wrestled him onto his back and shoved his big thighs between Gabriel's more slender ones, cock against cock. He jammed an arm under Gabriel's back and brought their faces so close he felt the man's breath on his lips. He pressed his weight into Gabriel, gave him all the aggression and domination he loved, gave himself all the frightening physical contact he'd grown so addicted to.

"Tonight, you said?" Shane asked.

"Please."

"That's an improvement. Beg me. Beg me and maybe I'll give it to you."

"Please."

Shane kissed him, quick and deep.

"Please, Shane."

He kissed him again, dirtier and rougher, fingers digging hard into his back.

"C'mon, Shane. Please."

For a minute or more Shane fucked Gabriel's mouth with his own, thrust their pounding cocks together, ground their hip bones and reveled in their slick, mingling sweat. He pulled away abruptly, stood and watched Gabriel's violently rising and falling chest, his glassy expression.

Shane's heart beat so hard he thought it'd crack his ribs open and tear through his skin. The wine was working, blurring everything, opening Shane's mouth and pushing out words he couldn't predict but didn't fight. "Get on the fucking floor."

Gabriel moved to his knees on the rug facing the couch, dug his elbows into the cushions. The most tempting invitation in the world.

Shane swallowed. God, that ass. Tan skin over firm muscle, no chance of imagining this into some heterosexual denial fantasy. Shane didn't want to, anyhow. He wanted this man, even more than he wished he didn't. He fell to his knees behind Gabriel.

"Take me, Shane."

His dick pounded and he gritted his teeth against the ache. He ran his hands over the taut skin, ripe flesh, squeezed and kneaded, got so hot from the sight it felt like a fever. He ran his thumbs along Gabriel's crack, found his asshole, spat across his fingers and stroked it. The man's groan set Shane's cock pounding.

He worked two fingers in, penetrating that tight ring of muscle and holding until Gabriel's body relaxed and let Shane's fingers fuck deeper.

"More," Gabriel groaned, pushed his hips back to meet Shane's hand.

"Slow down. I need you ready for me."

"I want you to fuck me so bad. Don' care if it hurts."

Another jolt pulsed down Shane's cock, made him harder and hotter than he knew he could get. "You taken anybody as big as me before?" he asked, desperate for the ego-stroking.

"Nobody big as you," Gabriel said, voice straining as Shane twisted his fingers deeper. "Nobody near big as you."

"Good." He eased his fingers out and spat in his hand again, spat straight onto Gabriel's eager hole and shoved the slick digits back inside, adding a third.

"Yeah." The shift in Gabriel was visible, a fine layer of perspiration breaking out over his skin, a faint tremble quaking his muscles. "I need it, Shane. Now. Fuck me."

Shane stared, transfixed by his fingers, by Gabriel's perfect ass, this sick invitation setting his body on fire. He slid his fingers out, back in, fucking Gabriel with all the control he could muster. "Beg me," he ordered.

"Please. Fuck me, Shane. Please. I need your cock."

"Say it again." He took his fingers away, reached for his jeans and wrestled his wallet from the pocket, found a condom.

"Fuck me, Shane."

He ripped the plastic open and rubbed Gabriel's asshole with a thumb as he slid the rubber down his cock. He grasped his erection, brought it close, feared he'd come the second his sheathed head brushed against that ready, pink flesh. He ran his cock along Gabriel's crack.

"Say it again." Shane swept his crown up and down over the hole.

"Please, Shane. Fuck my ass."

Shane spat in his palm again, wet his cock. "You look good, boy." He clamped his hand to Gabriel's hip. "Hold still."

He held his breath, angled his pounding dick to Gabriel's entrance, pushed his head past that first tight barrier. Gabriel gasped. White spots popped and danced in front of Shane's eyes. He willed himself to breathe.

"More," Gabriel begged.

Shane had done anal before, a few times with a few ambitious lovers, with mixed results. Nothing he'd done had felt like this, didn't come anywhere near to as forbidden or dirty or scary or wondrous. He felt Gabriel adjusting, easing his way. Shane pushed in deeper, another inch, then another. He drew himself out then slid back to that tight depth. He ran an appraising hand over Gabriel's ass. "That's good, boy. You ready for more?"

"Please, Shane. Fill me up."

He licked his lips, grasped Gabriel's cheeks and pushed in another inch, rough this time. "Come on. Lemme in."

A shuddering moan rattled out of Gabriel then Shane felt his body relax.

"Good... Fuck, you feel so fucking amazing." He looked good too—even if this never happened again, Shane knew he'd conjure this image as he jerked himself off, that hot, firm ass begging for his cock, taking it. He eased himself out, spat in his hand and slicked his cock. He pushed in deeper, half his length wrapped in that tight, forbidden heat. Gabriel's groans and gasps set the fire blazing out of control and Shane started pumping, not caring if they were ready or not.

He watched Gabriel's jutting shoulder blades, his back muscles flexing to brace himself against each thrust of Shane's hips.

"This worth your wait?" Shane asked.

Gabriel craned his neck to flash his dark eyes at Shane. "Yeah."

"You want more?"

He nodded, looking too lost in the pleasure to form words. Shane grabbed his hips, pulled him hard into the thrusts, entranced at the sight. "That's so hot, boy." He rammed himself even deeper, nearly all the way. "Goddamn, you feel like heaven. Tell me nobody's ever fucked you this deep before."

"Never."

He squeezed Gabriel's cheeks together, more friction against his throbbing shaft. Shane felt himself getting ten times drunker than he had from the whiskey or wine as the seconds wore on. Each push felt better than the last, almost *too* good, and he wanted to flop down and collapse on Gabriel's back, wrap his arms around the man's waist and ground himself in reality for a moment.

"Pretend you're forcin' me," Gabriel hissed, just loud enough for Shane to hear.

The idea sent a shiver down his spine. "How?"

"Hold me down. Fuck me rough. Lemme fight you."

Shane swallowed, unable to speak. His body communicated for him, hands clamping to Gabriel's hip bones, thrusts speeding. For a minute it was straight-up hard fucking, then Gabriel changed. He lunged, reaching for the back of the couch. Shane shook off his surprise and yanked him by the hips, pulling him back hard and ramming his cock deeper.

"Don'," Gabriel said. He looked over his shoulder, eyes wide and hungry.

Shane's throat went dry and tight but he was game. He tugged Gabriel into his thrusts, driving even deeper until the sound of skin slapping skin punctuated each violent motion.

Gabriel grunted between thrusts. "Stop."

Shane had never heard a single syllable crammed with so much need.

"You made me do this," he said, keeping his hips pounding. "You made me *want* this. Now you get fucked and take what I give you."

Gabriel thrashed, interrupted Shane's rhythm and pissed him the fuck off. He leaned forward, grabbed Gabriel's shoulders and dragged his arms off the couch so he landed on his elbows on the rug. Shane pushed a palm against his back and pinned him, grasped his ass cheek with the other hand and slammed into him, fast and mean.

"God, you feel so fucking good. Take that cock, boy."

He slid the hand holding Gabriel's ass around to grip his dick, as stiff and pounding as he'd ever felt it. "Yeah, you fucking love this." Shane squeezed him tight, gave him mean pulls, abandoning rhythm and control in favor of intensity.

Gabriel moaned, sounding wild and scared and needy all at once. He turned to stare at Shane's body, lips parted, eyes slits.

Shane looked between his legs, watching the steady motion of his cock disappearing over and over. It didn't scare him, only got him hotter and harder. He felt obscenely big and strong, holding Gabriel down and making his body beg for this punishment. He'd never felt anything near as intoxicating and he let it take over, rode the high.

Gabriel's legs and hips tensed and shook as his noises turned harsh, cock going hot and thick in Shane's fist.

"You gonna come, boy?"

Another moan answered him.

"You say my name when you come. Say my name and remember who's fucking you." Shane was close too. His body was burning so hot he didn't actually know how much longer he had before the pleasure came to a head.

Below him Gabriel cried out, his hips bucking as his cock shuddered. Shane gasped as Gabriel's ass clenched his cock, tight as an angry fist.

"Say it."

"Shane." It came out a gasp, choked and disbelieving.

"Good boy."

He cupped the head of Gabriel's dick as he came, spurt after hot spurt filling Shane's palm, more than he'd known a man could give. He stroked the cream up and down Gabriel's cock, milked the last drops from him.

Free to give his own body what it wanted, Shane slowed his thrusts. He grabbed Gabriel's waist and took him deep, savoring the tightness of his body, the view of his slick back muscles and the rise and fall of his ribs as he fought for breath.

"You're so hot. You're so fucking hot. Look at me."

Gabriel turned his sweaty, flushed face and met Shane's gaze. He looked just how Shane wanted, just the opposite of how he'd looked dancing with those women. Shane stared straight into those heavy-lidded eyes and rammed himself home with a fast, relentless beat.

"Oh fuck." The climax hit him like a wall—pure, incapacitating pleasure. He doubled over, wrapped his arms around Gabriel's middle and jammed his cock as deep as it could go, shooting for what felt like forever, warm come filling the condom.

The room spun as Shane came down from his orgasm and he smelled them at once. He felt his palms on Gabriel's hot skin, one slick, one sticky. He eased his sensitive cock out, stripped the condom and sank back on his haunches. Gabriel sat and they watched each other's chests as they struggled for breath.

Shane wasn't sure what he wanted. If this had been a woman he'd have succumbed to a brief bout of romantic affection, wrapped his arms around her and fallen happily into satisfied sleep. He might've done that with Gabriel if he couldn't still feel a bit of that ugly jealousy from an hour ago. He got to his feet.

"C'mon."

Gabriel followed him in silence to the bathroom. Shane got the shower heated up and stepped inside, Gabriel following. Shane soaped his hands, cleaned himself first, then Gabriel. He pulled him closer, felt their slippery stomachs and chests touch as the hot water streamed between them. He grabbed the shampoo bottle, lathered Gabriel's hair, leaned in and kissed him. Not gentle, not rough, just deep and slow and passionate.

They kissed until Shane tasted shampoo then he broke away so Gabriel could rinse his hair. Shane reveled in the eye contact, how it felt to let himself stare at this face so openly, without fear. He wanted to get lost in the heat and steam and the white noise and never find his way back to reality. They kissed 'til the hot water waned and drove them out into the cool, dry air.

They toweled off, brushed their teeth side by side in front of the foggy mirror. Shane didn't know what to make of their blurry domestic reflection, but he was still so blissfully spent he just admired the man beside him.

Shane flipped off the light and fan and went to his dark bedroom, threw the covers back and got beneath them, Gabriel following suit. Shane moved, straddled Gabriel's waist and slid a hand under his head, his damp hair. The man tasted like mint, smelled like soap and spring, felt like heaven. Shane kept the kissing shallow, just a faint passing of his lips across Gabriel's.

He cleared his throat, a sudden thought making it feel tight. "How long you think you're sticking around here?"

Gabriel nipped Shane's lower lip. "Long as you let me, I guess."

A mix of emotions flooded his chest. Hope and relief, and selfish, nearly violent satisfaction. It felt a lot like safety, but not quite. Shane flopped to the side. He grabbed Gabriel around the waist and pulled his back tight to Shane's chest. Shane's cock nestled against Gabriel's ass though he was too worn out to muster lust, only contentedness.

"You sore?" he asked, lips against the back of Gabriel's neck.

"Yeah. Don' mind though." The next time he spoke Shane heard a smile in the words. "Means I'll think about you all day tomorrow."

Shane was glad it was dark, that there was no chance of Gabriel turning and catching how broad his grin was. He palmed Gabriel's ass with one hand, held him tighter with the other.

Sleep came down hard, buried Shane's fears so deep inside his body's satisfaction he couldn't feel anything aside from peace and relief. Somewhere in the distance his intuition drummed a warning, the sound ignored, lost behind two steady hearts beating in the dark.

CHAPTER SIX

S hane was pushed from sleep by a stressful dream in which he was
trying to masturbate but seemed to have been paralyzed from the
waist down. When he woke he discovered a hard cock in his hand. It
wasn't his.

Gabriel's back was plastered against Shane's chest, ass against his
crotch. Shane's own dick was rousing, growing right along with the
one in his fist. He squeezed his hand tighter, earned a low, sleepy
moan from his bedmate. He breathed in the smell of Gabriel's hair,
pressed his face to Gabriel's neck and tasted his skin. The man's hips
moved, sliding his cock in Shane's grip and rubbing his ass against
Shane's erection.

"Mornin'," Gabriel murmured, the words thick with sleep.

Shane kept stroking, wanting those sounds, needing to feel this
strong body tremble and beg. The wait was short. In a few seconds'
time Gabriel was writhing under Shane's touch. Shane got his other

hand between their bodies, fingers between Gabriel's cheeks. He found that sweet spot and Gabriel gasped.

"Sore?" Shane asked.

Gabriel nodded, seeming incapable of coherent speech.

Shane gave him a final, taunting rub and shoved his hand between Gabriel's hip and the mattress. "You forgive me?"

Gabriel laughed, a soft, breathy noise. "Course."

Shane stroked him with a slow, tight fist, tried to make the touch sensual, motherfucking *romantic,* wanting to be the one doing the seducing for a change. Gabriel thrust himself into the strokes, reached a hand overhead to fist Shane's short hair.

"What're you thinking about?" Shane asked.

"Las' night."

"Tell me."

Gabriel swallowed and when he spoke he sounded pained. "Thinkin' 'bout how rough you fucked me. How good you felt. How much I been wantin' that…how long you kept me waitin', Shane."

Shane laughed and tightened his fist. "You callin' me a cock-tease?"

"Yeah," Gabriel moaned.

Shane's body tightened momentarily but he let it go, embraced the label. "Bet you're used to gettin' whoever you want, whenever you want 'em."

Gabriel didn't reply, just pushed his cock into the caresses, let Shane's hair go so he could stroke his own stomach and chest, clasp Shane's fist and follow the motions. "Tell me 'bout last night," Gabriel mumbled.

"'Bout how I bent you over my couch and fucked your ass?" Blood flooded Shane's cheeks and groin with equal heat as the words tumbled from his mouth. "How I held you down and rammed my cock inside you, fucked you 'til you got so hot you were begging me for it?"

"Yeah."

"How you felt so fucking tight and dirty and hot I thought I was gonna pass out?"

Gabriel moaned. Shane stared at his black stubble, breathed in his smells, stronger in the morning.

"Last night was the single hottest thing I ever experienced," Shane said, only able to utter that frightening truth because the man who had him so hopelessly spellbound was currently plastered against him, a sloppy, horny mess.

"Make me come," Gabriel gasped.

Shane smirked at the command, imagined making him wait…making Gabriel get him off first, fumble through it in a cloud of taunting arousal. Shane damn-near came at the idea. Gabriel moaned again as Shane took his hand away—a sound of disbelief now, not pleasure, but Shane knew how this man loved to suffer.

"Don't stop."

"It's my house, I come first." Shane piled a couple pillows and leaned back, half-reclined.

Gabriel turned over, lips parted and swollen, brows pinched together, so fucking close it had to ache…but his discomfort was overshadowed by his excitement. This was the man who haunted Shane's thoughts every second they weren't together. The man who made him feel more powerful and craved than any woman ever had, made him feel strong and filthy and drunk and goddamn invincible.

"Suck me," Shane said.

Gabriel got obediently between Shane's knees, stroked his stiff cock until Shane was nearing the edge himself. Just the expression on that man's face was almost enough to pull his trigger.

"Come on. Do it." Shane reached down, took over the stroking as Gabriel leaned in. Shane's eyes rolled back as warm, wet lips closed over his head, as that skillful mouth sucked in time with Gabriel's rumbling, muffled noises. So much wrong about this—a man's rough fingers, five o'clock shadow—but so perfect.

Shane grabbed a fistful of Gabriel's hair, gave himself over completely to how right dominating felt. "Good. Don't you dare stop." How good hypocrisy felt.

Skillful lips coaxed blood and pleasure into Shane's cock, made him feel so heavy and swollen it hurt.

"Good. Suck that cock, boy. Show me how much you love it."

Gabriel obeyed, intensified everything he was doing, angled his black eyes up to Shane's face. From nowhere, a laugh rumbled through Shane's chest. He smiled and shut his eyes, let himself get lost in this moment. He heard and felt Gabriel's smug grunt of a laugh as well, opened his eyes to find the most beautiful man in the world smiling with his lips wrapped around Shane's cock. When he came, it wasn't lust that was flooding him but pure happiness. He held Gabriel's head as the spasms rocked his body, voice lost to crazy, undignified groans and sighs.

Gabriel slid Shane's cock from his lips, swallowed and grinned. "Like when I make you smile like that."

"Get up here."

Gabriel made his way up the sheets, locked knees then eyes with Shane.

"Love makin' you feel good," Gabriel murmured, brown eyes boring through Shane's skull and rewiring his brain.

Shane reached between them and took hold of Gabriel's stiff cock, stroked him slow and cruel.

Gabriel moaned, shut his eyes and pressed his face into Shane's neck.

"You like that?"

Another moan heated Shane's neck and his cock was already primed for round two, a phenomenon he hadn't experienced since he'd been a teenager...not until this man had shown up. Shane brought his body closer, shifted his hips and pressed his dick against Gabriel's, earning a faint nip of teeth against his throat. He got both their shafts in his grip and stroked them together. He felt Gabriel's hand join his, squeezing them tighter, forcing the rhythm.

"Slow down," Shane whispered. "We got all morning."

Gabriel obeyed, let Shane's hand lead. He moved his mouth to the hollow behind Shane's ear. "You think you might ever suck me, Shane?"

He groaned, more from surprise and fear than pleasure, though the idea didn't terrify him the way it had a week ago. "Dunno."

"I fantasize about it," Gabriel murmured. "'Bout your strong hands holdin' me down and your mouth on me."

Shane let his own cock go, focusing his hand on Gabriel alone, not wanting him to feel it if Shane lost his erection. He was less afraid of the act than he was of being terrible at it.

He wasn't even sure he was all that good at giving women head…God knew how hopeless he'd be with a man. Then again, his sexual strengths revolved around his rough selfishness, a quality most ladies didn't request when Shane was camped out between their thighs, but a quality the man currently clawing at his ribs worshipped as an idol. Still, there was only one position that'd leave Shane more vulnerable than sucking cock and he was afraid to start down that slope, afraid of where the momentum might ultimately land him.

"We'll see." He stroked Gabriel's cock until the man's sounds were irrefutable proof of who was in charge. "You fantasize about whatever you want, but remember I'm callin' the shots."

"Course, Shane." The words escaped through a tangle of groans, barely audible.

"Good. Now you think about last night. You think about that big cock I fucked you with."

"Yeah." Gabriel thrust his hips into Shane's pulls.

"I know you been wantin' that. And if you ever want it again you remember whose house you're in."

Gabriel mumbled, "Shane," his voice caught between plea and rapture.

Shane switched hands, took Gabriel's cock in the lower one, reached the other around to palm his ass, slip his fingers between his cheeks.

"Spank me," Gabriel whispered.

Shane got to his knees as Gabriel did the same, a position they knew well now. Shane added a new feature, rubbing his own cock until it was stiff again, resting it against Gabriel's crack. He reached around and took hold of Gabriel's pounding dick, stroked him light and taunting, the other hand rubbing his ass cheek.

"Tell me what else you fantasize about."

"About fucking *with* you...fucking someone else. A woman."

"You really like both, huh?"

"I love women," Gabriel choked out, overcome by Shane's tightening fist. "I fantasize about seeing you with a woman, us taking her together, making her come, then you finishing with me while she watches."

Shane could handle that fantasy. He let it take shape in his mind, the palm rubbing Gabriel's ass coming down with a smack.

Through the gasp, "Shane."

"Is she watching us right now?" Shane asked.

"Yeah."

He spanked him again, harder, rubbed him faster. He kept it up until Gabriel's hips were pumping, ass teasing Shane's cock as he fucked his fist. Shane stared at the burning pink skin he'd branded with his palm, knowing it must feel scorched and blistered. He gave Gabriel's ass a soothing graze then slapped him again, inspiring a groan that had to be at least half actual pain.

"Shane."

"I'm gonna keep spanking you 'til you come, boy."

"Hurts."

"I'll bet. And I bet you fucking love that."

Another strained moan.

Shane was as good as his word, punishing—or perhaps more likely, rewarding—Gabriel with a fresh slap every few strokes. Then Shane felt him reach the brink, hips lost to a graceless rhythm as he came, spilling against Shane's hand and the bedding, a little more encroachment into the territory Shane used to think of as his own.

Shane wiped his hand on his rumpled sheet and turned Gabriel onto his back, wanting to study his flushed, spent face.

"Happy?"

Gabriel grinned deeply and nodded.

"Good. Now up you get. I got a zillion things to get on with." A load of laundry, for starters. "Don't need you under my feet." *Or my skin.*

"You the boss, Shane."

"Yeah. And don't let me catch you forgettin' that again."

* * *

The slap of the screen door yanked Shane out of his own head. He looked up from the papers scattered over the bar to find his Aunt Marie trotting across the porch, her corona of frizzy red hair glowing pink around the edges from the sun streaming in behind her.

"Holy—cow," Shane said, veering to avoid cursing in front of his sixty-something aunt, the closest thing he had left to a mother. "What're you doing here?"

She smiled and held out her arms. "Surprise!"

"You look gorgeous, Miss Marie," Shane said.

They met halfway across the floor in a tight hug. She smelled as always—rose-scented lotion and menthol cigarettes.

"What brings you back to this dump?"

"Checking on my investment." Her eyes, the same gray-blue as his momma's, darted around the club, checking that all her handiwork was still as it should be.

"You mean the investment you signed over to me two years ago? It's the same as always."

"I don't know about that. It's looking a lot more worn since the last time I came for a visit," she said.

"I ordered some new stools, I promise."

"Good."

"So why're you really here?"

"I've got a new grandchild to see," she said, puffing up grandly.

Shane made a skeptical face. "You ain't got any kids, last I knew. Do I have cousins hidden someplace you never told me about?"

"No. But Rhonda Johnson's daughter Katie just had a son. I changed Katie's diapers and made her dress for prom, so that gives me some kind of surrogate rights, I think."

"Fair enough. You want a drink?" He nodded toward the bar.

"No," she said, wandering to a chaise lounge to take a seat with a weary huff. "These cushions are shot, Shane."

"I know. Sure about that drink?"

"I've got to get back on the road in a few—the christening's at two. I'm staying the night there but I might make you look at my car when I pass back through. It started making a knocking sound 'round when I passed through Shreveport."

Shane sat on the table in front of her. "Anything for you, Miss Marie. Sorry—Missus. How's that husband treating you?"

"Like a princess," she said, and the glow in her cheeks was all the corroboration Shane needed.

"He better."

"And how about you, darlin'? You seein' anyone special these days?"

Images from the past couple weeks flashed across Shane's mind, made his heart race from lust and fear and shame. He pictured that face, those dangerous eyes and lips that kept him up nights. "No one special."

"Shame."

He sensed the lecture coming and cut it off at the pass. "Don't start. I'm thirty-five, barely."

"Your folks got hitched when your momma was twenty-one."

"Yeah, and it was a fuckin' train wreck. Friggin' train wreck, sorry. So no thanks. Plus *you* settled down at, what? Fifty-eight?"

"That is impossible," she said carefully, "as I am only forty-two. As everyone knows. As I have been for many years and shall continue to be until I drop down dead."

Shane smiled. "Right, my mistake."

Marie sighed. "Well, I really just stopped in to say hello and use the powder room and to let you know I'll bring my car by tomorrow afternoon."

Shane slapped his hands on the table beside his butt and stood. "You old tease, you, making me think you came here to see me. Hey, you want a bottle of something to bring to the party?"

"It's a christening, Shane."

He knew that face anywhere, that put-on, sanctimonious propriety. "Yeah, and it's the Johnsons. What d'you want? Bourbon?"

She pursed her lips then nodded. "Bourbon would be best."

Shane grabbed her a bottle out of the stock room while she used the ladies' and they said their goodbyes.

He stood by the front door for a long time after she drove off, looking around the club in the weak winter sunlight. This place was his, but it wasn't really. He ran it how Marie always had, kept things as close to her vision as he could manage. He'd never changed the upstairs rooms from his grandparents' taste aside from moving the furniture around and cluttering it up with his modest collection of bachelor possessions. The auto shop was a quarter his, but he'd come into co-ownership decades after the place had been established, didn't do much aside from his own fair share of hard work. More than his share, lately.

No kids. No wife. No nearby family, at least none he cared to see. Not even a fucking dog.

Who the fuck was he? What did he have that was actually *his?* His truck, maybe. He'd fixed that up from the junk heap. Maybe he ought to just climb into the driver's seat and get the fuck out of Shiloh and this bar and the shop, out of the cloud of confusion and annoying self-analysis that one strange man had brought with him from...from wherever Gabriel had been haunting before he'd deigned to make torturing Shane his latest hobby.

The door before him swung in, Zach holding it open and looking perplexed to find Shane planted where he was, fists on his hips, probably with an idiotic frown screwing up his face.

"Hey, boss."

Shane stepped aside. "Afternoon, Zach. Just thinking about if maybe I should paint this place."

Zach shrugged.

Shane glanced around, not really recognizing anything in the space that'd been the center of his world for nearly a decade.

"You all right, Shane?"

"D'you think I need a dog, Zach?"

"A dog?" Zach's befuddled expression ushered reality back in and Shane realized what a fuckwit he must sound like.

"You been drinkin', boss?"

"No... Just havin' a midlife crisis, maybe."

Zach smirked, walked to the bar and started the prep work. "My dad had one of those last year. Bought himself a muscle car and started dating this chick who graduated high school like three years ahead of me. It's not a dignified look, Shane. I don't recommend it.

So sure, get yourself a dog, if that'll help. Can't wait for you to send me out back to de-shit the yard."

"Nah, I'll save that for Ryan."

Zach laughed and began emptying the dishwasher. "Good. That guy's a dipshit."

CHAPTER SEVEN

Shane made the rest of the day into one long, somewhat successful distraction. He drove into Baton Rouge and spent nearly two hours in the hardware store, got dinner at his favorite diner and arrived home around eight laden with paint swatches and shiny new fixtures for the bar—a hundred little chances to keep his mind off Gabriel.

The man in question wasn't among the few dozen patrons when Shane walked in, though that was no surprise. Shane knew the man's routine the way one might find patterns in the comings and goings of a semi-feral cat, and Gabriel rarely sauntered in before nine unless he was playing, which he wasn't, tonight.

Shane wondered for the millionth time what that man got up to when he wasn't at the Shivaree and how he got where he was going. His charm must've worked on passing cars, since Gabriel didn't drive and it'd take at least an hour to get anyplace outside of Shiloh without hitching.

Shane dumped his purchases on an empty shelf in the stock room and went upstairs, flipped channels until quarter past ten before heading back down to the bar. He took a seat across from Zach and was handily passed a beer and whiskey.

"Thanks," Shane said over the evening's noisy blues ensemble. He scanned the crowd again, pretending to look for his favorite employee. "Where's Jeanne at?"

Zach nodded to the hall. "Out back."

"Ah. You seen Gabriel around?" Shane had never referred to the man by his name in front of anyone before and felt naked, as if those seven letters might come out loaded, trigger some air raid siren and alert everybody to exactly what was going on.

Zach finished pouring a beer and making change. "He was here earlier, flirtin' with somebody. Maybe he got himself taken home. Why? He supposed to be playing?"

"Nah." Shane made his voice so casual it didn't even seem to be coming out of his own mouth. "Just wanted to know if that mooch is planning on using my couch again before I lock up."

"Your lucky night, boss. I think maybe he found a better offer."

Zach went back to filling orders, leaving Shane adrift in a river of anxious energy.

Jeanne returned from the back hallway and offered Shane a passing smile.

"You seen Gabriel around, Miss Jeanne?"

She snorted. "Oh yes. He's out back with that redhead from Lafayette. If they dry hump any harder they'll catch fire."

"That so?" Shane kept his exterior cold even as ugly emotions were boiling in his gut.

He cleared empties from tables for a minute or two so his exit wouldn't look suspicious. The pounding of his heart was so violent he thought he heard it over the music as he strode down the hall to the back door. It opened on to the cement patio that housed the trash cans and bottle bins. The back light was bright and Shane felt caught, as if under interrogation. He took a few steps onto the grass then froze, his tiny little world spinning off its axis.

There he was, that stranger who'd got himself buried so damn deep in Shane's skin. Gabriel and a girl Shane vaguely recognized were glued together at the mouth, she on the edge of one of the picnic tables twenty yards away in the shadows, Gabriel standing between her legs. Shane had thought watching him dance with women was torture, but this was worse. This was way worse and it wasn't dry humping either. The girl's skirt was gathered at her waist, obscuring the action, but Shane had no doubt they were fucking. Gabriel's pants were riding low. No mistaking the rhythm of his deadly hips, those too-familiar moans, the way those talented hands held the girl's ass.

Pain—the most gut-wrenching feeling Shane had ever experienced—folded his body in on itself, wrung him out. His chest ached and his head swam and he wanted to be sick, to force all the hateful jealousy out of his body and just feel empty, feel nothing.

The girl pushed Gabriel's pants down farther, exposing his perfect ass, kneading it with her small hands. Her feminine grunts blended with Gabriel's harsh ones and Shane swallowed down one of his own, a territorial, primal growl trying to burst from his throat.

No way he could rush in and break this up. It might be his prerogative as a property owner but he didn't need that man knowing how much power he had over Shane. He tore his eyes off the sight and dumped the bottles, stole back inside, nearly staggering from the adrenaline. He looked down to find his hands shaking, crammed them in his pockets as he skirted the bar, hoping to make a clean break for the side steps and hide in his apartment.

"Hey, boss!"

He turned to meet Jeanne's eyes. "Yeah?"

"You got bandages hidden someplace? Zach just cut his thumb open."

Zach had a fist wrapped around the digit, face pinched up in a wince. "It's all full of frigging lime juice."

"Fucking hell," Shane said. Shame burned in his face as he caught Jeanne's eyebrows rise. He'd never lost his temper with his staff before, not unless he caught them doing something illegal or downright dangerous. He shoved the anger deep in his body, replaced it with half-assed paternal concern. He went around the bar, dug the first-aid kit from behind the register and got Zach patched up.

"Keep it dry," Shane said, tossing a latex glove at Zach's chest. He left the kit on the counter and headed for the exit, wanting to run but forcing his legs to act calm. Shit, it felt as though somebody'd slit his heart open and squirted *it* full of frigging lime juice.

"You okay, Shane?" Jeanne's voice behind him sounded meeker than usual, made him feel like a world-class shit.

"Fine." He strode through the lounge, broke into a run as he reached the steps. He kept his eyes glued to his door and off the backyard, forced his ears to hear only the muffled music from downstairs and block out anything he might not be able to handle coming from the backyard.

He shut the door, switched on all the living room's lamps in an attempt to drive away the images playing in a loop in his mind. He rubbed hard at his chest, needing to soften and break up the pain that had his muscles clenched tight and his heart pounding. There was nowhere safe to look—everything reminded him of that man. The couch, the kitchen, the shower, his own goddamn bed.

Shane shut himself in his bathroom, braced his palms against the cool countertop, took deep breaths for at least five minutes before he moved. He'd be okay. He'd felt jealous before and it always faded after a day or two. This hurt more, though, more than he could ever remember hurting except maybe when his momma had died.

He stared at himself in the mirror, stripped off his shirt, rummaged under the sink for his clippers and plugged them in. He switched them on and turned the setting to the second-shortest, needing a change. Something. Any-fucking-thing.

Shane put them to his temple, dragged them buzzing across his skull. His hands shook so bad the strip was jagged and wavy. Shane sensed movement in his periphery and the shaking turned near-convulsive. He tossed the clippers down, leaned against the marble again.

He felt that man's heat as surely as he might have heard him speak. After a long minute, a hand came to rest between Shane's shoulder blades, fingers rubbing gently. Shane straightened, met Gabriel's eyes in the mirror.

Don't you fucking ask me what's wrong.

He didn't. Instead he picked up the clippers, switched them on, coaxed Shane to face him with a hand on his shoulder. Shane obeyed, not feeling as if he had a choice. His body couldn't manage to rebel when this man was making requests.

He let Gabriel do what he couldn't, run the clippers over his scalp in steady strokes. He felt his hair fall away along with his jealousy. What was left was desperation, a violent need to reclaim what there'd been that morning and the night before, nearly every night for the past two weeks.

Gabriel clicked the clippers off and brushed his hands over Shane's buzzed head.

"Saw you with her," Shane said.

"Figured. I saw your lights come on."

"You used to bein' in a different pair of arms every fucking night then?"

Gabriel kept his eyes off Shane's as he brushed clippings from his bare shoulders. He shrugged. "I like sex."

The answer deflated him, drained all his once-justified-seeming anger and left him feeling helpless and idiotic. How foolish was he being, acting as though they were in any kind of committed relationship when he of all people would be the first to deny it?

"I like variety, Shane."

Those four little words stung like a slap.

"I liked las' night too," Gabriel went on, his light touch turning sensual, palms surveying Shane's throat and chest and arms. He leaned in close. "I been waitin' forever to give that to you. Can' wait for it to happen again."

Gabriel brought his hips to Shane's, the taunting contact sending Shane's blood rushing southward against his wishes.

"I can't offer you variety," Shane mumbled, resenting the tightness in his voice.

"Maybe no', but you give me other things I want. Other fantasies."

Shane swallowed before he spoke. "What kind of fantasies?" He knew the answer wouldn't be like what Gabriel had shared this morning, some simple threesome with a woman.

"Kind that involve a big strong man like you." He nipped Shane's ear. "Real nasty ones."

"How nasty?"

"I got prison fantasies," Gabriel murmured, lips at Shane's throat. "'Bout gettin' held down by a big man, like you done las' night. 'Bout bein' fucked hard an' tossed away."

Shane pulled away enough for Gabriel to see the skeptical squint of his eye. "You wanna get fuckin' ass-raped by a bunch of inmates?"

The corners of Gabriel's mouth curled in to a smirk. "Or guards."

Shane blew a breath through his nose and looked away.

Gabriel stroked his arms with worshipful hands. "Been hopin' I'd find a strong man like you, Shane."

"I'll fuck you but I ain't playin' dress-up and readin' from no twisted-ass script."

"I like you how you are," Gabriel whispered. "Love the way you fuck. Maybe you have some friends who could join us sometime." He ran his tongue over Shane's jaw.

Shane stiffened. "No. I don't."

"Tha's too bad." Gabriel leaned back to meet Shane's eyes with his dark ones. "I'd love for someone to watch us." He licked his lips. "Watch you fuckin' me."

A different part of Shane stiffened but his anger trumped his dick's curiosity.

Gabriel stared at Shane's throat, ran his finger along his collarbone. "He beg you to let him have a turn. Maybe you let him. Maybe you make me suck his cock while you fuck me. You make him watch."

"I don't like sharin'," Shane said, keeping his tone even to hide just how hot the jealousy had his blood boiling, from the mere thought of this man being anything but his sole possession. Especially if that other person was a guy.

"He can hold me down while you fuck my ass," Gabriel murmured. "Maybe you take turns."

Shane wanted to tell him to shut the hell up about other men but decided to make his displeasure and possessiveness known in terms Gabriel was more likely to understand.

He grabbed Gabriel's shoulders and spun him around, pushed him hard against the counter. Reaching around, he got the man's belt and pants open quick and yanked them down his legs, bunched Gabriel's shirt up around his waist to expose his ass. He gave him two hard slaps, designed more to hurt than arouse, though judging from Gabriel's moan they'd done both.

Rubbing his fingers between Gabriel's cheeks, he leaned in close to speak just behind his ear.

"So you think you need more than what I can give you?"

Gabriel slid seamlessly into his role. "I di'n mean it, Shane." He gasped as Shane pushed two fingers inside, soreness and preparation be damned.

Shane let him go a second, stooped to slide Gabriel's cigarette case from his pants' pocket and find a condom. He opened his own buckle and fly and took his rock-hard dick out, got himself ready. Whatever lube the condom came with would have to be enough—he wasn't about to let on that this was anything more than a hate-fuck to the man who had him so goddamn ripped up inside.

He pushed hard on Gabriel's shoulders, bent him over the counter with an elbow in the sink and his face right up against the mirror. His breath fogged the glass in time with his low moans.

Shane rammed himself deep with no warning and no gentleness, moaned in harmony with Gabriel's gasp. The man sounded fearful but his grunts turned unmistakably hungry after a few dozen thrusts. He pushed his hips back into Shane's, invited the violation, reveled in it. Shane gave him another hard spank and grinned at the way the man jumped with surprise.

He watched Gabriel's face in the mirror under the cheap bulbs' sour light, the whole scene looking like a fucked-up sex movie, one that would've frightened the ever-loving shit out of Shane if he'd watched it a month ago.

Gabriel's clenched eyes opened and met Shane's in the glass. He pushed back, tried to reach between his legs to jerk but Shane stopped him. He grabbed both Gabriel's wrists and pinned them at the small of his back, laying his chest and shoulder back down on the counter.

"You already had your fucking fun tonight," Shane said, hammering hard.

Gabriel groaned. "Yes, Shane."

"But you like this too, don't you? You love this."

"Yeah."

Fuck, how had Shane gone his entire life not knowing somebody could get him this hot? He let Gabriel's wrists go, grabbed his waist and just *fucked*. Took everything he wanted as fast and mean as he pleased, felt the climax building as if he were speeding toward a cliff's edge. He watched them both in the mirror, watched himself as if it were a stranger fucking this exotic man in this shockingly familiar room, a stranger with Shane's face looking high on some kind of brutal ecstasy.

"Fuck yeah." He came hard to the sound of slapping skin, the smell of sex and latex and the sight of Gabriel's white dress shirt, damp against his back with sweat. Shane pushed himself in deep as the climax rocked him.

The pleasure squeezed him out, replaced all his anger with relief. Violent screwing might be a temporary fix, but for the moment he felt serene, secure, spent and happy and human again.

"Shit." He ran a palm down Gabriel's back, and like a fool went straight back to worshipping the fucker.

He cleared his throat and pulled out, tossed the condom, let Gabriel turn around to survey his face with jumpy black eyes.

"You all right?" Shane asked between heaving breaths.

"Course."

Shane ran his hands over Gabriel's neck, opened the top button of his shirt, then the next. A white bandage was taped to his chest.

Shane frowned, pressing his fingers to it gently. "What's this?"

"Tha's you, Shane." Gabriel peeled the gauze away to reveal new notes—the raised black lines of a fresh tattoo edged in tender red skin.

"I can't read music. What is it?"

"I play it for you sometime," Gabriel said, smiling.

Shane stared at the staff and its notes, confused by what it meant. It meant he mattered, but it also meant he'd be yet another piece of music Gabriel was counting on forgetting, requiring a reminder for the day Shane faded to near anonymity with all those other lost souls.

Still, there he was. Branded right over Gabriel's heart, incidental or not. Permanent. Shane blinked at it, pressed the bandage back in place. He slid the white cotton off Gabriel's tanned and tattooed shoulders and rubbed his tight muscles. He aimed his eyes at the ink of a hundred others, afraid his returning anxiety might show.

"What d'you want?"

"Thought I already got mine for the night," Gabriel said.

Shane swallowed. "Think maybe I owe you something for what just happened. Didn't mean to be that rough."

"You were angry, Shane. It's okay."

He shot him a glare. "I don't need your fucking excuses, boy. You just tell me what you want and I'll make us even." *Make us good again so you won't go looking outside my house for what you need.*

Gabriel studied Shane's face, ran a hand slowly across his own stomach and fisted his half-hard cock, stroked until it was stiff and dark. "Anythin' I wan', Shane?"

"No. But try me."

"You wanna get on your knees for me, maybe?"

Shane's chest tightened but he oozed out a long breath. He could do this. He'd do most anything to guarantee this man kept coming back for more.

He held on to the counter and lowered to one knee then the other. Gabriel kicked away his pants and Shane put his hands to his warm thighs, unsure.

"You never sucked dick before, eh?"

Shane didn't dare acknowledge the question…plus Gabriel knew the fucking answer, just wanted to hear it. Same as how Shane wanted to hear he was the biggest Gabriel had ever had.

Short nails raked Shane's scalp, the sensation bringing pleasure and trepidation. Shane brought his face close, the smell of this man so potent he could damn near taste him.

Gabriel reached down and dragged his weeping head across Shane's lips, his scent making Shane's mind swim as though he'd downed a fifth of whiskey.

"Open up, Shane. Open your mouth an' I give you your first lesson."

Shane's hands trembled and he clamped them on Gabriel's hips to hide the shaking. He'd never been submissive with anybody before and it was terrifying, this impulse—this desperate need to please the man staring down at him.

He parted his lips, slid the tip of his tongue out to taste Gabriel's head. He tasted strange and tangy, not quite salty, not quite bitter. His skin was smooth and warm and slick, painting Shane's lips with his pre-come.

Gabriel grinned, evil if Shane had ever seen evil. "You're so hot. Jus' like I fantasized you'd look. Now open up for me."

Shane opened his mouth wider, let Gabriel ease inside.

"Cover those teeth, Shane."

Fearing failure, Shane tightened his lips.

"Good." Gabriel pushed in deeper. Shane took the first couple inches, bathed them with his tongue as he worked to keep the suction going. Gabriel pumped his hips, slow and shallow.

"Yeah. Suck that cock. I teach you how to do it good."

Hands gripped the back of Shane's head, the absence of his hair making him feel as vulnerable as the hard, cold tile under his knees, the sudden loss of his height. There was pleasure to what was happening but he was frightened too. He wanted to be good, the best Gabriel ever got, but this cruel streak in his lover was intimidating, taking orders humiliating.

"Good. Tha's good. I think you like that... I make you a good little cocksucker, Shane. Jus' do what I say."

Shane freed his mouth to take a breath. His jaw ached and it was way harder than he'd ever guessed. He owed women a load more credit for this.

"Get your mouth back on me."

Shane obeyed.

Gabriel cupped Shane's head, coaxing him to take more. For a couple minutes he let Shane find his rhythm, murmured encouragement and gentle orders.

Once Shane settled into the experience, Gabriel changed. The palms grazing Shane's buzzed hair turned possessive and Gabriel's hips pumped softly.

"Make it nice an' tight. Suck me hard." Gabriel wrapped his hand around his base, giving himself pulls that bumped his fist against Shane's lips. "I wanna fuck your mouth jus' like you fucked my ass. Wanna own you... Bet you never got fucked, eh?"

Shane took a deep breath through his nose, trying to banish the nerves that question ushered in.

"Sometimes I fantasize about takin' you," Gabriel whispered, stroking Shane's hair. "'Bout gettin' you on your hands and knees, fuckin' your tight virgin ass raw."

Shane moaned, the sound muffled.

"Keep suckin' me."

He obeyed, entire body tense with heat and confusion and fear and desperation.

"I fuck your ass," Gabriel went on, rubbing Shane's head affectionately, "an' I reach around and stroke that huge cock right in time with it. Pretend it's mine. How it'd feel to have a big, thick cock like yours."

Shane slid Gabriel from his mouth. "You're never fuckin' my ass."

Gabriel laughed as Shane's lips closed over his shaft again. "Maybe no'. But I can fantasize."

Shane backed off enough to mutter, "Fine."

"Wanna hear you moan when I fuck you. I do it nice an' slow, 'til I know you enjoyin' yourself. 'Til your body's beggin' me to make it rough." Gabriel groaned, lost in his imagination. His hips thrust his cock deeper into Shane's mouth, past his meager comfort zone and into his throat. Shane blinked his watering eyes, took what he was given and enjoyed what he could from it—total helplessness, that thing he felt all day long when he thought of Gabriel but never let himself show before now. He wanted to get it out, own up to it for a few brief moments so maybe it wouldn't dog him so hard the next morning. He clamped a palm over each of Gabriel's hips and met his thrusts.

"Yeah, Shane. Jus' like that."

Shane glanced up and found Gabriel's eyes shut tight, the hand not on Shane's head caressing Gabriel's chest and stomach, trembling. Even on his knees with a cock halfway down his throat, Shane clung to every scrap of control he could find. He upped his mouth's suction, rode a wave of satisfaction as Gabriel groaned deep, body shaking. And Shane felt big again, claimed ownership of what was happening, made it into something he was doing, not having done to him. He sucked with all the aggression he'd feel if he still had Gabriel bent over the sink.

"Yeah, Shane. Suck me. Open up and take my come."

With that, Gabriel lost it. For a half-dozen beats he fucked Shane's mouth, thrusting hard and deep, choking him until he pulled back, come lashing Shane's tongue in hot spurts.

Shane's eyes stung from the gagging and he swallowed as Gabriel pulled out, more to have the act done with than to appear obedient. He got to his feet and disguised the shaking in his legs, zipped his pants up and pressed his body against Gabriel's, staring him down.

"You want Friday night gigs and my couch, my cock, my mouth then you do what I say."

Gabriel took a deep breath, looking as though he were fighting for consciousness. "What you say, Shane?"

"You don't fuck anybody but me in my house or my club or my motherfucking yard." Shane worked to keep his anger under control, hating how torn-up he sounded.

Gabriel broke eye contact to stare over Shane's shoulder. "You can' give me what I need from a woman, Shane." His eyes reconnected. "Or you won'."

Shane took a seething breath, feeling so desperate he thought he might pass out. "Fine. You can go with women. Just not in my house... And you come to me for permission first. You do that, or else you get the hell out of Shiloh for good and leave me in fucking peace."

Gabriel blinked thoughtfully then met Shane's eyes again. "Okay."

There was no triumph in the bargain. Shane felt weak and defeated and he wanted to crawl into a dark room or a bottle and lose himself for a long time.

"Now you get out of my face. Go to the living room and don't talk to me 'til tomorrow. I can't stand lookin' at you right now."

It was one order Gabriel refused to follow. Shane got about ten minutes' solitude before one of the louvered doors to his dark bedroom creaked open, splashing warm light across the floor. Gabriel's silhouette approached on quiet feet and the mattress sagged as he sat down.

"You awake?"

"Course I am."

"Lemme sleep with you," Gabriel murmured and a hand grazed Shane's buzzed head. "Sleep next to you."

Shane didn't answer but he didn't protest when Gabriel lifted the covers and laid his naked body down against Shane's. His skin felt cool as he eased an arm under Shane's waist, set his palm on his back. Shane couldn't see his face, just the shapes of his ear and his hair, backlit by the hall light. Soft lips and a rough cheek rubbed Shane's jaw, tightening his chest. He wanted this, bad. He put his arm around Gabriel's shoulder and held him, kissed his temple, tasted the faint salt of his sweat.

"You scare the shit out of me," Shane whispered.

"Because I'm a man?"

He thought about it. "No…but don't go telling anybody about you and me."

"Why, then?" Gabriel slid a thigh between Shane's and one on top, locking them together.

Because you don't care half as much as I do about all this. About us. "Doesn't matter."

CHAPTER EIGHT

Shane didn't think he'd ever been so motherfucking happy to wake up and realize it was Monday. He stared at the ceiling, not quite ready to move and upset the warm arm flopped across his chest. He didn't want to wake Gabriel, didn't want to speak to him yet, but he wanted to get the hell out of the house, go in to work and escape the weird weather patterns inside his head. He could hear rain drumming the windows, mimicking the storm in his skull. Then he remembered he had a guest arriving sometime today and there'd be no going into the garage until Marie came by.

He pushed Gabriel's arm away and got up, tapped him rudely on the forehead. "Hey. Wake up."

Gabriel's eyes opened halfway and he smiled. "Mornin'. What time's it?"

"Almost eight. You gotta get up and out. I got company coming by sometime. I don't know when, but I don't need them finding your ass in my bed."

Two black eyebrows rose to express Gabriel's wry amusement. "I guess it your house, Shane."

"Yeah, you guess right. Get up."

They showered quickly and separately, shared a pot of coffee in the kitchen and barely spoke. Shane was feeling so many things they all blended together and cancelled each other out, left him floating in a cloud of numbness.

That cloud lifted as they wandered to the living room, and what Shane found underneath was an electric tangle of paranoid anxiety. The second he kicked Gabriel out of his house was the second he'd start wondering where he was. And who with. Sitting on the couch, he stared at the tread of his boot for a long time before pulling it on.

"Shane?"

He turned, met Gabriel's eyes as coolly as he could manage.

"What wrong?"

"What's wrong?" Shane repeated, attention back on his hands and feet. "Nothin's wrong."

"You still upset about las' night?"

"Listen…" Shane searched for the right label to tack on—*listen buddy, asshole, freeloader, darlin'*—but none of them felt comfortable, especially not *Gabriel.* "Don't you try and talk to me about last night, like you and me are some kind of happy caring motherfucking couple. 'Cause we ain't. I don't know *what* the fuck we are, and I don't know where I'll find you the next time I blink."

"Shane."

He met those black eyes again.

"You full of shit, Shane."

He sat up straight. "'S'cuse me?"

"You make it sound like I'm the one keepin' this from being somethin' real." Gabriel waved his hand around the room. "Up here you can' keep your hands off me, but downstairs you won' even look me in the eye. I'm not stupid, Shane. I know I'm your dirty little secret."

The option of being publicly open about what was going on between them was so far off Shane's radar that the surprise of the thought knocked him senseless. Furthermore he'd never heard Gabriel string that many words together before or say them quite so firmly—it was as though he'd feigned muteness then burst into song. He stared past Gabriel's perfect face to the rain streaking the tall back windows.

"You act like you got some right to be jealous when you barely even look at me downstairs," Gabriel said. "So fuck you, if you think you can fuck my ass one minute and ignore me the next. Fuck you if you won' tell people what we are."

"I can't do that."

Gabriel shrugged, a tight, cold gesture. "Fine. Jus' quit actin' like I done you wrong when I'm the one willin' to be honest about us."

Shane's heart thumped against his ribs as anger morphed into fear. "So what are we then?"

"We're lovers, Shane." *Lovers.* "But you don' get to keep me on a leash when you won't even acknowledge what's goin' on between us, outside this room."

What is *going on between us?*

Gabriel held his eyes for a second longer then turned away, trailed a hand over the back of the couch and gazed blankly across the dim room. "Maybe someday you find you can fuck me without bein' shitfaced or half-asleep, eh?" He turned to fix Shane with a cool stare. "Then maybe you get some of that power I let you think you got over me."

Shane's blood reached a steady simmer. "Fuck you, fuckin' ingrate. Don't forget who's a guest here."

Gabriel just smirked. "Yours ain't the only couch in town."

Shane narrowed his eyes to slits, fisted his hands then regretted the show of hurt.

"But yours is the one I want," Gabriel went on, smiling. He took a seat on the far cushion. "Day you kiss me with a witness'll be the day I tell my eyes to stop wanderin'. For now, we jus' enjoy each other."

It was an offer Shane couldn't refuse. "My aunt's coming by today with her car," he said, changing the subject. "I need you out of here when she's visiting. If she comes upstairs she's bound to notice you're not one of the original furnishings."

Gabriel shrugged as if Shane had just pled guilty to all charges.

"Don't give me that fuckin' saintly grin," Shane warned. "I'm not gay and even if I was, I'm not coming out to my sixty-something auntie."

"She the one who opened the bar?"

Shane nodded. "She's used to me leaving my socks all over this house, but stray musicians're another matter."

Gabriel stared at him with a weird little grin tightening his lips. He turned the tense chitchat into far more with a couple of relocated knees, lodging one on either side of Shane's hips and bracing his palms on Shane's chest. "When she comin'?"

"Dunno."

Gabriel licked his lips.

"Don't gimme that look—she's got keys. She grew up here."

Gabriel leaned down, heated Shane's neck with a couple deep exhalations before running his lips across the skin. Against his better judgment, Shane tangled his fingers in Gabriel's hair and cupped his head, succumbed to the temporary impulse to hold him there as long as possible.

"I got a deal for you," Gabriel murmured, that voice trickling malt liquor into Shane's ear and turning his brain to mush.

"What?"

Gabriel leaned back, ran slow hands over Shane's stomach. "You can have me, Shane…but if I see a woman I want to go with, I send her to you for permission. And you say yes or no."

Shane stared at the man's chest, fearing his eyes. He realized in a flash what they were, just what Gabriel had said a minute earlier—lovers. *Duh,* perhaps, but it hadn't truly occurred to him before. This man counted. Mattered. In fact, if Shane were the type who carved notches into his bedpost Gabriel's would be the deepest by far, damn near saw the fucking frame in half.

"I keep it discreet," Gabriel said, "but I send them to you. What you say?"

"And I can say no if I want?"

"If you say no every single time, you prolly won' keep me around forever." Gabriel fingered Shane's belt buckle. "But yeah. You get to decide."

"And I'll own you?" The verb he knew both of them got so fucking hot over.

"Oh yeah, you own me, Shane." Gabriel grinned, looking nearly coy if he didn't also look about three breaths away from sucking Shane's cock.

"Yeah. Fine then."

Gabriel's grin deepened to the shit-eating variety once more, a kid in the midst of his own birthday party. He offered a slender hand and Shane shook it, firm and quick.

Shane took a moment to stare at this man, to feel the warmth and fear and excitement churning in his gut. He reached out and cupped Gabriel's hips, felt his muscle and strength and eagerness and realized it was all his.

"Want you," he grunted.

Gabriel blinked at him. "Then take me."

Shane pushed him away, got up and set the chain lock on the front door. He stood over Gabriel, surveying his official territory for nearly a minute. Gabriel sat up, linked his fingers through two of Shane's belt loops. Those black eyes darted, hands waiting for permission. Shane stepped closer until his ankles hit the bottom frame of the couch. Gabriel took the cue and ran a palm across Shane's fly, eager fingers tracing the outline of his erection.

Closing his eyes, Shane let himself melt into the feeling, that seductive mix of power and shame and relief. He let those familiar fingers open his belt and zipper, stroke him through his shorts.

"How do you get me so hard," he mumbled, not quite a question.

"Ooooh," Gabriel teased. "I got a gris-gris."

Shane laughed. "Spare me your crazy grandma's voodoo bullshit."

"Then I dunno, Shane."

The hold on Shane's cock tightened, lighting him up with impatience and desire and that ever-present and undeniably exciting anxiety.

"There something between us," Gabriel said.

A fuckload too much clothing, for starters. "Stand up."

He backed away so Gabriel could submit to the order. Shane memorized each button as he freed it, every square inch of golden skin as the white cotton slid away. He got Gabriel's pants off, pushed him gently back onto the cushions then went to work on his own clothes, got a condom from his wallet and tossed it on the side table.

"Turn over."

"You ever gonna fuck me face-to-face?" Gabriel asked, already obeying.

"I give you everything else you want," Shane said. "Lemme have my baby steps."

Gabriel got onto his knees, elbows on the arm of the couch. Shane sank down behind him, traced each knob of his spine, the muscles pinched between his shoulder blades, marveled at him a moment before lust pushed adoration out of the way.

He squeezed that hard ass, spanked it a few times, watched Gabriel's skin bloom pink and made him wait. He fucking loved this part—controlling this man's anticipation and excitement.

"Come on. Please."

"God, I love it when you beg." Shane wet two fingers and slid them over Gabriel's asshole, eased them in slow. Gabriel's arms trembled as he moaned, lighting Shane on fire.

"Need it," Gabriel mumbled.

"I know you do."

"Now. Please."

Shane fisted his cock with his free hand, got a jolt from his own hardness, from believing he was the biggest this man had ever had, from the thought he might be the best, the only one good enough. He stroked himself tightly, fantasizing that if Gabriel was with another man sometime—tonight, next week, five years from now—he'd only be able to imagine it was Shane who was fucking him.

His patience dissolved. He ripped open the condom and slid it on, spat in his palm and got himself slick.

They fucked hard and fast, each finding what they needed from the other, climaxing together in a sweaty heap of ticcing muscle on the beleaguered couch. Gabriel got his body under control enough to toss his leg over Shane's hips, straddle him and rest his face against Shane's neck, his ragged breaths heating and soothing.

Shane knew this wasn't love, at least not any kind of love that extended beyond the desires of two selfish bodies. No future, only fleeting pleasure. This was addiction, plain and simple…irresistible need coupled with painful consequences and regret, moments of pure happiness like islands, spread out in a thrashing sea of insecurity and interminable waiting.

But for as long as he had his hands on this man's skin, Shane had solace. The second he let go the pain would return, scary and intense but nothing compared to the highs.

Shane had quit smoking in his twenties, a month of pure hell that'd be nothing compared to the withdrawal he'd face if the warm body currently plastered to his chest and stomach were to up and disappear.

Gabriel whispered behind his ear. "You need me gone soon."

"Yeah."

"An' I always do what you say."

Shane swallowed. "We'll see."

Gabriel pulled away, peeled his hot skin from Shane's and stood, and Shane wanted to grab him and yank him back, wrestle him to the carpet and never let go.

Instead he stood and got rid of the condom and they dressed in silence. He stole glances as Gabriel pressed his bandage firmly against his chest, buttoned his shirt and slipped on his jacket. He raked his hair with his fingers, found his hat and put it on…perfectly ignorant or utterly cognizant of how magnetic he was, who knew which.

He met Shane's eyes with his deadly ones. "Maybe I see you tonight, Shane?"

"Maybe."

Gabriel grabbed his mandolin case from the counter. Shane followed his every move as he walked to the door, undid the locks, opened it. Gabriel turned in the threshold.

"You keep that bed warm for me, eh?"

Shane took a breath. "Yeah. Sure." He looked to his feet, kept his eyes there until he heard the click of the door closing, felt the chilly breeze wash over him, heard the thump of Gabriel descending the steps, taking away all his sweltering heat and leaving Shane stranded in the barren emptiness of winter.

And before he even started lamenting their latest parting, Shane was craving nine o'clock, craving red wine and heated glances, tenuous bargains and a tempting imitation of trust. He looked to the clock.

Only twelve more hours and he could breathe again.

SHIVAREE

CHAPTER ONE

A couple miles from the junction that would've taken her to Baton Rouge, Natalie's ancient pickup gave three rodeo-quality lurches and coasted to a halt. The engine sputtered to silence, headlights illuminating a neglected gravel road and the dense trees to either side.

"Beautiful," she muttered. She rested her forehead on the wheel and blew out a long breath. What had Chris told her? *You'll never make it without me.*

Well, shit. They'd been broken up for less than three days, and she was already possum meat. She could practically hear his mocking voice, humming the opening to *Dueling Banjoes.*

She tried turning the engine over a dozen times with no luck. Slamming her fist on the wheel was equally ineffective, though it felt pretty good. The air conditioner had died with the engine and its magic chill dissipated, replaced by the oppressive August heat.

The barest sliver of a crescent moon peeked from between the treetops. The clock in the dash said it was ten twenty-six, Miami time, which made it just about nine thirty here in Nowheresville, Louisiana.

Farther down the road, Natalie could make out a faint glow. A business or a house, she hoped, though she hadn't seen a single building or passed another car in the fifteen bumpy miles since discovering the too-cheap-to-be-true motel she'd been looking for was shuttered and derelict. That's what she got for trusting the decade-old regional guide book she'd paid a quarter for at a yard sale outside New Orleans that afternoon.

"Fuck it."

She pocketed her keys and grabbed her wallet, shoved her purse deep under the passenger seat. She swung the door open and the humidity closed around her throat. Her shoes were practical by her standards, but that wasn't saying much. The pointed toes and demure one-inch heels were wasted in the darkness, and as soon as she set foot on the ground, gravel found its way under her soles. She had sneakers in her suitcase, inside the cargo box in the bed of the truck, but fumbling around in the dark trying to unlock it seemed an invitation for frustration. Plus the glow wasn't coming from too far away.

Ignoring the questions bouncing around in her skull—most of which concerned what sorts of snakes might be causing the rustling noises in the undergrowth alongside the road—she headed toward what she hoped was salvation.

Could just be a streetlight. She wished she'd picked up a pay-as-you-go cell phone at a convenience store, as she'd been meaning to all day. More than that, she wished she hadn't chucked her smart phone out her truck's window, sick of finding Chris's name on its screen. *Oops.*

In the end she'd just kept driving, kept putting miles between her and Chris, between her and all those mistakes she'd made and the four years she'd wasted on him. She tripped on some unseen bump in the dirt.

"Fucker."

The glow wasn't a streetlight, though it wasn't as close as she'd hoped either. A quarter mile down the road, she heard the place before she could see it. Music drifted through the woods, haunting and eerie, like a spell. Like the sort of spooky metaphor Natalie wasn't inclined to draw. It carried her closer, making her forget the pebbles grinding into her raw heels.

As the melancholy song ended, a happier one began. The road curved and a building came into view, lighting up the night like a miniature carnival.

It was a three-story white house with a wide front lawn. Hastily parked cars and trucks were strewn over the unkempt grass, and a porch wrapped around the ground floor, lined in mosquito netting and draped with mismatched strings of Christmas lights and electric lanterns. A hand-painted sign hung above the front steps. The Shivaree, it said.

Clearly a bar. In addition to the music wafting out, Natalie heard glasses tinkling, floorboards squeaking, laughter, loud voices calling out to one another. Surely *someone* in this bustling club would be able to help her—take a look at her truck, or at least give her a lift to the nearest motel.

But her practical troubles dissolved as the screen door slapped shut behind her. Her gaze drifted past the bar, past the couples promenading on the creaky dance floor, past the scattered tables and loitering drinkers to the lone man on the little stage in the corner.

Natalie swallowed.

"Charisma" didn't go halfway to describing what he had. Tall. Lean, but substantial, utterly magnetic. He looked as if he'd stepped out of some other era, transported by time machine from the 1920s, maybe. Shined black shoes, dark slacks, a crisp dress shirt with the sleeves rolled up to his biceps. A watch chain dangled from his belt and a gray porkpie hat topped his messy hair. His face was placid. Tan skin, black eyebrows and sideburns. A wide mouth designed for whispering sinister promises.

Natalie looked to his hands and the instrument they were holding, something like a small, asymmetrical guitar, with strange curves to it—something she recognized, but only vaguely. Something from a film set in a different century.

A tap on her shoulder snapped her out of her trance. A couple had arrived behind her, and she mumbled an apology and moved out of the threshold. She kept her eyes off the musician and made a beeline for the bar. She'd planned to enquire about solving her engine troubles, but the thought flew away as the woman behind the taps smiled at her.

Natalie glanced to the bottles lined up above the register. "Blue Moon, please." Her truck would be okay for a few extra minutes, and her feet could use the break.

She took her sweating beer back through the crowd, settling herself at a high table. She resisted the temptation to look at the musician again, staring at the couples instead. The fast song came to an end, and the dancers paused to clap and whoop their appreciation.

"Thank you." His voice was low and deep, with a gentle rasp. Natalie's eyes snapped up against her wishes. They found the man smiling into the crowd as his fingers plucked idly at the strings. He eased into another song, its dreamy, dark notes oozing out into the space. Most of the couples stayed on the floor, beginning to slow dance, looking like lovers. Looking like sex, upright to a beat.

Natalie felt the music wash over her, as warm and languid as the air seeping through the screens. The man on stage raised the mic stand up a few inches, and he sang.

On some atomic level, Natalie felt the vibrations of his voice pulsating on a wavelength attuned to her own private rhythms. The lyrics were foreign—Spanish—but their meaning was unmistakable. Couples moved as singular bodies, cores pressed tight as they rotated. Hands drifted low, cupping backsides with fond flirtation, holding hips with possession. Parched, Natalie took a deep drink of her beer.

The magnetic man's eyes were closed for much of the song, fingers left to their talented devices, consciousness surrendered to the creation of the music. Natalie was staring at him when his lids finally rose, and she was caught.

For the rest of the song, he held her gaze, his eyes black in the colored glow of the motley lights. She couldn't have looked away if she wanted to. And she *didn't* want to. She wanted this man to sing to her. She wanted him to do everything to her, with an urgency that made her blush and made the damp, hot air feel cold against her fevered skin.

She was so far gone she didn't realize the song had ended until the clapping roused her. The man's gaze released hers. He looked down at his hands as he said, "Thank you," again, the last syllable drawn out into a sigh. He nodded to some unseen person and recorded music came through the speakers, a lazy country ballad. He flicked the microphone off and set his instrument on top of its case by the wall. Hopping off the stage, he snaked through the dancing bodies, heading toward Natalie. She felt her eyes go round.

He was tall, just as she'd thought, perhaps six-one. Slender but masculine, strides graceful and confident.

He stopped directly in front of her, a strange, subtle smile curling his lips.

"Hi." She clutched her bottle like a merry-go-round pole to keep from tipping over.

"You dance?"

"Not very—"

He cut off her protest, taking the beer from her hand and setting it on the tabletop. He led her by the shoulder to a small opening in the dance floor.

"I don't dance very well," she finished. It didn't matter. These were lazy steps, a dance with no title or conventions. He led her in slow circles, one hand on her waist and the other clasped around her fingers in the air beside them. She set her free palm on his shoulder, feeling his warmth. From this close, she could smell him and see the tiny beads of sweat along his neck. His eyes were shaded by his hat. It looked vintage, the felt brim worn and the black satin band frayed. She wanted to put her nose to it and be taken back in time to an elegant era when men still danced and wore hats.

"What's your name?" he breathed, and his voice so close to her ear felt like the faintest whisper of a fingertip over her clit.

She cleared her throat. "Natalie. Foster."

"You're from away."

She nodded. "Rochester, New York. And Miami for the last few years."

"You on your way to someplace?"

"Back north," she said. "What's your name?"

"Gabriel."

She let the syllables dissolve like sugar in her ears. *Gabriel.*

"What brings you to this place?" he asked.

She laughed. "Chance. My truck broke down, up the road. I came to try to figure out if I can get it jumped, or whatever it needs. But I got distracted." She paused before adding, "By your music."

He grinned, deep and indulgent. "Oh?"

She nodded. "I don't even know what your instrument is. A harpsichord?" she ventured.

"Mandolin."

"Oh right. Sorry."

"But I can play you something on a harpsichord, if you brought one." His accent was thick and unusual, nothing she could place.

She blushed, unseen under the colorful lights. "I was way off, wasn't I?"

"Only by about two hundred pounds."

She blushed deeper. It wasn't her way, but this man made her body's inner workings misfire, sending blood to her cheeks and lips and breasts and lower.

She found her voice a few steps later. "What town am I in?"

"Shiloh. Barely a town. You heading to Baton Rouge tonight?"

She nodded. She watched his throat as he swallowed, the tendons and the bob of his Adam's apple, the dark hair framed in the V of his open collar. She glanced at his arm, bare up past the elbow, tan skin beside white cotton. He had tattoos, dark lines and shapes, just the very edges of the design visible.

All at once, being near this stranger was too much. From a distance, he was a sip of liquor. This near, for this long, he was alcohol poisoning. Natalie felt woozy. His long body felt close, closer than the inch or two separating their chests. The heat coming off him put the southern summer to shame, and sweat trickled down her spine beneath her tank top.

She glanced around the club, over Gabriel's shoulder. It was an odd place. More Christmas lights hung from the ceiling, a canopy of candy-colored stars. Strings of random pendants and crystals and glass beads were strung there as well, and all the tall windows were draped with long white curtains. The fabric was strange and spangled, textured with tiny pearls and lace and sequins. The breeze from outside made them dance along with the music.

"You lookin' at the drapes?" Gabriel asked, amused.

"They're odd."

"Made from weddin' dresses."

Of course.

"Everyone from around here calls this place The Chapel."

She nodded. She kept her eyes trained beyond the intoxicating man in front of her, mustering sobriety. Despite the chaos and noise, it was a peaceful, ethereal, sensual place. She took in the patrons, a mix as colorful as the decor. Everyone looked content, dancing, chatting around tables, seated at the bar.

With one exception. A large man in jeans and a tee shirt leaned against the wall near the front door. He was tall and dangerous-looking, and he was staring straight at Natalie.

"You distracted," Gabriel murmured. His voice dripped honey down her neck, warm and sweet and sticky.

"It's that man." She pointed with her eyes to where he stood, nursing a whiskey and some invisible grudge. Gabriel craned his neck and smiled.

"That's Shane Broussard."

"Is he your enemy or something? He's giving us the evil eye."

Gabriel laughed, low and seductive. He moved her in dreamy circles over the scuffed wood, commanding with his hands, teasing with his breath and smile and the grazing of his chest against hers. Natalie felt lucidity falling away again.

"He's my lover," he murmured.

She tightened in his arms. "Your lover?"

He ran his palms over her bare shoulders, over the goose bumps that had risen there. He nodded.

Natalie glanced to the side, taking in Shane Broussard—well-built frame, nearly shaved head, boxer's arms. He had the air of a soldier, dishonorably discharged.

"He looks…cruel," she whispered.

Gabriel laughed again. He drew his head back to study her anxious face. The edges of his eyes crinkled with mischief and satisfaction. "He's a beast."

Against anybody's better judgment, she ran her fingers over his neck and through his unruly black hair. "Maybe we should stop dancing. I don't want to upset him." She'd inspired more than her fill of masculine displeasure in recent months. Make that years.

Gabriel pulled her closer. "He don' own me."

Natalie sucked in a breath. She could feel him, stiff behind his fly, his erection pressing against her hipbone as their bodies swayed. She hesitated, torn between fear and pleasure. The chill he'd given her moments before gave way to a flush. The sultry air enveloped them and its magnolia scent was eclipsed by Gabriel—by the smell of his sweat and skin and by his mere presence. She wanted him. She craved him as palpably as a castaway might crave water. That his possessive lover was watching them with unveiled hatred only deepened the ache. Gabriel moaned softly as her nails raked his neck beneath his collar.

Natalie was used to going after what she wanted and usually getting it…though recent history had taught her she didn't always like her prize once she'd claimed it. Still…

"Does he let you take other lovers?" she whispered, reckless.

"Only women."

"And you do as he says?"

Gabriel ran his lips up her jaw to her ear, warming her with a deep exhalation. "I do."

"Why? What's in it for you?"

"I have my reasons."

With that, he led her with the dance, each step bringing them nearer to where Shane leaned against the wall. Gabriel's body broke from hers as they reached him. Up close, the man was huge, taller than Gabriel by two inches, Natalie guessed. She swallowed, tilting her chin up to meet his cold blue eyes.

"Gabriel," Shane said with a small nod.

"Shane. This is Natalie. She got car troubles. Maybe you could help her?"

Natalie's eyes jumped between them.

"Shane's a mechanic," Gabriel said. He ran a hand over her back then curled his fingers around her shoulder, shameless.

"Where's your car?" Shane asked, impossible to read.

"Truck," she corrected. "Maybe a quarter mile down the road. It just sputtered to a halt after a couple of lurches."

His gaze jumped to her feet in their kitten heels. "You walk here in those?"

She nodded.

He breathed out through his nose, the gesture gruff and impatient, saying distastefully, *Women.*

"Why don' you help her, Shane?" Gabriel asked, and Natalie caught the tiniest flick of his tongue at the corner of his mouth. "I'd be so grateful."

"I'll pay you, obviously," Natalie added, hoping she sounded casual. Hoping she sounded as though she wasn't caught between two feral men, their tension as hot and thick as the stifling humidity.

Gabriel's fingers drummed her collarbone. "I have another set coming up." His arm slid from her back and he stepped to Shane. He brought his head close and whispered something. Natalie caught Shane's eyes close in a wince. They exchanged a long look before Gabriel sauntered off toward the stage.

Natalie stared at her feet, unsure of what else to do. In her periphery, Shane drained his glass and set it on a windowsill.

"Fine. Take me to your truck."

Her head popped up. "Are you sure? I don't want to make any trouble for you."

"Shut up and lead the way." His tone wasn't entirely unkind, but it wasn't far off.

They made their way outside and Shane stopped at his own pickup, grabbing a huge toolbox and a Maglite from the bed.

"Which way?"

"We're walking?" Natalie asked, suddenly able to feel each ripened blister.

He nodded. "I'm half-loaded."

"I could drive. It's not far."

"Nobody drives my truck but me," he said, stony.

"Fair enough."

They walked in silence along the dark road, slapping mosquitoes. Natalie was too nervous to break her stride to kick the gravel from her shoes. In the distance, Shane's flashlight beam winked against chrome.

"That's it."

"Pop the hood for me," he said as they reached the vehicle.

She did and he handed her the light. "Hold this." He prodded and poked. Twice he asked her to try the engine, but it refused to turn over.

"Shit," he said. "All you need's a new plug, but I can't fix this tonight. Tomorrow you better get it towed to the garage and they'll sell you one. Hell, I'll tow it myself."

"Fuck."

He let the hood drop and took the flashlight back. They trudged back up the road, the lights of the club glowing above the trees in the distance, music drifting as though on the warm breeze.

"Thanks for trying," Natalie said.

The beam bobbed and she suspected he'd shrugged.

"I hope we didn't miss the whole set. Gabriel's quite—"

"Don't you talk like you know him," Shane cut in, a warning.

She swallowed but refused to be bullied. "I was just going to say he's talented. Scary-talented."

"You don't know him. I do."

"Fine." She fell silent for a minute. "What is he to you?"

She looked to his face, faintly illuminated, and his eyes met hers, icy cold.

"He's a goddamn curse."

CHAPTER TWO

S hane yanked the screen door open and held it for Natalie, the protocol feeling like a knife against his nuts.

"Thanks," she mumbled.

The music had begun casting its spell from a quarter mile down the road and now they were plunged into it, over their heads. Deep enough to drown.

Across the floor, past the pairs of gyrating bodies, Gabriel stood on the little platform. He was lost in his playing, black eyes locked on some invisible object in the middle distance. Shane took him in, that long, tight body, gifted fingers, goddamn beautiful face, the faint jerking of his hips and arms as he played. So powerful, creating all this. So helpless when Shane had his way, when he punished Gabriel for making him love him the way he did.

Shane glanced to his side, to Natalie. She was lovely. Slender, with tasteful curves, long neck, dark, wavy hair against white skin, a mole on her jaw. Late twenties, he guessed. Her eyes were pale, blue or green or hazel or gray, he couldn't tell, not in the colored lights. A few months ago, he'd have wanted to fuck her himself... But now he just hated her. He hated her for the way she made Gabriel look at her and the way she looked back. Her attention was glued to him now, hypnotized, exactly how Shane must look when he watched too, which made him hate her all the more.

He nudged her with his elbow and she glanced up.

"Get me a beer and a shot of whiskey."

She blinked for a moment, thinking.

"Do the math and you'll find it's a bargain, for a half hour's work."

Her jaw tightened but she nodded. "What kind of beer?"

"Whatever."

She returned, gripping two bottles by their necks in one hand and a rocks glass in the other.

He accepted his drinks with an open scowl.

"What?" She took a pull off her beer.

"I didn't ask for no ice."

"Well, you should have been clearer."

"And this beer tastes like shit. I've had it before."

She rolled her eyes. "You're welcome. You said to bring you 'whatever'."

He took a deep drink. "Tastes like fucking celery."

"It's a witbier. That's wheat you're tasting."

"I know what I'm tasting. And what are you, some kind of expert?"

"No... My ex was a brewer," she murmured then met his stare. "I picked up a few things."

"He leave you for eye-ballin' other people's men?"

"No. I left him. For bringing his work home with him."

Shane stared at her a few seconds longer, thinking of his old man. He nodded solemnly and turned back to the stage.

The dancers paused and the room filled with lazy applause and a few whistles as Gabriel finished his song. He smiled his appreciation and looked up. His dark eyes caught Shane's. He plucked out the opening notes of the song he'd been playing the moment Shane had fallen in love with him—before they'd ever spoken or touched, before they'd come together, scalding hot, and well before the heat had corroded to cruelty. Cruelty Gabriel surely attributed to Shane… Falsely attributed. He brought it on himself.

Natalie's voice scattered his thoughts. "Do you dance?"

"No."

"Well, me neither. Can you sway to a beat?"

He looked her over, long and hard. "What're you after, little girl?" As if he didn't know.

"Just dance with me." There was something drunken in her expression. Something that had nothing to do with alcohol.

"Fine." He let her lead him onto the floor, and he put the hand not clutching his beer at her waist as she draped her arms over his shoulders.

They meandered in circles and Shane felt the song wash over him. He heard a tiny spark of feedback as the mic was adjusted then the deep, primal rasp of Gabriel's voice as he began to sing. He'd learned this song in Havana, where he'd lived in his twenties. Shane had no idea what the words were saying, but they felt like a wet pair of lips sliding down his cock. He moaned against Natalie's forehead as he stiffened.

"He's beautiful," she whispered.

Shane swallowed. "I know."

"Do you love him?"

Shane's feet lost the beat a moment and something thick lodged itself in his throat. "Mind your own business."

"He said you let him go with women."

His pulse spiked. "He does as he pleases, sometimes. You want him?"

"Yes."

"You ever been a heroin addict?"

She pulled her face away, uncertain.

"Me neither," Shane said. "But I bet the withdrawal's got nothin' on him. You think twice before you get in over your head."

She peered over his shoulder to the stage. "What is he?" she asked. "Cajun?"

"Part," Shane said. "Part Choctaw. His old man's Cuban. He was raised by his bat-shit-crazy grandma in town."

"He's beautiful," she said again.

"He'll ruin you," Shane whispered.

He heard her swallow. "Maybe that's what I want."

"Think it over, when you're sober. You come back tomorrow, maybe I'll let you have him. For a price."

"Fuck you," she said. "You're not his master."

He pulled her body close, not caring if she felt his arousal. "That's exactly what I am."

"What's your *price* then?"

"You let me watch."

Her frame went rigid against him. "No way. You're a fucking control freak."

"I'm tryin' to spare you a lifetime of pain." His own body relaxed, relieved. He watched Gabriel on stage and let that deep voice course through him. He'd hear that baritone soon enough, not singing. Moaning and grunting. Begging. Then commanding. Shane closed his eyes.

"You don't know the first thing about him. Get out of town while you can, little girl."

* * *

Natalie downed a pint of water as the bar clock's hour hand neared one, trying to counteract the three beers she'd drunk.

After their dance, Shane had retired to his broody corner with a final, mean squint in her direction. She glanced at him every few minutes, amazed. When she'd first sized him up a couple hours ago, she'd seen him as he must appear to the rest of the world—hetero and painfully so. Built like a marine, hard-drinking, handy in a fistfight. Not a jealous wreck. Not a man sick in love over another man.

On stage, Gabriel continued to weave his web. The couples were oblivious, too drunk and infatuated with one another to see, but there was no doubt Natalie and Shane weren't the only ones mesmerized. Scattered around the bar were a half dozen men and women with their attention drawn inescapably to Gabriel, dogs all eyeing the same steak.

At a quarter past one, he strummed off a song and murmured a thank-you into the mic. He departed the stage and his haunting music was replaced with canned zydeco to keep the lovers dancing and drinking until after last call.

He strolled to the bar, mandolin case in hand. Natalie watched Shane sidle up to him, carefully keeping their bodies apart by a few inches. He said something private, close to Gabriel's ear. Gabriel craned his head over his shoulder, eyes locking onto Natalie's. Her heart raced into overdrive, pulse pounding hard in her wrists and throat and between her thighs. She'd never wanted a man like this before. She'd wanted her ex, certainly—more than she ever should have—but he'd never made her breath catch quite this way, never made her body prime itself, aching for him.

Gabriel looked back to Shane. He turned a moment later, holding a glass of red wine. He made his way across the dance floor, floating between amorous couples to where Natalie sat at a small table by herself.

"Hello, again." He set his case on the tabletop and took a deep drink, eyes trained on her over the wineglass.

"That was wonderful," she said.

He tapped his glass against hers and smiled, two dimples forming beside his devil's smirk. "Thank you. *Ça viens?* He fix your truck?" He nodded to Shane.

She shook her head. "It needs a part. I'll get it towed tomorrow."

"Where you sleepin' tonight?"

"In the cab, I guess. I don't have the cash for a motel *and* a tow."

Gabriel laughed, so obscenely sexy. "No, you won'. You come home with us." He looked to Shane again.

"I don't think your friend likes me much."

"Sometimes, he don' like *me* so much. Or himself. Come with me." He swallowed the last of his wine and straightened his hat. With buzzing nerves, Natalie followed as he led her to where Shane waited by the bar.

"She's coming with us," Gabriel announced.

She caught Shane's nostrils flare with a deep exhalation. "Fine," he said. He set a shot glass on the bar with a loud clack and pulled a set of keys from his pocket.

"We're all drunk," Natalie pointed out.

"That's okay," Gabriel said. "We're not driving."

She grimaced, wiggling her savaged toes in her ruined shoes. "Okay."

Shane slapped the counter and shouted a good-night to the bartender. They headed for the side porch, past passionate couples sequestered in the shadows. Natalie was surprised to be led not out into the darkness but up a set of steps to a balcony.

"You live here?" she asked.

Shane unlocked the door to the second-floor apartment. "Yup. I own this place."

She blinked. "You made me buy you a drink in your own bar?"

"Looks that way." He pushed the door in and for the first time, he smiled at her. She shook her head, as amused as she was annoyed, and followed Gabriel inside. Shane flipped on a light and locked up behind them.

Natalie glanced around the living room they'd entered, taking in the decor—plain walls painted a deep gold, tall windows, old mahogany furniture. Worn but tasteful. Probably the taste of some former denizen, not this man.

Gabriel set his case on the tiled counter that separated the living room and kitchen, tossed his hat on a coat rack and sank into an old velvet armchair. Like a cat, long and lazy and graceful and predatory. Scheming, to Shane's brutish bulldog temperament.

"You'll be sleeping in here," Shane said. He pointed to the couch.

"Looks ten times more comfy than my passenger seat. Thanks."

"Bathroom's in the back, straight past the kitchen. Don't steal nothin'."

"I hadn't planned on it," she began, but his narrowed eyes posed an addendum. *Don't steal my man.*

"I'm just grateful to have someplace to sleep."

Shane disappeared for a minute, returning with an armload of blankets and a pillow. He tossed them onto the couch.

"Thanks." She caught Shane flash Gabriel a stern look before leaving the room. Gabriel raised his eyebrows at Shane's retreating back and rose. He stepped slowly to Natalie, eyes on the floor, a smile on his lips.

"And thank *you* for getting him to let me stay," she said.

His head came up. His dark eyes flickered over her face, and she could smell the wine on his breath, the scent of his sweat. She wanted to run her tongue across his throat and taste his salt. In the lamplight she studied the ink on his neck and below his collarbone, as on his arms—sheet music. Notes on staves, scribbled on his skin in blue and black by different hands, as though the composers hadn't had paper handy when inspiration struck. As Gabriel's hands ran up her arms to her neck and cradled her head, Natalie surrendered to the kiss she felt coming. Her palms slid down his chest and stomach to his hips, hungry. Sadly, his lips found her forehead, not her mouth. Gabriel ran his rough thumbs over her cheeks a few times.

"Sleep well." He stepped away, taking his warmth and energy and heading into the dark hall.

"Good night."

* * *

Natalie sat on the couch beside the pile of bedding for twenty minutes or more, rolling a twenty-pound dumbbell between her feet on the throw rug, turning Gabriel's old porkpie hat around and around in her hands. She listened to the muffled music drifting up through the floorboards and stared into space. Eventually the music died, replaced by murmuring voices and flares of laughter then cars starting up, the clinking of glass as the staff put the club to bed. At the other end of the apartment, doors opened and closed and water was turned on and off in the bathroom. Then nothing but the whirring of insects and chirps of frogs.

She padded through the kitchen to the bathroom, eyes drawn to the left, to the room she assumed was Shane's. Lights were on behind the louvered doors, a warm glow seeping from between the closed wooden slats and the crack above the floor.

She splashed cold water on her face and combed her fingers through her messy hair. Her stomach made an angry noise and she realized she hadn't eaten since lunch. Maybe she could scavenge something from Shane's kitchen and leave him a couple bucks in return. That wouldn't technically be stealing.

But her appetite shifted when she flicked the bathroom light off and stepped back into the hall. Rumbling, masculine voices sounded from Shane's room. She tiptoed to the threshold, trying to peek between the two doors. She couldn't see anything, but she heard them.

"It's humiliating," Shane said.

"She a perfectly nice woman," Gabriel replied in his languid way. "You jus' don' like her 'cause she no' intimidated by you."

There was a pause. "You want her?" Shane asked.

"I do."

"You let me watch then."

"Up to her," Gabriel said, sounding light and conversational.

Natalie reached a shaky hand up and tilted the slats of one door open slightly, until she could see them. The room was big, and the two men were maybe six feet from where she stood. Shane's broad back was to Natalie, and he obscured her view of Gabriel, who was sitting on the arm of a couch, facing Shane. She could see his bare feet and one bare arm, more tattoos decorating his biceps. The men were quiet, trapped in some intimate face-off.

Shane finally broke the silence with a groan. "Why do you do this to me?" He sank down, crouching before Gabriel, defeated. Gabriel made a shushing noise and ran his hands over Shane's buzzed hair, consoling. Natalie studied his face and naked torso. He was lean and wild-looking, a long body draped in taut muscles.

"You do this to yourself," Gabriel whispered. He tucked a messy lock behind his ear.

She heard Shane mumble something that sounded like, "I hate you." He stood up a moment later. Gabriel stood too and tried to wrap his arms around Shane's waist, only to have them knocked away.

"Don't touch me."

Gabriel's reply came low and sweet. "I love touching you. Jus' like you love touchin' me."

"I like fuckin' you," Shane spat. "That's all it is."

"I don' believe that any more than you do." This time Gabriel was allowed to wind his arms around Shane's middle for a moment, his fingers raking the cotton of Shane's tee shirt. His hands slid to cup Shane's ass, pulling him close for a second before he was shoved back, rough. They were still for a heartbeat then Shane took control.

Natalie held her breath. Shane stripped off his shirt, revealing the toned expanse of his back, pale beside his tanned arms. She heard a slap, the sound of Gabriel's hand being swatted away again, she guessed. She eased the slats wider, greedy eyes demanding more.

They grappled for a moment but Gabriel, though muscular, was no match for Shane, who had a couple inches and a couple dozen pounds on him. Shane turned Gabriel around, and Natalie watched his triceps flex and heard the metallic click of a belt being unbuckled.

Gabriel muttered, "No." But it wasn't the voice of a man protesting. It was an invitation. A tease.

Shane yanked Gabriel's pants down his hips and bent him over the arm of the couch. Natalie froze, mesmerized and terrified and aroused beyond belief. And *frustrated*. She wanted to see everything— their faces and chests and stomachs, their eyes at the moment of penetration. She could make out one of Shane's hands on Gabriel's lower back, pinning him. The other fumbled in a pocket a moment then there was the sound of another buckle. He grunted as he pushed his pants down an inch and took his cock out. Gabriel moaned. Natalie heard plastic rustling as Shane got a condom ready. He spat in one palm and his arm muscles twitched as he made one or both of them slick.

"No," Gabriel murmured again, sounding hungry. He gasped as Shane groaned, and Natalie felt desire, wet between her thighs. She wanted to be both of them at once. She wanted to fuck Gabriel and get fucked by Shane. She drank in the sight of them, of Shane's hips pumping, slow at first. His jeans slid halfway down his ass, letting her see those hard muscles working as he pushed deeper. Gabriel moaned, the sound suspended somewhere between rapture and torture.

"You brought this on yourself," Shane muttered, voice shallow. "You made me do this."

"No—"

"Take me. Take my cock. You made me do this, now you take it." Shane's hips pumped harder. He raised a hand and brought it down on Gabriel's ass with a sharp smack.

Gabriel mumbled again between thrusts, something ending in "so big".

"That's right. Say it again."

"You're so big." Gabriel's voice dissolved into primitive grunts and groans.

"That's right. And you're so fucking tight." Another smack. "Tell me who's fuckin' you."

"Shane," he moaned.

Shane's voice deepened. "Good boy. Say it again."

Gabriel grunted the syllable, over and over. Natalie wanted to scream it herself, wanted to reach down and stroke her aching clit and join them in this pleasure and pain. She watched Shane's rhythmic thrusts grow fast and rough until control abandoned him. His arms trembled, hands grasping frantically at Gabriel's hips. His commands gave way to animal sounds as he lost himself. He gave a final, deep thrust and held there as his moan crescendoed then died.

Natalie snapped out of her spell as he withdrew. She could smell him, or both of them, the musk of their sex suffusing the air. She slid the slats nearly closed, ready to flatten herself against the wall should Shane head for the bathroom.

She heard the rasp of breath being reclaimed. Shane stepped back a pace, holding his jeans up with one hand. He snapped the condom off and wandered out of Natalie's line of sight to dispose of it. Gabriel stayed bent over the arm of the couch. She could make out the rise and fall of his ribs and the red mark on his right cheek where Shane had struck him.

Shane returned, buckling his belt. He ran a hand thoughtfully over Gabriel's back and hip.

"I'm sorry," he said.

Gabriel said nothing.

Shane sank to his knees, in profile to Natalie, and buried his head in his palms. Through his fingers he muttered, "I'm so sorry." His shoulders hitched, and she thought he'd actually begun to cry.

Gabriel righted himself. He pulled his pants up while Shane repented at his feet. He took a seat on the couch and brushed a hand over Shane's head.

"You're so hard on me."

Shane nodded his agreement, still rubbing his face.

"Why d'you do this?"

Shane looked up, face damp and contorted. "You make me want you so bad."

Gabriel stroked his thumbs across Shane's tear-streaked cheeks. "You can' blame me for this, you know."

He nodded again. "I know."

"You have to make it up to me now."

Another nod.

Gabriel sat back against the cushions. His lap was obscured by the arm of the couch as Shane reached forward to open his fly. Both of their mouths fell open, eyes fixed on Shane's hands. Natalie wished she could see what they could. She wanted to see Gabriel—his black hair and tan skin, every private inch of him.

His eyes shut and he grunted. Shane's powerful shoulders flexed as he pleasured him.

"Good," Gabriel murmured. He ran his palms over Shane's ears and neck. "Take me." He guided Shane's head down until Natalie could only see the back of it, cupped in Gabriel's hands.

"Yes." His voice filled the air, that dark baritone lost to moans as he arched his spine and claimed the pleasure due to him. "Deeper. Like I took you... Show me how sorry you are."

Natalie tried to swallow but her mouth was dry as cotton. Her body hurt, longing to see this act in all its details and to take part in it. To be Shane, taking orders. To be Gabriel, feeling that power, able to bring a man like Shane to his knees. Her fingers twitched against the slats and Gabriel's head turned, slow. His eyes left his lap to settle on the door, aimed right where her own were spying. Her heart stopped. Gabriel didn't look away for several long seconds. Even when he turned his head back to the matter at hand, his eyes stole glances in her direction. If he knew she was there, it only seemed to excite him more.

"Harder, sweetheart. We both know you love it. You love sucking my dick."

Shane's head and shoulders bobbed, taking every instruction. He moaned, the sound muffled and desperate.

"You look so thirsty," Gabriel whispered, stroking Shane's hair.

Another moan came in reply.

"You want to taste me?"

More grunts, as Shane's entire body communicated his need.

"Suck me good an' I'll let you taste me. Suck me. Suck me." It became a mantra, the words growing rougher and harsher by the moment. Gabriel's hands trembled. He stroked his palms over his own chest and neck, over Shane's shoulders. He cried out as he came, hunching forward, fingers digging into Shane's back. He relaxed against the cushions as Shane pulled away. Natalie saw Shane swallow and watched his chest rise and fall with frantic breaths.

"You're so good," Gabriel said. He touched Shane's face fondly then coaxed him to straddle his lap on the couch. They kissed, deep and long, tender lovers suddenly, not master and servant.

Natalie instantly felt like what she was—a voyeur. She slid the slats closed and backed away, one quiet step at a time, until she was back in the living room.

CHAPTER THREE

Natalie woke to the sound of a screen door slapping shut. She sat up, staring around the room for several seconds before she remembered where she was. Weak morning light slipped between the curtains, making the deep yellow walls glow. She rubbed her eyes and checked the clock on Shane's cable box. A few minutes past seven. She wondered which one of the men had snuck out so early.

Gabriel answered her question, appearing at the edge of the kitchen. He had a towel wrapped around his waist, though his skin and hair were dry. Natalie took a thorough, greedy look at him, stripped to the hip. Not an ounce of fat. Strong like a dancer and wrapped in those long, lean muscles. A sprinkling of black hair at his chest tapered down to a line at his navel. She drank in the twin crests of muscle at his hip, the start of more dark hair behind where his hand held the towel, low.

He let her stare a good long time before he spoke.

"You sleep okay?"

"Yeah." She chewed on her lip, wondering again if he'd seen her watching him with Shane. "Thanks again."

Gabriel's eyes snapped to his hat, sitting where Natalie had left it on the floor by the couch. She blushed. "Did Shane just leave?"

"Come with me," he said.

She held the blankets tight against her chest. Gabriel's pull was just as strong in the morning light, sober. Scarier, without the dim glow of the bar and the buzz of the beer numbing her judgment.

"Come with you where?" she asked.

He turned and walked down the hallway, letting her see the intricate muscles flexing in his back as he disappeared. She stood, body obeying his order even as her brain hesitated.

She found him in the bathroom with the door open, leaning on his hip against the sink, watching her approach. Waiting. He'd knotted the towel around his waist.

"How long is he gone for?" she asked, shy.

"Long enough."

She stepped close, close enough to smell him. She studied his face in the bathroom light, trying to guess his age. Thirty? Older? Younger? He had a few fine lines around his eyes, deep ones bracketing the corners of his lips, but smooth skin behind a couple days' stubble.

"You still want me?"

She nodded and he grinned.

"Can I brush my teeth?" she asked, and when he laughed, she relaxed.

"Yeah. Whatever you like." He found her a new toothbrush from Shane's cabinet and they stood side by side before the mirror as she brushed and he shaved. When they were done she breathed him in, shaving cream and sweat—the good kind of sweat.

He leaned back against the sink, facing her. "Ready now?"

"Yeah. Now."

He tilted his head down and kissed her, soft and light, then pulled away, grinning again. He licked his lips, black eyes darting over her face. When his mouth came back, it was hungry. His teeth nipped her bottom lip. He tasted and suckled, teased and coaxed. When his tongue slid between her lips to glide against hers, she felt her core tighten and wetness breaching between her thighs. His hands held her jaw, fingers tangling in her hair. He consumed her and she gave back. He tasted primal, raw and faintly salty. His skin was bitter from the shaving cream, like a sip of cheap gin, and she dragged her teeth down his throat to his shoulder as her hands stroked his chest. He let out a deep breath above her ear.

"I saw you last night," she whispered. "I saw you with him."

"I know."

She kissed his skin as his fingers raked her scalp.

"It change how you feel?" he asked.

She ran her tongue over his collarbone, surveyed his abdomen with her palms. "I want you more, now." Her fingertips flirted with the soft curls at the base of his belly.

"He possessive."

"I don't care." Her hands roamed his back, tracing his spine and the ridges of muscle flanking it. He stepped away, reached an arm behind the shower curtain and turned on the tap.

"Let me see you," he said.

Nerves returned, tensing Natalie's body as she peeled her tank top over her head and let her jeans slip down her legs. Gabriel's eyes followed each movement. She caught his tongue flirt with the corner of his mouth as she took her bra off. She pushed her plain black briefs down her legs and stepped out of them.

He swallowed. "Beautiful. C'mere."

She came close, letting her bare breasts brush his chest, nipples going taut as his hair teased them. He cupped her, squeezing gently, making her ache and arch.

"Gabriel."

"Wan' you so bad," he murmured. The steam that leaked out from behind the curtain made their skin sticky then slick.

Her hands slid between them to free his towel. The length of his erection pressed against her stomach, heavy and thick. Ready. He moaned as she stroked him.

"Thought of you, las' night," he whispered.

"When?"

"All night, at the bar. When we danced. And when he sucked me, I imagined it was you."

She held her breath.

"I imagined it was your mouth on me. That I came for you."

"I wanted it to be me," she admitted, barely audible.

"It can be, now. I'll give you anything you want."

She nodded. She tightened her grip, giving his cock long, slow pulls and memorizing every inch of him.

He led her into the hot heaven of the shower. Their wet bodies came together, his hard dick sliding against her soft belly as they kissed, deep.

He moaned against her lips. "Tell me what you want."

She thought a moment. "I want to know what else your fingers can do." The image of them from the night before, so eerily talented, flashed through her mind. She wanted to be mastered like that mandolin.

He turned her around, strong arms circling her waist. Hot water coursed between their bodies. Cooler air leaked in from the room, tensing her nipples. He teased them for a cruel minute before his hands slipped lower, snaking over her wet curls to find her swollen clit.

She groaned as one calloused fingertip stroked her.

"Good…"

He pulled her tight, his cock against her ass. Two fingers strummed her clit as the other hand crept lower still. His chest pressed into her shoulders and he leaned close, the sounds of his excitement right at her ear. He moaned as he ran two fingers up and down the length of her lips.

"Gabriel."

He slipped inside her to the second knuckle. "Fuck. You so warm." He moved her with his hips, pushed her forward until her arms were braced against the front wall of the shower. She felt him adjust then his cock slid between her legs as his fingers penetrated deeper. They weren't enough. She needed him filling her, deep and thick.

"I want you," she gasped.

"An' you get me. Jus' not yet." He thrust his length slowly between the sensitive skin of her inner thighs and his fingers dove and stroked, explored and teased. His moans were deep and chilling, so close behind her. Her pleasure and need mounted until her knees shook.

Just as she thought he was going to give her release, his fingers withdrew. He spun her around again and dropped to his knees. He coaxed one of her feet onto the rim of the tub, and his mouth claimed her. His tongue flicked her clit, reigniting the fire. She raked her nails through his wet hair, studied the angles of his brows and nose, the black spikes of his eyelashes as the water streamed over his face. His hands held her thighs and he feasted, a man in thrall.

"Gabriel…"

He moaned against her, the touch of his tongue intensifying. She watched his shoulders flex, fantasizing about how they'd look if she could somehow watch from behind as he fucked her. How they'd look to Shane when he took this man, rough and greedy.

Her orgasm grew, nearly peaked, then dialed back as his tongue slowed. He brought her close, three, four, five times, until she was clawing at his arms, desperate. She heard the tiniest laugh escape him as his tongue finally gave her the pressure she needed and kept it coming as she rode out the spasms. Her leg twitched as she relaxed, and she nearly fell out of the shower. Gabriel held her steady, smiling up at her with wicked eyes.

"Beautiful."

She giggled, a silly sound she hadn't made in months. She combed her fingers through his dripping hair and he gave her clit a last flick with his tongue, a little zap to those ravaged nerves.

"Come." He stood and shut off the taps, dripped water all over the floor as he found her a clean towel. They dried off and she studied him again in the yellow glow of the cheap vanity lights. The climax had left her feeling high, her vision crisp and acute. Gabriel looked stark and dramatic, like an actor in a stylized piece of film.

She let him lead her to Shane's room, to his bed. He took her towel, tousling her hair one last time and grinning at her. The towel dropped and his mouth claimed hers again. She heard him sucking harsh breaths in through his nose, desperate sounds. Her hands found his cock, stroking until he lost the coordination to kiss and groaned against her lips.

She stepped back a couple paces and found the edge of the bed with her calf. She sat down, wriggled over Shane's rumpled comforter and lay her wet hair across his pillow with its man-marinated smell. This bed where two strong men fucked the living daylights out of each other... The thought made her feel obscenely feminine.

Gabriel crawled to her, covering her naked body with his. His weight felt sinful as he pushed her into Shane's mattress.

"How do you want it?" he asked, forehead pressed to hers, eyes glittering.

"Whatever you like."

He leaned over to grab a condom from the bedside table, and she studied his cock again as he unwrapped it. Fairly long, nice and thick. His curls were still wet from the shower.

"Let me." She took the rubber and unrolled it, measuring him as she went.

His hips pushed her thighs wide and he reached down to angle himself. He stroked his head up and down her lips, eyes locked between them. She cupped his ass and pulled him close, until she felt every inch sink deep inside her swollen pussy, until their hipbones touched.

"Gabriel."

He held there, making her feel it—feel him pulsing, needy beneath the veneer of patience and self-control.

"Fuck me," she said.

He drew back slow then drove in hard. He laughed at her gasp. The thrusts came fast and rough, punctuated by his grunts and the sound of his thighs hitting hers.

"Yes." His eyes shut, face reverent. His forearms locked tight against her ribs. She watched his tight, tattooed chest and shoulders, flexing with each push and shining with sweat. He fucked like an animal, greedy and primal.

"Well, lookie here."

Natalie jumped at the sound of Shane's voice. Gabriel's hips slowed but didn't stop. They both looked to where Shane stood by the couch, arms crossed over his chest.

"Big fuckin' surprise," he said, staring them down. "Can't believe my shock."

Natalie wasn't sure what to do, but she didn't have much choice as long as Gabriel had her pinned. He caught her eyes for a long moment then lowered his mouth to hers. His hips sped up as the kiss deepened, the display clearly designed to excite or enrage Shane. He released her mouth and leaned back on his haunches, hands holding her knees, letting all three of them see his cock surging in and out of her, fast and rough.

Natalie heard Shane make a noise, a gruff sigh, accompanied by a thump. She turned to see his other boot hit the floor. He glared at them with the air of a man weary from a long day at work and stripped off his socks. "I let you stay here as a guest in my house, little girl. This is how you repay me?"

She glanced at Gabriel, still fucking her, unperturbed. She glanced back at Shane, looming about ten feet tall, looking like heaven and hell and purgatory all rolled into one pissed-off, muscular package. She tugged at Gabriel's hips and he lowered back down, arms locked at her sides.

"I want *him* too," she whispered, pointing to Shane with her eyes. "I want him to join us." She caught Shane's cold stare and ran her hands down Gabriel's back, cupping his ass, kneading the hard muscle there. She spread his cheeks and stroked her fingertips between them.

Gabriel sucked in a breath. "He's territorial," he warned.

"That's what I'm counting on." She circled him with the pads of her fingers until he groaned.

"Fuck me," he whispered. He reached over and grabbed the lube bottle off the table, snapping it open. He smeared a measure across her fingers, hips never missing a beat. "Fuck me."

Her slick fingers teased him until he was panting. She could sense Shane in her periphery, his anger feeling as though somebody had maxed the thermostat.

"Come on. Please." Gabriel's voice was strained. "Please."

She slid the tip of one finger inside him and he rewarded her with a gasp and a buck of his hips.

"Yes. More." His cock hammered, excitement mounting.

She pushed into him deeper, another half inch, eliciting a moan that reverberated in her bones and made her feel high.

"More. Fuck me. Fuck me like he does." He was playing her game, baiting Shane, and across the room she could see the other man's fisted hands shaking at his sides.

Without warning, she plunged another finger inside Gabriel, fast and deep. His cry was bestial, surprise and pleasure wrapped in a dark groan that raised the tiny hairs all along her arms. He continued to pump her, but his body grew distracted, losing its grace.

"You're so tight," she murmured, the comment designed for Shane.

"Deeper."

"That's as far as I can take you," she said, her fingers withdrawing then sinking again to the third knuckle.

"I need more."

"You need *him,*" she said. She flashed her eyes at Shane. "We both do."

The man's face was steely. He approached the edge of the bed in slow strides, stripping off his shirt as he neared. Natalie took in the cut shape of his chest and stomach and arms, the sheer size of him. He opened his belt and fly and dropped his jeans, revealing gray boxer briefs tented by a huge erection. Gabriel turned to look.

Natalie kept fucking him with her fingers. "Is that what you want?" she asked Gabriel.

Shane stroked himself through the cotton.

"Yes," Gabriel groaned.

"Show us, Shane," she said.

His lids looked heavy as he fondled himself. His erection was long, curving up to the right, filling his shorts to the waistband. He pushed the fabric down, exposing the biggest, thickest cock Natalie had ever seen in person.

"Come on, Shane," she whispered. She slid her fingers from Gabriel and held his ass, squeezing him, raking his skin as an invitation. "He needs you."

Shane stood, stoical, jerking himself. Natalie wanted to see the length of his tall, strong body working, and feel his weight behind Gabriel's. She wanted to see his face as he gave himself over to his darkest desires and succumbed to the pleasure. She pulled Gabriel's cheeks apart and stroked her wet fingers over his asshole.

"I'm not enough, Shane."

He held her eyes for a long moment then stepped out of his jeans. The mattress bucked as he joined them. He forced both their pairs of legs wide as he knelt behind Gabriel, pointed to the table and snapped his fingers. Gabriel fumbled for a string of condoms and the lube.

As Shane got equipped and guided himself close, Natalie watched Gabriel's face. He looked fearful and excited, flushed with dark anticipation. He choked out a gasp and she knew Shane was starting to penetrate. She rubbed her hands over his face, transfixed by all the intimate evidence of his pain and pleasure. She kissed him, soft, then deeper.

He moaned against her mouth as she felt Shane pushing into both of them.

"Better?" she whispered, loud enough for Shane to hear.

Gabriel nodded, frantic, the cock-sure master of seduction reduced to a desperate, panting mess. He slid his arms beneath her back and buried his face against her throat.

She found herself looking right into Shane's eyes.

"Fuckin' my man in my bed," he said over Gabriel's shoulder. "You got some goddamn nerve, girl."

Gabriel moaned as Shane took him deeper. The thrusts forced Gabriel's cock hard inside Natalie's pussy, making her feel as if she were being taken by both of them. She watched Shane's body, upright and commanding. She could see the nest of brown hair and the base of his thick cock as his length disappeared and then withdrew from the cleft of Gabriel's ass in steady strokes.

"I wanted *you* too," she said.

"Selfish," he spat, and there was a gleam of cruel triumph in his eyes.

True, she thought. She feasted on Shane's hard body as it drove into Gabriel, drove him deeper inside her cunt with each pump of his hips. A moan escaped as she imagined those thighs slapping against her own, giving her that huge cock, anger underscoring each thrust.

She looked to his face. There was pleasure there and something more. Something vulnerable and helpless behind the animal desire. The emotion was so raw Natalie had to look away. She watched Shane's cock hammering Gabriel, owning him. She reached down to grasp his ass, kneading the firm flesh to excite Shane, aching to know how it must feel to dominate such a beautiful, magnetic man.

"He loves it, Shane. He loves the way you fuck him."

Gabriel moaned against her throat, confirming her words. He pushed up onto his elbows, craning his neck to look at Shane. In profile, his face and ear were flushed pink. Natalie felt the fever in her own skin—that hot, impatient need.

She whispered, "He's so big."

Gabriel groaned, still watching.

"Big and thick," she said. "Is he hard?"

Shane answered for him. "Like fuckin' steel." His hands were clamped on Gabriel's hips, arms tensed, roped with muscle. He rode him harder, and Natalie felt the impact echoed through Gabriel's body.

She caught Shane's wild eyes. "Let's make him come, Shane. Let's make him helpless, like he makes us."

Shane pounded Gabriel a few beats longer, then pulled out, stripping the condom and tossing it aside. Natalie pushed Gabriel away enough to slide the rubber from his throbbing cock. She drew him back, drew his length against her swollen lips, hearing him gasp, feeling him shudder at the contact. She coaxed a few thrusts, soaking him in her wetness.

"I want him to taste me when he sucks you," she whispered.

Shane was still kneeling, chest rising and falling fast, eyelids heavy, sweat gleaming on his skin. Natalie slid from under Gabriel and urged him onto his back.

"Let's make him beg," she said to Shane.

Shane went to his jeans and unfurled the belt. Natalie straddled Gabriel's chest and grabbed his wrists, sliding them through the tubing of the metal headboard so Shane could bind them. He joined them again on the bed. Natalie licked her lips, studying Shane's erection with its weeping slit, the definition of *ready*.

"May I?" she asked, making her meaning plain with her eyes. Shane nodded and she touched his dick, weighing it in her hand, marveling at his size. Her fingertips touched the pre-come at his tip, teasing his head, then making the shaft slick. Making Gabriel watch.

"You're so strong." Her eyes roamed Shane's powerful body. "I loved watching you fuck him last night too."

"You saw us?"

She nodded, blushing but unafraid. "Through the slats in your door. I'm sorry."

"No you ain't."

She offered a sheepish grin. "Well, no. Maybe not."

Shane's lips parted as she stroked him in long, slow, tight pulls. "Nobody's ever seen me with him before."

She met his eyes. "Thanks for letting me be the one."

For a few seconds, it was just the two of them, her cool palm wrapped around his hot, pounding cock. There was an odd tenderness in the touch and to Shane's features as he watched.

"Can I watch you suck him?" she asked.

His gaze slid to Gabriel's supine body and the erection hovering above his tight stomach. Natalie saw hunger in his eyes.

"Go on. He needs you." She released Shane's cock and he sank down between Gabriel's spread legs.

She tried to identify the emotions passing over Shane's face—fear, excitement, longing, shame. He wrapped his big hand around Gabriel's shaft and put his lips to his head. His eyes closed as he took the first inch. Natalie held her breath, transfixed, and her pussy tightened. Gabriel moaned as Shane's tongue gave him some unseen pleasure. Shane moaned too, a thirsty, greedy sound.

She reached out to touch Shane's short hair, and he let her. She raked his scalp, the way Gabriel had when she'd watched them in secret. Another inch disappeared in Shane's mouth and the tendons in his arm tensed as he stroked Gabriel.

"Don't let him come yet," she said, running her hand over his strong shoulders. "Make him wait."

He pulled his head back and she watched him lap at Gabriel's head, slick tongue torturing. She stole a glance at Gabriel's face; she never would have imagined he could look this powerless.

"Can I have a turn?" she asked Shane.

He moved to Gabriel's side but kept his fist pumping, slow and mean. Natalie took his place, breathing in Gabriel's scent as she lowered her lips. Shane slid his hand lower to cup Gabriel's balls, giving the man's cock over to her. She rubbed the smooth skin of his head across her lips then flicked her tongue to taste him. She made a happy noise and tightened her fist.

They pleasured him together. Each time Gabriel seemed near to coming, they traded who sucked him, cutting off the climax. Soon he was whimpering, arms tugging against the headboard, all his muscles strained and desperate. Shane lowered down to his arms and nudged Natalie out of the way.

"Milk him," he said, and ran his tongue over Gabriel's swollen head.

She sat up, moving to Gabriel's side. She gave his cock long strokes as Shane suckled him, his moans filling her ears. Shane's voice joined in the hungry chorus.

"C'mon, boy. Give it to me."

Natalie jerked Gabriel harder, dying for his climax. Dying to see Shane take it, to watch him sacrifice his persona for the sake of pleasure, right here next to her.

Gabriel's voice dissolved into grunts, their rhythm attuned to Natalie's touch.

"Here he comes," Shane said between licks. "Come on. Come on." His hand grasped Natalie's as Gabriel came, holding it tight and still. She saw Gabriel's come lash Shane's lips and tongue before he closed his mouth over him, sucking. Both men's eyes shut, and Gabriel's moans faded to silence. Natalie felt her heart slamming against her ribs.

Shane let her hand go, rolling onto his back on the other side of Gabriel's panting body. He began to jerk himself. "Let him loose," he said.

She rose on wobbly knees and unbuckled the belt. Gabriel slid his hands free and curled his body against Shane's. His hand took over. Shane turned onto his side and their faces met.

Natalie knelt, watching, knowing it was the single most erotic experience of her life. Shane cradled Gabriel's face as they kissed. She saw the flush deepen in his cheeks, saw his fingers twitch as Gabriel brought him closer and closer, until Shane buried his fingers in Gabriel's hair and held his head, losing himself. He moaned—a harsh, bestial noise as his come spurted on Gabriel's stomach in long spasms.

Natalie shuddered, rocked to her marrow by the intimacy humming in the air, tangible as the smells and the heat and the sound of them reclaiming their breath. She looked down at their panting bodies, no clue what to do with herself. Gabriel preempted her panic, reaching out to touch her arm. He coaxed her to lie behind him, to press herself into his back and join them in the reverie.

CHAPTER FOUR

B right noontime sun was streaming through the tall windows
when Natalie's eyes opened. She was alone in the bed, though its
owner was nearby, putting clothes away in his bureau.

She sat up, wrapping the comforter around her bare chest and
searching the room. "Where did he go?"

Shane kept his eyes on the drawer, expression tough to read. "He's
a stray. Wanders in and out as it suits him. Always comes back."

She bit her lip. "Is he playing again tonight?"

"It's Latin dance night."

"Is that a 'yes'?"

Shane finally met her eyes. "Come and find out." There was a
threat or a challenge in his voice, something sinister she couldn't
pinpoint.

"I will."

"Your hair's a damn mess."

She ran her fingers through the tangles.

"Don't you need to get back north?" he asked.

She shrugged. "Nobody at home's expecting me. I'm going back with my tail between my legs. Can't say I'm in a hurry."

He pushed the drawer closed. "You hurt your family or something?"

"No. Well, maybe."

"What'd you do?" he asked.

"I ignored all their warnings and ran off with my no-good boyfriend, all the way to Florida."

He nodded. "I got a hitch ready to tow your truck. I'll bring it to my shop this afternoon, if you're good for the money."

"You couldn't just bring the plug back?" she asked.

"I wanna charge you for the tow."

Natalie sighed and flopped back on the bed. "Neanderthal."

"Homewrecker," he countered, but she heard teasing in his voice, one of the warmer tones he'd offered her since they'd met. She suspected what she'd seen and what they'd shared had changed their dynamic. How could it not?

"Do you need me to get out of here soon?" she asked.

Shane turned to look right at her, and she saw him as if it were the first time. He was handsome—and not just big and built and hot, some caricature. A good-looking man stood in front of her, with an honest face and sad eyes the color of slate.

"You can stick around," he finally said. "For the day. Just do your own dishes and don't go snooping through my shit."

"Can I watch your TV?"

He nodded. "But don't order Pay-Per-View or nothin'. I'll be back around six."

"When do you think Gabriel will be back?"

The corner of his mouth twitched. "Darlin', if I had the first clue how to predict that, I might actually be able to sleep at night."

* * *

Natalie spent most of the day lounging and flipping channels. And poking through Shane's drawers trying to figure out who he was.

Most of the junk cluttering up the closets was clearly leftover from the previous inhabitants—ancient vacuum cleaners and mothball-stinking, out-of-date clothes, ironing boards and musty furs. His bedroom was the only interesting room in the apartment, but it didn't hold many secrets. No porn—none she could find, anyhow—no letters, no sex toys, no X-rated snapshots of old lovers. Dull, dull, dull. If she hadn't watched with her own eyes as he'd fucked the holy hell out of the sexiest man she'd ever seen, Shane Broussard wouldn't have struck her as all that remarkable.

She went downstairs around five and sat at the bar. It was quiet, just her and a handful of early drinkers. She nursed a beer, eyes and attention on the door, waiting for Gabriel.

Shane arrived just after six, lugging two cases of beer. A deliveryman was on his heels, wheeling a dolly stacked with more of the same. They disappeared into a back room and then emerged as Shane was signing an electronic pad. He noticed Natalie and headed to the bar. He smelled like a man—motor oil and leather.

"You stay out of my stuff?" he asked, then addressed the barman. "Usual, Zach. Thanks."

"I looked through all your closets and drawers and under your bed. Total waste of time." She smiled at him with her eyes as she took a deep pull off her bottle.

His mouth twitched, trying not to smirk, she suspected. "'Bout as much as I expected from you."

"When does the Latin dance portion of the evening get under way?"

He glanced at the clock. "Starts in an hour, but like everything in this place, it doesn't come to a boil until ten or eleven."

"Will he be here?"

He nodded. "Yeah. And you'll get exactly what you deserve."

"What does that mean?"

"Stick around and find out, Miss Natalie."

She rolled her eyes at his cocky tone.

Shane reached over the bar and conjured a portable phone from some unseen shelf. He punched in a number and swiveled his eyes to Natalie's. "You want a burger or something?"

"Sure."

Shane ordered delivery for them and the two bartenders on duty and tucked the phone back behind the counter.

"I'm out of cash," she said.

"I'll add it to your tab at the shop."

"Thanks for taking my truck in."

Shane grinned. "Hold those thanks 'til you've seen the bill."

"You know," she said, "I don't think you're half as big a jerk as you want me to think."

"Must be losing my touch."

The food arrived awhile later and Shane divvied up the orders. "Grab us a table," he said to her.

They sat and ate and Shane people-watched, and Natalie pretended to people-watch, but mainly just inventoried the folks coming through the door, filing them all under "Not Gabriel". A stout man carrying a trombone case arrived just before seven. He waved to Shane.

"Evenin', Luke. You're first." He nodded to the stage, where Luke went to fiddle with the speaker cords and mixer. More musicians trickled in and someone set up a drum kit. The sounds of tuning instruments peppered the air.

When Gabriel finally sauntered through the door, Natalie's pulse rocketed as if she'd been shot full of adrenaline. He had his mandolin in one hand, another gigantic case in the other. He was talking with another man as he entered, and he flashed Shane and Natalie his dark eyes as he passed the table. Her heart leapt into her throat.

"Is Latin dance night popular?" she asked Shane, partly to make sure she could still talk.

"Sure. As popular as any other night around here."

"It certainly was bustling yesterday," she offered.

"Latin dance, blues, jazz, Gabriel on his lonesome. It all just means foreplay here." He waved his hand around the bar, the sultry space lit like Christmas. "People don't care what they're listening to or how they're dancin'. They just care who they're with. Or who they might get with, if they play their cards right."

Natalie nodded. "Folks were getting pretty amorous on the floor last night."

"You ain't seen it at last call. This place does something to people."

She nodded again. Her eyes drifted to the musicians, to Gabriel tuning an upright bass, face shaded by his hat.

"What else does he play?" she asked Shane.

"I ain't seen an instrument he can't play."

"Wow."

He shrugged. "Just what he does. I never seen him read a book or drive a car or use a phone, but he can play. But it's not his playing you should be worried about tonight."

She sighed. "Thanks for the warning, Dr. Ominous. I've seen some shocking things in the last twenty-four hours, though, and lived to tell. Is this place about to go all *Eyes Wide Shut* on us?"

"Nah. And anyhow, the show's gonna be right here." He tapped the table then pointed at her face.

The lights dimmed everywhere but the dance floor and stage. The drummer counted them off and the band launched into a raucous number.

The half-dozen couples already on the premises hit the floor immediately. The women, young and old alike, wore heels, and knew what they were doing.

Natalie half-shouted over the music to Shane. "Is this salsa?"

He nodded. She watched the dancers, enjoying what these people could do. She tapped her feet, wishing she'd taken classes so she could have a bit of their charisma. As the bass player, Gabriel didn't have the most dynamic role, but it was hard to imagine anyone watching the band and seeing anyone else. Natalie studied his fingers flashing deftly along the length of the person-sized instrument, wishing she could magically inhabit it and feel his masterful calluses coaxing those deep notes out of her.

They played a couple more songs like the first one, then the band reassembled, swapping out some strings for more drums and a flute and a tambourine, and other things Natalie couldn't identify. Gabriel leaned the bass against a wall and took the hand of a young woman in a swishy skirt, coaxing her out of her seat. He led them to the middle of the floor as a new song began.

"Do they know—" Natalie never finished her question. Gabriel and the woman began to dance, and Natalie lost her mind.

She'd heard people say that a man is just an accessory in ballroom dancing, just there to make the woman look good, but she didn't take her eyes off him. The only times she noticed his partner were when their bodies came together so closely and so smoothly and so *erotically* that Natalie had to grit her teeth to keep a territorial shriek from erupting from her lungs. He may as well have been fucking the girl for all her body cared. And not just the one girl. He switched partners between songs, working his way through the room, sampling from one big tasting menu.

It was going to be a long-ass night.

* * *

Shane returned from the bar around nine with a third round of beers. He caught the predictable sourness pursing Natalie's lips, and that all-too-familiar heat burning in her eyes. He got her attention and jerked his head toward the back of the room, away from the stage and the dance floor. She followed him to the sunken lounge area on the screened-in porch. The couches and chairs were all full so they stood by a tall table, lit pink by a neon sign mounted on the wall from some defunct drive-thru wedding chapel.

Shane handed her a bottle. "Now you know how I felt yesterday when he danced with you."

She met his eyes. "How does he do this? Make us feel this way?"

He shrugged and took a pull off his beer. "Beats the hell out of me. It's just him. I hope he up and disappears one day and never comes back. Just lets me go... Or he grows old and sick and loses whatever it is that makes me want him this way."

She nodded, solemn, then laughed a small, private laugh.

"What?"

She smiled down at his hand, wrapped around his bottle. "I was so surprised when I found out you two were lovers. I never would have guessed you were—"

"I'm not," he cut in, hackles rising sharply.

She blinked. "No?"

He shook his head. "It's him. I like women. Always did, until he showed up."

"Oh." She nibbled her lip.

He felt frustration flash hot through his body. "I ain't lyin', you know."

"I believe you." She took a deep drink. "I mean, I never slept with a man whose last name I didn't know before him. Or had a threesome. Or slept with somebody else's lover," she added, and looked him in the eye. "I'm sorry."

"He makes people do things," Shane offered. He was tempted to clap her on the shoulder, a truce, but wrapped the hand tighter around the bottle instead. "If you'd come here six months ago, before he did, I'd have been all over you."

She held his gaze and took another drink. "Yeah?"

He nodded. "Sometimes I think he's ruined me."

"You're awfully cruel to him too, you know."

He cocked a brow at her. "That's what he likes. With men."

Her gaze drifted through the open French windows to where Gabriel commanded some hapless woman out on the hardwood. "He seems so in control."

"He is. He makes himself into whatever people want him to be. You wanted to get seduced last night, so he seduced you. I want to use him and treat him like shit, so I don't have to admit how helpless he makes me. And he lets me."

Natalie's eyes widened, clearly surprised he'd come out and said this.

"Then I do," he went on. "And afterward I remember how we used to be, and then *I* feel like shit." Where had those early days gone? They'd faded, in a blur of drunken memory. Those first cautious nights when Gabriel had been the seducer, when empty bottles of wine had multiplied on the living room floor, enough to numb Shane into forgetting how much the feelings he was fighting disgusted him. Enough to let the lust overpower the fear and revulsion, enough to make them stumble to Shane's bed, tearing at each other's clothes, jerking one another until they were blind with need.

Over the weeks, they'd shifted. The trust had dissolved as Shane noticed how openly Gabriel's eyes wandered and tenderness had given way to aggression and jealousy. Gabriel seemed only too happy with the change. The only scraps of affection they found these days were in the fleeting moments just after the peak of their cycle of brutality and apology and penance. And this morning they'd been that way, a show for Natalie.

Her voice broke through Shane's thoughtful haze. "You hate him because you can't stand the thought that you're attracted to a man?"

He considered it for a moment. "No."

She raised her eyebrows.

"No. I hate him because he makes me love him, and he doesn't love me back. The sex… I've come to terms with that. It doesn't threaten me. Not the way it did at first."

Natalie looked him over. "You're one of the manliest men I've ever seen," she said. "I bet you can open beer bottles with your teeth. It'd take more than bedding one man to diminish that."

Shane laughed, humorless. "Look at him."

She turned to where he was leading a woman across the floor, in complete and utter control. Tall, built, surely whispering in that deep voice, promising dominance with those deadly hips.

"He's beautiful," she murmured.

"Fuck beautiful," Shane said, and she turned to face him. "He's a man. A strong one, who can hold his own in a fight and knows how to fuck a woman senseless."

"Yeah," she murmured.

"You wanna know somethin' strange?"

She took a drink and nodded. "Sure."

"I've never felt bigger or stronger or more powerful than the first time I fucked that man's brains out." He pointed with his beer. "The first time I turned that man right there into a pleadin', helpless mess…no woman's ever made me feel so fuckin' big. Not even close." He drained the bottle and slammed it on the table between them, making Natalie jump.

"It's a goddamn addictive feeling," he said.

"I'll bet."

Shane wiped the back of his hand across his lips. "I can't stop unless he leaves me. Cold turkey or nothin'—just years more of this." Moments of bliss spaced out by hours or days of torture. "All that waiting and jealousy and feelin' like shit after I get what he makes me want."

"How were you before him?"

Shane sighed, remembering those days of free will like scenes from a movie—scraps of a life that didn't belong to him. "It was easy."

"Were you with a lot of women?"

"I suppose. A few times a week I'd bring someone up to bed with me after the bar closed. The chase or the hunt or whatever. The take-down. All that shit."

"Love 'em and leave 'em?"

He shrugged. "I made them breakfast."

Natalie laughed. He studied her face, her mouth in that wide smile, showing off her perfect white teeth. It made him want something he hadn't in a long while.

"Come upstairs with me," he said.

"Why?" Her eyes darted to Gabriel for a split second before returning.

"I want you."

She smiled again. "Is this how you seduced women before he wrecked you?"

"Just about. I guess I'm the kind of man a drunk woman wants."

She nodded, seeming to agree. "Pretend this was before he ever showed up. That you and I just met. You just spotted me and put me in your sights."

He nodded. He left her to wander to the bar and snag two more beers. When he returned he handed her one.

"Thanks, stranger."

He clanked the neck of his bottle against hers. "Enjoyin' yourself?"

"I suppose." She took a sip, eyes glued to his.

"I'm Shane Broussard. I own this place. I never seen you here before."

She smiled, game on. "I'm Natalie Foster. I'm just passing through."

"From where to where?"

"Miami to upstate New York."

"That's a long drive." Shane took an equally long pull off his beer. "Not a real direct route either."

She shrugged. "I wanted to see New Orleans."

"Where you stayin' tonight?"

"Motel, I guess. My truck's in the shop. Mechanic's a real dickhead."

"I'll bet." He nodded toward the ceiling. "There's a bed upstairs you're free to use."

She smirked at him, eyes narrowing. "An empty bed?"

"It's empty right now." He moved, standing in front of her and bracing one arm on the wall behind her. He felt his cock growing, straining against the fly of his jeans.

"That's a very tempting offer, Shane Broussard."

He drew closer, so she had to turn her head to take a drink. "I got lots to offer."

She set the bottle down. "Like what?"

He took her hand with his free one and drew it between them, not caring if anyone saw what was happening in their little corner. He cupped her palm over his swollen cock.

She kept her face calm but he caught her eyes turn glassy. "I'm lousy with subtle flirtations, Mr. Broussard. You'll have to spell it out for me." Her fingers tightened around him.

"I'll make you breakfast."

She laughed. "What? Cold cereal?"

He shook his head and pressed himself close. "Eggs. Bacon. Toast and coffee."

"Home fries?"

"I'm out of potatoes."

Natalie slid her hand out from between his legs and turned to drain her beer in two long swallows.

He grabbed the bottle from her and set it down, took hold of both her wrists. He pinned them to the wall above her head, leaned down and kissed her.

It had been months since he'd felt a woman's mouth. Smooth skin, soft lips. He made her feel the opposite—his neglected, stubbly chin. He drank in her beer taste and let his tongue penetrate, let her feel his aggression and dominance, all the promises he wanted to make to her. She was sensual and receptive, following his lead, sweeping her tongue against his to spur him on.

His mouth broke free just as his mind began to swim. "Lemme show you where you'll be sleeping."

She nodded as he released her wrists, her eyes round and half-drunk.

He heard her quiet footsteps following as the music faded and the voices blended to a hum behind them. He felt her energy with him as he mounted the outside porch steps, unlocked the door, flipped on the lights. He grabbed her hand as soon as she stepped inside and pulled her onto the couch.

Her breasts were soft and full, and she let him fondle them as their mouths came together again. He squeezed her, tweaked her nipples into hard peaks through her tank top. Her hand slid up his thigh and settled between his legs, palm running along his pounding cock. Her moan vibrated against his lips.

"Take me out," he said.

She fumbled with his buckle then got his jeans open. He abandoned her breasts to push his shorts down and free his erection. "Touch me."

Her small, smooth hand grazed him, light and appraising. "You're a big man, Shane Broussard."

He clamped his fist over hers, making her strokes tight and rough. He pushed his face against her neck and moaned. "Make me come, darlin'." *Make me forget. Just for a few minutes.*

"Tell me about the first time you were with him," she said. As much as the thought stung, the memory made him high. Made him hard as sin.

"It was right here." He wrapped his arm around her shoulders and let her hand take over. "Right on the floor."

"Tell me."

He moaned, remembering. "We'd split a bottle of wine. That's what we always did when he first started inviting himself up. We'd get trashed and end up on the carpet, kissing and groping each other and watchin' each other jerk off. I let him suck me a few times."

"When did it go further?" Her touch slowed, pure torture.

"I dunno," he sighed. "After a couple weeks of that. We were in here, drinkin', in our underwear. Suddenly he's on his knees on the floor, elbows on the couch cushions, sayin', 'Take me'. I was hammered, and he looked so damn good... I got behind him and pulled his shorts down." Her other hand found his balls, fondling. He groaned, remembering just how he'd felt that night. "He looked so *fucking* good. And he wanted it. I spit on my hand and I fingered him, and he was in goddamn heaven. I never seen anybody get so hot."

"You wanted it too?"

"Fuck yeah, I wanted it. He said, 'Do it, Shane', and I found a rubber from someplace and suddenly I was there. He was beggin' me to. God, he was so fuckin' tight." Her hand gripped him, jogging the memory. "It took awhile, to get in deep, but then I was fuckin' him. And he turned his head and said, 'Pretend you're forcing me'."

Natalie's hand paused. "Take me, Shane."

He stood and got a condom and kicked away his pants and shorts, and Natalie got on her knees, arms on the couch just as he'd described. He knelt behind her and tugged her jeans down. He sheathed himself in the rubber then her. Her moan made his neck hairs stand on end.

It'd been ages since he'd sunk into a woman, and her pussy was wet and deep, slick and hungry for him. He pumped her slow and deliberate. "This what you needed, little girl?"

"Shane…"

He pushed her shirt up and clamped his hands on her waist, liking the softness of her. He kneaded her flesh. "You make me feel real big."

She looked over her shoulder. "You are."

He pushed as deep as he could, until he felt his balls slap her. He pulled out and gave it to her again.

"Tell me how it ended," she said, voice hitching each time his hips bumped her ass.

"I fucked him, like I'm fucking you now." He thrust harder and rougher, mean. "Like that. And he struggled, pretended he didn't want it, but he did. He said my name, over and over, and I felt like the biggest fuckin' man ever to walk the Earth."

She grunted as he slammed into her.

"You say it now," he ordered.

"Shane."

"Again."

She obeyed, moaning his name as he pounded her. He reached around to stroke her clit, as he'd done to Gabriel's cock all those months ago. He teased her until she was crying out, begging for him.

"Yeah, that's right. Come on my cock, girl."

He felt her pussy tighten and shudder, milking him, and he let go, shooting until he was empty and limp and near to fainting.

He pulled away and she sank down next to him, their backs against the couch. He glanced between them. Both panting, both flushed and sweaty and undignified, stripped from the waist down. He decided he didn't give a shit what they looked like. He wrapped an arm around her and pulled her against him, tipping them over into a spent heap on the carpet.

CHAPTER FIVE

Natalie awoke to a big hand jostling her shoulder. She squinted her bleary eyes to where Shane stood over the bed. They'd slept there together, or pretended to, both secretly waiting, listening for the sound of the door opening, but it never came.

"You best get up if you want that breakfast," Shane said.

She took the world's fastest shower and dressed, greeted by the smell of bacon as she stepped into the kitchen. Shane was busy at the stove. She sat on a tall stool at the center island, watching his back and arms as he worked.

She smirked at him when he turned, holding a plate of eggs. "You weren't kidding."

He shared a look with her, not quite a smile, but not too far from it. He piled a few strips of bacon and some nearly burned toast beside the eggs and slid a mug of black coffee next to her elbow.

"Well, thank you kindly, Shane Broussard."

"Eat it quick, I got a job to get to."

She dug in.

He loaded himself a plate and leaned on the other side of the counter, eating on his feet. "Your truck's ready," he said between bites. "Has been since yesterday afternoon. You get a lift with me to the shop and go on your merry way."

She nodded. His tone was brusque, but friendly in a no-nonsense way. She knew she'd overstayed her welcome or was about to. "Thanks for all your hospitality."

He shrugged, eyes on his food.

"I have some errands to run in the city," she said. "If I stopped by tonight for a goodbye drink, would I be pushing my luck?"

He met her gaze and she watched him chew and swallow. "Nah. You're welcome here. Downstairs," he amended. "Long as you tip my staff well."

"Will you be around tonight?"

"I'm around most nights."

She nodded. She took a gulp of coffee, too hot, too bitter. It burned going down and she rubbed her sternum. "So has this place always been yours?" she asked. "The decorations don't seem like your style."

"Like you know my style, little girl." He smirked at her. "But since you ask, this house was my memaw's. All the decoratin' up here, that's just how she left it. My Aunt Marie inherited it in '02 and made the first floor a bar and did the stuff down there."

"What's with the wedding dresses?"

"My aunt used to own a bridal shop, since before I was born. She said it's a real shame how many dresses get returned, when women get cut loose and need the money when their men up and run out on them. She said it's bad luck to buy a weddin' dress that failed, so she wouldn't resell any of 'em. But she didn't believe in wasting good fabric."

"I see."

"She says this place is haunted by the souls of a hundred jilted brides." He laughed. "She also told me, 'Never marry yourself some poor girl unless you're goddamn sure her dress won't end up in those windows'. So I didn't."

"What's a...whatever this place is called?"

"A shivaree's a big raucous racket the old-timey townsfolk used to make when a couple got hitched. Sort of a weddin' reception crossed with a riot."

"I see. So where's your aunt now?" she asked.

"Got married herself a couple years back. Moved to Texas. Said I was the best barman she'd ever seen and sold me the place for damn near nothing."

"Sounds like she's had better luck than her old customers."

Shane nodded, sopping up yolk with the last bite of his toast. He took their plates to the sink.

"Let's get you back on the road, Miss Natalie."

* * *

Natalie wandered to the open door of the garage and poked her head around. Shane was standing beside a scrawny teenager, pointing at the underside of a sedan jacked up close to the ceiling. When he turned to leave the kid to whatever instructions he'd imparted, he caught sight of Natalie. He wiped his palms on the rag tucked through his belt loop and walked over.

"Don't you dare come in here and conk yourself on something," he said. "Last thing I need's a lawsuit."

"I want to talk to you about my bill," she said, holding up the yellow copy of the invoice the front desk guy had given her.

"Fees are nonnegotiable," Shane said.

"You didn't charge me anything."

He shrugged. "Lucky you. Must be a clerical error."

"And my wiper blades look suspiciously new. Let me pay you *some*thing. How much did the plug cost, at least?"

"Never you mind, Miss Natalie."

She gave him a flustered smile. "You do a really good impersonation of an asshole, you know that?"

"My old man set me a real fine example."

"Well, I'm going to swing by tonight, after I go into Baton Rouge." She paused. "If that's still okay with you. My stopping by."

"Free country," he said. "But I know you're only after one last taste of what you can't have."

She pursed her lips then nodded slowly. "Maybe I am." True, she wanted one more confirmation that Gabriel hadn't been a figment. But she wanted more than just that now. She gave Shane a long, casual, up-and-down look.

"Well, then," he said. "I guess I'll be seein' you tonight. You drive safe." He turned away to check on his apprentice.

* * *

When Shane got back to the Shivaree just past six, he hid a little smile as he spied Natalie perched at the bar. He took a good look at her back and her ass and her dark hair, glad to find those things distracting again. She'd changed her clothes—some kind of stylish short-sleeved blouse and different jeans and shoes. He strode over and set two pizza boxes on the counter beside her.

"You tip my staff like I told you?" he asked.

She smiled her greeting and clinked a tidy, bare nail against the glass jar, pointing out a fifty-dollar bill. "I did my best. That's all I could afford, but I know it's less than you should have charged me for the parts and the tow and the labor."

"True." He caught the bartender's eye and tapped the pizza box. He grabbed a couple singles out of the tip jar and folded them into his wallet. "You're welcome to a slice too," he said to Natalie. "I gotta go get cleaned up. Maybe you'll save me one last sway-to-the-beat, later."

She smiled again, looking shy, and Shane headed up to shower.

When he came back down twenty minutes later, Gabriel was by the stage, setting up with a couple other guys. Shane took a seat next to Natalie and slid a cold slice from one of the boxes still littering the bar.

"So what night is it?" she asked, nodding toward the stage. He could see that glimmer in her eyes—that hungry, intoxicated look. He didn't glance at Gabriel, not wanting to turn back looking identically glazed and helpless.

"Blues."

She nodded, eyes still trained over his shoulder across the club.

"Truck running okay, then?"

"Just like new, thanks." She made an uncertain face then fished around in the purse set before her on the bar. She took out a new prepaid cell phone, popping off its packaging and turning it on.

"I don't suppose I could have your number?" she asked. "I've got a long trip ahead of me the next few days. I'd feel better if I had someone to call, if something happens on the road." Her expression and tone were hard to read. There was a flirtation in it somewhere, but some kind of softness too.

Shane took the phone from her and messed around until he figured out how to add a contact and punched in the numbers for the bar and his cell. "There you go. Just don't call me up drunk."

She smiled as she put it back in her purse. "I won't, thanks."

He ordered a beer and a whiskey and nursed them in silence for a little while. Stealing glances to his left every couple minutes, he felt strange toward the woman at his side. Strange and warm and familiar. And grateful.

"So," he said, once the band started up, wanting the music to keep their conversation private. "What'll you do, back north?"

She bit her lip. "Nothing immediately. I'll stay with my mother or my sister for a week or two and figure out my next move. I haven't seen my family in a while. I'm sure they'll be happy to let me stay, since I owe them some major I-told-you-so-ing about my ex. Then when I'm done licking my wounds I'll probably start applying for jobs."

"What d'you do?"

"What do you think I do?" she asked, and tossed her hair.

Shane gave her a long looking-over, trying to guess. Casual, pretty in an approachable way, stylish but not glamorous. "I dunno. Some sort of marketing or advertising or something?"

She shook her head. "I have a nursing degree," she said. "I worked at a hospice in Florida for the last two years. I wouldn't mind doing that again."

He laughed, a small, impressed noise that was drowned out by the music. "Well, that's awful admirable."

She shrugged. "I suppose. But I get aggravated like anybody else. I'm just real good at pretending to be cheerful and patient, even when I want to scream."

"My momma was real good at that," Shane said, and took a drink.

"I shouldn't have too much trouble finding a job," Natalie said. "God knows I could use a change of scenery."

"Gets real snowy up there, right? You're pretty close to Canada?"

She nodded. "Yeah, we get tons of snow because of Lake Ontario."

"I ain't seen snow since New Year's Eve, maybe fifteen years ago," Shane said. "Maybe a hundred flakes fell outta the sky here and you'd have thought it was the Rapture, the way people carried on."

The bartender delivered Natalie's second beer and she smiled. "Well, Shane Broussard, if you ever want to see some real snow, like the kind you can build forts out of, you can come on up to Rochester and find me." Her eyes held his as she took a long drink. "We can go sledding," she added as she set the bottle back down.

He laughed, tapping his fist on the bar. "Don't leave the light on for me, darlin'… Though that's a real pretty invitation." He went quiet, staring at the bottles twinkling behind the register for a couple minutes. He monitored his breathing, making it steady and deep in his chest. When he felt calm enough, he craned his neck to watch the band.

That man… As welcome a distraction as Natalie had become, she could never match the jolt that buzzed through Shane's body when he caught sight of that face.

Gabriel's dark eyes were fixed through the windows opposite the stage. He looked serene, fingers dancing over the strings of the bass, independent of his brain. The brim of his hat cast a shadow over one eye, the other side of his face bathed in red light then blue-green, from the slowly chasing Christmas lights strung above him. Shane wondered where he'd been last night and who with. His heart tightened, a jealous fist gathering and twisting the tendons in his chest. He was used to this. It was a torture he was all-too-familiar with, one he wouldn't wish on anybody as decent as this girl. He stole a glance at her, those eyes glued right where anybody could've guessed they would be.

He owes her, Shane thought, and downed his shot. And even though he could argue that he'd warned her that very first night, this was his fault as well. He'd wanted her to suffer this way, to punish her for the way she made Gabriel look at her. Shane owed her too.

They both owed her one goddamn unforgettable night.

* * *

An energetic song wrapped. Natalie stepped back a pace on the dance floor from Shane's warm, strong body to clap for the band, careful to keep her eyes off the stage. They waited a few seconds for the next number to start, but instead the rumbling bass of the singer's voice thanked the crowd and announced they'd be taking a ten-minute break. No canned music came on to replace them, and the silence was filled by a few dozen spirited conversations and the tinkle of glasses. Natalie looked up at Shane.

"Guess our dance is over," she said, but his attention was focused somewhere past her shoulder. She turned as Gabriel strolled across the floor to meet them. That predictable feeling quickened her pulse, tightened her throat.

"Evenin'," he said, black eyes moving between their faces.

Shane nodded as Natalie said, "Nice set."

"How's your truck?" Gabriel asked. Such simple, innocuous words…yet they may as well have been whispered against her pussy, for the shiver that traced her spine.

"It's ready for a road trip," she said, smiling at him. "I'm heading back north tomorrow morning."

He nodded, the gesture lazy and indifferent.

"I need to talk to you," Shane said suddenly, looking square at him, man to man.

Gabriel nodded again and they excused themselves, disappearing through a door beside the bar, into what Natalie suspected must be an office or a break room. She wandered back to the table where they'd left their half-drunk beers and drained hers. The men reappeared quicker than she'd expected. Shane walked to her and Gabriel headed back to the stage as the band reassembled.

She licked her lips, uncertain. She searched Shane's face, not seeing any of that glassy expression he usually wore after having a private exchange with Gabriel.

"You boys been talking about me?" she asked, playing coy, feeling nervous.

He nodded and looked at the bottles, finding his. He swallowed its dregs before he said, "I told him we owe you a proper goodbye."

Her lips twitched. "Oh yeah? What exactly does that mean?"

"You come upstairs after last call and you tell us."

She wished another drink would appear in her hand to give her something to do with her mouth while she chose a reply. "I'll be honest with you, Shane… It sounds like you're offering to be nice to me. I hope it won't sound too rude if I ask you why."

He kept his eyes on the band as he thought. They launched into a harmonica-heavy number.

Shane finally spoke, bringing his mouth close to her ear. "He owes you for how you'll feel when you leave here. All that withdrawal. And I owe you for lettin' you get close enough to him to have to go through that."

She pulled her face back and held his eyes. "You think I'll regret all this?"

He nodded.

She tried to look amused and cool to cover up the fact that he didn't know the half of it. "This was just a two-man rebound, Shane. Probably the best rebound a girl could ask for. I'll be fine. In fact, I'll mail you a thank-you card as soon as I'm home."

He swallowed, expression solemn and a bit drunk, eyes back on the stage. She joined him, watching Gabriel and welcoming his spell.

"You just think about what you want tonight," Shane said.

She smirked to herself, unseen. She didn't have to think about it for a second.

CHAPTER SIX

When the lights came up just after two o'clock, Natalie shook herself out of a dreamy haze. Shane had gone to help man the bar a couple hours ago, letting one of his staff head home early. Natalie was seated across the wood from him, picking the label off her empty bottle.

Shane caught her and frowned at the mess, then leaned in, blowing all the little flecks of paper off the bar and into her lap. He ran a wet rag over the wood and grinned at her. "There's all that snow you been talkin' about."

She watched him close the club down. Or half-watched. She also half-watched Gabriel, putting his bass away and bidding the other musicians good night.

Twenty minutes later the last of the patrons and staff disappeared through the front porch and Shane locked up behind them. He and

Gabriel moved toward Natalie at the same time from opposite directions, making her feel like a deer trapped between two wolves.

Gabriel reached where she was sitting first. He took hold of her leg and uncrossed it from the other. He stepped between her thighs and stroked his hands over her jaw and cheeks. He leaned in to nip at her lips with his teeth. If there'd been any breath left in her lungs, it would've been sucked clean out as Shane's hands snaked around from behind to cup her breasts.

He whispered into the hair above her ear as Gabriel deepened his kiss. "You know what you want from us?" His fingers coaxed her nipples into stiff peaks and stroked them, heating her chest and neck.

She spoke against Gabriel's mouth. "Yeah, I know." Gabriel stood up straight, hips pressing close, his erection hard against her thigh. She grazed her palms over his sides and he touched her face.

"Upstairs?" Shane asked. She felt him now too—his cock against her lower back.

"Yeah." She swallowed. "Upstairs is good." In Shane's bed, she thought. Those smells and aggressive sounds, two hard bodies against her soft one. So fucking right. Pity she couldn't mail a video of it to her shithead ex-boyfriend.

Shane led the way, through the side porch and up those familiar steps. She listened to the key sliding into the lock, the knob being turned, the light switch flipping—tiny, torturous triggers, making the anticipation flare as they entered the apartment.

"In your bed," she said to Shane, and he led the way.

She kicked her flats off beside the couch and sat on the edge of the mattress, watching the men unlace their shoes.

Shane finished first, and as he approached she caught his expression darken, predatory. She felt her eagerness falter, daunted all over again by his height, his size, that look in his eye. He pushed her down onto the bed, bracing himself above her. Her fear transformed when he kissed her. As his tongue penetrated, she slid her hands beneath his shirt and raked his back with her nails. She needed to touch him again—to feel the brutality of his desire, the impolite roughness of it, so different from the smooth seductions promised by his lover. Shane pushed his hips between her thighs and leaned back, tugging her by the waist of her jeans until their centers touched.

"Take your shirt off," she said.

He surprised her by obeying. Pearl snaps ran up the front of his checked western shirt, and he ripped it open in one motion. His hips pumped as he slid it from his shoulders, his erection rubbing her, the two layers of denim feeling like a punishment. She watched his triceps flex as he peeled his undershirt up from his waist to show her every square inch of his broad chest and tight stomach. His belly swelled and contracted with rapid breaths. To the right, still standing by the couch, Gabriel had his dark eyes fixed on them.

"I want him to watch," she whispered to Shane.

He nodded. He let her sit up enough to get her top off, to reach behind and unclasp her bra. Shane's mouth and hands found her breasts as she lay back down. She ran her hands over the soft bristle of his buzzed hair while he suckled and plucked, coaxing that hot, impatient buzz into her chest, down her arms, right to her fingertips. He teased her until the longing turned to demand. She shoved at his shoulders and he leaned back again, showing her those long, tight muscles. His face looked flushed in the dim glow of the lamp beside the couch. The light cast Gabriel as a near-silhouette, making him seem dangerous.

"Fuck me, Shane," she murmured, loud enough for both men to hear. "Just like you did last night."

He nodded, eyes half-lidded. "Turn over then."

She moved to her hands and knees, feeling Shane's big fingers at her fly. After he eased her jeans and panties down to her knees she heard his buckle release, his zipper lower. She looked to Gabriel. He watched them with his lips parted, as distracted as she'd ever seen him.

"Come closer," she told him as Shane leaned over her for a condom.

Gabriel crossed the room slowly, slow as Shane's fingers penetrating her lips. She moaned, from one man's touch, the other's mere proximity.

Shane clamped a hand to her waist, setting a rhythm as he fucked her with his fingers. "Get your clothes off," he said to Gabriel.

Natalie watched him undress. His hat, each button of his shirt, his belt, his pants.

"Stop there," Shane ordered, and Gabriel stood in his boxer briefs. To Natalie he said, "Tell me what you need."

"You know what I need." She pushed into each thrust of his fingers. "I need to get fucked, Shane."

"You want my cock, darlin'?"

She twisted her body to look back at him. His cock was already sheathed, hovering just above her ass. "Just like last night," she said. "And more."

His fingers left her as he angled himself to her pussy. He pushed in a couple inches, so goddamn thick. She moaned. He pulled out then drove deeper.

"What's 'more'?" Shane asked, setting his pace, slow and steady.

"Faster, for starters," she said.

He obeyed, hands on her hips, thrusts quick and smooth. She turned to Gabriel. His cock was hard, curving up to one side and tenting his shorts. He stroked it lightly, two fingers running up and down its length, his gaze glued between their bodies.

Shane fucked her harder and deeper and rougher, some show to make Gabriel jealous. Jealous of which one of them, Natalie wasn't sure, but it seemed to work.

"Harder, Shane," she said.

"You like the way I fuck, don't you?"

"I love it. I love your cock," she said. "And how full you make me feel."

He pumped hard. "I'm gonna make you come on me, just like last night," he promised.

"I'm sure you will," she said, glancing back at him. "But I'm not in any rush."

Beside them, Gabriel stroked himself harder, his fist hidden behind his underwear. He looked mean and hungry but not half as hungry as Natalie felt.

"It's Gabriel's turn," she said to Shane.

He released her after a few more thrusts and she turned over, kicking her pants off, relaxing against the comforter and pillows. Gabriel climbed onto the bed as Shane moved aside. He spread his knees between hers, lowering down to rub his hard cock against her wet pussy, drenching his shorts.

"Get him ready, Shane," she said. "Tell him what I like."

Shane found another condom and knelt behind Gabriel. She watched him push his underwear down and nearly came at the sight of Shane's big hand stroking Gabriel's dick.

"Is he hard?" she asked Shane.

"Oh yeah. He wants it, darlin'." He stroked him faster, and she could see the droplet of pre-come beading at Gabriel's slit.

"Let him have it then."

Shane ripped the plastic open and rolled the condom down Gabriel's cock.

"Fuck her," he commanded.

She held Gabriel's hips as he closed the space between them. He slid in, smooth, pushing deep and holding for a few breaths, savoring.

"Fuck her," Shane barked.

Gabriel complied. His thrusts came fluid and steady, tensing the muscles of his chest and shoulders and arms in the low light, the most gorgeous spectacle Natalie had ever seen. The illusion of his calm was wrecked by the low moans rising from his throat, desperate little noises that made her feel powerful. She fingered her clit as he fucked her, drinking in every square inch of his bare flesh.

"Nice and fast," Shane said.

Gabriel obeyed. His lids looked heavy, lips swollen. He turned to where Shane knelt at their sides. "Fuck me," he begged.

"It's not about you tonight," Shane said, stony. "It's about her."

Gabriel looked back to her but addressed Shane. "What she want then?"

"Good question," Shane said. "What d'you say, Miss Natalie?"

She glanced between them. She reveled in Gabriel's cock as it slid into her, steady and deep.

"I want both of you," she said.

Shane watched for a few beats longer before he spoke. "That's what you're gettin'."

"At the same time."

She caught his eyebrow twitch. "Front and back?"

She shook her head. "Not my scene."

"How, then?"

"In my pussy. Both of you." Whether that was possible, she couldn't say. But it was what she wanted, undeniably.

The men exchanged a telling look, and Gabriel pulled out and moved to the side. In seconds, Shane was between her legs, cock driving deep. He pulled almost all the way out then pushed in fast and harsh. "Both of us... You think you can handle that?"

"I don't know. But you better get me real wet if we're going to find out."

"Selfish," he said, his grin wicked.

"Have you ever done it?" she asked. "I haven't. I'm not actually sure how it works."

"No," Shane said. "But I seen plenty of porn. I'm sure we can figure it out." He fucked her hard for a few moments then paused again. "Who d'you want to be facing?"

She thought a moment or pretended to. "Him."

Shane withdrew and turned to Gabriel. "Get on your back."

Gabriel lay down. Shane reached for the lube, kneeling between Gabriel's legs and stroking him, making him slick. He prepped himself next then turned to do Natalie, wet fingers slow and gentle.

He snapped the bottle closed. "Straddle him."

She swung a leg over Gabriel's hips and felt him sink in, deep and easy. She rode him, luxuriating. Then she felt the mattress sink as Shane got in position behind her, grasping her waist. She held her breath.

"Relax, darlin'." His voice was dark but kind. "And lean forward as much as you can. I'll go real slow."

Natalie slid her arms under Gabriel's back, settling her chest against his. His skin, like his cock, was slick and hot.

"Tilt your hips a little. I'm gonna start," Shane said. One hand left her side and she felt his head at her lips, pressing.

"Yeah," Gabriel breathed. His hands kneaded her back, and she felt his body twitching, aching for this. "More."

"I'm not yours to command tonight," Shane told him, cocky. "What d'you say, girl?"

"Go ahead," she said. "Try a little deeper."

Shane made a hissing noise, and Natalie caught her breath as he pushed, his head sliding in, spreading her open.

"Oh God."

Shane paused. "It hurt?"

"Not in a bad way."

She felt his hands roam her back and waist, giving her a reprieve before he pushed deeper.

Right by her ear, Gabriel moaned.

"You're so tight," Shane whispered. He withdrew, slow, and reached for the lube bottle again. "You tell me if it's too much."

She squeezed Gabriel harder in her arms as Shane returned, sliding in as deep as before.

"Fuck."

"I want you how you are, Shane. Once you're in, don't be gentle."

He drove deeper, feeling like some beautiful, perfect violation.

"More," she begged.

She could hear him, his short breaths and tiny grunts as he took her, inch by thick inch. Gabriel's fingers snaked into her hair and he whimpered.

"You feel amazing. Both of you," she said. She wished she could see Shane. She wished there was a mirror, so she could watch all this happening to her.

"Ready to get fucked?" Shane asked, that familiar, mean tone returning to his voice, thrilling her.

"I'm ready."

"You move first. Show us the speed."

She pushed up onto her elbows. She drew her hips forward an inch then pushed back, taking both their cocks as deep as she could. A deep moan rose from her chest, and she thought she might die from the sensation, from all that power pulsing inside her.

"That's right," Shane said. "Be greedy."

She led for a few more thrusts then Shane's hands clamped her waist, holding her still. He slid out a few inches, then back, hard. She gasped.

"Good girl." He set a slow rhythm, the bump of his hips steady and controlled. Gabriel began to move too, first matching the beat, then alternating his thrusts with Shane's.

She lowered her forehead to his chest, overcome.

"Oh you love that," Shane said. She gasped as his hand came down on her ass.

"Yeah."

His hips pumped harder. "You like gettin' fucked by two guys, don't you?"

"I love it."

Gabriel moaned, writhing beneath her. "She so tight."

"Yeah," Shane said. "We're gonna make you come, little girl."

She grasped Gabriel's shoulders, digging her nails into him. "How does he feel?" she whispered.

"So hard."

"I'm fucking you next," Shane warned, thrusting fast.

Natalie felt her hold on reality slipping. Two big, hot male bodies pounded her, chaotic and rough. Her clit stroked Gabriel's pubic bone with every thrust of Shane's cock, each motion like the strike of a flint, sparking, bringing her closer.

"I think she's gonna come," Shane said, cruel and taunting.

"Oh God."

"Come on," he said. "Come on."

"Come," Gabriel whispered, and the rasp of his voice in her ear pushed her into free-fall.

Her body clenched, wanting to possess theirs, wanting to stop them, before the pleasure split her in two. They both pushed in deep and held there as she rode out the spasms.

As reality returned, she heard herself first, a low, luxurious moan, then them, heavy breathing, deep sighs. Their skin was slippery, Gabriel's chest and stomach against hers, Shane's hips against her ass. After a few exquisite moments, Shane withdrew. Natalie felt empty but unspeakably satisfied. Shane's hands ran over her, from her shoulders to her thighs.

"Good girl."

She pushed herself up on trembling arms and flopped over beside Gabriel. "Holy shit," she said, and laughed.

Shane smirked at her then his attention shifted. He knelt between Gabriel's spread legs and stripped both their condoms off.

"You feelin' taken care of, Miss Natalie?" Shane asked, reaching for a fresh rubber and cocking an eyebrow at her.

"I feel broken, thank you."

He nodded and got himself re-equipped. Gabriel watched, hungry as always. He tried to turn over but Shane pinned his hips. They exchanged a brief, tense look then Shane slid a hand beneath each of Gabriel's knees and pushed them up, spreading him open.

"Get yourself ready," Shane said.

Gabriel grabbed the lube bottle, prepping himself then Shane. Shane entered him, balls-deep in a handful of thrusts. They both moaned, and Shane leaned forward, locking his shoulders against the backs of Gabriel's knees.

Natalie wrapped the covers around herself, just watching. She could sense something about this was different for them. The darting of Gabriel's eyes told her they'd never fucked this way, face-to-face, that this was something Shane hadn't allowed before tonight.

Shane's words came out thick and drunk as his body worked. "Lemme watch you shoot."

Gabriel reached a hand down to jerk himself, Shane's eyes taking in every movement.

"Good. That's good. Take my cock, boy."

Gabriel's face was flushed and Natalie could see the fingers of his other hand shaking against Shane's ribs. He started to gasp—frightened, disbelieving sounds.

"Good boy. Come on. Lemme see."

"Shane."

"That's right."

Gabriel said the name, over and over. His fist pumped fast and rough, mimicking Shane's thrusts until he gave in. The come lashed his clenched stomach, and Shane joined him. His back arched and his hips froze, pushing deep, and his groans filled the room, punctuating each spasm. For a few seconds, the men were still, chests rising and falling violently. Natalie caught their eyes lock, sharing some intimate message she'd never dare try to understand.

* * *

The mattress bucked as Shane left the bed, rousing Natalie. Early morning. She kept her eyes shut and listened to his steps grow faint then the hiss of the shower behind the bathroom door. For reasons she felt but couldn't articulate, she knew she had to leave before he got back. She wasn't supposed to say goodbye to Shane.

She opened her eyes to study Gabriel, still stretched out next to her, eyes half-open like a contented cat.

Gabriel. She ran a hand over his tan skin, over the dozens or hundreds of black and blue staves tattooed across his chest and shoulders and arms. His dark eyes followed hers.

"That Shane's, right there," he said in a sleep-sticky voice, putting his fingertips to the staff inked below his left collarbone.

Natalie felt her brows rise as she took in all those ribbons of notes. One tune for every lover? For every person he considered meaningful? Every person he'd ever hurt?

"What music is it?" she asked.

Gabriel closed his eyes, drawing his finger along Shane's notes and humming a bar of *Summertime,* the Gershwin standard. His eyes opened again and he smiled. "What will yours be?" he asked.

"My what?"

"Your music, when I add it. And where?" He sat up and touched a few ink-free spaces, prime real estate.

Natalie thought a moment. There was a sting that came from knowing she'd be one tiny scrawl among many. But there was a thrill of pride too, from the intention and the permanence of the invitation. Some small guarantee against being forgotten.

She got to her knees and ran her fingers over a bare spot just under his shoulder. "Here," she said, and sat back down.

"What song?"

"I'll let you pick," she said. "Maybe you could write something special for the occasion." Frankly, she didn't want to know what it would be. She didn't want to spend the rest of her life doomed to mourn this man's absence each time she heard the notes. "Don't tell me."

Gabriel grinned, nodding slowly. "All right then."

"I better go," she said.

They both got up, and as Natalie dressed she looked around Shane's bedroom one last time. She tried to memorize the smell of it, and the way the light came through the tall windows...though she knew that in just a few weeks, she wouldn't even remember how many windows there were, or whether his sheets were gray or blue. She thought about writing her new number down and leaving it for Shane, but she knew he wouldn't use it any more than she'd use the ones he'd put in her phone.

Gabriel tugged his pants on and walked her to the front door. He framed himself in the threshold as she stepped onto the balcony, into the cool, damp morning air. She turned to smile at him, one last taste of that face and body, those deadly eyes, that criminal's smile. She wondered if he'd ever let Shane go free.

"Thanks for everything," she said. "And thank him too."

Gabriel nodded. His expression changed as a thought distracted him. He stepped back inside for a moment and returned with his hat, setting it on her head.

Natalie took it off and studied it, admiring the worn felt as she turned the brim in her hands. "Thanks," she said and gave it back. "But no."

His smile was tight as he nodded. "You have a safe trip now."

She looked at her feet for a few moments then back up at that face. "You treat him good."

She watched his lips part, and then she turned and left him behind.

GETAWAY

CHAPTER ONE

Natalie clocked out at five past three, dead on her feet. Another Thursday done. One more day to get through and the relief of a lazy weekend would be hers. She waved to the new front desk girl and the elderly residents milling in the sunroom. She tugged on her hat, heading outside to face the stinging cold—good old Rochester in the dead of winter. Gray sky like a hangover, dry wind like a punch to the lungs.

She fumbled in her purse for her gloves as she made her way to her parking space. Then she spotted something that slowed her steps—a man. A familiar man, leaning on the closed tailgate of an equally familiar, faded blue truck. She knew that face, vaguely, but it was all displaced, tough to label surrounded by her familiar work parking lot, the white expanse of the nearly frozen pond and the snow-covered trees. Then—

Ho-ly shit. Shane Broussard.

They'd shared a lover—simultaneously, in fact—for a couple of steamy nights in Nowheresville, Louisiana. Two men, one woman, a rebound to be reckoned with.

She covered the last few paces at an ice-cautious jog, a smile overtaking her mouth. She stopped in front of him and craned her neck to meet those blue-gray eyes. Seeing him triggered a change in the atmosphere—from Rochester winter to the bayou in August in a blink.

"Hi, Shane."

"Hi yourself, Miss Natalie." That warm, lazy accent brought a faint blush to her cheeks. His tan was gone and heavy stubble peppered his jaw. He had a distinctly travel-worn look about him, but otherwise it was the same old Shane she remembered.

"What are you doing in my parking lot?" she asked.

"It's still a free country north of the Mason-Dixon, ain't it?" Shane's surliness hadn't faded in the cold.

She offered a teasing, not entirely flirt-free smile. "Are you here to see me?"

"If I wasn't this'd be one fantastic coincidence."

"I just finished work. Do you want to go someplace? Get a coffee or something? Tell me what the heck you're doing in Rochester?"

Shane nodded. "Sure. It's fucking freezing out here. How d'you people live this way?"

"We're very hardy. You want to follow me?"

"Sure."

"Can I hug you first?"

"Have at it." He opened his arms and Natalie wrapped herself around his middle, squeezing his strong body and marveling anew at how big this man was. He didn't squeeze back but gave her shoulder a few friendly pats. She pulled away, offering him a final fond smile as their few seconds of shared heat dissipated.

She crunched through the salted parking lot to her own truck off in the employee section, stomach suddenly souring. As the windows defogged she watched Shane in her rearview, ramrod straight in his driver's seat, hands on the wheel, staring into space. Natalie only had two guesses why Shane might have driven all the way to see her with no warning, and they weren't pretty. She backed out with anxiety clenching her middle, Shane following her onto the road.

Maybe Gabriel died. It was a bizarre thought. It made logical sense, given Shane's appearance, but it was impossible to imagine a person so lively not...alive. Maybe Shane's lover had just up and gone, the way Shane had told her he sometimes wished might happen. Just suddenly disappeared, leaving Shane free to get on with his life, pick up the pieces in the wake of crippling infatuation.

Natalie led him six blocks to a chain coffee shop and they parked, slamming their doors in sync. She noticed as they approached the entrance how underdressed Shane was.

"You really ought to buy a winter coat." She gave the sleeve of his light jacket a tug. She held the door for him but the gesture was met with a glare. Natalie shook her head, letting Shane do the door-holding and preceding him into the café.

"You haven't changed," she told him as they got in line.

He shrugged. "It's only been about six months."

"Huh. I guess you're right. Feels like a lifetime ago. To me, anyhow."

Shane unzipped his jacket and she was relieved to see he at least had a sweater on.

"So, you going to tell me why you're here, Shane?" Her gut twisted again, fearing one piece of news, praying for the other.

He became rather distracted by his zipper pull. "My, um...my aunt passed away."

"Oh no. Your aunt who opened the bar?"

He nodded, clenched his jaw in a way that forced Natalie to fight off an urge to hug him again.

"I'm so sorry, Shane. Is that related to whatever brings you here?"

"I s'pose. I just got to thinking..." His attention moved to the front window as he trailed off.

"Next!"

Natalie jumped and hurried to the counter, ordered her coffee then looked to Shane.

"Large...whatever. Nothing fancy. Not decaf."

They fought for a moment over who paid and Natalie won, elbowing Shane and his bills out of the way.

"Thanks," he mumbled.

Their drinks were handed over and Natalie led Shane to a free pair of easy chairs in the front. They had a view of the parking lot, the wind pushing old flakes off the roof to dust the mud-splattered cars, a rather uninspired snow globe.

"Here, have a seat." Natalie pointed to a chair.

Shane sank down with an almighty huff.

"So your aunt passed away," Natalie said, settling in with her cup. "When?"

"Couple weeks before Christmas."

"That's awful, Shane."

His jaw shifted again. "Yeah. So, anyway. I got to thinking how, now that she's gone, I got no family left. None I want to know, anyhow. And you know..." His voice trickled to a mumble. "Me and Gabriel."

She nodded, tried to ignore the flush that crept up her neck at the mere name.

"The way that's headed... Nowhere, I mean. I dunno."

He shrugged and Natalie leaned forward, putting a hand to his knee—a more tender gesture than they'd managed in those three bygone days they'd spent banging one another's brains out all over the apartment above Shane's bar.

"It was just time." He sipped his coffee. "Marie passing was like a brick to the head. I got nobody, family-wise. I'm not working toward a family of my own, and him…he's no partner, you know. Not even if we were like, out there with everything."

As far as Natalie knew, the only people who were aware of the sexual status of Shane and his bar's resident musician were the women sent to him for permission when Gabriel wanted to take an outside lover. Natalie had been one of them, though she'd largely violated the whole permission clause.

She nodded. "So why are you here? Did I grossly underestimate how charming you found me?" The recollection of their not-wholly-sexual tension from those few days the previous August buzzed in her veins, stronger and hotter than the coffee in her hands.

"I'm real happy to see you, Miss Natalie. But mostly I came because this is as far away as I can get and still know somebody. I needed to get away. Cold turkey."

"Gotcha. You afraid of a relapse?"

Shane grinned and nodded guiltily. Gabriel was a damn hard fix to quit and Natalie could appreciate that she was lucky, having escaped as cleanly as she did.

"Maybe you came because I kicked the habit you couldn't. Maybe you need a sponsor." She offered another smirk, suddenly charmed to have this huge man in her hometown. It wrecked the fantasy quality of the strange few days she'd passed in Louisiana, but Natalie didn't mind. She liked Shane the person more than Shane the memory. "In any case, you're welcome to stay with me. My apartment's not crazy roomy, but the couch folds out."

He nodded. "That'll do."

"For how long, do you think?"

"No clue. Couple weeks? As long as you'll have me. I'll give you rent, obviously."

She sputtered her lips at him, dismissing the idea with a wave. "Is that what you think of northern hospitality? Keep your money, thanks."

Shane shrugged.

"I still owe you for the work you did on my truck." She leaned back in her seat and crossed her legs. "How was the drive, by the way? You ever driven in snow and ice before?"

He shook his head. "Nope. And it is *fucked* up. Why'd you idiots settle up here in the first place? In the tundra? It's fucking miserable."

Natalie put a finger to her lips and glanced pointedly at nearby parents and small children.

"Sorry. Frigging miserable."

"Plenty of us would say the same about your humidity and bugs, you know."

"Maybe, but I hear the food up here sucks too."

She rolled her eyes. "Oh, you are going to be one charming houseguest, I can feel it."

"Sorry. Just hate the cold." He looked down at his hands, flexed his fingers. "My knuckles been aching since Cincinnati."

"Poor baby. Well, I'll crank up the heat and keep you full of warm home cooking, how about that?"

Shane smiled, the expression looking cagey as always. "Sounds just peachy, Miss Natalie."

"Good. Actually, I'll need to get some food… You want to go to my place and take a shower or nap or whatever, and I'll head to the store and stock up?"

"I'll go with you. I don't mind."

"Okay. Oh," she said, frowning. "How did you find me, by the way?"

"Googled you. Saw your name listed in the staff directory at your work."

"Ah. A bit of a heads-up wouldn't have hurt, you know."

He shrugged. "Wanted to be free to change my mind at the last second."

She nodded and stared into her open paper cup, still trying to wrap her mind around this man's presence. She wondered if he was being honest—with either of them—about why he'd chosen to run to her. She wasn't sure but she guessed she might still be the only person who'd really seen Shane with Gabriel. Not just literally. She suspected she was the only one who really understood just how helpless Shane could be around his lover. She took another sip, studying Shane's somber face over the rim of her cup. He couldn't have shaved in the last three or four days and his brown hair looked a month overdue for its buzz cut.

"So who's running the Shivaree with you gone?" she asked.

"One of my barmen, Zach. Finally shut him up about what a waste it was earnin' his business management degree. He'll do fine."

"That's good. What about the garage?"

"I had a bunch of vacation time due to me. The other guys can manage without me for a few weeks." Shane took a deep drink, weary eyes on the parking lot.

"You've been staying in motels?"

He nodded. "Just the one, outside Lexington."

Natalie toyed with the lip of her cup then met his eyes again. "Can I ask how old you are, Shane?"

"Thirty-six."

She nodded.

"How about you?"

"Thirty-one, since just after Christmas." She laughed. "It's weird the things we don't actually know about each other, considering the things we *do* know."

Shane smiled tightly, looking as if he agreed but didn't want to make a conversation out of it.

As they nursed their coffees, Natalie stole glances at Shane, wondering what was troubling him. Grief or withdrawal, plain old exhaustion? Some invisible blow to his manhood, coming here to ask his erstwhile sexual rival for a place to stay. Maybe all those things. Natalie made a decision to forgive Shane's attitude. For as brief as it'd been, their relationship had been a complicated one, muddied with jealousy and exposure and resentment, rolled in unbelievably hot sex and hard-won kindness. Over as quickly as it had started.

She took a deep breath and stood, tossing her cup in the nearest trash can. Shane followed suit and they confronted the cold to climb into their trucks. Natalie watched him in her rearview, this character from the most surreal chapter in her life to date, following her to someplace as mundane as Wegmans…and it didn't dull his shine.

On the contrary, having Shane here made the old snow and the dingy ice sparkle in the day's dying sun. He made her skin flush as warm as it had at the height of August, and as good as it felt, Natalie knew it was doomed to get complicated.

CHAPTER TWO

Shane slammed his door and followed Natalie across the ugly brown crust of the parking lot. So far that's what Rochester was to him—an endless slideshow of identical slippery, salty parking lots under a bland gray sky. But there was Natalie too. She had on a long red coat—some style Shane didn't know the name for—pink gloves and matching pink hat. She looked like a Valentine against all the gloom and Shane reminded himself to not be such a grumpy asshole for a change.

Natalie turned to look at him as the automatic doors slid open. She kept giving him that same smile, some mix of amusement and resignation, he guessed.

"What?"

"It's just so weird, having you here suddenly." She gestured at him with an up-and-down sweep of her arm then tugged her gloves off.

"You look the same, you know. You're still all huge and your voice is the same except now you're in Rochester."

"Why would I be any different?"

"I know, of course you're the same. It's just strange." Shane caught a pinkening in her cheeks as she pulled a cart from the line. Maybe it was just from the cold.

She lowered her voice. "Everything that happened when I was with you last was like a dream. Like a three-day dream. If I'd known I'd see you again, I wouldn't have expected you to seem so…familiar. It's nice," she added, poking him softly with her elbow.

"Here." He nudged her out of the way and took over steering the cart.

He hadn't shopped this way in ages—browsing for potential meals. Too many aisles, way too many choices, he decided, scanning the huge store. Big enough that you could multiply Shiloh, Louisiana's sole market by fifty and house them all inside this place with room to spare.

Shane only ever bought breakfast stuff, nearly always skipped lunch and had takeout for dinner. He couldn't guess what a person might fill an entire cart with.

Natalie led the way through the produce section, which looked more like a garden center to Shane.

"Shit," he said, glancing at signs and displays. "I don't know what half these things are. How'd you guys manage to make vegetables so damn complicated?"

Natalie gathered potatoes and bell peppers, adding them to the cart. "We like variety up here, Shane."

He winced at that word—*variety*. Gabriel's need for *variety* had kept Shane up any number of lonely, sleepless nights.

"You like pot roast?" she asked.

"Sure."

"Good. I haven't had an excuse to make mine in ages. Actually, I'm supposed to have dinner at my mom's on Monday. You'll have to come. Now *she* can cook."

Shane had to smile at that, at the prospect of a mom-cooked meal. Or a Natalie-cooked meal. Both ideas made him feel a little warmer, a little comforted. He couldn't remember the last time he'd been handed food by someone not wearing a restaurant uniform. And even if it made him a sexist caveman, Shane would be happy to watch a woman like Natalie lean in and set a plate of steaming meat in front of him. Especially if her top was low-cut.

There were two things Shane wanted out of this trip. One was a friend, and the other was a chance to figure out whether or not he'd wrecked his heterosexuality irreparably. He hoped Natalie might be the right woman to help him with both.

He stopped the cart at Natalie's request and she stacked some cans inside. He watched her selecting items and considered what she'd said earlier. He didn't know what he'd expected when he saw her again. He'd been so numb on the drive north—even before the temperature dropped below thirty—he hadn't considered his plan. Hadn't considered it when he'd stopped at the library to use the internet or as he'd driven over to her work, or when he'd been told she was off at three by the front desk girl. In fact, he hadn't wondered about her reaction until it had been too late, until she'd been walking out into the parking lot toward him.

She'd said Shane looked the same, and she was the same too. Dressed different, her cutesy shoes swapped for winter boots and her sexy blouses by that disappointingly unrevealing sweater behind her open coat. Still, she was as pretty as before. Pale skin and eyes, shiny dark hair. Same mole on her jaw, like a *put thumb here and kiss* marker.

Prettier now that she wasn't an active threat to Shane's precious, codependent wet dream.

They finished shopping and Shane managed to wrestle a few twenties into Natalie's hand, even if she was the one who got her bank card into the swipey device first.

He pushed the cart out to where they'd parked side by side, loading the bags onto Natalie's passenger seat. He spotted a shiny silver tube in one of her cup holders—lipstick. He frowned to himself, wondering who she'd be wearing lipstick for these days. Then he reminded himself of his resolution to not be such a moody motherfucker, and let it go.

He started up his own truck and followed her through the city for five minutes to a quiet neighborhood of modest, two-story houses. Natalie parked on the street in front of a yellow one with a small porch. Shane grabbed the shopping bags to tail her up the steps. She slid her mail from one of two boxes and unlocked the door. Shane followed her to the left down a short hall, where she unlocked a second door with a brass A nailed to it.

"You got a neighbor?"

"Yeah. My landlady lives on the second floor."

She pushed the door in and they stepped into a decent-sized kitchen, probably a cheerful space when the sun was still out. Beyond the counter was a big living and dining room. Shane set the bags down and went back out for his meager luggage. Natalie took his coat and hung it alongside hers by the door then disappeared down a hallway. He looked around the room, noting she had a thing for spider plants and those weird hanging vases, glass globes suspended in artsy wire frames dangling in the windows, leaves tumbling out of them.

Natalie reappeared, having replaced her boots with spangly, pointy-toed shoes. She stopped to flip open the thermostat panel and punch some buttons.

"Wondered how long you'd last in practical footwear." Shane pointed at her sequined feet.

"These are slippers," she said defensively, looking down and modeling them for herself. "And you should see the Frankenstein shoes they make me wear at work. I need these for my spiritual well-being."

"You liking your job?"

"Not as much as the hospice where I worked in Miami…but it's okay. I mean, any job's a good job in this economy."

"Guess they can't outsource the nurses."

She laughed. "Don't give them any ideas. So, are you like, dying for a shower?"

"Wouldn't hurt."

"I'll show you where everything is."

She gave Shane a quick tour of the bathroom and the living room, the futon where he'd be sleeping. Natalie seemed to like red…red shower curtain, red drapes and slip covers, red cloth on the small dinner table parked at the far end of her living room. Shane wondered what color her sheets were. He wondered if he'd be finding out soon. Soon like tonight.

But he elbowed his libido aside, body infinitely more interested in the comforting over the carnal for the time being. He shaved and took a long, steaming shower, melting his muscles only to have them tense up again as he stepped out of the tub. He changed into fresh jeans and a tee shirt, mercifully clean socks. When he strolled back into the cool dryness of the hall he could already smell dinner—spices, onions.

Natalie was in her kitchen cutting potatoes, a lump of beef taunting Shane's empty stomach from the center of a casserole dish. He leaned on the opposite side of the counter, his primitive brain fusing the smells and the profile of Natalie's breasts and the relief of being inside, in the warmth, in clean clothes, feeling human again. Feeling distinctly male again.

As she arranged the potatoes around the meat in the dish, her gaze jumped up and held his, smile warming his insides. "So what's up, Shane? What have I been missing since I moved back north?"

"Just the usual. You and...you and him are the only interesting things to come my way in the last year or so. The rest's all work."

She nodded, rinsing carrots.

"How about you?" he asked. "You happy to be back with your family? Your mom and sister live close, right?"

"Yeah. My mom's just up the street, actually. My sister Alicia lives about a half hour away."

"Cozy."

"Yeah, it's great." She set down a carrot. "Plus my sister's like..." She put her hands out, miming massive pregnancy.

"Oh. That your first niece or nephew?"

"Niece, yeah. First grandkid in the family, all that good stuff." She picked up a cleaver and chopped the carrots, smiling to herself.

Shane swallowed down a little hurt, that same old dull ache he got when he thought about family. He'd lost all the relatives he'd loved and avoided his dad's rotten side like the plague.

"That's nice," he said then cleared his throat of the stickiness. "You think you ever want that? Husband and kids and all that?"

She made a face, part surprise, part ambivalence. "Yeah, sure. I like kids. Not sure where I'm going to conjure a husband from anytime soon, but yeah, that'd be nice. Something to aim myself toward in the next few years." She met Shane's eyes as the carrots tumbled into the pot. "What about you? Now that you and him..."

He shrugged. "That's kinda why I had to pull the plug."

Her smile came slow and a touch mischievous.

"What?" Shane asked.

"I dunno. I know we don't know each other that well or anything, but it's a little surprising. You're not the cuddliest man I've ever met."

Shane frowned and Natalie reached a damp hand across the counter to touch his wrist. "I'm not saying you wouldn't be an awesome husband or dad though. I mean, you're hardworking and good-looking, and when you're not busy acting like an asshole, you're really quite thoughtful."

Shane mulled it over, decided she had him pinned pretty well and filtered the compliments from the slights. "Thanks."

"And you're great in the sack," she added, lips pursed to hide her grin.

Shane's neck warmed and he rose happily to the invitation to flirt. No doubt his dick had had a say in where he'd chosen to escape to when he'd left Louisiana, no shock he wanted to resume where he and Natalie had left off, minus the third party.

"I do believe you're flirtin' with me, Miss Natalie."

She turned away to grab a pepper grinder. Shane watched her twist it over the ingredients, watched the tendons in her throat as she chose her response.

"I don't hear you denyin' it," Shane said.

"I'm not trying to flirt, Shane." She licked her lips. Probably had no clue how fucking sexy she looked when she did that. "I know what it was like between you and him. That's not a rebound I want any part of."

Fine, they could play that game. "Seem to recall being tapped to take part in *your* rebound."

Her smirk told him he was winning. "Yes, and an epic one it was, Shane. But I dunno. You two were complicated. You should give yourself some time to…"

"Grieve?"

She shrugged.

"I been doin' too much of that lately."

"Time to get over him then. Let the next woman you go after get all of you. Not just whatever's left right after he goes away. I mean, don't act like you two were just some random, yearlong fling."

No, definitely not.

"You said you were in love with him."

"I don't know about that anymore. Don't know if that was love. Felt like somethin' else, somethin' ugly sometimes."

"Like jealousy?"

"Like...like whatever love feels like when you don't trust the other person any farther than you can throw them."

She nodded. "I hear you."

"Anyhow, it's over now." He hadn't exactly told Gabriel that in so many words, but he would...if his sudden absence hadn't already made the break plain.

Shane decided to let Natalie focus on her cooking, let himself avoid talking about his ex-lover.

"You mind if I just zone out to the TV for a bit? I could use a nap after the drive."

"Of course. Go crash in my bed, if you want. Dinner won't be ready for ages."

"I'll just switch on the tube, maybe pass out on your couch."

"Knock yourself out." She waved a hand in the direction of the television. "You want a drink? I've got some beers, I think."

Shane perked up. "Please."

He waited until she came back from the fridge and grabbed the hand she had wrapped around the bottle. He smiled, aiming his eyes at the beer, the food, her chest. "You just get better and better."

Natalie raised a skeptical brow and he released her hand. She pulled a drawer open and got a bottle opener, popped the cap for him. "You haven't changed," she said again.

"Beer, hot meal, permission to nod off on the couch watching TV? How'm I not supposed to hump your leg for that?"

She laughed, pretty face turning damn sexy. "You're rusty with the ladies, aren't you?"

"Maybe you'll give me a little practice then?" Shane inched his free hand closer to where hers rested on the counter.

Natalie picked up the opener and rapped his knuckles with it.

"Ow."

"Take a seat, Broussard. Go cool yourself off."

He scowled at her and walked off with his bottle. He deciphered her remotes, finding the evening news and zoning out for a few minutes. The ads came on and Shane glanced around the room, let comfort ooze over him for the first time in ages. Warmth, the smell of real food, the faintest buzz from the alcohol, a stronger one from Natalie's proximity. He could get used to this…maybe not this region and its fucked-up idea of winter, but this family-type feeling. He'd missed this. His eyes settled on the hearth beside the TV stand.

"You got a fireplace," Shane said, pointing his bottle at it.

She glanced up from behind the counter. "Yeah. It works and everything, I think."

"You got any wood?"

She shook her head.

"Shame." Swirling his beer, he stared out the window into the dark backyard. He drained the bottle and stood. He pulled on his boots by the front door and grabbed his jacket from the hook.

"Heading back home so soon?" Natalie teased.

"I just got to check on something."

She opened the oven door with a creak. "All right. But be careful—it's icy."

Shane braved the frigid wind and the slick sidewalks, and tried three houses before he was met with success. He arrived back at Natalie's after ten minutes' absence, balancing his newly acquired firewood in one arm as he got the doors open.

"You ready to kiss my feet?"

Natalie turned from the sink, brows rising. "Whoa. Who gave you that?"

"Diane."

"Who?"

"Older lady across the way in the green house," he said.

"Wow. I've never even talked to most of my neighbors."

Shane set the wood on the tile by the door. "That's 'cause you're from the north. You guys know nothin' about neighborliness."

"Well, good work. I'm sure *Diane* found your accent both charming and perplexing."

"You got a light?"

"Someplace." She set the cutting board in the dish rack and dried her hands, disappearing into another room then returning with a big box of matches.

"That your bedroom?" Shane nodded toward where she'd gone.

"Yeah."

He took the box. "These your matches for lighting candles when you seduce hapless men into your bed?"

She shot him a withering look. "So what if they are?"

He shrugged. "So nothin'. You got any newspapers?"

She dragged a recycling bin stuffed with junk mail in from the kitchen. Shane got to work building them a decent fire then relaxed back into the couch cushions, domestic bliss complete. Once dinner was over there'd be just one base desire left to meet. He scanned Natalie's body from across the room, curious. He hadn't been with a woman in a long while—not since he'd been with Natalie six months earlier, in fact—and he missed it. Missed the softness, the smooth skin and a comforting female voice, small hands. He shifted in his seat.

"You almost done over there?" he called.

"Just about." She turned off the faucet. "I'm having a glass of wine, if you want one." She pulled a bottle from a cupboard to show him.

Shane got lost in his head for a moment, lost in the memory of a hundred hangovers and the face he'd never be able to divorce from the taste of red wine. Natalie must have read his mind, as her shoulders slumped and she set the bottle down. She crossed the living room to sit on the arm of the couch.

"Sorry. That a sore spot?"

Shane did his best imitation of a bored shrug. "Nah. Don't worry about it." He imagined kissing her later, tasting wine and how it'd make him feel... Fuck it. He'd driven cross-country to escape that man. He wouldn't let a goddamn beverage get to him now.

"Go get yourself a glass, Miss Natalie."

She squinted at him as she stood. "Why do you always call me that?"

"It's your name, ain't it?"

She headed back to the kitchen counter. "Why the 'Miss' bit, I mean? I feel like you're making fun of me or something."

"It's considered polite where I'm from." Shane watched her uncork the bottle and pour herself a healthy glass before grabbing another beer from the fridge. She crossed the floor and handed him the bottle.

"Thanks. You want me to call you something else?"

She shook her head. "No, just wondered what that was about."

Shane took a deep drink, cold beer to balance out the warm, dry heat of the fire. "How about you move down south with me and I'll make you a missus?" A tease, but Shane didn't mind the thought of such a thing.

She laughed. "Yeah, right."

He glanced at her over the bottle as he drank, one fucking beautiful sight in the firelight. "Why not? Natalie Broussard's got a nice ring to it. Plus our kids'd be so damn good-looking."

"Oh yeah, you and me and our brood of surly babies." She sipped her wine. "Gimme a couple more bottles of this and maybe that won't sound like the worst idea ever."

Shane cupped a hand over his crotch. "Thanks a lot. Didn't know it was possible to get kicked in the nuts without a foot being involved."

"You know what I mean. We've got thousands of miles and a weird bit of history between us."

"I like our history," Shane said. More than he could tell her. Natalie was the one woman he knew—the sole person—who could begin to understand what he was going through, post-Gabriel.

She sipped her wine. "You didn't like me much at first."

"I fixed your truck and gave you a place to sleep."

"Yeah, you did. Even after I kind of crapped all over your wishes."

"Damn straight." Shane took a drink, fixing her with a cocky look.

"The other thing we've had between us is Gabriel."

He flinched at the name.

"Literally between us," she added. "If you're looking to move on, I'm not the cleanest break you could pick. In fact I'm probably the worst."

"You trying to tell me you ain't interested?"

"In marrying you and birthing your many gigantic, angsty children?"

Shane laughed. "Nah...just, you know, interested in me?" He bobbed his eyebrow at her, kept it up until she laughed.

"Too complicated."

"Sex was great though, right?"

She pursed her lips, stared into her glass.

Shane frowned. "Feel free to lie."

Sighing, she aimed her eyes toward the ceiling. "The sex was awesome, Shane. Duh. But I'm not ready to just jump right in and be like that with you again."

"Why not?"

Her gaze dropped to meet his. "It's just messy. *We're* messy."

"And we're drinking." He held his bottle up to illustrate. "Things'll be less complicated after you have another glass."

She smirked and shook her head. "Shameless as always."

"Not as shameless as some houseguests."

Her gaze drifted away again. They sipped their drinks, watching the news until Natalie stood to check on the roast.

Shane leaned into the cushions and let the smells and the warmth and the comfort of female company wash over him. He nodded off for a while, waking to Natalie's hand squeezing his shoulder.

"Dinner's ready."

Shane glanced at the hearth. "You let the fire practically go out."

She headed back to the kitchen. "I don't know anything about fires, Shane. You're the man. That can be your job while you're here."

He stood with a grunt, feeling the last few days' driving and anxiety in his stiff back and achy muscles. He added a couple logs to the embers and met up with Natalie as she was carving the beef.

"That's another man-job." Shane elbowed her out of the way. He sensed the eye-roll he couldn't actually see in his periphery. Elbows and eye-rolls, him and her to a tee.

"Meat and fire and trucks and whiskey," she said through a sigh. "You're just a walking stereotype of American manliness."

He laughed. A combination of sleepiness, gratitude, intimacy and alcohol led him to add, "Yeah, except for that whole banging-another-guy thing."

"Yeah, I guess that one doesn't quite fit the mold." Natalie accepted a thick slice of roast and scooped vegetables from the dish.

Shane swallowed, determined to use this visit as practice for wrapping his head around everything he'd been struggling with for the past year. "Meat and fire and whiskey and good old, patriotic cock sucking," he said grandly. "Drape a flag on me and cue the bugles."

She gave him a sarcastic salute and he grabbed his bottle and followed her to the dinner table.

He felt small just now, naked and vulnerable. It felt surprisingly nice.

He trusted Natalie. He had to, or else why would he have come here? As close as they were to strangers, she knew him better than any other living person, save one. It would've been a depressing thought if he wasn't here with her now. "Thanks for taking me in," he said.

"Happy to have you. Sorry this didn't happen at a nicer time of year."

"Not your fault your forbearers settled in such a miserable place."

"Ahem, humidity? Mosquitoes? West Nile virus? Hurricanes?"

"Louisiana's got enough troubles without you adding your two cents," he said.

"True. And you're right, it is sort of miserable here this time of year. I didn't realize it until I'd spent a winter in Miami. It never occurred to me that in some parts of the world, people don't have to shovel their cars out."

"In the South we drink to cool down," Shane said, taking a sip of beer. He nodded to her glass. "You kids drink to warm up."

Natalie smiled and swallowed. "Actually, I should own up and say the summers here can climb into the nineties, and it gets humid and there's tons of mosquitoes."

"See?" he said, triumphant. "You're going to love moving down and being my wife."

She shook her head and Shane let the conversation trail off, the drone of the TV and the crackle of the fire filling his head; warm, home-cooked meal leaving him sleepy and content. He stole a glance at his hostess every few seconds, eyeing the threshold of her bedroom door and wondering how long it'd take him to get himself invited there. Not long, he hoped. She owed him a hell of a rebound.

CHAPTER THREE

Firelight and a full belly, the proximity of a warm male body Natalie knew well enough to have kept herself entertained with on any number of lonely nights since she'd returned north. Tempting. That body worried her too, since she didn't entirely trust herself around it.

She shifted in her seat beside Shane, wondering if he was taking in any of the action movie they'd agreed on after twenty minutes of Netflix browsing. She stared at the images, but other ones were running through her mind. Shane's strong, naked body, the mean face he wore when he was aroused, the sheen of sweat on his skin in the summer heat.

He reached for her hand and she jumped. He slid the remote away. "I'm not really watchin' this. Are you?"

"No, not really. I'm pretty wiped out."

He clicked the TV off and set the remote aside, the weight of him shifting the couch and the nearness of his body filling Natalie with bad ideas. He leaned one arm along the back of the futon, turning toward her.

"And I need to be up by six to get ready for work," she said.

His broad, warm hand cupped the back of her neck.

"Shane."

He leaned in to kiss her and she ducked to the side. He pulled away with parted lips and a raised eyebrow.

She sighed, mainly from frustration. "Sorry, Shane. I'm sort of seeing somebody."

He withdrew his arm to clasp his hands in his lap. "Sort of?"

"Yeah, sort of. I don't know what we are but I don't think I'd want him kissing other women behind my back, so…"

"What's this sorta-somebody do?" he asked.

"He's a doctor."

"Oh." His brows knitted. "Well, you coulda told me all that a couple hours ago."

"I know…and I should have. But it's nice, you know. Flirting with you again."

"Uh huh. Not as nice as the fucking ache between my legs. Thanks for that."

She checked his expression and saw he was just teasing her. She tried her best to return the smirk but sexual energy was still flooding her body, clouding her head in tandem with the wine. The last time she'd seen Shane before this afternoon, she'd been naked in his bed with another man between them. The next morning she'd slipped out while Shane was in the shower. Having him suddenly here in her world, the offer of more sex on the table… If she'd known this were going to happen she'd have absolutely kept herself a hundred-percent free.

She patted his thigh, wanting to squeeze it and remind herself how hard his muscle was. Instead she set her curious hand on the back of the couch.

"Even if I wasn't sort of seeing someone, you getting into something like that with me when you're trying to get over Gabriel… It doesn't seem like the best idea."

"Methodone," Shane said.

She slapped his cheek lightly, disparaging the metaphor.

"Sorry," he said.

Natalie sighed, combing her fingers through her hair and staring into the fire, trying to ignore her nagging, hungry body. "Don't be sorry. I'm glad you're here. I'm really happy you came up."

He nodded, eyes cast down at his knees. "Wasn't sure if I should. I mean, you left without sayin' goodbye."

"I know. In the end, it was weird. I didn't feel like I was supposed to say goodbye to you. As strange as it sounds, it would've been harder to say goodbye to you than Gabriel. You did a lot for me. Saying goodbye would have felt like closing a book, I guess."

"Oh. Well, maybe that's why I'm here then." Finally, another taste of that familiar, smug grin. He leaned back into the cushions. "Maybe you can finish your story. I bet it ends by me driving you up the fuckin' wall until you kick me out on my ass."

"A girl can hope. And you know…I've thought about you more than him."

Shane laughed, either embarrassed or disbelieving.

"No, really. I know Gabriel's…well, he's magic," she said. "He's beautiful and he's scary-talented, but he's like a dream, like I said. You get away from him for a week or two and he fades to two dimensions. But you're real, Shane. You don't fade like he does. If you hadn't been there I might have started to think I hallucinated that whole weekend."

Shane stared down at his hands. "He don't feel like no dream to me."

"No, I bet he doesn't. Did you tell him where you were going?"

"Left him high and dry."

Just as Gabriel had surely left Shane dangling any number of long, sleepless nights. Natalie had shared one of those nights with him, lying beside Shane in his bed, waiting for Gabriel to come through the door and ease both their impatient minds. He hadn't. They were strange, those two. On the outside Shane was the cruel one, the one who seemed to have all the control, but underneath it was the complete opposite. Gabriel could play people as surely as he could a mandolin or a fiddle or any other set of strings he got his masterful hands on. At the same time, she'd seen the way he looked at Shane... Her guest might not agree, but she bet this breakup wasn't any easier on Gabriel than it was on Shane.

"I better get to bed soon," Natalie said.

"Sure."

"I'll get you some blankets and pillows. Anything else you need?"

"Don't think so. What's happening tomorrow?"

"Well, I work seven to three. I've got spare keys, so I guess you're just on your own. Sorry."

"Don't be sorry. Not like I gave you any notice."

"Feel free to use my computer and eat whatever you want. Call me if you have any questions tomorrow."

"I'll be just fine. I'll surf for the nastiest, most fucked-up porn I can think of and leave your computer a mile deep in pop-up windows."

"That's fine, just don't break anything."

Shane smiled at that. She returned it, then stood and went to her bedroom to gather spare bedding from the top of the closet. She caught Shane trying to peer inside her room as she headed back to the den.

He followed her to the couch, watching as she stripped off the futon's slip cover, unfolding the bed with a creak and making it up with clean sheets.

"Thanks very much."

"This might be a bit short for you," she said, nodding at his legs. Her bed was plenty big but she bit back the flirtation fighting to pop through her lips and mention that fact.

"Beats the shithole I crashed in last night, trust me. You're quite a hostess, taking me in like this."

"Like I said, it's nice to have you here. Lovely change from the boring end to January I'd been imagining." She handed him a couple of folded blankets then headed back to her room to bring him a pair of pillows.

"Anything else?" she asked, crossing her arms over her chest.

Shane gave her a last taste of sexual harassment, running his eyes up and down her body. "No, think I'm good."

"Cool." She stifled a yawn then stepped close to peck a sisterly kiss on his jaw and pat his chest. "Sleep well. Have fun tomorrow if I don't talk to you before I leave in the morning."

"Call me when you're done with the old folks," he said. "I'll meet you someplace for dinner, if you want the night off from cooking."

"Will do. Sleep well, Shane."

* * *

Shane watched her saunter to the bathroom then sneaked to her bedroom's threshold, scanning her bed and nightstand, the entire setup, so he'd know what to picture when he doubtlessly jerked himself to the idea in a few minutes' time.

As he went back to the foldout, a thought dogged him. How ruined must he be by now? In the year since he'd met Gabriel, that man had been the only thing on his mind when he came, either while fucking the guy or by himself. That'd never happened with a woman before, that kind of effortless mental fidelity. He tried to blink away the man's face and replace it with Natalie's, but already he was having a tough time picturing her.

"Fucking doomed," he muttered.

He closed up the fireplace and turned off the lights, stripped to his underwear. As he settled beneath the blankets, his formerly eager body had already cooled by a few degrees. He stared at the ceiling, mind simultaneously blank and racing. He snaked a hand down his stomach and palmed his cock. A few thoughts of Natalie's mouth got his blood moving, his dick growing hard and heavy in his hand. He'd never been sucked by her before, though he'd seen her do it to Gabriel. He imagined that, imagined spreading her thighs with his in her bed, feeling her soft skin and watching her breasts bounce as he fucked her. His fist tightened but even as his orgasm built, he felt other memories tugging at him, his brain splicing in unwanted images, a beautiful man staring up at him, strong hips pinned under Shane's hands.

"Fuck." He let his cock go, fisting the covers. He'd rather go to sleep hurting than let those memories win. Cold turkey, he'd promised himself.

He forced deep breaths, getting his foggy memories of Natalie's naked body cued up and waiting until his cock was pounding from her and her alone. The thoughts sped with his strokes, got him to the brink of coming before he lost them again, brain swapping in a flash of tan skin, five o'clock shadow, Gabriel's black eyes on Shane's face and his mouth wrapped around his cock.

"Fuck." He released his dick again and turned onto his side. His body was a clock, wound too tight, drawn around and around in circles, pulse ticking away the maddening seconds as he prayed for unconsciousness to come. Prayed these restless nights wouldn't dog him 'til his death.

* * *

Shane slammed his truck door, hoisting the bundle of firewood he'd bought at the supermarket and lugging it up the porch. Only a little past two and already the sun seemed to be fading. He fished for the spare keys Natalie had left him and shuffled out of the frigid wind and into the warmth. He left the wood by the fireplace and ditched his jacket, went to work searching her cupboards for coffee.

He froze as his phone buzzed to life in his jeans pocket. Pulling it out, he frowned at the familiar number on the screen. He'd told his staff at the Shivaree that he was on vacation, to be contacted for emergencies only. Still, if someone was calling from the bar, at least that meant they probably hadn't managed to burn it down in his absence.

"Shane Broussard."

"Hello, Shane."

His heart stopped. From confusion, since he'd always assumed Gabriel didn't know how to operate something as modern as a phone. From joy too—cocky triumph that he'd driven this man to seek him out. And from terror, realizing his worst addiction had learned to inject itself independent of Shane's will.

"Hey," he said, cool. "Didn't know you had my number."

"Zach did. I'm in your office right now."

Shane pictured it, that magnetic man with his black eyes and hair, that lean, strong body lounging in Shane's chair in the club's shabby back room.

"Zach let you in there?" he asked.

"He did."

Shane sighed, faking irritation as his heart pounded so hard he thought he might pass out. "What's up?"

"Where you at?" Gabriel asked in his lazy voice, a raspy baritone crippled by two insanely heavy accents, Cajun and Cuban. Cubajun, Shane called it.

"I'm in Rochester, New York, visiting Natalie Foster," Shane said, so casual he knew he wasn't fooling anybody.

"Oh. How she is?"

"Fine. She met a doctor." He walked to the futon and took a seat.

"Tha's nice."

"Yeah, ducky."

"When you comin' home, Shane?"

He swallowed, hating the thrill that question gave him. "Dunno. Why? You missin' havin' someplace to sleep?" Gabriel came and went like an ownerless cat, crashing with Shane most nights, shacking up who-knew-where the rest of the time and robbing Shane of his sleep and sanity.

"Miss *you*, Shane."

"Uh huh. Well, I'm staying here for another week, at least. I earned some vacation time. You'll just have to fend for yourself, I s'pose."

He heard the soft, satisfied grunts of Gabriel stretching. Shane could picture it—that long, slender body leaning back in Shane's ancient office chair, shined old shoes propped on the desk, maybe that worn-out porkpie hat set on Shane's laptop, a clash of eras.

For a long time there was silence, so long Shane wondered if maybe Gabriel had wandered away and left the phone off its cradle. Then, "Miss your body, Shane."

Blood rushed south to get Shane's cock as heavy and warm as if the very man's hands were at his belt buckle. "Do you then?" *Idiot. Hang up now.* An addict didn't just have a little taste of heroin and Shane knew he probably couldn't handle just a taste of his intoxicating lover. Still, addicts lived for their relapses.

"I'm lonely, Shane." His voice sounded dark and hungry, just as it did when he sang.

"You'll live."

"Miss your hands on me."

Shane's cock went stiff and insistent and he glanced to the clock. At least forty-five minutes before Natalie got home...not that she hadn't seen it all before. Still, this'd be like catching Shane with a rubber tie strapped around his arm as he primed a needle full of something regrettable right here in her living room, guilty as the sweetest sin he knew.

Shane pinned his phone between his cheek and shoulder and unbuckled his belt. "Tell me," he said. "Whose hands are on you right now?"

"Mine."

Shane swallowed and took the phone in his left hand. "You lock the office door?"

"Yeah."

He eased his fly down and cupped a palm over his erection, light—that teasing way Gabriel was such an expert at. "Tell me what else you're missing, boy."

"How you taste," Gabriel murmured, voice reminding Shane of hot breath warming his cock.

"It's my hand on you now," Shane said, pushing his own underwear down to free his dick. "Make it tight."

Gabriel moaned into the phone and Shane imagined those talented fingers fisted around his lover's hard length. He swallowed a moan of his own.

"What're you missing most?" Shane asked.

"Your cock."

Shane tightened his grip, stroked himself slow. "You want it now?"

"Yeah."

"Tell me how."

"Fuck me," he begged. "Fuck my ass, Shane."

"I'll bend you over that desk." Shane groaned, picturing such a thing. "Shove those pants down your legs and spit in my hand, get you nice and wet."

"Yeah."

"Tease you with my cock 'til you're begging for me." He could feel it now, the smooth, tight skin of his head taunting Gabriel's spit-slick, puckered hole.

"Please, Shane."

Fuck, those two words that never failed to suck the sense right out of his brain. He made his stroking hand into a tight circle with his thumb and forefinger, eased it over his head. "Yeah. I'm pushing inside you. Lemme in."

Gabriel grunted, sounding real for a moment, more than a voice coming through the ether, so real Shane thought he could smell the man's wine breath. He licked his fingers, squeezing them over his crown and mourning the warmth that was missing.

"Yeah," he murmured. "You're so tight."

"More, Shane. Please."

He drew his fist down his cock, slow and mean. "Fuck yeah. I'm fucking you deep, boy. You feel so damn good."

Gabriel moaned again and Shane wondered if he was jerking or finger-fucking himself…pants down to his knees, bare ass against the sticky, fake leather of Shane's desk chair. He imagined pulling those pants all the way off, pushing Gabriel's knees against his chest and slamming himself in deep, sending them both rolling across the floor to slam into the wall, maybe earning a curious knock from one of the staff.

"You so big, Shane. Fuck me hard."

"I am."

"Turn me over. Push me back on the desk."

Shane reassembled the scene in his head, shoving everything off the table and pushing Gabriel onto the wood with his thighs spread, dark eyes on Shane's cock as he rammed it home. "Oh, you're takin' it, boy. Lemme watch you stroke."

Gabriel's grunts sounded pained, sounded so exactly as they did when he was getting fucked for real that Shane damn near lost his mind. "Fuck... I'm gonna come. Take my cock. Take me." His fist stroked, tight and fast and frantic as he imagined Gabriel doing the same exact thing more than a thousand miles away.

"Shane."

He knew that sound anywhere, the sound of both of them losing control.

"Good. Here I come, boy. Here I come." Shane's own moans drowned out his lover's as he lost it, coming like a force of nature into his hand. "Fuck yeah."

"Shane."

For a few moments there was only panting on either end of the line, two men fighting for breath and bidding good riddance to their dignity.

Shane looked to the clock on the cable box, to his hand, feeling the high abandon him as reality punched him in the face. "I gotta go. She's due home any minute."

"All right, Shane."

"You take care." He fumbled with his phone and jabbed the end button, tossing it to the far cushion. "Fuck. Fucking idiot."

He stood and got his jeans buttoned then went to the bathroom to rinse his right hand and the front of his shirt of the mistake he'd just made. He stared at himself in Natalie's oval vanity mirror and shook his head. "Good fuckin' job, genius. Way to go."

"Shane?" Natalie's voice came from the kitchen and he heard the door click closed.

He shook his head and wandered out to meet her. "Hey there."

She met his half-assed smile with a confused frown. "Hey yourself. Your shirt's all wet."

"Accident with a cup of coffee. You're back a little early." He glanced to the couch, relieved there was no evidence of what had just gone on there.

Natalie set her purse on the counter and rummaged in it. "Yeah, it was pretty quiet so I clocked out. Listen, Alex—the guy I'm seeing—he wants to meet up for an early drink. Just the one. You want to come?"

Hell no, Shane didn't want to have a drink with *Alex*. What had just gone on had ripped him open, left him frustrated and humiliated. Left him eager to find somebody to absorb all the anger he was feeling toward himself. "Don't he know you got a houseguest?"

"It's Friday." She took out her wallet and counted her cash. "And he's the closest thing I have to a boyfriend. Aside from a ninety-seven-year-old Korean War vet named Howie who pinches my ass every time I pass him in the residence. And Alex wants to buy me a drink. Come along if you like, otherwise I'll be back in an hour or so with a pizza."

Shane sighed, openly petulant. "In that case a drink'd be just plum-dandy."

"I can hear your eyes rolling, Shane." She zipped her bag and met his gaze. "I'll be ready in a couple minutes."

She left him to disappear into her bedroom, emerging shortly in snug jeans and a sweater that showed off the tops of her breasts.

"You'll catch a cold in that, Miss Natalie."

She raised her eyebrows at him and pulled the elastic from her hair, letting her dark waves unfurl from a bun and mussing them with her fingers.

Shane pursed his lips, leftover aggression from the phone call still stirring up his blood. "That hair always looked better spread out across my pillow."

She glared at him then took a few steps closer to tap a finger against his lips. "And that mouth always sounded better when it was full of Gabriel's dick."

He laughed, burned by the remark but willing to let her win. "Low blow."

Natalie smirked. "Get your layers on."

"Yes ma'am."

"And Shane?"

He smiled at her, as innocently as he could muster.

"Be nice."

CHAPTER FOUR

A half hour later they arrived in Rochester's gray and modest downtown. Natalie parked her truck and led Shane to a flashy, new-looking bar. He flared his nostrils as they entered, glancing around in the low light at the flat-screen TVs and the young professionals chatting at high, brushed-aluminum tables. Shane lived and breathed the Shivaree, and being in another bar felt like cheating.

He didn't like this place, not its fake-vintage beer signs or canned pop music, its professionally printed menus or its cold, northern clientele. He especially didn't like the man who stood from his stool to touch Natalie's arm and kiss her on the mouth when they approached.

She turned to smile at Shane. "Shane, this is Alex; Alex, this is my friend Shane I mentioned."

Alex sized Shane up with a flash of his eyes then slapped a too-friendly grin on his pretty face. "Nice to meet you, Shane. Welcome to Rochester."

"Thanks."

They shook quickly, Shane's tight grip probably racing past confidence and right over the cliff into meatheaded intimidation. Being in this foreign bar made him feel even more eager to assert his dominance than usual. He had a good three or four inches and fifty pounds on this guy, and he hoped his caveman shake underscored that fact.

Alex took his seat and Natalie followed suit. "Natalie said you're from Louisiana," Alex said.

Shane stayed standing, crossing his arms over his chest. "Yeah, near Baton Rouge. You from here?"

"I grew up in Buffalo, actually. Just moved here a couple months ago for work."

"What sort of doctor are you?" Shane asked.

"Surgeon," Alex said, neither proud nor humble.

"Uh huh."

"What about you?"

"I own a bar."

"And he's a mechanic," Natalie offered. "Shane fixed my truck when I was on my way back from Miami."

And banged her ever-loving brains out, Shane added to himself. *Natalie ever tell you she fucked two Southern gentlemen at the same time? No? Oh, too bad. Good luck sleeping at night.*

"Can I get you a drink, Shane?" Alex asked.

Shane felt drunk already, high on a hundred dangerous brain chemicals from the phone call. "Sure. Bottle of something domestic and a shot of whiskey. No ice." He pulled out a couple bills to kick in but Alex waved them away. "Thank you kindly," Shane said, shrugging on airs of overdone Deep South friendliness, more bees than honey.

"Babe?" Alex said to Natalie.

Shane's fingers tensed, itching to form fists.

"Genny Light, thanks."

Alex left them to seek the bartender at the far end of the long metal counter.

Shane shoved his hands in his pockets and raised an eyebrow at Natalie. "Surgeon, huh? You're moving up in the world."

"From brewer? Yeah, I guess so."

"I meant from mechanic and musician, but if we don't rate, then—"

"Shane." She glared at him, disapproving but not angry. "Don't be like that. Neither of you were ever mine. *He* certainly wasn't. He was yours, and you made that abundantly clear. Please don't make this awkward. Alex is a really good guy."

Shane ground his teeth and got control of himself. "How long you been seein' him?"

"Just a couple weeks."

You fucked him yet? "He treat you good?"

"Yeah, he does."

"But he ain't your boyfriend?"

Natalie shrugged. "Not yet. Maybe soon. Maybe soon if you don't keep flexing your arms like you plan on putting him in a headlock."

He smirked at her.

"Maybe your red-blooded-thug shtick plays well with the ladies in Shiloh," Natalie said, "but up here we like our wishes respected, thanks."

"Understood."

"Good. So behave yourself if you want my futon."

Shane laughed softly. He leaned in close to murmur, "Remember tellin' you the exact same thing, Miss Natalie. And I don't remember you complyin'."

She looked poised to snap right back then shut her pretty mouth, shook her head with a smile. "Touché, Broussard."

Alex returned, juggling their drinks.

"You ought to be a waiter." Shane picked up his shot as Alex set the glasses on the bar.

The guy grinned. "I was, all through med school."

Shane scowled to himself, wanting Alex to be a spoiled rich kid whose mommy and daddy had paid his way. Disappointed, he shifted his judgment to Alex's hair, which he suspected had been coiffed with the aid of some kind of mousse to get that wind-proofing. He glanced at his hands next, equally relieved by his way-too-tidy fingernails, the hands of a man who was useless with tools.

"You, uh, you work on Natalie's truck for her, now she's back north?" Shane asked, knowing damn well his open skepticism was bordering on rudeness.

Alex laughed. "It hasn't come up yet, but I don't think I'm the best guy to turn to with mechanical issues...unless Natalie's truck needs a bypass."

Shane grinned tightly. *Scalpels versus socket wrenches. Fine. We can play that game, doc.*

* * *

Natalie returned from a trip to the ladies' room, anxious as she rounded the bar. Shane and Alex were just as she'd left them, twenty minutes into semi-awkward small talk, two mismatched examples of what it meant to be a man. South, North, crass, polite. Brutishly sexy versus the breed of non-threatening handsomeness moms and dads alike prayed their daughters might land. Natalie shook her head at her own libido for always picking the Neanderthal.

She touched Alex's shoulder as she passed him to take her place, reminding herself to keep making better choices.

"What'd I miss?" she asked.

Shane answered, offering her a cheerful grin she didn't trust one bit. "Just shootin' the shit about your beautiful Rochester weather."

She laughed. "No comment. I stayed in Miami as long as I did for a reason, and it wasn't just because of my lousy taste in men. Present company excluded," she added with a warm glance at Alex.

Shane cleared his throat and stood. "Listen, I've horned in on your little date for long enough. I'm gonna grab another drink. Why don't you two cozy up at a table or somethin'?"

Natalie knew what that meant. If Shane didn't excuse himself, he'd say something they'd all regret. She could *feel* him itching to pick a fight with Alex. A perverse part of her wanted him to...just being near the both of them together, she knew which type of man her body preferred.

No. Bad. Give the nice guy a chance. Shane was being good and she'd be well advised to follow his example.

"Sure. Thanks, Shane." Natalie flashed her eyes at Alex and picked up her drink, and he followed her to a small table by the window.

"That was decent of him," Alex said, pulling her chair out.

"Surprisingly decent, yes."

He pulled his own chair closer and sat, leaning close. "I'm glad he did, actually. I have a surprise for you. And a question."

Natalie felt the room go cold and her mouth fall open. She closed it, but not quickly enough to cover her horror.

Alex laughed. "Don't panic—it's not a ring."

She put a hand to her chest, relieved beyond belief. "Oh my God, you scared me. No offense."

"None taken. It's only been a couple weeks."

"Yes, exactly. Okay, breathe." She laughed, fanning herself.

"But my question—or rather my surprise, since I hope you'll say yes, since it's already paid for... I was hoping..." He drew a brochure from his back pocket, unfolded it and handed it to Natalie.

She stared at the palm trees and aqua sea and swoopy wording, not quite understanding. "Montserrat?"

He grinned. "For a week in March, right when the snow turns from gray to brown around here. What do you think?"

She laughed, confusion morphing into alarm. "I think that's very generous of you, but I don't know. I mean, it's not always easy to get time off from work. And my sister's baby will be here. And..."

"And?"

"And I didn't know we were even like, a couple or anything. I don't think I'm ready to go away with you. As delightful as it all sounds. I mean, a weekend in New York City, maybe, but not a vacation in the Caribbean." She slid the brochure across the table toward him. "I'm sorry, but no. That's too fast for me."

Alex smiled tightly. "It's a trip, not a proposal. And we're in our thirties...now's the time to take chances, you know? No time to waste, right?"

She stared at him, realizing suddenly what he was.

Alex was a particular sort of boyfriend, the kind a woman tried on to see if he'd make a good husband. But Natalie didn't want a husband, not anytime soon, at least. She wondered what she was to him...probably more of the same, a potential life partner audition as the opening night for traditional adulthood edged ever closer.

Natalie made a poor decision and looked to the bar, at Shane's back and ass, arms propped on the counter. He didn't seem the type to spontaneously whisk her off to the tropics for a week, but he'd certainly be happy to take her home and do terrible things to her all night long. And for better or worse, that's what she wanted from a man at this point in her life.

She stood, chair squeaking against the floor. Rifling in her purse, she set a five on the table beside Alex's brochure in an attempt to even out the balance of the entire date. "Thank you, really, for asking me. But this isn't what I'm looking for. I hope I haven't wasted your time too badly, but I'm not ready for what you are."

"It's just a trip."

Natalie could feel him backpedaling and didn't give him a chance to talk her into it. "And I hope it's refundable, because I really can't go. I don't want to go."

"Nat—"

"I should go. Sorry, again. Have a lovely weekend."

He called after her as she headed for the coat rack. "I'll call you tomorrow, okay? Sleep on it."

She turned to shout, "No, I'll call you," knowing she probably wouldn't. She grabbed her coat and Shane's and tugged at his arm. "Come on, drink up. We're leaving."

He aimed a beady look at Alex. "He get out of line with you?"

"No, worse. Let's go."

"You need me to straighten him out?"

She shoved his bottle into his hand. "Here, drink. Drink drink drink."

Shane drained his beer obediently and followed her out, tugging his jacket on. "What happened?"

"He asked me to go to the Caribbean with him."

Shane laughed. "That bastard."

Natalie made an overblown shuddering noise and dug out her keys as they reached the truck. "I seriously could only have been more terrified if he'd come out with a ring."

They climbed inside and she cranked the heat, not caring if it came out frigid for the first couple of minutes.

"Caribbean," Shane said. "What kind of a sicko offers to take you there when you've got all this to enjoy?" She sensed him gesturing at the street scene as she turned them onto the road.

"It's just way too much, way too fast. Plus don't pretend you're taking his side. I saw you just dying to fuck with him when you guys were talking."

"I won't deny that. But I did what you said. I was good. Even excused myself and everything. Model wingman."

"It's not really a wingman I'm looking for tonight, Shane."

A pause. "Oh?"

"I don't know exactly what it is I want…but it's not a one-way ticket to Husbandville."

"Surgeon, though…"

She shook her head. "All I'm looking for at this point in my life is a chance to make all the mistakes I missed out on while I wasted four years on my idiot ex."

"Right. Well, you let me know if I can help with any of that."

Natalie nodded, eyes on the road, adrenaline pumping as though she'd just avoided a deadly collision with a tanker truck. "Will do."

CHAPTER FIVE

As they drove, Natalie's initial panic eased, mixing with relief then mingling with Shane's odd energy and sparking. She parked and as their doors slammed in the still winter air, she felt free. Even if Alex hadn't spooked her, she didn't really want to be at the bar with him. She didn't really want to be anywhere with Alex. After just a day's reacquaintance with Shane, Alex felt too tidy and too polite. Too slender. Too logical.

Natalie's body had an aversion—an allergy—to good choices when it came to men. She heard six feet three inches of bad decision crunching on the flagstones behind her, felt two hundred-plus pounds of it thumping up the front steps at her heels.

Once inside, they ditched their shoes and coats. Natalie hung up her scarf with a weary sigh, feeling wrung out as both the adrenaline and alcohol left her system. She turned to Shane. "You want a drink?"

His expression was tough to read…part deferential, part smug. "Yeah, sure."

Too wiped to play hostess, she didn't bother asking his preference. She got two glasses and filled them with red wine. When Natalie turned she found him crouched by the fireplace, arranging wood in the hearth.

"Where'd you get all that?" She walked to the couch and set the glasses on the coffee table.

"Grocery store."

"Oh. Thanks."

Shane finished the prep, got the fire started and closed the screen. He stood and tucked his hands into his back pockets. Natalie walked over, keeping a couple feet between them as she joined him, staring into the flames. They stood without speaking for five minutes or more and she felt her body shift again, from exhaustion to curiosity.

Shane broke the silence, clearing his throat. He swallowed before he spoke. "You might feel different tomorrow. 'Bout his offer."

"I won't, but thank you for pretending to want me to make the grown-up choice."

"You deserve somebody good," Shane said softly. "You deserve a surgeon."

The statement made her feel acutely guilty. "Maybe," she muttered. "Just not anytime too soon."

"Somebody who's got their shit together," Shane added.

"You sound like my mom."

He shrugged. "Just some advice from a man who wasted the last year on his own mistakes."

Huffing out a long breath, she registered the workweek's toll in her brain and body. She stepped to the couch to take a seat and patted the spot beside her, slid one of the glasses over on the coffee table.

Shane walked over and sank onto the cushion, the feeling of his weight another sinful reminder of what Natalie should be trying to keep her mind off of. Was he right? Had she just made a stupid mistake? Her sister would probably think so.

Shane picked up his glass and they clinked. "To the surgeon who got away," he said.

She stared at her wine.

He caught the chill in her mood and bumped her shoulder with his big one. "All done talking about it, I take it?"

"It's fine. I'm just tired." She stretched her neck from side to side. "But hey, it's the weekend now. Nothing but sleeping in and being lazy."

"Sounds good. If we don't freeze to death trying to make it to the movies or something."

She shook her head. "Wuss."

"You and me are kinda the same," he said.

Natalie looked up and found him wearing an expression she'd never seen on him before—somber regret. "How do you mean?"

"We're lousy at commitment, but when we do manage it, we pick the worst possible people to do it with."

She nodded. "It's just that the lousy ones are so damn good in bed."

"Heh."

"Maybe the well-adjustedness gene cancels out the decent-lay gene…" She trailed off, brain going fuzzy as her body warmed with ill-advised cravings.

They drank in silence, zoning out to the fire. Natalie wondered if Shane's body was full of questions too, wondering how close they might be to reprising their experience from the previous summer. Without quite meaning to, she let her knee nudge his the next time she leaned forward to set her glass down.

Shane glanced over and caught her eye, then looked away. If he wanted something to happen, he was clearly waiting for her to initiate it.

"You know what I always liked about you, Shane?"

"What's that?"

"How pushy you can be when you want something."

"Like last night?"

Natalie nodded. She toyed with the ring on her middle finger, wondering what he was waiting for.

He cleared his throat but didn't speak.

She eyed him. "What's on your mind?"

"Not sure how I feel about you thinkin' of me as a mistake, I guess."

"I never said that's how I think of you."

"But I know that's what it'd be. Like you cleansing your palate after your doctor left some sour, grown-up, good-decision taste in your mouth."

"And what would I be?" she asked. "I know you came here with something to prove to yourself, about you and women. And I'm fine with that. In fact, I'm honored. I don't want to overthink everything...if we're both looking to use each other, let's just use each other."

"I never used to be the kind of man who overthought things..."

"So don't. Just do what you want."

After a moment's silence, he did. In a flash his hands were on her—holding her jaw, tangling in her hair as his mouth took hers. His aggressive sexual energy knocked reality aside and she met his pace, kissing him back and devouring everything familiar and foreign about his taste and tongue and the low noises rising from his throat.

She pulled back to take in the mean edge in his expression. "That's better."

"Seein' you flirt with him made my blood boil."

"Good."

"Never did play nice with other guys."

She smirked. "Except one."

He leaned into the back of the futon and laced his fingers behind his head. He addressed her knees. "Yeah, 'cept one."

When he next looked up there was fire in those blue eyes. He ravaged her for another minute, kisses steadily slowing until they seemed to simply be sharing the air between their lips.

"Feels like I'm losing you, Shane."

He flared his nostrils and closed his eyes.

She hunched forward and dropped her head into her hands. "Sorry. I shouldn't have said that. Brought him up like that." She sighed deeply and felt Shane rub her back.

"It's okay. Last thing I want's to be all sensitive about it. I just want to be done with it, finally." He kept his hand circling in firm, steady strokes that didn't match the subdued tone of his voice.

"Feels nice," she muttered. It felt different as well, this show of affection from Shane. After a minute she sat up straight, studying his face in the low light from the kitchen. She watched his jaw flex and his Adam's apple jump as he swallowed.

"You want to just call it a night?" she asked, praying he didn't.

"I just wish all this was as easy as it used to be for me. Being with a woman."

"I don't know exactly what you want from me, but whatever it is, you can have it."

No reply, but she felt his heat a split second before his lips touched hers, broad hands cupping her shoulders. He gave her a brief, polite kiss, one that didn't belong to the man she knew. She opened her eyes as he pulled away.

She bit her lip. "If I wanted to be kissed like that, I'd have skipped off to the Caribbean with Alex. You're pretty hopeless at being gentle, Shane. Just kiss me like the thug you are."

He smiled, eyes crinkling with a silent laugh. "Yes ma'am."

The next kiss came swiftly, sloppy for a moment until Natalie's mouth caught up with the ferocity of his. His tongue plunged deep, accompanied by a hungry growl and the rough press of his fingers along her jaw. He let her up for air after a minute's plundering.

Natalie gulped a breath, feeling drunk as she met his gaze. "Much better."

"Yeah, it is."

"What else have you got for me?"

He pulled her closer by the arm, plastering a hand to her back and holding her tight as his mouth crashed down on hers once more. Natalie felt gravity dissolve, felt the cold, dry air dissipate as a heat wave closed in around them. Her hands found his upper arms, squeezing the hard muscle of his biceps and shoulders through his sweater. Sweater…that was all wrong. She tugged at the hem and he broke away enough to peel the top over his head. Natalie's palms took in his warmth and energy as his tongue made promises she knew the rest of his body would have no trouble keeping.

So many things were familiar about Shane—his weight and size, the rough hum of his breath, even his smell. Foreign too, without Gabriel between them, figuratively and otherwise, without the heat and sweat, the dim kaleidoscope of the bar's lights getting her as drunk as the beer.

Natalie wasn't normally one to make a man into a piece of meat, but she knew what Shane had to offer and she wanted it again. Bad. She cupped a palm over the bulge in his jeans and squeezed, his hardness sending a blush from her chest to her cheeks. His mouth released hers as he groaned, eyes shut tight.

"I have to admit, I missed this," she said.

He laughed, the noise sounding choked. "Oh yeah?"

"Yeah."

Shane sat back to unbuckle his belt and open his fly. He'd never been subtle with his sexuality but Natalie didn't want seduction tonight, she wanted the big, bossy, dominant man she'd met in that intoxicating Southern bar—and she wanted him mean. Wanted him jealous and pushy just like the very moment they'd met.

She stroked his thick erection through his underwear and swore she could smell magnolia and the wood of Shane's old house, the sweat of bodies swaying in the shadows.

"You remember the first time we fucked?" he murmured.

"Of course I do. In your living room, that night you made me watch him dance with other women."

Shane nodded.

Natalie peeled his underwear down to expose every hard, tempting inch he'd punished her with all those months ago.

"Yeah." His eyes closed as she touched him, squeezed his shaft and stroked him from the base to the head.

"You're just as big as I remember," she said.

"I bet you're just as warm and hot and wet."

She let him go, stood and shimmied out of her jeans, shed her top so she was in her underwear. She sat, Shane's hands already on her as she took his cock in her palm again. "Find out," she murmured, wedging one knee in the cushions and the other between Shane's thighs.

He accepted the invitation, sliding a coarse hand up her leg, big fingers slipping under her panties to tease her folds. He groaned from deep in his chest, the sound tightening Natalie's fist around him, tightening her pussy.

"Have you been with any women since me?" she asked.

Shane shook his head.

"Good."

"What about you? You fucked that doctor yet?"

"Yeah, I did."

Shane huffed a contemptuous breath through his nose.

"You want to hear all about how much better you are?" An undiplomatic offer, but Natalie liked that about Shane—he had a tacky competitive streak that suited him like an old pair of jeans.

"Yeah. You tell me all about it."

"You're bigger, for one." She held his gaze as she ran a greedy hand up and down his cock. "And harder. You fuck deeper."

He shut his eyes and groaned. "Yeah."

"And you look good when you fuck, Shane. You look good when you fuck Gabriel too."

He groaned again and this time the sound was loaded—loaded with longing and the sting of self-denial, she bet. His free hand pushed hers away and clasped his erection, not stroking, just holding.

"You have no idea how much I've thought about you two when I get off," she whispered.

"You ever think about it when you were with your doctor?" His fist slid up and down, slowly.

Natalie pursed her lips and made a choice to be both indiscreet and honest. "Yeah, I did. I thought about that time you caught me and Gabriel...how your body looked when you fucked him, right on top of me." God, that memory had been her ticket to a speedy orgasm on a hundred lonely nights. Shane's cock pounding his beautiful lover's ass, the gorgeous, happily helpless man pinned between them, Shane's hips driving Gabriel deep inside Natalie with each thrust.

But tonight wasn't about that. It was about the two of them, and to bring in memories that Shane was trying to run from was cruel of her, selfish. She shifted gears, making the fantasy about Shane alone, about getting him all to herself.

"And I've thought about when it was just you and me...the things we did on your floor." She nudged his hand away, squeezed his dick with an eager fist. "And all the things we didn't get around to."

"Before you left without saying goodbye."

"Yeah. Before I escaped."

He swallowed. "Like what?"

"I always wondered how you'd be, with your mouth."

Shane laughed, the sound strangled from whatever her touch was doing to him. "I better warn you now, I expect I'm pretty lousy at going down on women."

"Is that code for you don't want to?" she asked, hand slowing.

"Nope, just a friendly warning. I'm good at all the rough, mean stuff. I never been begged for any repeat oral performances, let's say. Don't think I'm much good at the intricate stuff you ladies need down there."

"Mechanics versus surgeons again," Natalie teased.

The thinly veiled challenge seemed to perk him up. "But I'll give it a damn fine effort." He stood, pushed her coffee table back a couple of feet and nearly toppled the glasses. He got to his knees before her, peeling her panties off in a flash.

All she could think to say was, "Shane." She stroked his short hair as he brought his face close, watching his eyes close as he smelled her. Suddenly she wanted this very much. It was a small, weird gift to bestow, but she wanted to make Shane feel good at this. Plus if he was truly lousy at it, she owed it to womankind to offer some helpful redirection.

"Can I give you constructive criticism?" she asked softly. "If you need any, I mean."

He seemed to consider it a moment, his face retreating an inch, eyes opening to stare at her without focus.

"Never mind, Shane. Just do whatever you—"

"It's not my ego. It's just some stupid fucked-up memory started playing in my head."

"Oh. About him?"

Shane dipped his chin, the tiniest nod. "This ain't the first time in recent history I been on my knees, taking instructions. It's…"

"Here." She tugged at his arms until he stood, urged him to sit beside her. "Tonight shouldn't be about that. Some other time. Tonight I just want you how you are. Big and rough and mean."

"You sure? We got wine and fire and all that. You got candles beside your bed. I'm on your turf. I'm happy to play by your rules, be the sort of man you…you know. Deserve."

"You're the sort of man who makes a woman like me run screaming from a man like Alex." She turned toward him, rubbing her palm up and down his thigh. "Don't let the romantic candles fool you. I've got awful taste in men, Shane. I like bossy, meatheaded jerks who fuck like they're in heat."

"I can do that."

"I know you can." She moved her fingers to his cock, covered again by his shorts.

He moaned softly. "Stand up a sec."

She met his eyes and obeyed.

Shane stood and kicked off his jeans, took the rumpled spare comforter from beside the futon and spread it out on the floor, a couple of feet from the hearth. She approached with slow steps.

"Promise I'll be nice and mean and dirty," Shane said. "But come on, there's a motherfucking fire going. This is the first time I'll get laid up north, so meet me in the middle. Bit of girly romantic ambiance." He nodded to the fireplace. "Remind me what it's like to be with a woman."

"Sure."

Shane let her push his undershirt up his chest then tugged it off for her. His body was just as she remembered, hard and toned from good old-fashioned sit-ups and free weights and manual labor, no gym membership needed.

"Wow." She muttered it without meaning to, her hands compounding the sentiment as she took him in, the contours of his stomach and sides and arms. She'd seen him naked, just the two of them, but they'd been drunk. She'd also seen all this while one hundred percent sober, but with Gabriel suffusing the room with his crazy charisma, she'd still been effectively intoxicated.

Right now Shane seemed stark and alarmingly real, especially coming on the heels of styled, slender Alex. Her hands kept exploring, eyes hypnotized by the swell and contraction of Shane's belly as he breathed. She put her palm to his heart, feeling its beat, faint and rapid behind his firm flesh. Her gaze jumped to his face, plain but handsome, stern features offset by melancholy eyes.

"You may be the sexiest man I've ever seen."

He laughed. "You're forgetting at least one who's got me beat."

She gave his chest a tiny push to feel his solidness. "The sexiest *real* man I've ever seen."

"What d'you mean by 'real'?"

She considered it. "When I'm close to you, I feel like I'm…close to you. With him…I was with him, but it felt like I was just visiting. Or dreaming. You," she said, and stroked his chest and arms, sliding her hands around to admire his strong back. "You feel very tangible. And tomorrow I'll still be feeling it. Sore. He bruises people's psyches. Takes little chips out of people's souls. But you're something else, Shane. Something real." With that, she slid her hand to his cock, felt him go from half-mast to rock-hard in five seconds.

He groaned, hips thrusting in time with her strokes. "Fuck, you make me feel big."

"You are big."

"I know. But lately, even when I feel big, I feel weak too. But not just now." He pushed his shorts down for her, both their pairs of eyes glued to her hand on his dick.

"I want you in charge." Her free hand palmed his hip, feeling muscle and bone and the combined heat of Shane's body and the fire warming his skin. "Just be how you are, tonight."

"How I am ain't something I really know anymore."

"Then find it again."

He nodded. "Hang on." He left her to kick away his shorts and go to his bag, rummaging and returning with a box of condoms.

Natalie smiled. "Looks like you had me pegged when you packed."

He mirrored the grin, getting a rubber out and peeling the plastic open. "You taught me the importance of a good rebound."

Her smile tightened at the word, but there was nothing to be offended by. She and Shane were temporary by virtue of logic and geography, by their own fraught history, by her own disinterest in establishing anything serious. And he'd been one half of her epic rebound, a role she'd never designated as cheap in her memories. Nothing dishonorable in being a rebound.

She took the condom from him and slid it from the wrapper. Shane gave his cock a couple of rough pulls, getting himself as hard as he was in Natalie's fantasies. She rolled the rubber down his length, bit her lip to hide a grin.

"Why don't you lie down?" he asked. "You need a pillow?"

"Nah." She sat, fire dry and hot on one side, the air cool on the other, floor hard beneath the soft blanket. She reveled in the sight of Shane looming above her in the dramatic lighting for a few seconds before he dropped to his knees between her legs.

He nodded at her bra. "Take that off."

Natalie obeyed, reaching behind to unclasp it. Being a guy, Shane probably hadn't noticed she'd worn matching underwear—not quite lingerie but a pretty, lacey midnight blue set—worn it when her intentions had been to see Alex briefly and fully clothed, then head home to sleep alone. Leave it to Natalie's subconscious to prepare for the inevitable.

Shane lowered to his elbows, hands cupping her bare breasts, mouth taking her nipple. Instantly she felt that elemental harshness. She raked her fingernails across his scalp to reinforce the greedy tone of his touch. With the encouragement, he suckled her, roughly, hands squeezing possessively. Her pussy was begging for him already, tight and hungry and impatient. And he was right there, hard and ready to go.

"I want you, Shane."

"You'll get me."

"Make it selfish."

He kissed her breasts until the heat pooling there made her lightheaded, then all the blood rushed between her legs as he braced himself on hard arms. He shifted his knees and hips, cock brushing her folds.

"You ready?"

She reached a hand between her legs to be sure. "You have no clue how ready."

"Good." He angled his cock and Natalie guided him to her entrance. He slid inside with just a hint of resistance, the tiniest taste of enjoyable pain.

"Fuck," she muttered.

"Tell me I'm the biggest you ever had." He pushed deeper.

"You are."

"Tell me you ain't lyin'."

She laughed. "No way. No contest."

"Good," he said again, so exactly the way she loved him—crass and self-satisfied.

"Fuck me, Shane. Be selfish."

The thrusts started slow and deep, punctuated with a shallow moan from Shane each time their bodies met. Natalie watched his cock, everything about the visual precisely what she wanted from a man right now. Strong, hard, on top. She stroked his shoulders and arms, groaned as his thrusts sped.

"Damn, you feel good." His body surged, the impact harsh for a few beats. "So fucking wet."

"So fucking hard," she countered, reaching between them to squeeze the base of his cock between her thumb and first finger. "And thick."

"Take me." Rougher now, the mean slap of his skin against hers mimicking the snap of the firewood. He was taking her order to heart, and as much as Natalie wanted this to be his chance to be greedy, she wanted to come. She moved her fingers to her clit, and caught the change in Shane as she touched herself. His hips slowed.

"Keep it rough," she said.

"Selfish, huh?" His words were broken by his panting breaths.

"I'm so close." Laughably close, considering how intensely she'd needed to do this to climax with Alex the last time they'd had sex.

"Do it," Shane said. He sat back on his heels, hands on his pumping hips, his gaze and the firelight warming Natalie's belly and breasts. The controlled motions of his body contrasted with the wondrous glint in his eyes, his expression belonging to a man who'd never seen a woman naked before. "Goddamn, you look good."

Nowhere near as good as he did. Easiest orgasm ever. Natalie took one last glance at his face then glued her eyes to Shane's driving cock, teased herself for half a minute and lost it. The climax came fast and intense—a flash, not waves. A punch of pleasure that left her dim-witted and still hungry. If there was another one poised to take her, she didn't have a chance to find out. Shane dropped back down, fucked her so hard and fast it nearly knocked her breath out. His grunts were harsh, almost ugly. Wounded and desperate.

"Shane."

"Say it again."

She uttered his name a half dozen times and he came apart, cock thrust deep deep deep as his hipbones ground into hers. Another strangled noise and a few soft pumps then his muscles went slack, chest and stomach lowering to meet hers.

"Wow."

He made a sound like a laugh or cough, took a couple of steadying breaths and collapsed beside her. Natalie turned onto her hip and elbow and slung her other arm across Shane's ribs. She kissed his collarbone.

"Thanks," he mumbled. "You got no clue how bad I needed that."

"Ditto."

He laughed.

"You want to sleep in my bed tonight?"

He met her gaze, eyes shifting in tiny zigzags between hers. "If that's cool with you."

She nodded. "That's how all the best home wreckers operate," she said, teasing herself. "One night on the couch, then the real impositions begin."

Something shifted in Shane's expression. A flicker of sadness passed over his features, lasting just long enough for Natalie to wonder if that wasn't also how Gabriel's path to sharing Shane's bed had unfurled. Then she blinked and found his smile right where it had been.

"Take me to your lair, Miss Natalie."

CHAPTER SIX

S hane awoke to several exotic discoveries. Long, dark hair was tangled around his fingers, soft, full breasts plastered to his chest, smooth sheets enveloping his naked body and Natalie's quiet snores warming his throat.

"Hey." He freed his hand and touched her face, a bit sad to banish her goofy and undignified mouth-breathing sleep expression.

"Hey," she mumbled. Shane could pinpoint the second she remembered who he was.

"It's the weekend," he said.

"Right you are." She glanced beyond Shane's shoulder at her alarm clock and yawned. "Man, I haven't slept past nine in ages. You must have exhausted me."

He smiled, pleased their flirting was getting off to such an early start. "Can I make you breakfast, for old time's sake?"

"You can try...don't know if I have enough eggs, though."

"I'll just bum some off a neighbor if you don't."

She yawned again, so fucking adorable.

Shane licked his thumb and rubbed at the mascara smudge beneath one of her eyes.

"Oh God, I must look awful," she said, instantly alert.

"You look like a woman who got all her sense fucked out," Shane said. "No prettier sight in the whole world."

"You're in charge of coffee." She slid from his arms and the sheets and stood. Shane admired her body in the dim, pink light leaking in through her red curtains. "I call the shower," she said, grabbing a robe off a hook by the door and spoiling Shane's fun.

He lay in her covers a few minutes longer, feeling calm. And calm was something he hadn't felt in a long time. When the water shut off in the next room he got up, cursed at the cold and hurried to the living room for a fresh change of clothes. Natalie emerged just after he'd figured out how to work a coffee bean grinder.

"What have you done to my kitchen?" She clutched the robe closed between her breasts and eyed the black grounds peppering the counter.

"Your coffee's too complicated. But don't worry, I'll tidy up."

"How much did you put in the machine?"

"Plenty." Shane took a good look at the vee of skin between her lapels and got exactly what he'd hoped for—filthy ideas. "Get dressed before I maul you."

"Yes, sir." She patted his shoulder and disappeared into her room.

Shane grinned, watching the drops become a stream as the coffeemaker roused. He hadn't felt this way toward a woman in ages. Fucking relief, too. He hadn't broken his heterosexuality. He'd let Gabriel dick around and rewire it for almost a year, but there was something there to be salvaged.

Shane found what he needed, eggs and butter, bread and frozen sausage patties. He made Natalie the finest breakfast he knew how to, even set the table.

"Wow," she said, coming out of her room in shamrock-patterned pajama bottoms and a button-up sweater.

"You want cream and sugar?" Shane asked from the counter.

"Just cream. Thanks." She took a seat and smiled at him. "We playing house today?"

"Works for me." He got her coffee poured and walked over to set it beside her plate.

"Why thank you." Her smile started out teasing but faded to shyness after a moment. A glimmer of sad in there, even.

Shane's own mood took a dip and he headed to the stove to flip the sausages.

"Oh Jesus, Shane."

He turned to find her with mug in hand, face pinched up as if she'd sucked a lemon. "Too hot?"

"A bit...*strong*," she said.

"Good. It'll put hair on your chest."

"Oh yes, just what every girl wants for herself."

Shane took a sip from his own mug. "That *is* strong. But that's how you like it up here, right? All shitty and burned-tasting like Starbucks?"

She smiled. He liked making her smile. He'd be doing as much of that as possible while he was here. *While* he was here... Then what? Back to the bar, back to his empty bed with no romantic prospects. He'd have to get on one of those online dating sites, like a twelve-step program to keep him from falling back into his old, weak patterns with Gabriel. Maybe Natalie would be willing to help him put a profile together, one that'd appeal to a woman like her.

Shane grabbed the toast when it sprang up then carried the pan over to the table and slid food onto their plates.

She picked up her fork. "Thank you very much. If this is half as good as the sex, I owe you."

"If this is half as good as the sex, the sex wasn't near good enough," Shane said. "Like to think I fuck better than frozen sausages."

She shook her head. "Semantics. You mind if I turn the radio on?"

"Go for it."

She went to the stereo by the TV and turned it on low, a soft drone of monotone voices that made Shane's eyes roll.

"What?" she asked, sitting back down. "I like to hear the news."

"Fucking NPR."

She laughed. "Tell me you wouldn't prefer Rush Limbaugh, please."

"Nah…just don't think I'm listening to that liberal bull once I convince you to move down south and have my kids."

She laughed so hard she snorted. "Wow, what a very tempting offer, Mr. Broussard. I'll leave my shoes here, shall I? Doesn't sound like I'll be needing them down there, all barefoot and pregnant."

Shane enjoyed joking with her, felt only a tiny sting that she clearly found the idea impossible.

They traded regional insults for a few minutes, then a story about Medicare reform came on the radio and Natalie shushed him. He freshened their cups and she shook her head as the segment wrapped, annoyed by whatever the droning had been about.

"Government trying to mess with your precious old people?" he asked, taking his seat.

"Don't get me going." Her mood had clearly darkened, lips pursed to a tight line. Silence reigned for a few minutes as they sipped, and Shane knew whatever was going on between her ears wasn't about health care.

He poked her shin with his bare foot beneath the table. "Hey."

She met his eyes, smile weak. "Hmmm?"

"I lost you there. What's on your mind?"

"Oh, I'm just trapped in my own head."

"Join the club."

She smiled again, gaze on her mug. "It's really nice having you here…"

"But?"

"I just want to make sure this is the same for you as it is for me."

"How do you mean?"

She winced through another sip of coffee then finally looked at him. "You keep teasing me about marrying you, and I know you're kidding. But I want to make sure there's not any grains of truth hidden in there. Because I'm not looking to settle down anytime soon."

Shane kept his face neutral, casual, hiding the sting to his ego. "Course not. This is a rebound."

"Good. I just wanted to make sure we're on the same page."

"You upset you decided to screw up what you had with your surgeon for a few nights of southern comfort?" he asked, nudging her again.

"No, not at all. I wasn't really feeling that, with Alex. He's a good guy but I won't be losing any sleep over him. I just know you've spent the past year not really knowing where you stood with Gabriel, so I want to be the opposite. Crystal clear." She smiled at him. "But this is really lovely, being this way with you for a little while. You're pretty much exactly what I go for in a nutshell, except not all the terrible parts."

"What do you mean?"

"Well, you're sort of a bully. And an ass. No offense. But you aren't really. Well, you are…but not just for the sake of being that way. Anyhow, you're stubborn and tacky and a bit annoying. All the things I fall for, but I bet you treat women nicely."

"I try. They don't usually stick around very long though."

"What's your longest relationship been?" she asked, and the question chilled Shane's blood.

"With a woman," she amended, but no matter, the truth would still condemn him.

"Maybe six months."

Her face fell. "Oh."

"I know, my track record ain't so hot."

"No, it's not that… I was afraid I just jabbed your bruise there. I didn't know you and him…"

"I don't count that as a relationship," Shane said quickly.

Natalie made a little noise, not exactly a laugh. "You don't?"

"No. I mean, you're practically the only person who knows about it, anyhow. You and a handful of drunk women who've passed through the bar."

"Heh. Well, not to be contrary, Shane, but what you and him were, that's got to be more intense than most people's marriages. I can't believe you wouldn't *count* it."

"He was never just mine," Shane said.

Natalie licked her lip, holding back a thought.

"What?"

She frowned then drained her cup. "Whose fault is that, Shane? That you guys weren't…you know. More?"

He rankled. "He needed more than I could give him."

"Maybe he needed to be with somebody who'd admit what you were to more than just the spare women who passed through your bar."

He didn't reply, not willing to explore that idea.

"Maybe he wanted acknowledgment as much as you wanted fidelity. How did he take it, anyway? You never told me how the breakup went."

Shit, busted. Shane cleared his throat, eyes escaping just as Natalie raised her own to stare at him.

"What?" she asked. "Was it awful? I mean of course it was awful. Was it ugly?"

"It ain't technically happened yet."

"Oh."

"Don't worry, you ain't like, the other woman or anything."

She laughed. "I have been before… Oh great. Now you've both cheated on each other with me."

"It ain't cheating when there's no commitment."

She squinted at him. "What did you do, Shane? Just drive away? Tell him you're going on a road trip?"

"I didn't tell him shit. I just left."

She blinked, dark brows pinched together into a perplexed line. "What about your staff? You told them but not Gabriel? He's going to hear it from them instead of you?"

"He knows. He called me yesterday, actually. Told him where I was. He don't care. Just misses having a place to sleep."

"He doesn't have keys? After a whole year together?" she asked.

"Like I said, it ain't a relationship."

"That is such a load of bullshit. And anyway, he called yesterday and you didn't tell him you're through with him? What did you talk about?"

"Nothin' important. He just wanted to know where I was… But I'll tell him we're done, next time he calls. If he calls."

She shook her head, clearly exasperated. "You better. You owe him that much."

Shane started. "I don't owe that man shit."

"You love him. Or you did. You did when I was with you both."

"I don't know *what* that was anymore."

She huffed out an annoyed breath and leaned back in her chair. Winding her hair in her fingers, she asked, "What do you want for yourself, Shane? How do you want things to be in five years?"

"I want… I want a little bit of what my momma gave me. You know, nothing fancy or anything, just like…closeness. Like family."

"And you can't see Gabriel as a part of that?"

He stared at the floor. "No. He's the opposite of that. He's the thing that keeps me from changing and moving forward."

"And you don't think any of the blame for you guys not being more than—"

"Listen. I know where you're going with all this, but come on. What future is there? We can't start a family—that's ridiculous."

She opened her mouth but he cut her off with a raised hand. "Not just 'cause it's two dudes. Because he still does what he did with you, with other women. He still needs more than I can give him. Even if I *was* gay or whatever, we're not ever going to be me-and-him, happy rainbow flag couple with two kids and a lap dog, because there's always going to be some woman sneakin' into our Sears-fucking-family portrait. Like, 'Gee, where's Daddy tonight?' 'Oh, I dunno, Shane Junior, he didn't come home so he's probably busy fucking some random chick someplace. Let's hope he gets bored with her and comes home soon.'"

"That's harsh."

He pushed a laughing breath through his nose. "That wisdom from the woman who fucked him in my bed while I was out fixing to tow her car."

She made a grim face.

"Anyhow, forget it. I love him the way a drunk loves booze, and as long as I act like the habit's doing me any good, the further away my chance at a cozy little family life drifts."

Natalie sighed, sounding as fed up with the topic as Shane was. "Fine."

"I appreciate what you're trying to do though," he added. "I know you're a chick and you think love conquers all and that happy-sappy bull, and like him and me are destined for each other or something."

She laughed. "I'm not that obnoxious, Shane. I just...I dunno. Whatever weird glue holds you two together, it's not just sex. I know you're going to roll your eyes at me for saying it, but it's special, whatever you two have."

Shane did roll his eyes, as hard as he possibly could.

"Fine, forget it. Don't know why I'm trying to talk you out of it when here I've got you all to myself for a couple weeks."

Shane warmed to the change in topic. "See? Flirtin' with you's so much better than free relationship counseling."

"Yeah. Anyway. What do you want to—" A tinkling noise from someplace cut her off and Natalie got up and disappeared into her bedroom. Another tinkle and Shane heard her say, "Hello?"

He tensed, wondering if it was Alex.

"No, Mom. I just had breakfast. What's up?"

Shane relaxed back in his seat.

"Oh crap, seriously? I guess I could... I have a guest visiting. How long will it take?"

Shane stood and gathered the dirty dishes.

"No, I can swing that. Is Dan helping? Oh good. That shouldn't be too bad then. Yup. Yeah, see you over there."

Shane heard a beep then Natalie joined him in loading the dishwasher. "I have to abandon you for a couple hours, to help my mom with her aunt."

"I can help," Shane said.

"That's sweet of you, but it's not the intro you want to my family. My great-aunt's pretty much bedridden and me and my brother-in-law are going to head over to her place and help her bathe and dress, then my mom's taking over for the afternoon. I guess her caregiver got in a minor car accident this morning, had to go to the hospital for an X-ray."

"Bummer."

"Yeah. This sort of drama's never-ending in my family. We all seem to live into our nineties, but we don't do it very gracefully."

Shane nodded. "That how you got into nursing?"

"Yeah, probably. I had two sets of really awesome grandparents, lots of relatives from that generation." She laughed. "I like old people. They tell it like it is."

"You sure I can't help?"

"No, thank you. Dan is man-power enough for the task. And my mom would be mortified if that was how you got jumped into the clan. Let her do it her way, over dinner."

"I won't argue with anybody's momma. I'll just snoop around your apartment while you're gone, make a list of things that need fixing. That'll keep me busy while you're at work next week."

"Oh that'd be good actually…my landlady's sweet, but she's a bit slow about fixing things."

Shane swelled a bit, pleased for the mission. "I'm your man then."

"For the next two weeks, yes. You're my man."

* * *

Shane returned from the hardware store, two bags full of boyfriendly assignments dangling off his arm and his toolbox in hand. He shut the door with his hip and dumped the purchases on Natalie's counter, flexed his fingers to banish the stiffness. Distraction might not be the same as actual relief, but it felt pretty damn close.

Shane looked around as he ditched his coat, trying to decide which project to tackle first. Her broken burner was a good place to start, that or the slow leak under her bathroom sink—

His pocket buzzed, and, idiot that he was, Shane assumed it'd be her. He smiled as he fished his phone out, prepared to brag about his to-do list.

Two-two-five area code.

"Fuck me." Well, it had to happen sometime. Best that time came when Natalie was out. He pushed the talk button. "Yeah."

"Hello, Shane." Goddamn, that voice like angels fucking.

He wandered into the den. "Hey. Been waiting for you to call again." Shane toyed with a coaster on Natalie's side table.

"Oh yeah?" Practically a purr.

Shane cleared his throat, which did nothing to banish the invisible hand now choking him. "Yeah. I wanted to tell you, you and me, we're done."

A long pause. "Done?"

"I can't have you in my life anymore. I'm sorry. I got to fire you too, and I don't want you comin' round to see me or to have a drink or anything else."

"What I done, Shane?"

Shane sighed. He'd forgotten how hard breakups were even when you weren't in love with someone, and this was the first time he'd attempted one with someone he *did* feel something for. Maybe not love, maybe something far more dismal and obsessive, but it still hurt as though his ribs were being snapped, one by one. He sank into Natalie's recliner.

"Don't make this sound like some kind of regular old breakup," Shane said. "I didn't know what the fuck you and me were when we started, and I still don't know. But I know we ain't growin' old and losin' our teeth together and it has to end sometime. So it may as well be now." He took a deep breath. "Don't...don't think it's not hard. But I gotta move on with my life and we both know that can't happen with you in it."

More silence, then a soft, "I see."

Shane wondered if anybody had ever been the one to try to shake Gabriel first before...he doubted it. Well, Natalie, maybe.

"I'm sorry about the job," Shane said.

A faint laugh, the one Shane was used to feeling warm his neck. "You sorry 'bout the job?"

"And the place to crash," he offered.

Another laugh. "Fuck you too, Shane." An old-school click as Gabriel hung up from six states away.

Shane took a deep, shaky breath to keep from vomiting. "Fuck…" Then suddenly, vomiting was looking pretty desirable. Shane's sinuses stung and he panicked. No fucking way he'd cry. Not over this, over the end of a year of hot, messed-up sex, not over hearing that warm voice go so utterly icy. His nose began to run, tear-making machinery clearly backfiring after months of disuse. "Fuck."

He went to the kitchen for a paper towel and blew his nose, stared at the ceiling and blinked until the sensations faded. Shane took a deep breath, another, a hundred more, gathered his wits and looked around Natalie's apartment.

Item one, broken burner. He flipped the TV on, loud, flipped his toolbox open. Flipped a switch in his head and got down to work.

* * *

Natalie returned home later than she'd hoped, not quite one o'clock. Spotting the tools and bits of hardware scattered all over her counter, she was pleased to see Shane hadn't been left at a loose end in her absence.

"Shane?"

His voice came from the bathroom. "Ow."

She walked to the threshold to find him rubbing the back of his head, crouched before the open cupboard beneath her sink.

"Sorry to startle you. Don't tell me you're fixing that drip."

"Yep."

"You're amazing. The mildew's been getting worse by the week."

"All set." He got to his feet and rinsed his hands, checked his handiwork and shut the tap off. "Just a rusted-out washer."

"Well, I'll cook you whatever you want for lunch as payment. Thank you."

"Cook it on the back right burner, if you want. I fixed that too."

She bounced on the balls of her feet and clapped. "What do you want to go back to Louisiana for, anyhow? Just stay here and be my handyman. Just adhere to the no-shirt rule next time." She plucked at the sleeve of his tee.

"Tempting." Shane smiled, but she could sense something off about him, a strain in the gesture.

"You okay?"

"Yeah. I'm fine." He gathered up his tools, the world's worst imitation of blasé.

"I won't pry, but you don't look very fine." She touched his shoulder, studied his deepening frown.

He headed back to the main room. "I just talked to him." He kept his back to her as he replaced things in his toolbox.

"Oh. Who called who?"

"He called me."

"Did you...you know. Tell him?"

"I told him." Shane shut the lid, the sound making her jump.

"How'd he take it?"

Shane tidied up the mess of hardware, putting things back in their shopping bags. "He took it. Message received."

"Right. So, if I can ask, how do you feel now?"

He seemed to think about it, rubbing his chest, massaging the ache he must be feeling there, the one Natalie had nursed the entire drive north from Louisiana.

"It fuckin' hurts," he said, voice quavering on the final word.

"I'll bet."

He walked to the dining area and sat, dropped his head into his hands and pressed his fingers to his temples.

"You want to talk about it?"

"Nothing to say, really. It's over. He was pissed but he couldn't care less. Didn't ask me to reconsider or offer to change or nothin'. Just a fuck-you and he hung up on me. Probably just called wanting more fucking phone sex, anyhow."

More phone sex? Natalie sighed and pulled a chair up next to his, circling her palm over his back. "Sorry, Shane."

"Yeah."

"Do you feel relieved at all, now that it's done?"

"No."

She slumped in her seat, gave his strong arm a squeeze.

"But I will," he went on. "Just feel like my heart's been turned inside out right now, that's all. It'll fade. I'm glad it's done with, anyhow, even if I feel like shit."

"Anything I can do to make it easier?"

He sat up straight and blinked at her, eyes bloodshot but no tears glinting. "Nothing special. Just put up with me, I guess. I hope I don't spend the rest of this visit mopin' around all miserable."

"You can if you want," she offered.

"Give me one day, maybe two."

"Two days after the breakup of a year-long…whatever you guys were? You can mope for longer—"

"Two days. Tops. I wasted enough time on that freeloader already."

"If you say so."

Shane stood. "I say so. When the smoke clears I'll feel fucking fantastic, sweetheart. First day of the rest of my life."

And I'll be the first woman who lets you down, first one who won't come anywhere close to replacing him. "Whatever you say, Shane."

CHAPTER SEVEN

Though it hadn't been the most cheerful weekend in history, Natalie wasn't ready to head back to work on Monday. Even with a cloud of heartache hovering above Shane, it'd been nice relaxing with him for a couple of days. They'd accomplished little aside from watching movies, cooking meals, building fires and zoning out together, but it had been the right prescription.

They'd had sex on Saturday night, slow and a bit melancholy, a bit drunken. Sunday they'd tried, but it had dissolved into a long make-out session, pleasant and easy, no pressure. It was strange to see Shane rendered even remotely delicate, though it didn't dampen Natalie's affection for him. She wanted him to feel safe with her, and it seemed a good sign that he was opening up as freely as he was.

Natalie stood up straight at the residence's front desk as her phone vibrated in her pocket. She feared Alex's number but breathed easily at the sight of her older sister's. She flipped it open. "Hey, sis."

"Heya. I'm calling about dinner tonight," Alicia said.

"Is it still on?"

"Yeah, but I asked Mom if we can move it to my place. My hormones are going all psycho-nurture-mode on me and I really want to cook. Does that work for you? Around six?"

"Yeah, no problem." Natalie shuffled some papers on the counter. "I um, I was going to bring a friend along, if Mom didn't say."

"She did. Is this the famous doctor we've been waiting to meet?"

Natalie laughed. "Oh no. That's over, actually."

Alicia offered one of her flustered sighs of amusement, overdone, older-sister false superiority. "Sounds like old ricochet rebound Natalie is back in full effect then."

"It's not quite like that. He's really just a friend. I met him on my road trip home last summer. He came to visit unexpectedly."

"O-kaaaay…"

Natalie wandered to the break room around the corner, finding it mercifully empty. "Well, maybe we're slightly more than friends, but there's nothing technically romantic going on. He just ended this insanely complicated relationship. I'm not looking to follow that."

"Sounds very dramatic."

Natalie smirked, trying to think up an analogy her librarian sister would appreciate. "He's got a sort of Humbert Humbert thing going on with his ex."

"Oh… Natalie."

She cringed then laughed. "Sorry, not like that…*nothing* like that. He's just a bit tortured about the whole thing. Anyhow, don't ask him about it, he's here trying to move on."

"Well, he sounds like a baggage salesman, but bring him over. Dan will be happy for some male company for a change. Does this guy like football?"

"I have no idea, actually…but he's very man's mannish. He drinks whiskey and swears a lot. I'm sure they'll find something to talk about while you and me and Mom go on and on about birth plans and baby names. In fact, I might just join them."

"Sounds intriguing. Can't wait to meet him."

"See you at six."

* * *

Shane looked up from the newspaper as Natalie's key sounded in the lock. She stepped inside and spotted him, offering a warm smile to offset the pink in her wind-chapped cheeks and nose.

"Hey you." She set her purse on the counter. "How you feeling?"

Like I'm dying. He shrugged. "Just peachy. How was work?"

"Pretty quiet, actually." Natalie unwound her scarf and hung up her coat, glanced around at the droning TV and the lights on in the kitchen and living room. She made an "it's hot" *whew* noise and fanned herself with the mail. "I'm not made of money you know, Broussard. What did you set the thermostat on?"

"Eighty."

"Jesus. Does that pass for room temperature in Louisiana?" She tossed her mail on top of the microwave.

"Well, the sun sets here at about noon, best I can tell, and it's so cold my joints ache like I'm some old grandpa. Plus I figured if I made it hot enough you'd just drop your clothes right there on the floor." He stood and wandered to the counter, slapping on an evil grin he hoped would hide how damn much his insides still hurt.

Natalie pursed her lips, disapproval on her face.

"What?"

"You don't have to act all brave around me," she said quietly.

Shane rolled his eyes. "And you don't have to act like my whole family just died. I broke up with him. It sucks. I'll be fine. You gave me my two days of self-pity. Now I suck it up like a big boy."

"If that's what you want me to believe, I'll pretend to."

He bit back a defensive reply, smiled grimly instead. "Thanks."

"So we're heading to my sister's for dinner tonight, if you still want to meet my family. My mom will be there too, and my brother-in-law. Do you like football?"

"I like beer."

"There will likely be beer."

"Then I like football just fine."

Natalie disappeared to shower and change, and Shane toyed with an urge to join her. In the end he decided against it, fearing he might not be able to rise to the occasion. Shame. He could have used the distraction, and a reminder that Natalie made him happy too. Made him happy and made him dinner, made him welcome. Hell of a lot better than making him lie awake nights, wondering where she was.

Then again, she didn't make his brain and body convulse when she sang or spoke or walked into a room.

"Fucking magic," he muttered, and went back to not paying attention to the TV and paper.

At half past five they shrugged into their coats and Shane insisted they take his truck. Driving on the stupid icy roads would keep his mind off the sour ache in his belly. Natalie navigated them twenty miles east to her sister's place, a duplex among dozens of others in a tidy little personality-free development. Natalie led them up the steps, heading inside without bothering to knock.

"Hello?"

A man's friendly voice came from down a short stretch of hallway. "Heya, Nat. I'm in the den. Girls are in the kitchen."

"Hey, Dan." She took Shane's coat and hung it beside her own in a closet. They headed to the den, where Dan was camped out in a recliner watching a pre-game report. Natalie waved.

Dan stood upon noticing a stranger, walked to Shane and gave his hand a solid shake. "Hey, I'm Dan. Natalie's brother-in-law."

"Shane. I'm her…" He raised an eyebrow at Natalie.

"Friend. Date. Something," she concluded with a shrug, clearly comfortable not knowing the answer. "Shane's visiting from Louisiana for a couple weeks."

"Wow, did you ever pick the worst time to visit upstate," Dan said. "I grew up in Arizona and I barely made it through my first fall here. Then the first blizzard hit. Jesus."

Shane smirked, decided Dan was all right. Tall, clean-cut, solid in that previously athletic, now-slowly-going-to-seed fashion.

"Anyhow, intrepid of you to make the trip. You fly?" Dan asked.

"Nope, drove."

"Brave soul."

"I better introduce Shane to the ladies," Natalie said.

"Go to it. If you like football, there's beer in the crisper," he said to Shane, taking his seat again.

"Noted."

Natalie led Shane down the hall and through the dining room.

"Seems like a good guy," he said.

"Yeah, they've been together for like eight years now. I heartily approve. Hello?" she called into the kitchen.

"Come on in!"

Two women were at the far side of the counter, matching cups of tea steaming beside a furniture catalog. They looked up at the same time, so clearly mother and daughter, both with practical haircuts, brown eyes, curious smiles.

"Hey guys. This is Shane. Not the doctor," she elaborated. "He's the one who fixed my truck when I broke down last summer on the way back from Florida."

"Oh right," Natalie's sister said, and Shane wondered exactly what kinds of details Natalie may have shared about that trip. She rounded the counter to greet them, bringing her extremely round middle with her.

"Wow," Shane said. "How many months are you?"

"Eight and a bit. Nice to meet you, Shane. I'm Alicia." She gave him a handshake, the feminine kind, with her other warm palm set on top of Shane's cold knuckles.

Their mother came next, shaped not unlike Shane's own late mother, slender and plump at the same time. Soft. She too gave Shane's hand a shake. "I probably won't trick you into thinking Natalie's got two sisters, will I?"

"You can try, ma'am."

"Oh, ma'am? It's that bad?" she teased, patting her face.

"It's a Southern thing," Natalie said.

"Anyhow, Sandra will do," she said.

"Miss Sandra," Natalie added with a grin.

Shane smiled. "Miss Sandra, then."

"Much better. You two take a seat. Have some wine," Sandra said, waving at the breakfast bar stools.

"Excuse me, who's hosting this dinner?" Alicia asked. "But yeah, help yourselves. We're just bickering over changing tables." She tapped the catalog.

Natalie took a seat and looked around. "Where's dinner?"

"In the oven."

Natalie flared her nostrils. "It's not pot roast, is it?"

Alicia frowned. "Are you not doing red meat?"

"No, it's fine. I just made it for Shane the other day."

"It's the only thing the women in this family know how to cook," Sandra said.

"Are you guys competitive?" Shane asked, glancing between Natalie and her sister. "Am I going to get the third degree about whose is better?"

"Mine's better," Alicia said.

"I beg to differ," Natalie cut back, faking offense.

Sandra shook her head. "Mine's better, but no matter. Have some wine, you two."

"I'll just have a beer, if that's okay," Shane said, heading to the fridge.

"Whatever you like."

He grabbed a bottle of microbrew from the crisper drawer. Sinking into an easy chair and zoning out to the TV wasn't a bad invitation, but Shane liked the company and the voices of women, especially in conjunction with the smell of roasting meat. Alicia passed him a bottle opener and he popped his cap, took up his seat beside Natalie. He felt instantly if irrationally comfortable here, listening to her relatives argue about beech- versus pine-finished wood. Shane scooted his stool closer to Natalie's, close enough for their thighs to touch. She glanced at him, and Shane felt his stomach unknot itself. He felt his pain lessen before he even took a sip of alcohol.

* * *

Dinner was pleasant, Natalie's family all at ease teasing one another. Shane's good mood stayed with him. He didn't say much, just answered all the questions they had about his trip and was then allowed to relax. Alicia's upcoming due date dominated most of the conversation, and Shane was happy for the chance to lean back and simply enjoy the atmosphere.

Alicia looked a lot like Natalie...a sort of future version of Natalie. Alicia's dark hair was shorter and straighter and she had a healthy length of gray in the roots coming in on top, about eight months' worth, Shane imagined. She was Natalie with no frills...a bit frumpy, though Shane figured the woman had bigger concerns than stylishness at this point in her life. He tried to picture Natalie pregnant and practical, but those heels he associated with her wouldn't go away. Neither would her words from a few days ago. *I'm not looking to settle down anytime soon.*

Alicia set her fork aside, leaning forward to eyeball Shane with a smirk. "So come on, Shane. What's your verdict?" She nodded at his plate.

He honestly couldn't say one pot roast was better than the other. The only difference he could find was that Natalie used regular potatoes and Alicia used sweet potatoes, and he liked both equally. "If you're twisting my arm, I have to say Natalie's, since she could poison the next meal she cooks me."

"Good answer," Natalie said.

"But if Miss Sandra wants to have us over before I head back down south, I might have to change my answer."

"Yes, you would," Sandra said, with a teasing squint at her daughter.

Natalie turned to the window as a gust of wind rattled the blinds. "Yikes. I didn't think it was supposed to start snowing again until after midnight."

"Yeah," Dan said. "It might change to freezing rain too."

"We should head out before it gets nasty." Natalie pushed out her chair and began collecting dirty dishes.

"I'll do that." Alicia stood and hurried to take over hostessing duties.

"No, *I'll* do that," Dan said. He wrested the plates from his wife's hand and got to work cleaning up.

Natalie and Shane and Sandra got their layers on and many good-nights and nice-to-meet-yous were tendered. Shane tailed Natalie's mother through the snowy night until her little sedan turned down a street a few blocks from Natalie's house.

Shane turned to her. "I like your family, Miss Natalie."

"Thanks. I think they liked you too."

He smiled to himself. "I like that you're all girls, right down to the bun in your sister's oven."

"What's Dan? Chopped liver?"

"Anyhow, that was nice, just being around women."

Natalie nodded, eyeing Shane, nibbling her lip. "Your dad wasn't around much, was he?"

Shane shook his head and looked to the road. "They were married until I was ten, but even then I didn't see much of him. He was a world-class shit. Still is."

"So it was just you and your mom, for the most part?"

"And my grandmother and my Aunt Marie, and a heck of a lot of gossipy neighbors and clients... My momma worked as a hairdresser, out of our house. I was like one of those feral kids, lost in the woods, raised by wolves. The lone boy raised by a giant pack of Southern women."

"You still turned out to be a big old macho mechanic. I guess nature's stronger than nurture."

Shane laughed. "I think that was necessity—had to pick up the skills my mom and aunt and grandmother wanted me to have. Handy, manly skills they couldn't be bothered with."

"Gotcha. And Gabriel..." she began.

Shane hid a flinch and took a deep breath through his nose. Still, it didn't hurt as much as it had even a few hours ago.

"He was raised by his grandmother too, wasn't he?"

Shane nodded. "I think 'raised' might be a strong word, but yeah. He grew up in her house."

"What happened to his mom?"

"I don't really know. He never talked much about her. I assumed she's dead, maybe killed herself."

He turned to catch Natalie's eyes widening in the orange glow of the streetlights. "That's a pretty big assumption to make."

"Just a feeling I got, from the way he goes all blank when the topic comes up."

He sensed her nodding in his periphery. "And my folks got divorced when I was four, and me and Alicia only saw my dad a couple times a month… I guess we're all in the same camp. Raised by women."

"Okay when you're a girl, yourself."

Natalie laughed. "Didn't give me the best instincts when it came to the guys I tend to get mixed up with. But yeah, my mom did a good job. Just like yours. Maybe not so much Gabriel's grandmother."

"Not his fault she's crazy."

"What kind of crazy?" Natalie asked.

"Couldn't tell you for sure, but it sounds like maybe schizophrenic. Some kind of delusions—he said she talked to ghosts like they were right there, in the room. She'd look right through you and talk to someone who wasn't there."

Natalie turned the heater up a notch. "Wow, that's creepy."

Shane nodded. "But she was deep into all sorts of old-school voodoo bullshit, so I think everybody just figured she was eccentric, or like a real-deal witch, if you believe in that crap. He said everyone called her a witch when he was growing up. Anyway."

She made a sound, not quite a laugh. "Jeez, I'm sorry. I keep asking about him and you're here trying to forget."

"Yeah, like that'll ever happen."

She met his eyes at a red light. "Do you regret your decision?"

He shook his head. "It was a necessity, not a decision. But I have to say, I get what everybody means when they talk about heartache. Since I left town it's been fucking hurtin', right here." He rubbed a spot on his chest. "Worse since that last phone call. Feels like some sadistic surgeon snuck in while I was sleepin' and took it out with a dirty scalpel."

"That sucks."

"You got no idea."

"And you're done with him, because being with him precludes you having a family someday?"

"Or getting any fucking sleep at night, wondering what he's up to. We've been over all this before."

"You could have both, maybe."

"Both what?" He slowed the truck and parked in front of her house.

"Well, I'm not sure what the women in Louisiana are like, but there's got to be a few who'd like you, who want a family…and who'd understand and wouldn't mind you still seeing him."

Shane huffed out a breath, incredulous. "What kind of woman would ever put up with that? With her man bangin' some other guy on the side?" He shut the engine off.

Natalie smiled. "Some woman like me, maybe."

"No, you wouldn't."

"Maybe not *me*, but some woman. Maybe. Who'll see you're a good man. You're a hard worker. As bad as you have it for Gabriel, I bet you've never missed work over him, or let your employees down. I mean, I was in your house basically as the enemy and you were still kind to me. In your way."

"You'd put up with your man going behind your back with another man?"

"Going behind my back? No, of course not. But if it somehow was you and me and Gabriel again, it wouldn't be behind my back. What you two have, as sort of obsessive and intense as it is… I think there's a purity about it. I think the fact that you two have been together for a year when you claim the relationship's nothing but lust is really saying something."

Shane aimed a skeptical look her way.

"I'm not suggesting you guys need to become a married couple or anything. I'm just saying there are sane, open-minded women out there, ones who might be cool with being your partner and maybe the mother of your kids, and they'd be okay with you still getting what you need from Gabriel, for as long as it's important to you. I mean, why settle, Shane?"

"That is *the* most retarded idea I've ever heard."

Natalie shrugged. "Fine then. Have a blast going the rest of your life without whatever it is he makes you feel. That, or have a fucking blast going back to him and wallowing in your dirty little secret and never having the family I'm pretty sure you want. And deserve."

He shook his head, utterly unconvinced. Cold air seeped into the cab, making him shiver.

"Or," she went on, "find another woman like me, who not only gets that you need him, but who's felt it too. One who doesn't think you should have to choose, as long as you can keep your priorities straight if there's a kid involved."

"Can't raise a kid in the middle of a years-long threesome, girl."

"Kids have been raised in way worse. Kids grow up in families where their parents can't stand each other. Maybe you'll find the right woman and yours will be raised by three people who're all nuts about each other."

"And get the tar beat out of them in school 'cause everyone knows they got three parents gettin' up to sick shit together."

"There's such a thing as discretion."

Shane frowned, body antsy and agitated. "You know what? I appreciate all this happy, free-love liberal bullshit you're trying to comfort me with, but I'm all done talkin' about it now. I want my normal life back. Period. Hetero or bust."

"Fine."

He pocketed his keys. They climbed out and slammed their doors in the thin winter air, the noise startling Shane and setting his nerves back on edge. He followed her up the steps, body screaming with its own ideas to drown out his brain. He waited for Natalie to hang her coat up in the front hall then he grabbed her—a firm hand around her wrist, the other on her shoulder. Probably rougher than was polite, but the look on her face was amusement, not alarm.

"You need some distracting, Shane?"

He narrowed his eyes, cast them down at the gritty floorboards between their feet and let his irritation drift away. He looked back up at her face in the dim light. "You're better than just a distraction."

Her lips pursed to a narrow line and her gaze dropped to his chest. She peeled her gloves off and took his zipper pull, opened his jacket and stroked her knuckles over his sweater, his heart. "You have room left in there for anybody after him?"

The words hit Shane like a sock in the gut, and for once he didn't try to hide the flinch. "I got room. If anybody'd want to be with me. With whatever's left of me now."

"There's plenty, Shane."

He swallowed, studying her smooth, pale skin in the ambient streetlight. He leaned in, pressing his cold mouth to hers. Their breaths warmed each other's skin, her hot, wet tongue reminding Shane of a reality beyond the snow and ice and black night, reminding him of other parts of Natalie, someplace he wanted to be, to lose himself in for as long as humanly possible.

"Why don't you go light all them candles you got beside your bed," he said, lips against hers.

She stole the lead from him, kissed him so deep and dirty his cock ached when she let him go. "Fine."

CHAPTER EIGHT

Natalie went inside and disappeared to the bathroom then her bedroom. Aggression was humming in Shane's veins, a need to prove something to her. To himself. Prove he had a sexuality that wasn't hopelessly tangled up in that man.

That was the tough thing about Natalie. She was the only one who knew about or understood his hang-ups, which made her a comfort but also a source of worry. But tonight he wanted it to be just the two of them, Shane and Natalie, man and woman, so fucking simple and perfect. No kinks, no baggage, goddamn textbook, All-American, missionary-position screwing.

He met her in the bedroom just as she finished lighting the candles. Shane took her hand. "It's just you and me tonight. No ghosts creeping in, you got it?"

"I won't mention—"

He cut off the name with his mouth, kissing her again, dirty but not too rough. Her cool hands stroked his face and neck and he returned the study, enjoying the softness of her body, the differences in their sizes and smells, the pitch of their breathing.

Her fingers tugged at the hem of his sweater and Shane pulled it off. He felt each button as she opened his shirt, moaned when her palms found his bare skin. He returned the exploration, stripping away her top, hands turning clumsy as his cock grew hot and curious. Lust washed over him, banishing fear and hesitance.

He yanked her down on the bed with him and two sets of hands went to work fumbling with jeans. As they kicked them to the floor, Shane pulled her hard against him. Her thighs spread to invite one of his, her welcoming body and his hard cock grinding as they devolved to teenagers.

"Shane."

"You feel good, girl."

"Get on top of me."

He spread his knees between hers, lowering his hips to taunt them both with the rough contact. Natalie clawed at his sides with her nails, slid her hands beneath his shorts and kneaded his hips. Shane stared at her breasts in the candlelight, pale skin and cream-colored satin. So feminine and perfect and, halle-*fucking*-lujah, so exactly what Shane's body craved.

"Take your bra off," he whispered.

Easier than he'd even guessed. She flicked her fingers between her breasts and the cups fell away. Shane couldn't get his hands on her fast enough. Soft and warm and just a bit more than a handful, none of it wasted. He dropped to his elbows and brought his mouth to her nipple, breathed in the sweet smell of her sweat as he tasted her skin, teased her flesh, lost himself in her moan. He felt her foot pushing at one side of his briefs. He managed to reach a hand down and shrug them partway off, Natalie's toes doing the rest. The seduction dissolved into frantic grasping as the need clouded his head, spurred by the glide of his bare dick against the smooth fabric of her panties. He angled his hips and stroked her clit and lips through the satin.

"Jesus," she muttered.

Shane's patience dissolved. He knelt back and lifted her calves, nearly ripped her panties getting them down her legs and off her ankles. Natalie grabbed a condom from the box on the nightstand and he watched her open it and roll it down his cock, mean and slow. The aggression they always found together had him panting and eager, but the second he sank into her warmth, Shane's mood shifted. Someone yanked a rug from under his feet and he fell headlong into new and unfamiliar cravings, warm and strange and intoxicating.

He imagined there being no condom, imagined this as the first step toward a family. A relationship that extended beyond his tiny kingdom, bringing him something real and lasting instead of a series of hangovers. A relationship that lost him sleep over worries that actually mattered. He let his body take over, the possession plain in the hammering rhythm of his hips and the groans tumbling from his throat.

"Shane."

Warmth pulsed through him. "Love when you say that." He stared her down, lost in how good it felt to be here above her, inside her, the only thing on her mind. He thought of it again—no condom— and the distance between sanity and orgasm evaporated. The room melted away and he saw more...his house, finally cleared of his grandparents' old junk, an actual home again, with Natalie there. Natalie on the front porch with a baby on her lap. The scene made Shane's brain skip, but his body stayed steady.

He took her in with his eyes, this beautiful, smart woman who seemed to like the bull he dished out. She could keep him in check, call him on his shit, bring him to his knees with the tiniest smirk. In a quick and graceless motion, Shane flipped them over.

There was surprise in her grin. "Well well."

"Can you come this way?"

"With a little help, sure." She got her legs where she wanted them beside Shane's, lowered down an inch. "Touch my breasts," she whispered.

"Yes, ma'am."

Shane drove his own pleasure to the back of his mind and simply watched hers grow and deepen. Then another taste of that fantasy flickered across his brain—the image of her angling her hips back, sliding him out, stripping the condom away. Shane bucked with excitement.

"What're you thinking about?" Natalie murmured, sounding distant.

"Just how good you fucking feel."

"I'm so close."

Shane intensified the teasing of his fingertips, met her body's motions with his own thrusts. "Come on."

She lost it, took his cock all the way inside as her body squeezed him tight, made him feel welcome and wanted and powerful, even on his back.

She sighed and collapsed onto his chest.

"Good." He stroked her hair as her breath slowed, waiting until she was good and relaxed before he took his turn. Good, husbandly manners.

"You now," she said against his neck.

Shane turned them onto their hips, hugging her thigh to his waist as he found a fast, hungry rhythm. "Kiss me."

She offered quick, deep tastes that mimicked the urgency of his thrusts.

Again, that guilty thought of coming inside her, bare. Shane lost control and hammered his way home. He grabbed her ass and pulled her as hard against him as he could, buried himself deep and hoped to die there.

As sanity returned, the fantasy faded. Shane watched her face as she grew sleepy against him. He stroked her cheek. The mother of his children…? She'd told him that wasn't in their cards in no uncertain terms, and it was a mild relief to find the idea lost potency in the wake of the sex, a taboo fading along with Shane's lust. His heart sank to realize the impulse had been fleeting, a product of the evening's warm atmosphere. Shane saw only her now, only Natalie. Perhaps not the woman he'd spend forever with, but a damn great lover. An even better friend.

A good woman who deserved a lot better than half a man.

* * *

Shane awoke in utter confusion. Gabriel's body, warm but too soft, hair too long, tattoos gone. He jerked to full consciousness, realizing who he had his arms wrapped around.

The mix-up terrified him for a few seconds then he let it go. He'd been with the man for ages. Had to only be natural his body might still expect to find him there.

He squeezed Natalie tighter, trying to recapture what he'd felt with her last night. Some comfort came, along with a shadow of disappointment to remember how his picket-fence-family fantasy had fallen apart as soon as the lust had ebbed. *Like a Christmas tree*, he thought. A pretty idol for its time, but once the season was over, just a sad, brittle reminder of passing wishes. He sighed into her hair and felt her stir. The alarm clock beeped seconds later and Shane faked sleep, let her go to begin her morning.

The day felt different. Calmer. Still melancholy, but not as dismal as the first few. Shane took a long shower after Natalie left, made himself an entire pot of coffee and tackled a dozen more items on his home improvement list. He was running out of projects and wondered if maybe he'd offer his services to the landlady upstairs. Keeping busy felt like the only thing anchoring him to solid ground.

After lunch, Natalie called to ask if he'd meet her downtown for dinner, then drinks. Alicia and Dan joined them at the restaurant, and as much as Shane genuinely liked them, the weird magic of the first meeting was gone. As much as Shane genuinely liked *Natalie*, he couldn't look at this happy couple and honestly see it as a life he'd truly want. A fluke fantasy for one night, but who was he kidding? He'd been wrecked by his ex-lover, and Natalie deserved way better than a man who'd surely grow bored or resentful when she couldn't match the attraction he'd found with Gabriel. He just hoped he'd find a woman who could, someday.

Alicia and Dan left early and Shane and Natalie finished their drinks before bundling up for the short trip to the next destination.

"This ain't the same place we went to when you made me meet what's-his-name, is it?" He held the door open for her.

"I didn't *make* you meet anybody," Natalie countered. "And no, it's not. That other place is a bit too slick for me. Tonight I just want to drink a beer, shoot the shit with you, maybe play some darts or pool."

"Sounds good."

"This place is way more laid-back. It's where I learned to drink, back in nursing school. Probably more your speed too."

Shane unlocked her door. "Shadier the better."

"This'll be just perfect then." She cranked the heater up and pointed Shane in the right direction. "Thanks for driving. I know the bartender and a bunch of the regulars. It'll be nice to accept the free drink offers for a change."

"Bet you get lots of those."

She flipped her long hair out from under her scarf. "I do all right."

"I'm sure you do."

They stopped at a red light and she turned to him. "But you and I... Are we like, together, for as long as you're in town? Should I not flirt with anybody else in front of you?"

The question left Shane feeling shifty. They might not be destined for a house full of babies and moonbeams, but seeing her flirt with other guys would burn. Still, the answer he chose felt right, in light of how clear she'd made her intentions. "You flirt with whoever you like. Just remember who's takin' you home."

"Will do."

"I was thinkin'," Shane said as the light turned green.

"About what?"

"About gettin' a tattoo while I'm here."

"Oh yeah? What of, do you think? Left at this next sign."

"My mom's name. And my aunt's and my grandma's. On my shoulder, maybe?"

"I think that's a very nice idea," she said. "You'll have to explain to any girls you meet that it's not a roster of your finest conquests, but I think it's cool. I approve."

"Good. I always wanted one, but I couldn't think of something I'd *keep* wanting year after year. But those women, they're all gone now, but how I feel about them won't ever change."

"Very logical. And sweet."

"Yeah. Like a tribute. Anyhow, I might go out and set up an appointment this week. Little souvenir of my trip north."

Natalie laughed softly. "The claw marks I left on your back aren't enough? Need something a bit more permanent?"

Shane grinned at her then let the conversation fade to comfortable silence as he drove them to the bar. The word "permanent" lingered in his mind. Was he giving up too quick on the idea of him and Natalie as something real? Would she even want that from him someday? He wasn't sure. But he wasn't sure either if he'd ever find a woman back in Louisiana who understood him as well as she did. In fact, he doubted it mightily.

Shane parked the truck in the bar's front lot, already liking the look of this place. It was no Shivaree, but it'd do. No frills, and no gigantic TV screens glowing from within. No fancy cars in the lot, just cheap sedans and old salt-chewed trucks. Shane nodded to a couple of hypothermic smokers as he trotted up to hold the door for Natalie.

"Thank you kindly."

He followed her inside, relaxing instantly. It wasn't quite a shithole but it was definitely a dive. And a popular one, relatively bustling for a frigid Tuesday night. Living in Rochester must drive folks to drink, Shane decided.

"This okay?" she asked over her shoulder.

"Perfect. What're you havin'?"

"Oooh." They stopped at the bar and she eyed the taps. "Black and tan, please."

"You got it."

The thirty-something bartender wandered over and he and Natalie exchanged a pair of warm greetings. He went to pour their beers and she turned to Shane. "Ray's been my bartender since I was like nineteen and 'acquired' Alicia's driving license." She made quotes with her fingers.

Ray turned. "What was that?"

"Nothing."

Shane eyed the guy, thinking of his staff back home. It took a lot to keep employees in one place that long, and Shane figured he himself must be an okay boss if his two favorite bartenders were still with him after two years. No signs of leaving, either. Zach knew Shane was grooming him as a manager and Jeanne had just settled down close by with her new boyfriend. Shane hoped they'd both stick around as long as the veteran behind this bar. After all, they were the closest thing to family he had these days. The thought warmed him even as he missed his home with a potent pang.

The barman returned with their glasses, told Natalie the first round was on the house.

"Well, thanks very much. Are there any decent darts back there?" she asked.

He dug around beneath the register and came out with a small basket. Natalie fished for the three with the least-dull tips and led Shane to the back to a small table closest to the old board.

They nursed their beers, played game after lazy game. Both were decent at darts, though the two times a local cut in to challenge the winner, Shane and Natalie got trounced. Didn't matter. Shane felt happy. Buzzed and relaxed and normal. Not like a man with a debilitating condition for a change.

After a couple of hours they took a break from the game to sit and sip their third beers. Light snow was falling outside yet again, but it looked pretty now. Shane stared at Natalie and the dartboard behind her under its little spotlight, trying to memorize the moment. Trying to decide if this could ever be enough for him.

Natalie cocked her head, squinted.

"What?"

Her brows shot up, eyes trained over Shane's shoulder, toward the front of the bar. "Oh my God. Shane, turn around."

"Is it your ex?"

"No. It's yours."

CHAPTER NINE

The blood froze in Shane's veins. He turned and the sight that greeted him was like a kick in the teeth.

They spotted each other at the same moment and Gabriel stopped in his tracks. He looked the same but different—same white collared shirt but rumpled now beneath his old tweed jacket, same ancient hat but with snow dusting the felt brim. Same dark eyes, except now the warm mischief Shane was used to seeing in them was gone, replaced with a stony blankness.

Gabriel removed his hat, whapped the snow off against his hip and put it back atop his messy black hair. He licked his lips and threaded through the small crowd, his battered suitcase clutched in a gloved hand. As always, he looked like a man who'd strode straight out of a different century.

Shane's heart hammered. He made it to his feet to face this head-on, determined to appear cold and resolute, to stick to his guns. Then a realization slapped him.

He came after me.

Gabriel stopped a few feet away and he looked damn tired, bags under his eyes and even more dark stubble than normal.

Shane heard a stool squeak then Natalie was at his side. "Hi, Gabriel."

He gave her a glance and a curt nod and looked back to Shane. He set his suitcase beside the wall then peeled his gloves off and shoved them in his pants pocket. He stepped back toward Shane, ran his hands over his lapels—then lunged.

Shane heard Natalie shout at the same moment a fist connected with his chin. He staggered a step but didn't fall, straightening after a pause and putting his hands up on pure instinct. He didn't hit back—didn't have to. Natalie had grabbed one of Gabriel's arms and a nearby man had the other.

"Take it outside!" the bartender shouted. "Take it outside or I call the cops."

Shane dropped his hands. Another staffer, a big, bald, meaty specimen, came over from his post beside the door and took over for Natalie and the patron, grabbing Gabriel by the arm and tugging him toward the exit. Gabriel held his ground a moment, still staring Shane down, then gave in and let himself be led away. Shane followed.

"Go home and sleep it off," the bouncer said as he pushed Gabriel out the door and into the icy air. He turned and spotted Shane. "Oh. Fine. Finish this however you want but do it quick or do it someplace else. If you're still fighting in two minutes I'll call the police." He gave them each a look, a ref leaving a pair of boxers to their own devices.

Shane waited until the door closed again, relieved the smokers were all back inside. "You come to fight?" His breath rose like fog between them.

Gabriel's tongue flirted with his lip, but not in the way Shane was used to. He looked as though he were tasting invisible blood. "I came to hurt you."

"Oh yeah?" It was a stupid reply, but the only words Shane could find to say. "How come?"

Black eyebrows rose and Gabriel blinked, incredulous. "How come?"

"Why're you here?"

"You mean how come I take six buses in the las' three days and spend another bummin' rides all over this fuckin' frozen wasteland looking for your fuckin' truck?"

Shane had never heard Gabriel talk this way before—aggressive and graceless and agitated. He didn't get agitated—he got what he wanted. Well, until that phone call, Shane supposed.

"I didn't ask you to come up here," Shane said evenly.

"You di'n give me no choice, neither. What I was supposed to do, Shane? Shrug and move on?"

"Somethin' like that." Shane narrowed his eyes, confused. "You here for a temper tantrum or some kind of jilted lover's revenge?"

Gabriel crossed his arms over his chest just as Shane felt the cold himself.

"I came 'cause you been the center of my world for the pas' year, then you tell me over the fuckin' phone you done with me," Gabriel said. "I came to make you look me in the eye and tell me why."

The cold air breached Shane's sweater, made his knuckles ache and his lips sting. "Fucking freezing out here," he mumbled, eyes on the parked cars.

"Tell me why."

"Jesus... Fine. But in my truck."

Shane heard Gabriel's footsteps behind him as he crunched to where he'd parked and unlocked the driver's side. He leaned over and tugged the lock on the passenger door, started the engine and kept it in neutral. Gabriel took a seat and Shane nearly laughed—a year they'd been together and he'd never seen this man in a vehicle before.

"Tell me why," Gabriel repeated.

Shane addressed the steering wheel. "I already told you. I got to move on. I might want a family or something someday. You…you're a distraction."

"A distraction."

Shane cranked the heater up as far as it would go, though he knew it wouldn't take the icy edge off his lover's voice. "Yeah."

"You make me sound pretty inconsequential, Shane."

Inconsequential. Easily the longest word he'd ever heard this man utter. He opened his mouth but Gabriel went on.

"Sound like I'm jus' your bad habit, the way you talk about it."

"That's the long and short of it."

A dead laugh.

"What you and me were," Shane said, "it was pure pleasure. I won't deny that. No woman's ever got me hooked like you did. But it *is* like a habit with you, like the best drug imaginable, but it's keeping me from what's real. You and me can do what we have been for another ten years, but I ain't willin' to wake up and be forty-five with no family life in sight, nothing to show for the past decade but a bunch of hot fucking sex."

"You think we friends, Shane?"

The question knocked him sideways. Sometimes, on rare, sober nights, yes, he did feel that way. When he was camped out at the kitchen table with his laptop, balancing the bar's books or reading up on something for the shop, Gabriel across the room on the couch, picking his way through some new song or other on his mandolin… Yeah, those nights he felt something else. Companionship. Easiness. Sometimes when they were in public, nursing drinks downstairs at the bar, it felt like what Shane wanted people to think it was—friendship.

"Shane?" That voice was softer now.

"I dunno. Maybe."

"Tha's what it is for me," Gabriel said. "Nothin' else would have kept me with the same man for a whole year. You know I ain' faithful, not with anybody but you. You make it easy."

Shane laughed, cold and mean. "Faithful. You're fucking hilarious, boy."

"That was our deal. You came up with it yourself. You give me women because you won' give me you—not in public, anyhow."

"Like you wouldn't go and do that anyway…God fucking knows how many men you've been with since we started up."

Shane sensed Gabriel staring at him but refused to turn and meet his eyes. He took a deep breath, registered the faint, nostalgic scent of clove cigarettes, as undivorceable from his memories of his mother as her eye color or voice. He shoved the thought aside. "Men who smoke, by the smell of it."

"Tha's me, actually. Congratulations, you drove me to a relapse."

Shane winced at the word, not sure how close he might be to one of those himself.

"You ain't the victim you think you are, Shane. Not only that, you're a fuckin' coward. You blame me for what we got together, what you say I *make* you feel, like you don' have no ownership or control of it. Fuck you. I never put a gun to your head and forced you to fuck my ass every goddamn night for the pas' year."

On instinct, Shane scanned the parking lot for witnesses.

"I gave you everythin' you wanted," Gabriel said, "even agreed t'your little rules about who gets to know, let you think you was the one bein' wronged when I wanted to go with women once in a while. When you wouldn't even acknowledge what we were to anyone? When you were single as far as the rest of the world was allowed to know?"

"I let you cheat," Shane said.

Gabriel rubbed his chin and grinned. "Yeah, thanks so fuckin' much. So generous, you are, givin' me some freedom in the relationship you refused to admit we had. That so like you—dishin' out rules for a game you won' even stoop to play."

For a minute or more, silence reigned. Between the shushing sounds of cars passing on the main road, Shane listened to their breaths, inhalations growing deeper and slower until the hum of the heater drowned them out. Weariness overtook him and he gave in, looked at Gabriel's face. The most beautiful wreck he'd ever seen— and Shane had done this to him. Shane had driven him to come here, to come after him. The thought made his sinuses feel gluey. He cleared his throat.

"What d'you want?" Gabriel asked. "What you need that I ain' willin' to give you?"

"Family, I guess. The option for it."

"Kids?"

Shane pondered it. It wasn't kids, not quite. As hot as that idea had gotten him with Natalie in bed, he wasn't entirely sure he wanted children, specifically. "I dunno. Just something real. Something permanent and real to come home to, to be a man for."

"And what was I, Shane? Your whore?"

He flinched. "No. You were like…like a year of one-night stands, I guess."

Another empty laugh. "Right. Well then, fuck you. Glad I wasted my time comin' to find you."

Gabriel pushed his door open but Shane grabbed his arm and held him there. Just that little bit of contact lit him up, same as it always had.

"This is so fuckin' like you," Gabriel said. "Treat me like trash then throw a tantrum when I decide to leave."

"Close the door."

"Lemme go."

"Close the fucking door," Shane repeated, voice raised.

Gabriel's nostrils flared but he obeyed. The cold air hovered between them and Shane released his arm. He wasn't sure what he wanted, or why he'd kept him here.

"You're a coward," Gabriel finally murmured.

Shane opened his mouth, closed it again, cutting off whatever comeback his brain had readily stocked. He took a long, deep breath. "I know."

"You're a coward, and a hypocrite, and I been a fool to stay with you as long as I did," Gabriel said.

Shane shut his eyes.

"But I can' help it," Gabriel muttered. "I always been the least faithful person I know, but with you, it's like I gotta remind myself to stray, so I don' feel like your fool."

Shane looked up, not sure what to say. Then Natalie emerged from the bar holding his jacket and Gabriel's suitcase, stopping just outside the door and looking in their direction. "Hang on," he said to Gabriel. "Don't go nowhere."

Shane left the truck idling and jogged to Natalie.

"Is everything okay?" She passed him his coat and the case and rubbed her arms. "You've been out here awhile."

"Everything's...weird. I dunno."

"Why don't you guys go back to my place? Ray lives like five blocks from me. I can get a lift home at closing time."

"No, you don't have to do that."

"You two probably need time to talk. That'd give you a couple hours."

"I can't leave you here—"

"It's not an offer, Shane. Go. See you at home."

He sighed. Natalie clapped him curtly on the shoulder and went back inside.

Shane stared at the suitcase in his hand for a moment then walked to the truck. He stashed Gabriel's bag behind the seats and pulled his jacket on, got buckled up.

"You too," he said to Gabriel. "This region's a fucking death trap."

CHAPTER TEN

Shane waited for Gabriel's obedient click then drove. Not a word was spoken between them on the way back to Natalie's. As they entered the house, Gabriel looked around, seeming to avoid Shane's face. He set his suitcase by the door and toed his shoes off, more to be polite than to get comfortable, Shane guessed.

"You want a drink?"

Gabriel shook his head. Shane realized he didn't really want one either. Drinking had only ever muddied his grasp of what they were to each other. He cleared his throat. "She'll be back in a couple hours. She wants us to talk or whatever."

"You got anythin' you wan' to say to me?" Gabriel asked, finally meeting Shane's eyes with his black ones. His tone was stiff and challenging.

"Beats the fuck out of me." Shane left him to head to the hearth, getting a fire going, a few more minutes' chance to avoid this conversation.

"This what you two been doin' since you left?" Gabriel asked, and Shane turned. "Cozy little visit while you leave me back there, no idea where you got to?"

"Don't you even start actin' angry about that. How many nights've you disappeared on me to shack up who knows where? Don't pretend like you're allowed to get jealous. And over a woman *you* fucking invited to come between us in the first place."

"I get jealous if I wan' to," Gabriel said quietly.

"Didn't know you were capable of it. Bravo."

"You know who I'm really jealous of, Shane? Each and every damn day?"

Shane shook his head.

Gabriel took a seat on Natalie's futon, clasping his hands between his knees and staring Shane square in the face. "Everyone. Zach and Jeanne. All your customers and your pals from the garage, every fuckin' delivery person who come through that door. Everyone you joke around with, who you barely know, when you won' even look me in the eyes when we got our clothes on."

Shane's head felt fuzzy and floaty. He'd wanted this forever, to hear Gabriel tell him he was special and different. Worth being faithful to. Now those words had come but Shane didn't feel relief or triumph, just scared. Gabriel was offering everything Shane wanted and he seemed sincere…and that meant the man was right. It was down to Shane to be brave, if he wanted this as much as he and Gabriel and Natalie all goddamn knew he did.

The step was too big though. Disbelief was easier. He walked to the couch and took a seat, leaving a couple of feet between them.

"You sure you ain't just pissed to be the one who gets left for a change?" he asked his knees. He glanced at his lover's tired face.

Gabriel blinked at him. "You think I don' know what it feels like to get left? I got left my whole childhood. Why you think I'm so good at makin' myself a guest? Why you think I need to be wanted so fuckin' bad?"

Shane shifted his attention to Gabriel's hands.

"You still want me, Shane?"

He took a deep breath and met those black eyes. "Course I do."

"Jus' my body?"

Shane shook his head.

"Say my name."

A chill washed over him. He never said Gabriel's name to his face, not when they were alone—a rare utterance to get his attention down in the bar, maybe, but even those made Shane nervous. For a year the man had been playing three or more nights a week at the club and crashing in the apartment upstairs, and more often than not, Shane still referred to him as "the mandolin player" to his staff. He swallowed the lump forming in his throat, took another almighty breath.

"Gabriel." The seconds before it left his lips were terrifying, the moments following like a gasp of air after a brush with drowning.

"I been with you for months now, Shane. You know the longest I been with anybody else, romance-wise?"

Shane shook his head.

"Maybe three nights."

Shane laughed, a joyless, sad huff of breath. He wanted so badly to believe what he was being told. He wanted to believe he was something special to this man, more than another weak and willing body in a long line of Gabriel's spellbound admirers.

"I don't know what to tell you," Shane admitted.

"Tell me you wan' me."

He mustered the courage to meet Gabriel's eyes as he muttered, "You know I do."

"You wan' me enough to make it public?"

Fuck, that was the hardest question Shane could conceive of… He might lose customers, lose staff, lose thirty-six years' worth of his own identity. And if he and Gabriel went public but didn't stay together, and Shane woke up with an actual wife and family in ten years, what shit would that decision put his kids through? Did that kind of scandal have an expiration date?

"You don' even have to admit it to anyone out loud, Shane…but I want people to know. I want them to know we're together, even if it jus' rumors."

Shane looked back at his knees.

"Deny it all you wan' in words, but I need you to treat me like your lover in the way you talk to me. And touch me. How you are with me when there's other people around. I can' stand how cold you are to me in that bar. It fuckin' *hurts.*"

"I'm scared of that."

"What you think you gon' lose?"

"I'm not sure. Maybe business, or people's respect. Maybe my own damn understanding of who I even am."

"Well tha's the chance you take. You figure out what hurts more, losin' that or losin' me. An' when you figure that out, you tell me." Gabriel stood but Shane grabbed his wrist and pulled him back down. Their eyes locked, Gabriel's full of heat and melancholy, exhaustion and hunger.

Shane didn't know his answer, but it was impossible to resist their connection, not with this man's body so close, so familiar and warm, so perfect at giving Shane's own body what it wanted. So exactly the right fit.

And not just his body. Gabriel. All of him.

"C'mere," Shane said.

He'd said it a hundred times in the last year and Gabriel knew what it meant. He swung a leg over Shane's lap, straddled his thighs. Here was where the groping usually began, frantic and rough, but tonight was different. Gabriel rested his forearms on Shane's shoulders; rested his chin at Shane's temple. Shane breathed him in, lovesick. Homesick.

His body had darker agendas but his heart didn't want to be cast aside, drowned out by the lust he always found between them. Shane settled for the middle ground. He put his mouth to Gabriel's neck, took in his scent, kissed his skin. He'd done dozens of sinful acts with this man, but this one, Shane's lips on his throat, was the one guaranteed to make Gabriel lose his mind. Shane kissed his way up his lover's jugular, light sweeps of his lips, a faint scrape of teeth, a tease of tongue. Gabriel pressed his cock to Shane's belly, already hard behind his pants. His mind was clearly on sex, but Shane's was still mired in emotion. He surveyed this familiar, contentious territory with his hands, held Gabriel's ass, squeezed his thighs, rubbed possessive fingertips up his spine.

"You miss me?" Gabriel whispered.

"Yeah."

"Not half as much as I missed you."

Shane doubted that. He didn't think anybody could feel worse or emptier than he had this past week without taking their own life. His heart ached even now, even with the object of his restless nights held tight against his body. He ached from knowing that as perfect as this moment felt, it wouldn't last. Any resolution they might find for the next night or month or ten years, it was just time Shane would lose, and later mourn once the inevitable caught up with him. He could choose Gabriel over a family for a while, maybe a long while, but he couldn't go to his grave with nothing to show for himself but years of mind-blowing sex, no lasting investment of his heart and energy.

His kisses grew distracted and he felt Gabriel's heat cooling right along with his own.

"What you thinkin' 'bout, Shane?" That fucking voice, right in his ear.

"I'm thinkin' about us. How long this'll go on before we have to give it up and face reality."

"This is reality, Shane. My reality, anyway. What's it to you?"

Shane swallowed. "This is… This is perfection. But it's all just play. We're physical."

"We friends."

"Are we?"

"No one I rather spend time with."

What about all those nights you go missing? "I dunno what we are, I guess."

"You think this is a game to me? That I spent a whole year of my life playin' with you?"

"Feels that way, sometimes."

Gabriel's dark eyes jumped between Shane's. "Sometimes with you…it feel like torture. Feel like I'm givin' you everythin' I got and you just tossin' it away."

Shane swallowed. "I know that feelin'."

Gabriel's gaze dipped to Shane's chest before returning to hold him captive. "You love me?"

The question eradicated the wall that kept them separated, dissolved their clothes and mutual anger and left Shane feeling as though he were slipping into a shared skin with this man. This man he'd known intimately for months but still considered a stranger sometimes.

"I guess I don't know what this is."

Gabriel's lips twitched. "I love *you*, you know."

His heart quickened. "Do you?"

"Course I do. I'm here. I been with you a year."

"Not every night."

Gabriel's eyes narrowed. "I got pride. If I came to you every night, accept all your cowardly rules and got nothin' back but sex and a place to sleep… I'm not your toy. I can' be jus' yours until you willin' to admit you're mine. But tha's jus' my body, Shane. This," he touched a hand to his chest, "this been yours for months."

Shane fumbled with the top buttons of Gabriel's shirt, spread his collar and stared at the little band of notes above his heart. Shane's music. His notes were one set among dozens, perhaps a hundred snatches of songs belonging to any number of people Gabriel had known. Still, there he was. Indelible.

Gabriel dragged his short nails across Shane's scalp. "You got any clue how long a year is to me, bein' with one person? It's you who been breakin' my heart, keepin' us a secret."

"You and me," Shane began. He mulled the words over and let Gabriel's shirt go. "I might want a family someday. I can't have that, and have you. I need to find somebody like Natalie, somebody who can offer that."

"You willin' to give me up for the rest of your life?"

Shane shrugged, exhausted. "I don't have a choice. Or I do. It's hot sex versus a real family, kids maybe. And no offense, really, but I'm not choosing hot sex. I can learn to live with missing that, but not with missing out on a family."

"So don' choose, Shane. Why choose?"

"I have to."

Gabriel put his hands on Shane's shoulders. "So choose both. We fin' someone like Natalie. Someone who let you have both. Who give you both. Be a part of both."

Shane swallowed, uncertain. "You can't raise a kid with three people all shacking up together."

"How come?"

"It's fucked."

"Makin' a choice to be miserable when you could be choosin' to have it all is fucked. People do this, Shane."

"Natalie tried to sell me the same bull... I can't spend the whole rest of my life sneaking around to make that happen."

"Then don' sneak. There's a difference between havin' a dirty little secret and havin' an arrangement. Bein' discreet ain't the same as hidin' some dark, unforgivable sin tha's chewin' away on your insides." He slid a hand between them and rubbed the spot over Shane's heart. "You're lookin' for ways that this can' work. Spend some time wonderin' if maybe it could."

Shane stared at a point on the wall past Gabriel's shoulder, lost.

"You're not your momma," Gabriel said. "You don' have to settle for bein' miserable. And anyhow, you turned into your daddy instead, in the end."

Shane's muscles stiffened. "'Scuse me?"

"You choose to be the asshole at every turn. And to keep your mind closed up." He tapped Shane's temple. "You always sayin' how much you hate him, how you never end up like him, but you are. Give yourself another ten years of wantin' two things but only givin' yourself one, or makin' excuses so you don' have to face up to the scary parts of either. Ten more years and you be one of them. A mean old drunk or a miserable, done-wrong victim."

"Don't you fuckin' talk like you know either of my parents."

"I do, Shane. 'Cause I know you, and you told me plenty in the las' year."

As much as Shane wanted to push him away, off his lap and onto the floor, all the way back to Louisiana or Cuba and out of his life and his memory, he couldn't. He needed Gabriel as he needed air. Just yesterday he'd thought of this as an addiction, something he wanted fiercely despite the damage it did to him. Now he knew better.

He needed this man for nourishment, like light and water and food and sleep, everything that made him whole. Made him thrive. Maybe it was time to admit defeat, give up on the traditional family excuse for holding back and see where he and Gabriel might go, if he'd let this become reality.

"If you and me were…official or whatever," he mumbled. "What would change?"

"Like if you admitted to people what we are to each other?"

Shane shivered at the thought. Never in the past twelve months had he wondered if he was gay. One singular man on the face of the Earth got him hot, hotter than any woman he'd ever known, but still, it was a fluke. He'd never be able to explain that to anybody, not his staff or his patrons or his partners at the auto shop. He loved where he'd grown up, but it wasn't exactly San Francisco. He had no doubt he'd lose customers if it got out he was sleeping with a guy. His businesses could get vandalized and his partners in the shop might be spooked…

But fuck them. He knew now, he couldn't live without this. He'd pay for it in lost income and lost friends and maybe a few fistfights and property damage, but the price was negligible if it meant this man was his.

"Yeah," he muttered. "If I told people."

"Then I'd be yours, Shane. Jus' yours. Nobody else's unless you invite them yourself."

"You capable of that?"

Gabriel smiled grimly, a glimmer of injury in his narrowed eyes. "Yeah, I am. You capable of givin' your identity up in exchange for it?"

Shane blew out a loaded breath and nodded slowly.

"You capable of givin' up your dreams for a regular family?"

"I think so. Think I have to."

"You still the only one who thinks that, but okay. If tha's what you want, I won' pretend I don' want it too." He leaned in, kissed Shane soft and deep. As he pulled away Shane wasn't sure if this face was the most familiar in the entire world or that of a complete stranger.

"I love you, Shane."

There it was, that sting in his sinuses again, heat flooding his throat and cheeks. He wouldn't cry. As scared and happy and confused as he felt, he wouldn't cry. He'd escape into sex again, as they'd done three hundred times before.

Shane drew his tongue down Gabriel's neck then blew cool breath against his damp skin. The contact made him high too—all the chemicals of attraction heating him up from the inside and taking over his hands.

He got Gabriel's top layers stripped off as the same was done to him. As always, their touching was part tender and part mean, greedy hands fighting for control of the pleasure-giving. Natalie's futon creaked under their weight.

They kissed for a long minute, hands drifting lower as tongues delved deep. Shane gasped as Gabriel's hand closed over his stiff cock behind his jeans. He never made moves like this without Shane's permission, but it was okay. It was better than okay. Shane didn't need to play the role of the bossy asshole tonight. He didn't want to. He wanted them on par for a change, at least to start.

Leaning back against the cushions and armrest, he tugged Gabriel forward, inviting him closer. A bit of the usual, Gabriel in his lap, a bit of the unusual, Shane feeling as if he were on the bottom, if barely. The weight of this other man felt right, felt sinful. Shane held his hips and pulled him closer still, bringing their two hard cocks together. The low moan he earned stole the air from his lungs.

These familiar sounds and sensations were more thrilling to Shane than any exciting trick a new lover might share. He moved his hand to Gabriel's ass, kneading until his breaths dripped with longing.

"That's my boy."

"Missed you, Shane."

Heat washed over him, along with the persona he wore most nights with Gabriel—the cruel roughneck. He growled an order into his lover's ear. "Tell me what you missed."

"Your cock."

"How d'you want it tonight?"

Gabriel's hips pressed harder, rubbed his erection against Shane's. "Wanna kiss you while we play with each other."

Shane hadn't known it until he heard the words in that scratchy, dark voice, but he wanted that too. No top or bottom, owner and plaything. Just two desperate bodies and mouths, two men giving and receiving equal pleasure, all that eye contact Shane sometimes shied from. But not just now. Right now he'd keep his own eyes wide open, not miss out on a second of the sins they committed together.

He took Gabriel's mouth, deep and rough, his own jaw tender from the punch he'd more than earned.

Shane moaned openly to let this man know exactly what he did to him. He let Gabriel kiss back, accepted his tongue's explorations and traded the control back and forth.

"I don't know how you make me this way," Shane mumbled. "I never wanted a man before I met you."

"An' now?"

Shane laughed, exasperated. "It's still just you."

"An' why me, Shane?"

He considered the question, and memories—dirty and tender alike—flashed through his skull. It all came down to those eyes, that smile. "I like the way you look at me."

"How do I look at you?"

Shane licked his lips, saw the very gleam right there, inches away. "Like I'm the biggest man in the world."

"You are, to me."

Shane shoved a hand between them to wrestle with the stupid, complicated clasp of Gabriel's dress pants. He tugged the zipper down, rubbing his knuckles against the hard ridge that greeted him through Gabriel's shorts.

"Yeah."

"Take me out," Shane said.

Gabriel shifted, used both hands to open Shane's jeans and tug them down an inch. Shane swore as his underwear was peeled down, his hard cock exposed to the cool, dry air. That familiar, calloused palm closed around him lightly. Gabriel surveyed him with slow, reverent strokes, seeming to weigh him.

"I've missed you," he whispered.

Shane's habit was to issue orders, make this man suck him or stroke him, make him strip and bend over and beg. But not tonight. Not after all that'd been said. Shane leaned into Gabriel's shoulder and watched their hands on each other's cocks, listened to his lover's moans.

"I missed you too," he muttered. He tightened his grip just to hear Gabriel's breath hitch. Their knuckles bumped as they jerked each other, cock heads touching on the odd stroke. Shane surrendered to a body-racking groan of his own as he gave in and gave up, wallowed in how unbelievable it felt, just being close to this man. He mashed his cheek against Gabriel's and drank in the scents of his breath and skin and hair.

"Fuck."

"Make it tight," Gabriel murmured.

Shane obeyed, fucked Gabriel's cock with a mean fist, didn't give a shit what off-limits fantasy might be running through the man's head.

"Yeah."

"Love when I make you pant, boy."

"Love when I make you mean," Gabriel whispered.

Shane loved that too. He'd kept them equal for long enough. Time now to do what they did best. Shane released Gabriel's cock and slid his hand down the back of his pants and shorts. He found his asshole, circled it with his middle finger. The groan Gabriel unleashed was wild and disbelieving.

"I need you," Shane said, more threat than plea.

In a flash Gabriel was on his hands and knees on the cushions.

"No," Shane said. He tugged at Gabriel's hip. "Face-to-face." Fucking this way was rare for them, precisely for the reason Shane needed it now. It made him feel vulnerable, Gabriel watching him and seeing how helpless he must look. Right now he wanted that feeling, and moreover he owed it to the man.

Gabriel turned over and Shane yanked his pants and shorts off, then stood and kicked away his own jeans and underwear. He gazed down at this man in the flickering firelight, skin looking golden, tattooed notes seeming to dance. For a minute or more they watched each other stroke, each second of waiting sharpening the urge. Then an annoying bit of practicality drew Shane out of the trance.

"Hang on."

He headed to Natalie's room for the condoms and lube, praying the reminder that he'd played around in Gabriel's absence wouldn't cool the man's mood.

When he got back to the couch all he saw was desire in those eyes, thirst with a touch of fear. Shane rolled the rubber down his cock.

"I missed seein' that look on your face," Gabriel said.

"I'll let you see a lot tonight," Shane promised. He stepped to the couch, bracing one knee on the cushions between Gabriel's thighs, other foot on the floor. He handed the bottle over. "Get yourself ready."

Shane knew he must look insane now, nostrils flared and lips parted as he watched Gabriel prep himself. He stared at the fingers working their way inside, slow and practiced. "Now me."

Gabriel slicked lube down the length of Shane's cock, the touch worshipful. Shane grabbed the bottle, snapped it closed and tossed it to the floor. Gabriel brought his knees up as Shane leaned in close, angling himself home. He eased in slowly, sinking to the base after a dozen measured thrusts. He held there as they both remembered to breathe.

"Shane."

That little syllable—a deliberate match flicked into a puddle of gasoline. He lowered his face to Gabriel's neck as his hips began to pump.

Fuck, he'd been without this only a week and he'd missed it as though it'd been months. Shane liked rough sex, fast and mean, faster and meaner than most women wanted. Not Gabriel. As rough as Shane liked it, Gabriel had him beat. His kinks and fantasies scared Shane sometimes. His honesty scared Shane too. Gabriel wasn't afraid to voice what he wanted, no matter how utterly fucked it was, no matter if he knew he'd never get it. Gabriel's sexuality was like a playground, everything open and on offer, ready to be enjoyed. Shane's felt more like a cage, keeping things in or out, keeping him protected and keeping him prisoner at the same time.

Except tonight.

Tonight he'd own his desires the way he always pretended to own Gabriel's pleading body.

"Fuck. I'm so in love with you."

"Then show me, Shane. I know I got your body, and I got some dark, self-hatin' corners of your head. But I wan' it all. And I don' have this." He reached between them to rub the skin above Shane's heart again.

Shane leaned back and took hold of Gabriel's calves. He brought his own body upright, gave the man a perfect view of whatever awe or reverence or fear was plastered across his features.

"Oh, tha's what I wan'," Gabriel muttered, gaze darting over Shane's face and chest. He put a possessive hand to Shane's ribs, the other to his own cock.

"I can't believe what you do to me."

"Make it deep. Only you get me now, Shane. Show me how lucky we are."

Lucky. Shane pondered the word, so the opposite of how he'd always thought of their connection. He'd made it out as a curse before, but fuck, he'd been so wrong. It was a goddamn jackpot-winning lottery ticket, two mismatched strangers finding a sexual connection that hadn't faded a jot in an entire year of hysterical screwing.

He pushed in deep, reminding them both what a filthy, sinful fit they were.

"Shane."

He bit his tongue, on the verge of ordering him to say it again. Not tonight. "Gabriel," he muttered.

"Yeah."

"Gabriel." He said it again, and again, a dozen times until the letters blurred to a guttural moan. He watched Gabriel's fist pumping, a rhythm he knew so intimately he could track the countdown to his climax like a Swiss clock.

"Good," he murmured.

"Shane..." A few more seconds' thrusting and jerking and Gabriel fell apart. His body tensed tight around Shane's cock, back arching as the come lashed his lean stomach. Shane got lost in the firelit scene and the heat wrapped around his dick but resisted an urge to fold forward and finish this with his face buried in the cushions or Gabriel's shoulder. No. Tonight he'd watch it all and get watched in return. Tonight his fear and vulnerability would be celebrated, not hidden.

"Love you," he muttered. The pleasure spiked, yanked him toward release. "Fuck. I fucking love you."

"Shane."

"Gabriel."

Bliss.

The orgasm roared up his spine like electricity, so hot it must've left blisters. He came down from it to find his fingers jammed into Gabriel's knees, head flung back and lungs wrung out. Probably looked a damn mess, but that was all that mattered—he'd been seen. He'd shown his lover what the man deserved, proof of how helpless their sex made him, no power games or drunken playacting.

"Holy fuck," Shane muttered, eyes on the fire. He looked down at the man panting against Natalie's weary futon. "I fucking love you."

CHAPTER ELEVEN

Natalie bade good night to Ray as he dropped her at her curb. "Best bartender ever," she reminded him with a tipsy grin.

"That's why they pay me the big bucks."

She slammed her car door and turned toward the house, then her breath caught. She could see her two houseguests through the picture window—Shane's possessive hands on Gabriel's neck as they kissed deeply. She waved distractedly at the car as it drove off, wondering if Ray had spotted the scene as well.

She barely breathed as she mounted the steps and unlocked the front door. Excitement yanked her in one direction, fear another. Had Shane merely given in to the sex, or the fact that they needed each other? *Please tell me you used your heart for a change, dummy, not just your dick.*

By the time she made it into the warm kitchen, the men had assembled themselves into an imitation of good behavior.

Shane was wearing a tee shirt and jeans, Gabriel just his pants. Shane had his arm draped along the back of the couch behind Gabriel's shoulders.

Natalie waved, feeling like a dope. "Hey."

"Glad you got home all right," Shane said.

She spotted the lube bottle on the floor beside the coffee table then glanced away just as quickly. "Glad to see you two haven't killed each other." She bit her lip, looking around at the dying fire and the *lack* of glasses or open wine bottles on the table or counter. That was a good sign. If things had gone well, Shane wouldn't be able to blame his surrender on alcohol.

"Well, I'm wiped. And I've got to be up at six, so…"

"No problem," Shane said. "Sleep tight."

"Oh." She stopped in her tracks. "What a crappy hostess I'm being. I can't let two six-foot-tall houseguests sleep on my foldout."

"I wasn' exactly invited," Gabriel said with a faint smile.

"Nonsense. You guys should take my bed."

"Don't worry about it," Shane said. "I like your futon."

"You sure?"

He nodded. "Away with you."

"I know better than to argue with the likes of you. Night, then." With that, she headed for her bedroom.

* * *

Six a.m. arrived all too soon.

"Fuck off." Natalie slapped her alarm clock into silence and sat up, knowing she'd drop off again if she stayed horizontal. Shuffling to the bathroom, she realized she'd slept with her necklace on, its beads leaving a caterpillar of pink dents across her throat.

"Oh, very classy." She took it off, eyeing the matching burgundy bra and panties she'd picked out with Shane in mind. She shook her head at her reflection. "Nice try, Foster."

She got her hair shampooed before she was awake enough to ponder what the heck might actually be happening with Shane…

Dick or heart? Ego or instinct? If it was even his choice. Gabriel had been pissed. Pissed enough to cross six state lines just for the chance to punch him. Natalie didn't know the man well, didn't even know his last name or his age. Until last night she'd never seen him as anything but calm and in control…well, or begging. But even then he'd held total mastery over the situation.

She toweled off and got her hair dried, made up her face a bit more than usual for a workday. She wondered what her role was, now. Until the bar, she'd been Shane's safe haven and therapist, his rebound. With Gabriel here she felt uneasy, and not in the way she had when she'd been Gabriel's little indiscretion instead of Shane's.

Sadly, unless they were light sleepers, she might not have the relief and the luxury of getting a read on the situation until she got home from work. She'd have to call Shane on her break if she wanted an update.

But a different and more uncomfortable opportunity presented itself once she'd dressed and entered the den. Gabriel was awake, sitting on the edge of the futon with his hand on Shane's bare arm. He rose as Natalie headed for the kitchen, sauntered over and crossed his arms atop the opposite side of the counter.

She had no sense how to greet him. They'd used each other's bodies in the most intense ways imaginable, yet a hug seemed somehow awkward, even obscene.

She spoke quietly, partly from nerves, partly to keep from waking Shane. "Morning. You two sleep okay?"

"Yeah, jus' fine."

"Oh good."

He held her gaze, not *quite* staring. Gabriel was a hard man to read. It was impossible to tell if those dark, weary eyes were seeing her as his rival in a love triangle, or a guest in a future threesome. If those were the only two options, Natalie knew which she'd pick…but she'd happily put aside her own selfish pleasure in deference to whatever affection the two men had discovered last night.

"You look well," he finally said.

"I am, thank you. You look…" She searched her vocabulary for a flattering alternative to—

"I been a wreck."

She smiled. "Yeah. I bet. And I'm afraid you look it."

He nodded.

Natalie grabbed half a bagel from the cupboard and popped it in the toaster. "I'm not sure how it's happened," she said, turning to meet his stare, "but I've gone from being *your* other woman to Shane's. When he got here, I thought he and you were officially over already. He didn't lie to me about it, but…well, anyway. I'm sorry if I've come between you two for a second time."

"I'm not angry." Gabriel's gaze drifted over her shoulders, taking some idle inventory of her kitchen. "And I don' think you came between us. I think you good for him. He said you been treatin' him real fine."

"I told him I didn't think he should have given up on you guys the way he did."

"Shane can' be told anythin'."

She laughed. "True. But I tried. Do you want anything for breakfast? I have to head out soon but I've got—"

"No. I'm good." He glanced back at Shane's sleeping form. "Right now I got everythin' I need."

* * *

Shane woke late. The weak northern sun was already halfway up the sky beyond the picture window, which made it at least ten. Gabriel was lying behind him, arm draped over his ribs. Shane didn't know if he was awake, but when he reached down to squeeze Gabriel's hand, it squeezed back.

Shane smiled, almost pleased by the anxiety his own optimism stirred. He needed to get used to this feeling, quit letting it make decisions for him.

He lay still for ten minutes, drifting in a thoughtful half-sleep. They'd never be a normal couple...not just because of the two-men thing, but because of Gabriel. He simply wasn't *normal*. Shane couldn't imagine what activities they might go out and partake of together like some regular twosome, and that was okay. As long as he had that voice and warmth and welcoming body to come home to, to find comfort and excitement in, Shane would be content.

He'd never really enjoyed the dating part of dating, anyhow. With women, he'd liked the companionship, the fucking, the chance to do things for someone, practical things. He liked someone he could put an arm around down at the bar, someone he could make filthy promises to with a pointed glance. He never let himself indulge in those sorts of secret signals with Gabriel... Could he ever? He didn't need to flaunt what they were or anything, but to able to acknowledge it. Heck, to flirt. Shane sighed.

He slipped out from Gabriel's warm hold, pulled on his jeans and tee shirt and a sweater to block the godforsaken Rochester cold. He strolled into the kitchen and turned the radio on low. He flipped the channel off of Natalie's liberal propaganda NPR nonsense and onto something with actual news and voices that didn't put Shane to sleep.

He inventoried the fridge and found he'd already cleaned her out of the good breakfast fixings. He heard a deep sigh and a groan of beleaguered springs. He looked to where Gabriel was tucking his shirt into his slacks.

"Hey."

Gabriel looked up.

"You wanna go out and find a diner?"

Gabriel blinked and it was clear he was pondering what this was as much as Shane. A date, basically. The first time Shane had invited his lover someplace aside from the bar's stage or his bed.

"Yeah. That sound good."

Frigid or not, something about the air and the silvery winter sunshine perked Shane up. He stole a glance at Gabriel as the man slid into his passenger seat. For the second time in two days, they were sharing a vehicle. The second time ever, after an entire goddamn year of the best sex of Shane's life.

He'd always thought this man would look odd camped out here in such a mundane and familiar place, but he'd been wrong. Just as his presence changed the atmosphere of Shane's bar, Gabriel did something to this space as well. He made places shinier. Instant Christmas.

"Like the way you look," Shane said, and started the engine.

"Oh?"

"Yeah. This truck might be my favorite thing in the whole world," he said, aiming them downtown. "And I like the way you look in it."

Gabriel didn't reply, just watched the streets passing by outside his window.

Shane swallowed. He was trying his damnedest to make an effort, be a nice guy. To prove to both of them that last night hadn't been a momentary loss of control, but a wall falling down between them, one Shane had been fortifying diligently for the past twelve months. He guessed it'd take more than one weird compliment to demolish the thing.

Finding a diner was easier than Shane had expected. Parking was a bit more of a challenge, but after a couple blocks of brisk walking the door jingled open to envelop them in warmth and good smells. Shane followed Gabriel to the counter and took a seat on one of the red vinyl stools. They ordered coffees, a full fried breakfast for Shane and an omelet for Gabriel. They made just the barest of small talk as they drank and ate, a handful of bland comments about the meal and the city.

Shane had never put much stock in his own intuition, but he knew a few things for sure in this moment. He knew Gabriel was waiting. He was waiting to find out if last night had been yet one more instance of Shane giving in to the sex, and if his tiny gestures of affection were just that—gestures. Empty ones.

He knew Gabriel was scared too. His eyes usually held Shane's like magnets, but this morning he kept them focused on the food, the windows, the other patrons.

Until now it had always been Shane who'd harbored the distrust. It hurt seeing it reflected back at him, seeing Gabriel doubting his intentions just as the man had surely hated seeing it written all over Shane's face these past twelve months.

Get your balls together and do it. Shane fidgeted in his seat, folded his napkin into tidy triangles.

"Check," Gabriel said as the waitress passed them.

Fuck. Now. Do it now. To his own astonishment, Shane did.

He swiveled on his seat and leaned in, smelled the faint and pleasant scent of that familiar breath, the peculiar scent of those clothes, the scent of the skin he'd tasted so many times. He took Gabriel's hat off and set it on the counter, cupped the back of his neck. As he brought his face down, Shane strained for any noises of protest he catch hear from other patrons…then the moment their mouths met, he melted.

He blocked out the rest of the universe and just felt those lips for a few seconds, lost himself to the simple, brief, closed-mouth kiss.

When he sat up straight again everything felt very…unremarkable. The diner made all its usual sounds. No jeers. No stares. No slurs or threats.

But as Gabriel's lips pursed then broke into a shy smile, it all changed. The restaurant seemed suddenly vibrant and alive. Not from love, nothing so stupid and gooey as that. Adrenaline, probably. Or endorphins. Who cared? Shane grinned, knowing he'd just done the thing that scared him the most, and he'd lived to stare his lover in the face.

After a full year of grasping, paranoid cowardice, he'd finally found his manhood again, conjured it out of the most unlikely gesture imaginable.

He wrapped his palm around the back of Gabriel's neck once more, pulled him close so their foreheads touched. He said it quietly, the barest whisper against Gabriel's lips. "I love you."

A tiny laugh warmed his skin. "I know you do, Shane."

* * *

Shane honestly couldn't remember ever feeling so damn comfortable with himself. Not the outcome he'd expected following his first public acknowledgment of his modified heterosexuality, but no complaints.

They hadn't passed the rest of the day strolling hand-in-hand or picking out china patterns, just headed back to Natalie's and lost a couple hours to kissing.

Shane never would have guessed that exposing himself could feel so fucking perfect. His entire life he'd been fighting to keep from turning into his shithead father, thirty-six years spent trying to *not* be a certain way. And he'd pretty much failed, in the end. Until this morning. This morning Shane had sacrificed a hunk of the self-image he normally clutched so tightly, and it felt amazing, choosing to let people think whatever they damn well wanted to. Toward every person they'd passed on the sidewalk heading back to the truck he'd thought, "Fuck you," in the lightest and happiest way possible. He imagined others finding fault with him and his new philosophy on the subject. *Don't like that I'm a straight guy banging another man? Well, fuck you too. Have a great day.*

Straight. He might need to amend that label. Straight with an asterisk. Or whatever. Like trying to fit in ever did anybody any good.

He eyed Gabriel where he sat at the dining room table, flipping through a photo album of Natalie's. That man didn't fit in anyplace, but it didn't bother him. Raised in a crazy city by a crazier woman. Probably had God-knew-what done to him, pretty as he was, and came out kinky on the other side, near-crazy himself. There was a lifetime's worth of details Shane still needed to learn about this man. He'd start collecting them on the drive south.

The door rattled and Natalie appeared with a bag of groceries, cheeks as pink as her hat and scarf.

"Hey, kids."

"Hey, Miss Natalie." Shane stood to take the bag from her. "How was work?"

She pulled her gloves off. "Bit hectic. How was vacation?" She looked at each of them in turn.

"Lazy," Shane said. "Our biggest accomplishment was venturing out for breakfast."

"Sounds lovely."

He nodded.

"Well, if you're looking for more excitement this evening, you'll have to find it without me, I'm afraid. I'm wiped. I need a nap, and then I'll start dinner if you two think you're sticking around."

Shane looked to Gabriel and shrugged.

"I'll cook," Gabriel said.

Shane started. He'd never seen his lover so much as boil a kettle of water.

"Oh yeah?" Natalie looked intrigued. "Cajun or Cuban?"

"I'll see what you got to work with."

"I won't stop you. Help yourself to whatever. I just need to collapse for a couple hours then I'll be fresh as a daisy. Well, closer to it, anyhow."

Shane waited until Natalie used the bathroom and disappeared into her room before he went knocking.

"Come in."

He entered and closed the door behind him. "Hey."

"What's up?" She looked tired, maybe a touch nervous.

"I wanted to ask how you're doing. Like, because of how we were until last night and everything. I didn't know if you felt ditched or anything…"

She smiled. "I can't pretend I won't miss borrowing your body, Shane, but I couldn't be happier that you guys are back together. Honestly. Is it going as well as it seems like it is?"

He nodded. "It's different too."

She took a seat on her bed. "How so?"

"Usually it's like I'm giving in to the sex, but now…I dunno. I'm giving in to myself or something. I just decided to not give a shit anymore, about what people think. About what *I* think."

"Good for you."

"I kissed him," Shane added. "In public."

Her eyes widened. "Really? That soon?"

"Yeah. I did it like as proof, because I don't want to lose him… But it was pretty weird. It like, freed me or whatever."

"That's great."

He nodded and took a seat beside her. "So me and him are back together. We're a couple, like I guess we always were even though I refused to admit it."

"Yeah."

"But it's still him and me. And we're still pigs."

She laughed. "Where are you going with this, Shane?"

"I don't suppose I could talk you into maybe joining us again? In bed?"

She frowned thoughtfully. "I don't know... I mean, my body would certainly like that, but if things feel cautious between you, I wouldn't want to complicate it."

"You and me have got close these last few days, right?"

"Sure."

Shane leaned in and spoke privately, as though they weren't the only ones in the room. "There's somethin' I want to happen tonight, and I need your help with it. I trust you, and I want you there with me. Woman's touch and all that bull."

"What?" she asked.

"The one filthy, scary thing left that I ain't ever done for that man."

She stared at his shoulder for a moment then her eyebrows rose. "Oh."

"What d'you say? You wanna help me finally demolish the old Shane?"

CHAPTER TWELVE

Shane watched Gabriel holding court in Natalie's kitchen, those fingers so adept with an instrument looking just as talented with a knife and a shelf full of spices. It intrigued the hell out of Shane. He'd happily learn to grocery shop if it meant he might get the odd home-cooked meal from his lover.

He turned words over and over in his head, trying to figure out how to frame his plans for the evening. When Gabriel seemed done with his marinating, Shane sidled up to him at the counter.

"So tonight," he said.

"Mmm?"

"I know today and last night...this has been all about you and me. And me being straight with you. And myself."

Gabriel washed and dried his hands then met Shane's eyes, curious.

"But I want to invite Natalie along tonight. You know, sex-wise."

"Right." So impossible to decipher, that squint.

"But it ain't about us not being enough, or me trying to hide behind a distraction or cling to my...whatever the hell my sexuality is anymore."

Gabriel's shoulders dropped, his expression seeming to soften.

"But me and her...we're close now. She gets stuff about me that nobody else does. Not even you. And I want her there tonight, like as support."

"And she agreed already?"

Shane nodded.

Gabriel made a face, a playful frown that said he was intrigued.

"So's that okay with you?"

"Sure," Gabriel said.

"Okay. Long as you don't think I'm just trying to take the edge off how intense it's been between you and me."

He grinned. "Don' think I ever heard you soun' so considerate before, Shane."

He shrugged.

"Hope it ain' permanent," Gabriel added. "I love you mean." He gave Shane's cheek a gentle slap then went to work prepping a rice dish.

Shane smirked to himself and he headed back to the couch. Good. He liked *being* mean, just as much as he liked all this newfound self-acceptance and warm-fuzzy bullshit.

He surfed channels as Gabriel puttered and Natalie napped, growing steadily more anxious as the evening settled in. In three or four hours he might be on his knees, doing that thing that scared him so much.

He watched the news. In two hours, it might be happening.

Natalie emerged from her room looking more rested and Gabriel slid a dish into the oven. *One hour,* Shane guessed. His throat tightened.

He missed his chance to find out if Gabriel cooked as well as he played music—Shane barely tasted a bite of dinner, barely heard a word the other two exchanged.

He could do this… He didn't have to like it, he just had to get through it for the sake of Gabriel's pleasure. He'd made that same plunge when he'd first dropped to his knees and sucked cock, and fuck if he hadn't grown to love that. Didn't have much to do with the act itself, just the perfection of hearing and seeing Gabriel turn helpless with what Shane could do to him. He hoped tonight would be the same. More pain to endure to get the payoff, but a price he'd pony up for a chance to blow that man's mind. A chance to prove he'd finally given up protecting that last scrap of his precious hetero identity.

The sound of forks and knives and plates clinking snapped him from his thoughts and he found Natalie gathering up the dirty dishes. He muscled her out of the way to take over the cleanup.

"You wanna open a bottle of wine?" he asked her.

She met his eyes meaningfully. "Sure."

Soon the three of them were loitering around the counter. Natalie and Gabriel were talking about plantains, Shane sipping his wine and finally feeling his muscles surrender some of their tension, making room for anticipation. Red wine had come to symbolize sex for him after a year of mental conditioning, and tonight it tasted as dark and exotic as the places he was determined to get taken with the help of his two lovers. The thought put him in an odd mood—seductive. That was Gabriel's department, normally, but Shane decided to explore it, the first of a few role-reversals he had planned.

He rounded the counter and took Natalie's glass, setting it aside so he could slide his hand up her arm to her neck. He paused to appreciate the difference in their heights before he leaned in and kissed her. He felt Gabriel's eyes on them, a flashback to Shane's bedroom the previous summer.

He broke away to speak to Natalie. "You want to get all those candles lit?"

"Sure." She flashed a mischievous smile and touched his arm on her way to her room.

Gabriel licked his lower lip. "What you got planned, Shane? We gon' give her a hell of a thank-you present for her hospitality?"

"Tonight's more about you and me."

"Oh?"

Shane stole a glance at the bedroom door. "Yeah. You'll see."

He drained his glass then took an extra swig straight from the bottle. He handed it to Gabriel and watched his throat contract as he did the same, an unspoken toast to a year of fraught and filthy sexual discovery.

Shane took Gabriel by the hand and led him to Natalie's candlelit room. She smiled as they entered. "I think there's something by the couch we'll be needing," she said to Shane.

He left them to grab the lube and condoms. Setting them by the bed, he drew Gabriel close by the arms. Then Shane kissed him the way he loved to, rough and deep and pushy. He slid his hands to Gabriel's hips and tugged him closer so their cocks brushed through two pairs of pants. When he felt the tension and impatience building in his lover's touch, he let go and moved to Natalie. He kissed her lightly and put his lips to her ear.

"I'm gonna fuck you," he whispered, "then you're gonna do to me exactly what you did to him when I caught you two together. If you remember it."

"Of course I do."

Shane undressed her slowly then did the same to himself. He looked to Gabriel. "You just watch."

Gabriel nodded.

Natalie lay down in the middle of the bed and Shane followed. This alone felt a little scary—Gabriel standing with a view of Shane's naked body from above, still safe in his clothes. Then Natalie's warm hand closed around Shane's dick and the fear faded.

"Good. Make me hard."

Her strokes had him panting in a minute flat.

Shane grabbed a condom and rolled it on as Natalie slicked lube across her pussy. As he sank inside he pondered the act—penetration. As a man, he only knew what it felt like to do the fucking...cock sucking aside. But with that, he'd always been the one in charge. Tonight would be the first time he handed the top duties over, invited Gabriel to use his body the way Shane had been enjoying his for months and months.

Natalie touched his face and he realized his thrusts had slowed as his nervous thoughts crept in.

"You don't have to do this," she whispered.

"I want to." He needed to. Not duty or sacrifice—something stronger. Proof, evidence that he was brave, that Gabriel was worth putting his identity and fears on the line for.

He focused on the pleasure at hand, tried to keep his mind off the vulnerability. This decision—this surrender—had taken on mythical status in his mind in the past year, always something he worried he might one night be coerced into. He took a final calming breath and looked to Gabriel.

The man's gaze was on Shane's pumping hips, patient but hungry. His eyes snapped to Shane's and stayed there until Shane turned to stare down at Natalie, praying he didn't look as scared as he felt.

"Do it," he whispered.

Her hands slid from his waist to his back, slow slow slow down to his ass. Shane adjusted, brought his body forward a bit to give her access. Small, smooth palms kneaded him, squeezed and urged in time with his thrusts. One finger ran along his crack and Shane shut his eyes tight, from nerves far more than the actual sensation. She teased his cleft, shallow tracing gestures that gave Shane time to relax and adjust.

"More?"

He nodded, eyes still shut.

Her fingers delved deeper, parting his cheeks, the faintest graze across his asshole tensing Shane's entire body.

"Open your eyes, Shane."

He did, looked down at Natalie's face and felt so naked it terrified him.

"You tell me if you change your mind and want me to stop," she said softly.

"No. Keep going."

Shane held his breath as the pads of her fingers rubbed his entrance. Entrance, fuck—not before this moment it wasn't.

The taboo was so distracting, Shane couldn't actually tell if he was enjoying this or not. His erection had waned and he wasn't sure when he'd stopped pumping her.

"Scoot forward a little more," Natalie whispered, hands going still.

Shane withdrew and moved up a couple inches, shifting his legs to straddle her hips, soft cock resting on her navel. He felt spread-open and exposed, no longer as if he were on top at all. Natalie's fingertips found his asshole again, rubbing him in a tight circle. To his left, he heard Gabriel make a noise—a shallow sigh, not quite a moan. Shane turned his head, afraid of what he might see on that gorgeous face.

What he found surprised him. Gabriel didn't look predatory or cocky or poised to pounce—he looked helpless. He looked just how he did when Shane had him bent over the arm of a couch or on his hands and knees on the carpet. Needy and excited with a streak of fear running through it.

That expression upended Shane's own fears. He didn't feel like the one about to be used, the powerless one. He felt in control, the one granting wishes and pleasure, the one holding the other under his spell. How Gabriel must feel when he had Shane hot and impatient, dying to use his lover's body. Shane realized he'd begun to move, shifting his hips faintly in time with Natalie's touch. His cock was growing stiff—not totally there yet, but on its way.

"Ready for more?" she asked.

Shane looked down at her and nodded.

She reached for the lube bottle, snapped it open behind Shane's back before setting it beside them on the bed. One dry hand returned, kneading his cheek then spreading him wider. Then, two slick fingertips, cool with lube, slid across his asshole.

Shane lowered his face to her shoulder and moaned, still more fear than pleasure, though his cock didn't wilt.

She pressed her fingers harder against him, one tip teasing more explicitly, threatening. No—promising.

"Shane." Gabriel's raspy voice tightened Shane's body and relaxed it at the same time.

"Yeah?"

"I can come closer?"

He swallowed, considering. "Yeah, fine."

Gabriel sat beside Shane and Natalie at the edge of the bed, turned toward the pillows. Shane was glad of where Gabriel had positioned himself—not behind, as if waiting in line for the turn Shane had been denying him all these months. Beside him, as though he cared about Shane's face and not just his ass, as though he cared about *Shane*.

"I can touch you?" Gabriel whispered. He set a hand lightly on Shane's hip to illustrate his intention.

"Yeah, okay."

He felt those musician's calluses, strong palm possessive and hungry.

"Do it," Shane said to Natalie.

She reached for the lube again, snapped it open and closed. Her slippery fingertips found Shane once more, teasing for a moment before the pressure came. Shane sucked in his breath as one of her slender fingers penetrated the first half inch. Not pain, not pleasure, just pure weirdness.

"Relax," she whispered. "Breathe."

He did his best to obey, to force his tightening body to open again. It was one finger, after all. Shane had been on the giving end of anal plenty of times—with Gabriel of course, and with a few women too, a couple of them fairly small, and they'd managed to take Shane's considerable cock. He could handle a fucking finger.

It felt odd though. Part violation, part...just...strange. It didn't feel sexual, not yet anyway. It felt clinical, as if he were being probed. Still, it didn't feel *bad*. He'd focus on that.

"More."

His body let her in deeper, each millimeter explicit and tight.

"Breathe," she said again.

Shane obeyed this time and her fingers paused while he steadied himself. The next time she pushed he felt her break through, past the next tight barrier. Weirdest fucking thing he'd ever felt, but goddamn, he'd go through with it. He imagined for a minute that he was Gabriel, getting this from himself. Must hurt like hell. Must be one fuck of a head trip too.

"Shane."

He opened his eyes and craned his neck to meet Gabriel's stare.

"You tellin' me what I think you are?"

Shane nodded and faced forward again, eyes shut.

"How's it feel?"

"Fuckin' weird."

"You sure you want to?"

"Yeah, I'm sure." Shane gasped as Natalie pushed deeper. She paused while he got control of his breath again, then she slid out slowly and slicked more lube across him and her fingers.

"Start...you know," he said.

"Sure." Her finger drove in, slow but insistent, and when she got it in as deep as it went, she started to ease it in and out.

Shane wondered how he must look to Gabriel…three-course meal, probably. Well, fuck it. That's how he'd feel then.

"More," he muttered to Natalie.

She worked two fingers inside him, the discomfort not too much worse.

"Good. Keep it coming."

Beyond the more dramatic sensations, he felt Gabriel's hand on his ass. Again he opened his eyes to see what the man's face had to say. Gabriel's lips were parted and his lids heavy, eyes glued to Natalie's hand.

Shane mustered the balls to ask, "You want a turn?"

Gabriel's gaze jumped to Shane's face. "Only if you wan' me to."

"Yeah. Do it."

Natalie eased her fingers out and passed Gabriel the lube. As he waited, Shane stared at the weave of the red bedspread beside her dark hair. The rough pads of two familiar fingertips pushed between his cheeks, found his asshole.

"You tell me when you ready."

Shane nodded. He let Gabriel tease him for a minute before he gave the word. "Fine. Just slow."

"Course." One finger again to start. When Gabriel added the second the men moaned in tandem. Gabriel kept his hand slowly working and relocated, straddling Shane's calves. The position was unnerving but inevitable.

A warm palm kneaded Shane's ass. *Just don't spank me.* Submission was fine, just nothing demeaning. Fucking hypocritical, but oh well.

Natalie grazed his ribs with her hands, a little calming taste of that safety he felt with her.

"You feel good," Gabriel murmured. Shane felt him twist his hand the next time he drew his fingers out.

"Bet you been waiting forever for this," Shane mumbled.

"Waited a long time for the things you said to me las' night an' this mornin'," Gabriel said. "If you wan' this too, it's jus' a bonus. I already got what I wanted most from you."

Holy shit, if that wasn't the most perfect answer Shane could conceive of...though he hadn't conceived of it. Hadn't even considered such a proclamation.

"Yeah," he said. "I want this. Wanna give this to you."

"What you tryin' to prove?" Gabriel asked, no challenge in his tone.

"I want—" Shane gasped as a third finger joined the exploration. "Oh fuck. I want to show you I'm done protecting my stupid fragile ego."

"Oh yeah?"

"Yeah. Just wanna give in to you."

"You ready?"

Shane took a few long, deep breaths and nodded.

"Like this? Or can I see your face?"

"Like this to start," Shane said. "I'll tell you if I change my mind."

Shane kept his eyes closed, felt Gabriel's fingers leave him. There was a crinkle of plastic, another snap of the lube bottle.

"Fuck, you look good." Gabriel finally sounded the way Shane had expected—devious. It didn't scare him though. He liked that meanness, that hungry edge in his lover's voice. Then Shane felt the sweep of slick, smooth cock head against his asshole and the pleasure dissolved.

"I go real slow," Gabriel promised, already pushing.

"Ah fuck."

"Tell me to stop."

"Don't stop," Shane said, eyes clenched shut, hands balled into fists under Natalie's pillow. The burning sensation grew, more painful than the fingers by tenfold. Gabriel pulled out and the bottle snapped again.

"Ready for more?"

"Yeah," Shane muttered.

The penetration stung a bit less this time, the friction smoother. Shane gasped as Gabriel worked himself deeper. His own ragged breath was drowned out by Gabriel's long, raspy moan.

"You okay?" Natalie whispered.

He nodded. "I'm all right." He got control of his breathing as Gabriel tested their limits, pushing in farther then backing off, adding more lube, taking Shane deeper.

"I'm in, Shane. All the way."

He blinked, surprised. "Yeah?"

"Yeah. You doin' good. It feel okay?"

"Sure. Don't feel good or anything, but I can take it."

"You wanna maybe turn over for me?"

He pondered it a moment, decided the chance to see Gabriel looking all flushed and needy outweighed the embarrassment of letting the man watch him flinch. "Yeah, sure."

He felt tender beyond words as Gabriel slid out and Natalie moved to the side. Shane lay on his back and peeled the condom from his dick. As he spread his legs, Gabriel knelt before him. Shane let his thighs be coaxed wider, goddamn humbling position.

"You look so good," Gabriel whispered, and his eyes were on Shane's face.

"Do it."

One last smear of lube and Gabriel angled his cock, slid inside halfway. Out again, then back in, until the friction seemed to warm Shane's protesting body from the inside and tame his edgy muscles. He kept his eyes on Gabriel's face above him, an angle he wasn't used to seeing. Beautiful as any other, though.

"You good?" Gabriel asked, barely a whisper.

"Fuck me." Shane spat the words out, as gruff as he might've told Gabriel to drop to his knees and suck his cock. Gabriel began to thrust, slow and considerate.

"Harder."

He pushed a little deeper, a little faster.

"Harder. I wanna see you lose your goddamn mind."

Shane watched it happening, heard it in Gabriel's strangled groan, saw it in the way he squeezed his eyes shut.

"Fuck me. I know you've thought about this."

"Yeah."

"Now I'm letting you have it, so fuck me right. Fuck me like I fuck you. Tear me up."

Gabriel's eyes opened, locked on Shane's throat. His hips sped, cock driving deeper. The sensations weren't quite pain now, not pleasure either. Felt like that mean, aggressive burn again, and Shane kept reminding himself it was the feeling of finally toppling the barrier that stood between them.

Better than that, it was the feeling of his lover going utterly insane from what Shane could offer. He felt his cock stirring again as he studied Gabriel's face and its perfect mix of helpless and horny. Needy.

"How's it feel?"

Gabriel slowed, clearly savoring. "So tight."

"How long since you fucked a guy?"

"Since before I met you, Shane."

Dark self-satisfaction warmed his blood. "And you know I never done this before, ever."

"Yeah." Something hot flashed in Gabriel's expression. "Only with me."

"That's right. Only you."

Gabriel shut his eyes again, a low, rapturous hum rising from his throat. "Feels so good."

Shane realized it felt good to him too. As his arousal mounted the rest of his body abandoned its suspicion. The deeper he let Gabriel inside, the better it felt. His lover's cock was hitting some buried trigger, sparking pleasure. It wasn't enough to make him come or erase the intimidation of the act, but he could admit it felt good.

What felt extraordinary, however, was watching Gabriel, seeing him as what he was. A man. The only man Shane had ever lusted after or loved; the only one he let get close to him. If that wasn't magic, he didn't know what was.

"Fuck me deep," he said, keeping the mean bark in his voice as he issued the order.

Gabriel obeyed, pushed in another inch.

"That's it," Shane muttered. "Keep going."

"It hurt?"

"Does it hurt when I fuck you?" Shane asked.

"Yeah, but I like it."

"Well, it don't hurt. Just feels weird."

Gabriel licked his lips. "I wanna make you feel good."

Shane palmed his own erection, the contact lighting him up, tensing his body around Gabriel's cock. "Fuck. More lube."

Gabriel slid out, soaked himself in another palmful of gel and squeezed back inside. Shane winced through the initial sting, let his hand stroke as Gabriel drove in.

"That's right," Shane murmured. He gave himself slow, tight pulls to match the thrusts.

"Jus' wait 'til I'm deep, Shane. You won' know what fuckin' hit you. Wait 'til you come with my cock fuckin' you. You gon' think you went to heaven."

Shane watched his lover's body, those trim muscles and tattoos, tan skin and gorgeous face, every inch of him strained with excitement.

He could feel it happening—he could come from this. He *would* come from this. Before today that would have felt like a defeat, a hunk of his dominance being ripped away. Now he craved it. He wanted to be everything for this man.

Gabriel's eyes were glued on Shane's stroking hand. "You so big."

"Yeah. And I'm gonna come. Gonna come with your cock inside me, boy."

Gabriel was lost to a sound, a moan wrapped in a gasp.

"Deeper," Shane ordered. "Deep and fast, like I fuck you."

Gabriel's hands slid from Shane's thighs to his knees and pushed him open wider. Shane felt his strength in that moment, something he forgot about when he was busy being the dominant male in their twosome. Shane groaned as Gabriel forced himself so deep his hips touched Shane's ass. Pain spiked then faded, replaced with filthy excitement. Gabriel slid out, then back in to the hilt.

"Good. Fuck me."

"Wanna see you come," Gabriel said.

"Do what I say and you will. Now fuck me." Shane tightened his fist around his cock, sped the strokes to match Gabriel's hips.

"God, Shane."

"This how you fantasized it'd be?"

"Better," Gabriel muttered. "Never thought you'd lemme see your face."

Shane never thought he'd want to see Gabriel's face at this moment either, but here they were, and his lover's wild expression was the thing that made this submission possible for Shane.

"Gabriel."

"Yeah." His eyes were glassy, face flushed. His gaze darted from Shane's face to his ass, to Natalie, to Shane's cock. "Can't believe I'm inside you."

"Yeah, you are. You're the only one who'll ever get this. You're the only one who could ever make me want it."

"An' you do? You want it?"

"I want to watch you lose your mind, gettin' this from me," Shane said. "Yeah, I wanna give this to you."

"Come for me."

Shane stared at Gabriel's sweat-gleaming bare body in the warm light and knew he could obey. He stroked himself fast and rough. "God, fuck me. Fuck my ass."

"Shane."

"That's right. Keep sayin' it."

Without warning, he was there. He shut his eyes and gave in. It was unlike anything he'd ever felt, an orgasm that started deep and erupted hot and violent, wrung him out to the sound of his name on his lover's breath. He felt the come hit his stomach, then more. More than he ever knew he could give. He opened his eyes to find Gabriel staring down at him, eyes wide, chest rising and falling fast.

"You," Shane said.

Gabriel withdrew, slowly, leaving a sore ache in his absence. He surprised Shane by stripping away the condom and lying down between him and Natalie, body turned to Shane's.

"Touch me," he mumbled.

Shane fisted Gabriel's cock, more swollen and stiff than he'd ever felt it. Gabriel interrupted him to collect Shane's come and slick it down his own length. Taking over once more, Shane knew the man was close. He stroked him tight and listened to him whimper.

"Kiss me," Shane ordered.

Gabriel brought his face close, tasted Shane's mouth with distracted sweeps of his tongue. Shane grasped Gabriel's jaw with his free hand and kissed him back, deep and dirty. He was overcome, flooded with relief and gratitude. Gabriel could've come as the aggressor but he hadn't. He wanted what Shane was so natural at, taunting domination.

Shane spoke right into his mouth. "Come on, Gabriel."

A deep groan warmed his lips.

"Think about how you fucked me tonight and come right here." He angled Gabriel's cock so the head brushed Shane's stomach with each pull.

"I fucked you," Gabriel muttered.

"Yeah, you did. I'm all yours now. Nobody else'll ever get that from me."

That did it. Gabriel surrendered to a body-racking shudder as his hips hammered his dick into Shane's fist. Shane felt wet heat burst against his belly and knuckles and slowed his pulls, coaxing every last warm drop.

As the high subsided, Shane remembered the restless body on Gabriel's other side.

Guilt swallowed him and he wondered if Natalie felt left out. She'd faded for Shane, at the height of this evening's explorations. It'd just been him and Gabriel, Natalie a near-invisible figment helping to orchestrate it. He propped himself on his elbow and caught her eyes.

"Hi," she said quietly. Her cheeks and lips were flushed.

"Hi, yourself." His gaze dropped to her breasts and legs, then back up to her face. Beautiful face, and the only one he could ever imagine wanting here, witnessing the two of them. With the high of challenging his own self-image still warming his body, Shane knew what he wanted to give her. He climbed over Gabriel to kneel between her calves.

"Think we owe you a thank-you," he said.

"I thought tonight was all about you two."

"And this is about me thanking you for making it happen...or trying to." He scooted back and lowered to his elbows as Natalie opened up for him. He slid his palms under her butt and leaned in close, breathed her in. Gabriel knelt beside them, his hand on Shane's shoulder.

Shane gave her clit the faintest flick of his tongue, rewarded with a twitch of her thighs.

"Good." All his usual anxiety about this act was gone, replaced with excitement. He lapped her again, firmer, earning a rough scrape of her fingernails across his scalp.

"Don't be gentle," she murmured.

Excellent—Shane's specialty. He tasted her with slow, explicit strokes that had her hips begging for more. He freed his mouth to speak to Gabriel. "You owe her too."

He nodded and Shane saw him lean in to kiss her. For the first time he could remember, sharing this man felt like a gift he was giving, not a theft.

As he teased Natalie's clit he stole glances at the two of them, watching as they found their way together after six months' estrangement. Gabriel moved his mouth to her breasts, letting Shane hear her sounds, all the little assurances that told him he was doing just fine.

"Your fingers," she muttered.

Shane obeyed happily, sliding two digits inside her, tongue still torturing. He smiled to himself as she swore, nails raking him harder. He reached up to grasp Gabriel's wrist, drawing his hand to her clit. She'd been treated to both of their cocks before, now Shane wanted to give her this—his tongue and Gabriel's talented fingers, two men once again sharing the honor of blowing her mind.

Shane could hear Gabriel whispering low words as he pleasured her breasts and Shane shared the thrill with her, a shiver from what that voice alone could do. His tongue teased Gabriel's fingers as they ravaged her together, his own hand turning aggressive, deepening their motions as her moans turned harsh. He hoped the rough thrusts had her fantasizing about everything they'd given her back in his bed, what must surely have been a lifetime ago.

Against his tongue and around his fingers, Shane felt Natalie coming apart. For a final minute he fucked her hard with his hand, tasted and smelled her and got swallowed by a wave of bone-deep gratitude as he felt her come for both of them.

When Gabriel took his hand away, Shane followed suit. He scooted up the mattress to plant a messy kiss on her neck.

He exhaled against her skin and smiled. "Thanks."

She laughed, exhaustion in her voice. "No, thank you."

Shane flopped down on the blankets. Natalie slung an arm across his chest and as Gabriel nestled his face against Shane's shoulder, Shane felt consciousness instantly fading. Good thing, too. After a year of overthinking every tiny thing that happened between his body and Gabriel's, careless oblivion sounded damn good. Sounded as good as the deep male breaths heating his throat. Sounded like perfection.

CHAPTER THIRTEEN

S hane awoke in a pile of warm limbs the next morning, feeling sore and content.

He felt alert as well, full of impulsive ideas. The clock said it was only four thirty, but he eased his arm from under Gabriel's back and stood at the side of the bed. He nudged the curtains aside to let in a bit of streetlight. He stared at the two people responsible for how damn happy he felt. He studied Natalie's placid face a long time then padded to the bathroom.

Why settle, Shane? Her voice echoed in his head as he showered. Why indeed...not that Gabriel wasn't enough. Shane knew now that the man was plenty, but if Natalie had meant that advice another way...

He turned the idea over and over in his head as he crept out of the house, driving to the first open convenience store he could find to buy eggs and bacon.

Natalie was up when he got back. She emerged from the bathroom with one towel wound around her hair, another her trunk. "Shane." Her eyes were wide.

"Mornin'."

"Oh Jesus, I thought you'd, like, freaked out in the night and run off." She laughed, clearly relieved. "I spent my whole shower worrying you'd had a breakdown."

"Nope, just had to replace your eggs. I'm making you breakfast before you take off for work."

"You don't have—"

"It's tradition," he said, heading to the stove to get things set up.

Natalie disappeared then returned in her work clothes a short while later, damp hair twisted into a bun. Shane set a mug of his patented too-strong coffee in front of her and went to flip the eggs. He returned with two loaded plates and what he hoped was an irresistible offer.

"So me and him—Gabriel," he corrected forcefully. "We'll probably head back down south soon. Maybe one more dinner with you?"

"Whenever you like. If you're sure you're ready."

He nodded. "I came here to run away. Now the thing I was runnin' from is here. And I ain't afraid of it anymore. Or not as much, at least. You know what I mean."

"Yeah."

"Plus I'll admit, I'm damn homesick. But listen…"

Natalie took a bite of her toast, waiting patiently as Shane assembled his thoughts.

"I got an invitation for you."

Her pale eyes jumped between his. "Oh? What's that?"

"I know you don't love your job here."

She moved her eggs around with her fork and made a face at them. "No, not especially."

"If you ever want a change of scenery, you should feel free to come back down to Shiloh. I'll fix you up a room of your own in the house. Free room and board 'til you find a job, maybe in Baton Rouge?"

She set her fork aside and nibbled her lip, thinking.

"Free beer, even."

"I dunno, Shane."

"Two men who work well with their hands, ready to do appalling things to you any night of the week you please?"

She smirked.

"Doesn't have to be a be-all, end-all thing. Maybe you give it a try for six months, a year... Give *me* a try." Saying it made Shane feel naked, melted away the usual tough expression on his face and must have left him looking like a pleading man, armor chipped and rusty.

Finally Natalie laughed, just a soft breath passed through a smile. "Mosquitoes."

"Yeah, so much worse than the Russian roulette you play here just stepping on the sidewalk," he countered.

"Hot summers."

"Fuckin' hot-ass sex, girl."

She sighed, eyes roaming her living room as she pondered. Shane looked around too—fireplace, front window, couch. God, couches. That's what Shane should get a tattoo of. Fucking furniture wouldn't leave him alone.

"Nice man?" he ventured, poking her shin with his toe. "Who'll treat you as good as you like in public, as bad as you want in bed?"

Natalie smiled and reached over to squeeze his thigh. "I won't pretend that's not a tempting offer..."

"But?"

"But no." She leaned back in her chair and held his eyes. "I'm like you, I think. I could handle being the guest for a little while, but I wouldn't be happy sharing you. I want a man of my own. One who's a heck of a lot like you, but..."

"But just not me?"

She shook her head. "Maybe in some parallel, simpler universe, where you live in Rochester and you and he had never met. But not in this life. Not when I know how much you two need each other. I'd like to feel that needed myself. Just on my own."

He nodded, disappointed but not entirely surprised. It would have been a lot to ask of anyone.

She touched his arm. "Thank you though. That's the most flattering invitation a greedy girl like me could hope for."

"I had to try."

They finished their food in silence and Natalie dried her hair, got her boots and coat on.

"So I'll see you guys for one more night?" she asked Shane by the door.

"Yeah, I'd say so."

"Cool. I'll call you before I leave work to figure out where to meet, if we decide to go out."

Shane nodded. When she reached for the doorknob he grabbed her wrist and stared right into her eyes. "Thanks. For last night. For this whole week too. I, um... I came here pretty fucked up in the head, and you took me in and set me straight."

"What happened last night was all you, Shane. It was very brave."

"Yeah, maybe... But anyhow, thanks. You gave me a heck of a lot more than the couch and the rebound you owed me."

She shrugged, a bit of pink in her cheeks.

"You're a good woman. If you don't come to your senses and join us down in Louisiana, I hope you find yourself a deserving man."

"Me too. Just not too soon, I hope."

He let her wrist go. "Anyhow, I'll see you tonight."

"See you later, Shane." She opened the door to the front hall, icy air seeping in. "You treat him good."

CHAPTER FOURTEEN

SIX MONTHS LATER

In the end, Shane hadn't explained himself to anybody once he got back to Shiloh. Step by tiny, brave step, he'd set out instead to simply confuse people.

When he sat beside Gabriel at the bar, Shane let their knees touch. At moments when he'd normally kiss the man, had they been alone, he'd begun putting his hand to the base of Gabriel's neck, giving it a gentle, possessive squeeze. It earned him funny looks from his customers and staff, but no one came out and directly questioned him for weeks.

Jeanne, Shane's favorite bartender, had cracked under the curiosity one warm spring evening. Gabriel had sidled up beside Shane at the bar, brushing casually but openly against him as he accepted a glass of wine between sets. He'd left with the now customary heated glance, headed back into the fray to resume musician duties. Jeanne had slapped her bar towel down on the counter in front of Shane.

"Yeah, Miss Jeanne?"

"Seriously, Shane. What's up?" She jerked her head in Gabriel's direction.

He'd just chuckled, took a swig of beer and smiled at her, obnoxiously innocent. "No clue what you mean, sweetheart."

"Bull."

"I really don't."

She'd sighed then left it at that as a drink order called her away.

Shane smiled at the memory. It was August now, the summer humidity and heat tossed over the Shivaree like a wet sheet. Shane swiveled on his stool as a blues song came to a close, clapped politely along with the rest of the drinkers. The band left the stage for a smoke break, Gabriel making a beeline for Shane. Shane loved the look of his skin on sticky nights like this. Loved his smell. There were no empty stools so Shane stood as Gabriel approached, handing him his glass of wine.

"Thanks."

"Good set," Shane said. "I like the new trombone guy."

Gabriel nodded and took a sip of his wine. Shane longed to lean in and taste that mouth, but he held back, as always. Not so much to protect himself anymore, but to keep from embarrassing the patrons.

By now most everybody suspected what Jeanne did, but Shane didn't see any reason to flaunt it. Rumors were enough to make it real for him. He gave Gabriel's shoulder a firm squeeze, a tiny promise to make good on later when—

Shane flinched at the pointed sound of a throat being cleared behind his back. He'd lived in worry over the moment some drunk would catch him cozying up to Gabriel and want to make an issue of it. Hand still clamped firmly where it liked to be, Shane turned to glare at—

"Natalie." He laughed.

She smiled at each of them. "Hey, boys. Fancy meeting you here."

"Well, holy shit." Relief gave way to pleasure and Shane let Gabriel go and hugged her.

"Don't tell me you've got vehicle troubles again."

"No, just here for a drink with the boss-man," she said, then nodded to Gabriel. "Maybe a dance with the resident musician later?"

"My pleasure."

"Plus I flew this time, so I'm living the lush life with a shiny new rental car instead of my faithful '98 Chevy shitbox."

The band began reassembling onstage. "'Scuse me," Gabriel said with a tip of his hat. "I find you later for that dance, eh?"

"Please do." She watched him walk away then smiled at Shane. "I see you've gone public. How's it been? Any major trouble?"

"None yet. We ain't bein' too in-people's-faces about it."

"And I can't imagine anybody would really want to take *you* on in a fight."

"Maybe not. But anyhow, it's gone pretty smooth. I've been real nice, just like you told me to be. He's got keys and his own room and everything," Shane said, nodding up to indicate the apartment above the bar.

"I'm glad to hear it. That means there's a couch free for me to crash on tonight."

"Always." An intriguing possibility made his body flash hot. "You ain't here to finally accept that old offer I made, are you?"

She smiled, eyes traveling all over the bar then back to Shane's face. "No, sorry."

He let his shoulders slump, petulant. "Well, a visit'll do. Though you coulda called first."

"I didn't actually come to see you two. Well, I mean I did tonight, obviously, but I'm in Louisiana for work."

"Oh? Permanently?"

"No, no. I just took a new job in Rochester, at a cancer treatment facility. Really nice place. It's sort of a promotion, and I got sent down for corporate management training tomorrow and Tuesday in Shreveport, of all places. Couldn't resist showing up here unannounced. Tradition and all."

"Anything else you were looking for?" Shane asked, voice low.

She shook her head. "Very tempting, but no. I'm seeing someone, actually."

"Oh yeah?"

She nodded, and the way she bit her lip and looked to her shoes told Shane she had it bad. "Yeah."

"And?"

"And his name's Eric. And you won't believe it, but we met when he was fixing my truck."

"Mechanic?" Shane asked.

"Yeah. And a good one, I promise. He drives an old Mustang he rebuilt himself."

"He a jerk, just how you like 'em?"

"Yeah. But only in the good ways."

He smiled at that. "Sounds like a real dreamboat."

She shrugged. "Time will tell…but yeah. Right now I'm very happy indeed."

"So I can see. How's your sister's new addition?"

"Don't even get me going. So adorable it's disturbing. How about you? Are you happy, Shane?"

He cleared his throat. "Yeah. I am."

"Doing okay without the whole traditional-family thing?"

He nodded and his hand moved to his opposite shoulder, to the names he'd gotten tattooed there a few months earlier.

"I sorta realized, after I got back and me and Gabriel quit being all secretive… I already got that. Or enough of that to make me happy." He dropped his hand and looked to where Jeanne and Zach were arguing behind the bar, swept his eyes over his regulars. He looked back to Natalie. "You were right. Both of you. The only thing keeping me miserable was me, not letting myself just want what I did. It still don't make any sense to me...but I'm happy. Can't honestly think of a single thing that's missing."

"Random woman to spice up your cozy little picture of domestic bliss?" Natalie aimed her gaze upward, to where she'd once been such a bonus female.

Shane grinned, felt a blush warm his cheeks. He kept his voice low. "Yeah, sometime maybe. Though I'm in no rush. Happy where I am, for now. You sure you ain't lookin' to reprise your role?"

"No, thanks. One man's plenty for me these days. Especially the keeper I've got waiting back home."

"That's quite the change of tune. Lemme get you a drink and we'll toast." Shane squeezed in between the folks at the bar, leaning over the counter to pour her a pint.

"There you go."

"Thank you kindly, Shane."

He tapped his bottle to her glass and took a deep drink.

They both stared out at the milling patrons under the spangled lights for a couple of minutes. Shane's attention settled on Gabriel, just as it always did...those magic fingers and black eyes and deadly smile, all his.

Natalie laughed and Shane turned to her.

"What?"

She shook her head as if banishing drunkenness. "I'd forgotten what this place does to a person's brain."

"And other body parts."

She rolled her eyes and nodded. "Those too."

"Shit, I better get upstairs and tidy up, now I've got a guest."

"After another drink," Natalie said, facing the band as another song began.

"If you insist."

Shane got lost in the music, mind feeling hazy and airborne in the sultry summer air. He shut his eyes and breathed in magnolia, listened to the fond bickering of his staff and the subtle play of fingers over bass strings. He opened them again and saw Gabriel, the warm, beating heart of Shane's weird little kingdom. He saw his home.

ABOUT THE AUTHOR

SINCE SHE BEGAN WRITING IN 2008, Cara McKenna has published nearly forty romances and erotic novels with a variety of publishers, sometimes under the pen names Meg Maguire and C.M. McKenna. Her stories have been acclaimed for their smart, modern voice and defiance of convention. She was a 2015 RITA Award finalist, a 2014 *RT* Reviewers' Choice Award winner, a 2012 and 2011 *RT* Reviewers' Choice Award nominee, and a 2010 Golden Heart Award finalist. She lives with her husband and son in the Pacific Northwest, though she'll always be a Boston girl at heart.

caramckenna.com
facebook.com/authorcaramckenna
twitter.com/caramckenna

ALSO BY CARA McKENNA

After Hours

Curio and the Curio Vignettes

Hard Time

Her Best Laid Plans

Skin Game

Strange Love: Remastered Tales

Unbound

Willing Victim

THE SINS IN THE CITY SERIES

Crosstown Crush

Downtown Devil

THE DESERT DOGS SERIES

Lay It Down

Give It All

Drive It Deep

Burn It Up

www.ingramcontent.com/pod-product-compliance
Lightning Source LLC
Chambersburg PA
CBHW070638180626
46817CB00006B/2160